The
Medallion
Client

Stefanie Marklind

MELHOUSE
PUBLISHING

The Medallion Client
Copyright © 2025 by Stefanie Marklind
First Published by Melhouse Publishing 2025
ISBN: 979-8-9999033-3-4

Quotes from *Zen Mind, Beginner's Mind* by Shunryu Suzuki are used with permission of Shambhala Publications.

Front cover design Sylvia Frost at https://www.thebookbrander.com

Contact publisher and author at https://www.stefaniemarklind.com

MELHOUSE
PUBLISHING

To my Aunt Anita

Your encouragement, wisdom, affirmation, editorial advice, emotional support, and overall availableness made all the difference.

Dear Reader,

This book contains information about sex trafficking, and while not explicit, the subject matter might be sensitive for some readers. This story is purely fictional, but I do draw from my general paralegal knowledge gained from working on sex trafficking cases. I hope that this story will contribute toward the continuing effort to raise awareness of this topic. Additionally, some of the characters in this book grapple with mental disorders, such as bipolar and depression. By treating their struggles with empathy, compassion, and relatability, I hope I will have aided in easing the stigma surrounding these specific disorders and mental health issues in general. Additional warnings: adult language, mature themes, sexual content, and an off-page domestic violence incident in one character's backstory.

Below are a few sources that offer guidance on what you can do to help prevent sex trafficking:

Human Trafficking Prevention:
https://polarisproject.org/human-trafficking/

If someone you know is struggling with a mental health issue or is in crisis:

Mental Health Resources:
https://nami.org/

The
Medallion
Client

Prologue

The windowless room was shrouded in the kind of pitch-black darkness in which it didn't matter if one's eyes were open or closed. Tara's were open as she confronted her bedroom door, at a loss as to what to do next. Thus far, she had avoided giving her current situation its due consideration by telling herself it was temporary. She'd be going home soon. Everything was fine. However, the fact that there were holes in her memory regarding how she'd ended up at the "clinic" in the first place was one indicator that things were in fact not fine. The other indicator had just revealed itself moment's ago when she'd tried to open her bedroom door only to discover that it had been locked – from the outside.

She had merely wanted to use the bathroom, something she should have taken care of before heading to bed, apparently, but her need to do so was quickly fading, the urge replaced by a sudden feeling of dread. The time had come to process through her jumbled memories and face her fear that all may not be as it seemed. With a sinking heart, she slowly turned in the direction of her bed and began to make her way back through the dark, grateful that the cold concrete floor beneath her feet helped to mask her footsteps. She hadn't bothered to turn on a lamp, and now she wasn't so sure that she should. The darkness fell thick and heavy around her as she reached the edge of the bed and sat down, poised, listening intently for any sounds outside her door. She took a deep breath in, then exhaled slowly. With each passing day, her environment was starting to feel less like a clinic – as she'd been led to believe – and more like a military compound. She began to wonder why she hadn't given much thought to the odd details she'd been pushing to the back of her mind, such as why the security guards were armed....and why were there security guards?

She continued to sit in the empty silence, pondering how she was supposed to conduct an organized review of her memories when she felt so disoriented. At least she knew what day it was: Wednesday, May 6th (gleaned from the evening news that she and the other women had been allowed to watch earlier that evening as part of "group" time). She thought backward, skipping through patchy memories of the last few weeks, reaching for what had led to her being here. She remembered that she'd been in Portland visiting her dad....they'd had an argument. She couldn't quite remember what it had been about. She'd left the house.....walked down the sidewalk.....it was dark outside ....but where had she been going? *Think. Think. Think.* She tried to remember what she'd been wearing, but her mind drew a blank. Had she been alone? Yes. She had been alone. Something suddenly edged itself forward, causing her to sit up straighter.

She'd gone to a restaurant.....no – it was a bar. It must have been Mickey's – it was the only one within walking distance of her dad's house. She'd taken a seat at the bar......a man had joined her. Did he buy her a drink? Yes, he must have. She tried to recall his face, but nothing came to mind. No hair color or facial features....nothing. Just a vague outline. She pushed herself to think harder, massaging her forehead with her fingertips. There had to be something else, something that had come after her drink with him and before she'd awakened one morning, alone, in this sparsely furnished room with no windows and no sense of how long she'd been there.

Her ears pricked suddenly at the sound of footsteps in the hall. Barely breathing and with her heart pounding in her chest, she quickly slid under the covers and threw them over her head. With every second feeling like an eternity, she waited for the footsteps to pass.

They came to a halt outside her door.

1

There it was again: the wide brick tunnel, shrouded in mist, its gaping entrance lit only from the glow of two staunch lampposts symmetrically flanking its opening. It was the same tunnel he saw every time he dreamed this dream. He looked over his shoulder and noted the familiar stairwell descending downward into the murky shadows beneath the football stadium. The night sky was black and desolate, starless. Above him, barren tree limbs creaked and groaned, scraping against one another in the inky darkness. He was alone. With a growing feeling of dread, he turned and faced the tunnel. The sound of the fans in the stadium became white noise roaring in his ears. Dead leaves crunched under his foot as he took a step backward and stared at the empty tunnel looming in front of him. They were waiting for him, counting on him, but he felt no motivation to move. None. There was no small reserve of willpower tucked away somewhere in a corner of his being. The thing that had once filled him with joy and satisfaction now only held emptiness. Dread pooled in the pit of his stomach as a refrain began to echo in his mind like a doomsday broadcast on a loop: *Your existence is meaningless. Your existence is meaningless.* Suddenly, the air became oppressive and heavy as if someone had thrown a weighted blanket over his shoulders. He had no mental strength or physical energy to fight whatever it was that was suddenly gripping him, this formless and unexplainable opponent that was pulling him under like a rip tide. Indecision continued to keep him rooted in place as fear slowly seeped into his muscles. It was back. He knew what this was now. He could feel it, like a black hole spreading wider and wider inside his chest. Depression. Somehow it had found him again...

"Ladies and gentlemen, we're expecting some slight turbulence. Please return to your seats and fasten your seatbelts."

The pilot's voice was loud enough to overcome the crackling static of the airplane's intercom system, jolting him awake.

"We'll be clear of it once we've reached a higher altitude. Until then, please remain in your seats with your seatbelts securely fastened."

Ryan tightened his grip on his armrest and slowly began to count to ten, grounding himself back in the present moment. He took one long, deep breath then shifted his thoughts to his five senses, to what he could see, touch, and hear. He stared at the faint pinstripes on his navy suit, the one his housekeeper had suggested for him earlier that morning, telling him that the color paired well with his black hair and brown eyes. Next, he shifted his concentration to the droning sound of the plane's engines and took another deep breath in, then out. It had only been a dream. It was all in the past, and things were different now. There was nothing to be concerned about. A moment later, he slowly opened his eyes and glanced vaguely out the window wondering if, like amputees, it was possible to experience "depression" phantom pain, because whenever he awoke from that particular dream, he always had to remind himself that he wasn't actually depressed, that there was no basis for the anxiety and everything in his life was going well. He took one last deep breath, allowing the tension from his body to fade, and relaxed his grip on his armrest. He glanced at the older gentleman seated to his left, next to the window. One arthritic hand was clenched tightly around a dog-eared book, while the other was balled into a fist. His body was rigid.

As the jolting began to worsen, Ryan leaned toward him. "I take it you don't like flying?"

The man turned his head slightly in his direction. "No, not really, but it's a necessary evil if I want to see my grandchildren."

Ryan didn't exactly care, but he needed something to take his mind off the dream, so he asked, "How many grandkids do you have?"

"Five," the man replied, his voice pinched and his face taut. "Two of them live in Chicago. The rest are in Minnesota."

"I'm sure they'll be happy to see you."

His seating companion merely nodded so Ryan decided it might be helpful to change the topic to something that could be sustained. "I saw the book you were reading earlier. 'The Count of Monte Cristo.' How're you liking it?"

"Well, I've read it before. Several times, actually." He turned slowly in his seat, his body still rigid, then asked, "Have you read it?"

"I have, although it's been a while."

The gentleman turned the tattered front cover towards him. "It was an anniversary gift from my late wife, on our 'something paper' anniversary. I take it with me whenever I travel."

"Isn't Dumas a little dark, for a wedding gift?" Ryan responded, raising an eyebrow.

"Yes," he chuckled. "But she knew he was my favorite author."

"The 'something paper' – what anniversary year is that?"

"The first one. I wrote her a poem as my gift."

Feeling a genuine sense of interest now, he asked, "And what was the next year's?"

The wrinkles on the man's forehead creased in concentration for a moment or two before he responded, "I think it was the 'something wooden' year...yes – yes it was. I gave her a rocking chair. And she gave me a box of Cuban cigars, in a mahogany box." There was fond reverence in his voice as he straightened and added, "I still have the box. I keep my watch and tie clips in it now."

Ryan smiled to himself. He didn't store his Cartier cufflinks in a cigar box; however, the sentimental tone in the man's voice suddenly made him feel melancholy. It had been two years and three months since he'd last been in a relationship, and he hadn't dated anyone since then.

His companion gave him a sideways glance. "Are you married?"

"No."

The old man chuckled. "Do you want to be?"

"Maybe." Ryan laughed lightly, noting that the turbulence had subsided. "Are people still doing that?" He tried to ignore the sudden pang of longing in his chest.

The man gave him a wry look. "Commitment isn't always easy, but the kind of relationship that makes for a good marriage is worth the work."

Ryan nodded absently, giving the rough stubble along his jawline a quick scratch, then added, "Do you think it's better to part ways though, rather than force something that wasn't meant to be in the first place?"

"Perhaps. I suppose sometimes you might have to discover what you don't want before you know what you do."

Ryan glanced across the aisle, noticing the attractive brunette whom he'd observed earlier at the gate, before boarding. He turned back to his companion. "Tell me, do you believe in love at first sight...soulmates...all of that?"

"Of course," he responded with a firm nod. "I knew it, right when I saw Jean. She was the one, you know? I just knew it. Married her three months later."

"Hmm." Ryan shrugged his shoulders. "Maybe it still works that way sometimes. I don't know." He tried to keep the cynicism out of his voice. "In my experience it's rare, if it does."

"Well, I believe it does." The man smiled and gave him a light nudge with his elbow. "You'll know it when the times comes. The trick is to not let her get away."

Their conversation was suddenly cut short by a commotion several rows behind them. Ryan leaned to his right, craning his neck to glance down the aisle. It wasn't hard to decipher that one of the passengers – a well-dressed, middle-aged man, with a thick beard and wire frame glasses – was quickly becoming irate.

"Where's my bourbon?" His question was directed toward a petite flight attendant standing in the aisle. "I've been waiting," he continued loudly, his words slurring together. "What's taking too long, do your job ferr Christ's sake."

5

"Sir, I apologize, but I'm not allowed to serve you any more drinks. That's our policy."

"I've had two drinks!" he replied angrily, rising from his seat. He thrust his hand in her face and used his fingers to count. "One. Two."

She took a small step backward. "Sir, I need you to remain in your seat."

Ryan could tell that she was trying to appear calm, but her voice trembled. He shifted in his seat, his eyes scanning the vicinity. There were no other flight attendants nearby. Quickly returning his attention to the scene, he now saw that the short, burly man was attempting to force his way out into the aisle while simultaneously shouting his desire to be taken to the pilot.

Not waiting to see what would happen next, he rose and briskly headed in the direction of the disturbance. His trim frame made it easy to progress quickly down the aisle; however, he had to hunch forward slightly due to his height. As he approached, two distinct smells assaulted his senses: alcohol and cheap cologne.

He gave the flight attendant a fleeting glance. "I can handle him. Go find one of the others and let them know what's going on."

"Ri-ight," she stuttered, backing away. "Thank you."

Ryan nodded then turned to face the unruly passenger. "I think it would be wise for you to sit back down and take it easy. The plane will be landing soon, and you can get a drink in the terminal." In an undertone, he added, "She's only doing her job. No need to take it personally."

"Out of my way!" he blustered, not backing down. "You can't tell me what'd do to!" He renewed his effort to enter the aisle.

Ryan waited until he felt the rough jab of the man's elbow against his ribs. If anyone was watching, he wanted it to be clear who had started the altercation. Without hesitating, he placed a hand on the man's chest and roughly shoved him back into the row, toward the empty window seat. "If you try that again, they might have to restrain you, you know."

With a snarl, the man viciously kicked his leg toward Ryan, but it wasn't long enough to make contact – a fact Ryan had considered before he'd shoved him back into the row.

Once more, the man stood and faced Ryan. "You're not in charge of the plane, asshole! Who do'ya think you are?"

Ryan remained silent, focusing on the man's stance and body language. He waited. The tension of the passengers around them was palpable. And it didn't help that a baby was wailing in the background.

The man lurched towards him again. "Move!"

"Calm down." Ryan attempted to keep the edge out of his tone, still hoping he could deescalate the situation. "Like I said, the plane will be landing soon. I know you're upset, but she's not allowed to serve you anymore – that's the airline's policy. And it's also federal regu -"

The man lunged forward, and this time Ryan stepped to the side, allowing him out into the aisle where it would be much easier to restrain him. By now, several concerned passengers had risen from their seats to take in the spectacle. Ignoring them, he watched the man fall forward and stumble against the adjacent row of seats. He quickly regained his balance, and Ryan took a deep breath, waiting for the punch that he was

99% sure was headed his way. He was proven right a second later, but before the man's fist could get anywhere near his face, Ryan took him down to the ground with a few swift moves. Careful not to injure him or restrict his breathing, he put his knee gently on the man's lower back then pinned his arms behind him. A moment later, the flight attendant returned with a male coworker who was holding a restraining kit. He promptly removed a pair of zip ties from it.

Ryan glanced at the attendant and reached for the ties. "I think it'll be easier if I do it."

Nodding, the attendant handed the ties over.

Once Ryan had secured the man's wrists, he gently eased him off the ground and back to a standing position. The sounds of startled passengers had subsided, and the aisle behind them began to clear as people returned to their seats.

Without releasing his hold, Ryan guided the still-struggling individual back into the row and waited until the flight attendant had a handle on him. He was just about to step away and return to the first class cabin when he felt a light touch on his arm.

"Thanks." The female flight attendant leaned toward him and gave him a shy smile.

"Happy to help." He was tempted to linger but decided against it.

As he slid back into his seat, he glanced down the aisle, listening for any further signs of protest. All was quiet. Hopefully, the guy would simply pass out for the rest of the flight.

"Well, that was something," said his companion, smiling. "Where'd you learn how to do that?"

"Martial arts," he grinned. "About fifteen years' worth to be precise. It was my mom's way of keeping me and my brother out of trouble." He refastened his seatbelt. "She always said that one boy equaled half a brain – two equaled no brain."

"Sound theory," the man chuckled, leaning back in his seat. "Well you certainly impressed that stewardess. She's looking at you, you know." He smiled and gave him a light prod with his elbow. "Maybe you should find out what her dinner plans are for tonight."

Ryan glanced briefly in her direction then shrugged. "I don't think she's really my type." Too much makeup. But that aside, he wasn't interested in a layover fling.

Above them, the intercom crackled again.

"Ladies and gentlemen," the pilot announced, "we hope you've enjoyed your flight with us. The current temperature in Chicago is approximately 75 degrees and the local time is 10:32am. We'll begin our descent shortly. Please take your seats and fasten your seatbelts."

Ryan leaned forward and gently pushed his briefcase underneath the seat in front of him. The pressure began to build in his ears as the plane pitched downward. Leaning back, he closed his eyes, enjoying the sound of the roaring engines and the aeronaut pull of gravity on his chest. It felt good to be getting out from underneath the cloak of dense clouds that had been hovering over Seattle for the last few weeks.

The landing was smooth, and it wasn't long before he was free of the plane and its stale air. On his way out of the terminal, he grabbed some coffee and a bagel then caught the next 'L' train headed downtown. He chose a seat on the right-hand side, toward the back. A minute later, a teenage girl with neon colored hair, multiple piercings, and a small dog tucked under her arm shuffled towards him. He breathed an inner sigh of relief when she passed his row. After being on the plane, he wanted his space. He could've taken a taxi to the hotel, but there was something nostalgic about riding the 'L.' Perhaps it stemmed from his childhood obsession with trains.

Twenty minutes later, the city skyscrapers came into view, and he started paying closer attention to the stops. Eventually, the 'L' slowly pulled up to his and jolted to a standstill. He gathered his things then moved towards the door. After the 45-minute ride from the airport, he was ready to walk around for a bit. Lithely, he stepped off onto the sidewalk and headed in the direction of his hotel. It was the same one he always booked, nestled between an old historic bank and a skyscraper.

As he waited at the next crosswalk, he took a minute to call the front desk, confirming that his room was ready. He hung up as the light turned, and he continued down the street, enjoying the vibrant energy of people going places and doing things. Eventually, the hotel came into view, and with a few brisk strides he was at the main entrance. He stepped through the revolving door and into the lobby. Overhead, hundreds of soft glittering lights extended their glow in the reflection of the marble tiles and ebony paneled walls. A hushed, rhythmic sense of movement flowed throughout the spaciousness, and the sound of footsteps softly echoed across the tiled atrium. He could almost hear the hint of jazz somewhere as he walked up to the front desk, rolling his carry-on to an abrupt stop behind his heel. He took out his wallet and placed it on the counter.

The receptionist looked up with a smile. "Checking in?"

"Yes," he replied. "I think I spoke with you on the phone a few moments ago."

She smiled again, this time with a slight blush. "Yes, that was me. Mr. Harker, right?"

He nodded. "Ryan Harker."

"Perfect, I'll pull up your reservation now." He listened to the sound of her fingernails clicking on the keys.

She stopped suddenly, keeping her eyes on the screen. Her face took on a confused expression as she moved the computer mouse in a circular motion then started typing again. "Sorry this is taking so long," she stuttered. "I hit a wrong button, and it took me back to the beginning." The color in her cheeks deepened further, and he sensed that he was making her nervous.

He smiled reassuringly. "No worries, take your time."

A few more minutes passed before she looked up again and breathily said, "Alright, you're all set. Here's your room key." She handed it to him in a lingering manner. "Is there, um....anything else I can do for you, Mr. Harker?"

"No, I'm all set." He reached for the handle of his carry-on, managing to keep himself from grinning at her obvious interest; it wasn't the first time he'd had this kind of effect on a woman. "Thanks for your help."

"Anytime," she responded, blushing. "Enjoy your stay with us."

He turned and headed for the elevator. Sometimes he wished he could bring himself to give in to his baser desires. He hadn't slept with anyone since he and Katie had split, and the receptionist would've been easy prey. However, after surviving the emotional wake of the breakup, he'd decided to go back to the basics: abstinence. The last two years without sex had allowed him to focus completely on his work and building the future he wanted. Plus, he'd been able to sit back from a distance and watch the relationships of family and friends around him: which ones were working and which ones had fallen apart. And why, to both.

Now, two years later, he felt like he'd figured a few things out: starting a relationship with sex first made for a very unstable foundation; going from relationship to relationship was a coping mechanism for loneliness; and a good relationship should get better over time, not worse. Ultimately, at the end of the day, he'd made a commitment to himself: he would remain abstinent until he found the woman he wanted to spend the rest of his life with. He wasn't quite sure if he'd have the strength to remain true to his commitment, but he planned on trying. And at least his decision wasn't being dictated by the religious belief system in which he'd been raised. He'd left that behind long ago.

Ryan smiled as his thoughts drifted to his parents. The passing years hadn't done much to change their views and opinions. If anything, life's turbulence over the years had caused them to become further entrenched in their beliefs. But as much as he disagreed with them over certain points, he'd recently begun to appreciate the differences between them, and he could see the value of a moral principle, like abstinence, outside of a religious encapsulation. Nonetheless, he was dead set on keeping his decision to himself. It was hard enough when friends asked about his non-existent dating life, and the last thing he wanted was for his parents to think that he was "coming back around" to their way of seeing things. That would certainly never happen, not after he'd experienced what life was like outside the matrix of organized religion.

As he continued to wait for the elevator, his thoughts returned to the woman at the counter. He tried to imagine himself in a romantic relationship without having sex first. It was hard to visualize.

A moment later the elevator doors opened, interrupting his thoughts, and he stepped inside its gilded interior. After a short ride, followed by a lengthy walk down the wide hallway, he located his room. Once inside, he rolled his carry-on to the closet then kicked off his shoes and took a seat on the edge of the bed. Next, he unzipped the leather shoulder bag that served as his briefcase and blindly rifled through the opening for his planner. After shoving aside a pad of paper, he pulled it out along with a silk tie that had looped itself around one corner. With a smile, he removed the tie, folded it, and gently placed it back into the narrow opening. His secretary must have slipped it in before he'd left his office that morning, making sure he had an extra one in case he needed it.

Opening the planner, he began to review his handwritten agenda for the following day. While most people his age favored digital methods for keeping track of meetings and notes, he preferred paper; there was just something about the feel of a pen in his hand and the reading of his own handwriting, which wasn't to say that he didn't utilize the organizational features across his devices, but his preferred method was the best option for simplicity and efficiency – two things he valued.

As he continued to analyze his schedule for the following day, he looked for anything he might have missed. After adding a note in the margins about asking his housekeeper to pick up some dry cleaning, he closed it and set it on the nightstand. It was perfect – plenty of time afterward to meet up with his former college roommate. He was a little surprised that Peter had insisted on making the drive up from St. Louis to see him, especially given the fact that they easily could have arranged something after his return to Seattle. Since Peter lived in Portland, the drive wouldn't have been far for either of them, but Peter had been adamant on the phone that it was no trouble at all since he was already in the area visiting family, and he didn't mind getting away.

It'd been a few years since he'd last seen Peter, even though they lived within driving distance of each other. Their professions kept them both busy year-round. And then there'd been the breakup with Katie two years ago, right after Peter's wedding – at the wedding was more accurate. He quickly turned his thoughts away from any mental track that was headed toward watching past footage of his relationship with her. He'd managed to pull off the role of best man at the wedding without raising any eyebrows, but the months that followed had been rough, even though he'd been the one to break off the relationship. The wedding was the last time he'd seen Peter. He vaguely remembered his mom saying something recently about him and a baby announcement, maybe? He felt bad for not knowing, but he didn't do the social media thing. From his brief experience with it, he had concluded that it was a means of turning some wonderfully nice people into complete narcissists. He was probably old-fashioned, but so be it.

The following morning, he was shown to Howard Lowell's office suite where he had a brief wait before the CEO opened his door and greeted him with a warm handshake.

"It's great to finally meet you, Ryan."

Closing the door behind them, Howard gestured toward one of the large plush armchairs facing his desk. "From what I've heard, you've earned quite the reputation as an innovative strategist." He grinned broadly and added, "I've also heard that you're an even better visionary – I'm keen to hear your thoughts during today's meetings."

Ryan nodded. "I'm looking forward to it."

As soon as Howard was seated behind his gleaming mahogany desk, he swiveled his chair around and asked, "So, how long will you be in Chicago?"

"Just for the day – I'm flying back to Seattle tonight."

2

Late afternoon sunshine fell in scattered patches along the sidewalk as Ryan made his way toward Milton's Coffeehouse. The series of meetings had flowed well, and he'd had an opportunity to speak with Howard after the other board members left. He hadn't intended to state his true intentions regarding Howard's business; this trip had been purely about gaining more information and seeing the structural condition of the building before considering making an offer. However, based on what he'd gathered throughout the day's meetings, it was clear that buying him out would be mutually beneficial for all parties. He expressed this to Howard privately and was met with some initial defensiveness, which didn't surprise him since Howard's father had founded the company and there was sentimental value. However, after explaining his proposal in more detail, Howard had warmed to the idea, and they'd ended the day on a promising note.

As he stopped at the next crosswalk, waiting for the light to turn, he took a deep breath and cleared his mind of all work-related thoughts. The air smelled fresh; it must have rained earlier that day because he could hear tires splashing through puddles. As the light turned green, a couple rushed past him, laughing and holding hands. He brushed by them and stepped up to the curb. Ahead, he could faintly make out the sign for the coffeehouse. It was an old favorite of his, reminding him of his first visit to Chicago with his dad.

A moment later, he opened the door and ducked inside. The scent of freshly ground coffee enveloped him as he quickly scanned the interior, looking for an open table. His eyes landed on a booth nestled in a quiet back corner, and he began to advance in that direction. He angled his way around a small cluster of customers then sidestepped a pair of children running in his direction.

An exasperated woman called after them. "Say excuse me! And stop running – this isn't a playground!"

She halted briefly and offered an apology as he passed by; he gave her an understanding smile and continued toward his goal.

The owners had made some renovations since the last time he'd been there: the cheerful yellow had been painted over with a rich, forest green, and patterned wallpaper now adorned a few accent walls. The space felt heavier, more intimate and brooding...studious. He liked it.

He continued toward the back corner, and a moment later slid into the empty booth. Sinking into the velvet covered seat, he rested his head against the back of the booth and closed his eyes. After spending most of the day in a suit and tie, it felt great to be wearing street clothes. He took a deep breath in, reveling in the overall atmosphere before casting a sidewise glance toward the bustling front entrance. He then shifted his gaze to a section of wooden tables arranged neatly in rows; the dark, polished surfaces of the tabletops and chairs gleamed brightly in the sunlight. Eventually, his eyes landed on a piece of artwork hanging on the wall opposite him. It was an abstract piece, with the colors running wild and free across the canvas, but it somehow gave him a sense of peace. Perhaps it was just nice to look at something chaotic and know that everything on the canvas was confined to the edges of the frame.

A jingling sound near the front of the coffeehouse directed his attention once more toward the service bar, and he watched as a familiar figure wearing jeans and a Notre Dame T-shirt emerged from the entryway. His short, sandy-colored hair was slicked back, and his face was clean-shaven.

Ryan slid out of the booth and walked briskly toward Peter, whose face lit up when he saw him coming.

"Hey, man!" he said, giving Ryan a solid hug with a thump on the back. "Good to see you!"

"You too," Ryan replied. He took a step back and glanced in the direction of the service counter. "Coffee?"

"I could definitely use some," Peter nodded. "The drive up took a little longer than I expected. Way more traffic than I'd thought there'd be, for a weekday."

As they waited in line, their conversation stayed light, with cursory commentary on sports and recent political happenings; however, by the time they were headed back to their table, coffees in hand, they were deep in a discussion regarding Peter's recent transfer to the sexual assaults' unit at the Portland D.A.'s office. He had just inherited a number of high-profile cases from a retiring attorney, and he was now prepping for a trial on one of the more difficult ones.

The flow of dialogue halted between them as they each placed their mugs on the table and scooted into the booth.

Once settled, Peter continued, "It's set for August, so I have some time." He took a sip of coffee then set his mug down slowly. "It'll be nice to have that one done before the baby comes."

Ryan grinned at the sheepish look on his friend's face. "My mom mentioned you guys were expecting. When's the due date?"

"December 10th," Peter answered, his eyes lighting with excitement. "We're finding out the gender in a few weeks."

"That's great, I'm happy for you guys." And truly, he was.

"We're excited and a little nervous at the same time." Peter took another sip of coffee then gave Ryan a sideways glance. "So are you and Katie still dating? You guys seemed pretty serious the last time I saw you."

Ryan looked down at the table for a second then replied, "We broke up right after your wedding." He shrugged his shoulders and reached for his mug. "The wedding made me realize that our relationship wasn't headed toward marriage, and we were both facing career choices; in the end, she decided that she wanted to move back to Virginia, and my life is in Seattle. So that was that."

"Hmm," Peter responded, giving him a brief glance. "Well, I'm sorry it didn't work out." He tilted his mug sideways, gently swirling the liquid around before taking a sip. "So what brings you to Chicago? Business?"

Ryan nodded. "I just got done with a series of meetings with the CEO of a food processing plant. I'm thinking about buying him out and converting it into a manufacturing center. They're struggling a bit, and I have a feeling they'll accept my offer." He felt a twinge of guilt. Howard and the other board members had been expecting him to help turn the business around, not offer them a deal on selling the building and equipment. But based on Howard's reaction to his initial offer, Ryan felt hopeful.

Peter leaned forward, resting his elbows on the table. "You're in manufacturing now?"

"Indirectly. I'm working with a start-up company that manufactures systems for rainwater harvesting and ground recharging. It's part of a larger project that I'm overseeing with a group of investors, and the goal is to help underdeveloped countries obtain clean drinking water. We want to provide something that's both affordable and efficient." He leaned back in his seat, lifting his mug as he did so. "And sustainable." He took a sip.

"Interesting."

"There's a lot of angles to it. The start-up we're supporting will need some major structural changes before the whole thing can be up and running. At least the building itself is sound. We'll only need to do some minor construction to make it fit our purposes." He took another sip. "I want to section off parts of the building in a way that gives us space to add engineering and research divisions, along with the manufacturing component."

"You're leading this project?" Peter asked, raising an eyebrow.

"You could say that." Ryan grinned, ducking his head self-consciously. "I originated it."

Peter gave him a wide grin. "Sounds like you've been busy over the last two years." He looked intently at Ryan for a moment then slowly said, "Your work must be pretty time-consuming, I imagine?"

"It can be." He absently shuffled his mug from side to side, stirring the dregs around. He got the strange impression that there was something more behind Peter's questioning. Idly stretching his arm along the top of the seat's back, he asked, "So how long are you here for?"

"Until Wednesday. I haven't been back in a while, so I figured I'd stay an extra day or two with my parents."

"They still live in the old neighborhood?" Ryan felt a sudden longing for the small town on the outskirts of St. Louis where he and Peter had grown up, a block away from one another.

"Yeah," Peter nodded. "Same old house, not much has changed."

"Seems about right," Ryan smiled good-humoredly. "You think you'd ever move back?"

With an abrupt laugh, Peter replied, "No, not planning on it. You have to really love it here." He looked sideways at Ryan and added, "I see you didn't move back."

"True." He stared down at his mug for a moment then grinned at Peter. "You remember the time your mom found that king snake behind the washing machine?"

"Yes," Peter responded, chuckling. "The way she was screaming, my dad thought somebody had lost an arm, or died."

"The thing was huge," Ryan laughed. "I remember it took forever to get it to come out. Honestly, I still can't believe your mom chose not to move out of the house after that."

"Yeah, surprisingly," Peter grinned, shrugging his shoulders.

They both took a sip from their mugs, a moment of silence ensuing before Peter hunched forward and casually said, "I'm glad the timing worked out on both our ends so we could catch up in person." He looked down at his coffee for a second then added surreptitiously, "Although I'm afraid this whole time I've had an underlying motive for seeing you. I need your input on something."

"I thought there was a little more to this meetup," Ryan grinned. "You didn't give me much information when we talked on the phone. I've been wondering when you were going to get around to it." He lowered his arm from the seat back and leaned forward in anticipation.

"Well, it's not so much about input. It's really more of a proposal."

Ryan studied him for a second. "You have that look on your face."

"What look?"

"Like you want me to do something that could end up with me getting lost in a cave." He grinned. Peter knew exactly what he was referring to.

"Hey," Peter smirked, "you followed me of your own free will. And technically, your brother was the one who suggested it in the first place. And," he pointed at Ryan," while we're at it, let's not forget the trip you planned. The one where we got stuck in a monsoon."

"So we got a little wet," he replied, remembering their excursion to Cambodia. He'd convinced the guys to go in the off-season to save some money, so they'd blamed him personally for the sudden downpour they'd been caught in; as punishment, they'd tied their wet gear to his pack, making him carry the extra weight until everything was mostly dry. He grinned and added, "You guys definitely needed the shower."

"Riiight," Peter scoffed with a smile. He was quiet for a second then continued, "Well, you're right about me wanting to propose something that has an element of danger to it." He leaned forward and folded his hands on the table. Slowly, his smile faded. "I wish I could say that I have some carefree adventure in mind." His face grew tense, and his eyes hardened. "This wouldn't be like anything you've done before."

Just as he was about to continue, a barista stopped at their table and asked if she could take their cups. Ryan quickly gathered them both and handed them to her. He waited until she was out of earshot then looked back at Peter. "Does this involve something illegal?"

"No," Peter laughed. "At least, I don't think so." His shoulders slumped as he sighed. "I don't know. I've been rehearsing this conversation in my head over the last few days, and now I can't figure out where to begin." His brow furrowed. "I'll just start at the beginning, I guess."

Ryan nodded for him to continue, his sense of humor fading as he watched Peter's face cloud.

"Well, I've already mentioned that most of my caseload relates to sexual assaults, which includes a few sex trafficking cases." He paused for a second, running a hand through his hair before continuing. "So anyway, last week we got a case involving a trafficking victim. The feds ended up taking it, but I've kept in contact with the investigating agent, Tom Mitchell. I spoke with him on Thursday, and well..." He looked at Ryan. "You might be useful to the case. I drove up here to see if you'd be interested."

Ryan simply stared at him, his mind blank. "Interested? In what exactly?"

"I'll explain." Lowering his voice, Peter continued, "The victim in the case was being trafficked by some sort of organized syndicate. Mitchell thinks they might be operating out of Seattle, but he's not positive. The victim hasn't given them much to go on thus far – Mitchell thinks she's still too scared to open up. She has a follow up interview this afternoon, so hopefully she'll disclose more information. At any rate, based on her responses thus far, we think the head of this particular trafficking ring is an upper-level executive of some sort." He leaned closer. "We're not talking about an average pimp, here. Somehow this guy's built a network of high-profile clientele, but no one has any clues as to his identity. Or those of the clients. It seems that he's able to maintain a reputable front." He shrugged his shoulders and added, "For all we know, this guy could even be a woman."

Frowning, Ryan hunched forward and placed his elbows on the table. "A woman would actually traffic other women?"

Peter nodded. "It can happen, especially in pimp culture. There's a lot of psychology and methodology to all of it but basically, once a pimp gets control over a woman and turns her out, she'll do pretty much anything that's demanded of her." He paused then explained, "'Turning out' is part of the pimp inside lingo. It refers to the process that a pimp follows to gain a woman's trust and establish a strong emotional attachment, usually by posing as a loving partner or a father figure." He lowered his voice even further and added, "Once a pimp's formed that kind of attachment, it's easy for him to use his influence to get whatever he wants – money, namely. But control is also a big part of it. That feeling of power over another human being. And to add another element to the picture, a pimp will frame everything in terms of 'being a family.' He takes care of them and gives them what they need when they 'behave.' And the women who have been thoroughly reconditioned will often work just to get his approval, along with any positive attention." He sat back and sighed. "There's just a lot to it, on both a psychological and emotional level. They usually target easy prey, like runaways from a foster home, or someone with a mental illness. Drug addicts – basically, any female who's financially unstable and looking for someone who can provide love and support."

"Hmm." Ryan glanced absently towards the open area of tables next to their booth, processing his thoughts, then looked back at Peter. "So whoever is running this sex trafficking ring is going out and finding young, vulnerable women? I mean, how's he able to do that? He's just picking them up off the street?"

"Not exactly. The majority of the women, from what our victim – Kristen – has told us, seem to have been enticed and were not necessarily in vulnerable positions. She said that the traffickers are targeting women who have more to offer than just a pretty face, so I wouldn't say 'off the street' either – they want educated and poised, along with the looks. Kristen said that most were promised lucrative jobs in the modeling industry." He leaned forward. "However, in Kristen's case, she was abducted. She met the guy at a college job fair in Portland – we're guessing he was posing as a recruiter. He asked her out to dinner, and he must have slipped something in her drink.

She has no memory of what happened after that. She barely remembers what he looks like. Never saw him again."

"But she remembers having dinner with him?"

"Yes. She just doesn't know what happened between the dinner and the moment she woke up alone in an unfamiliar room. She found out in stages that she'd been taken to some sort of underground complex."

"Hmm," Ryan pondered. "So the guy who abducted her is the same person who's running everything?"

"No, the feds don't think so. He's probably just one pawn in a bigger scheme." He rubbed the back of his neck then with a flourish of his hand, said, "I'll give you the short version of what we've learned thus far." He cleared his throat. "Kristen was taken to the complex where she was held, along with a group of other women, and 'trained.' Once she was deemed ready, she was moved on to the next stage: traveling with clients on board a superyacht for weekend getaways." He lowered his voice again. "Sounds like the person heading everything up operates his enterprise under the guise of a gentleman's club. The 'clients' appear to have paid memberships, with all the sexual activity taking place on the yacht."

"You're saying the club is on a yacht? And what do you mean by 'trained'?"

"Yes. From what Kristen's revealed, the yacht is the club. And by trained, I mean they're supposed to provide clients with the ultimate experience, and not just sexually. They're expected to be intelligent and refined. Sophisticated. Apparently, the club is quite exclusive and meant to cater to the very top." He gave Ryan a pointed look. "And that's where you come in."

Ryan raised an eyebrow. "How so?"

"Your mission would be to position yourself in a way that would get you access to whoever's running the club. You'd have to connect with someone who knows a guy, who knows another guy, etcetera, so you can get a membership." He squared his shoulders. "Like I said, you have the social status, business acumen, and financial credentials. And you've been publicly recognized for several successful entrepreneurial endeavors." He grinned at the look of surprise on Ryan's face. "Yes, I Googled you, you egotistical bastard."

Ryan tilted his head and laughed. "Go on..."

Peter rolled his eyes. "I was going to add 'networking capabilities' to your list of assets – that's key to all of this." He took a deep breath and leaned in. "You'll need to assume the persona of a wealthy socialite who's just looking for a good time – and a way to spend his money. It'd just be a matter of getting you into the right crowd of people, so you can rub some shoulders. And your profession is perfect for being able to do that. Plus, you live in Seattle..." His voice trailed off.

Ryan ran his thumb absently along the edge of his jaw for a few seconds, pondering, then looked at Peter. "You're really serious about this."

"Yes. I am. And it's not like the feds are looking for one person to go in and take the place down. There's already a task force in play. You'd simply need to establish some connections, maybe gather some intel. Law enforcement would take it from there." After a moment's reflection he added, "When I talked with Agent Mitchell, he didn't think anyone on the task force would be able to hold up to the scrutiny if they went undercover." He shrugged his shoulders. "None of them have any real business credentials or the necessary pre-established social connections." He grinned. "You, on the other hand, would be able to pull the role off without suspicion, and like I said, you already have a solid business network in place."

A moment of silence ensued in which Peter stared at the table, while Ryan glanced absently at the painting on the wall.

"So how time intensive would this be?" Ryan finally asked.

Peter leaned casually back into his seat. "I think you'd mostly be spending your evenings exploring what Seattle has to offer for adult entertainment, along with attending any kind of high-profile social events." His eyebrows furrowed, and he added, "You might have to scale down your business dealings in order to commit at a level that would produce results. However, on the flip side, there's strong financial backing for this project. The victim's family has contributed quite a sum to help support the investigation, so between their contributions and what the FBI will provide, you'd have everything you need, including contract pay and special training."

Ryan flicked his hand dismissively. "I don't care about the money, but this sounds like I'd be entering a whole new profession. It doesn't quite sound like a side-job to me."

"I suppose that's true." Peter's eyes gleamed. "But remember, your current profession is your cover." "Riiiight," Ryan replied, smiling jauntily. "I forgot."

Peter leaned back in his seat. "Well, at any rate, I think before considering the offer any further, I'd suggest you call Agent Mitchell." He removed a business card from his wallet and slid it across the table.

Ryan picked it up and gave it a brief glance. "This does sound interesting to me, but I just don't know if I have the time to make a real commitment." He looked absently at the card again. "I need to think about it."

There was an empty silence for a moment, then Peter slowly asked, "How much do you really know about sex-trafficking?"

Ryan took a moment to reflect before answering. "Honestly, not much. I just know it's a huge problem." He paused then added, "I think the mainstream public is aware and empathetic enough to donate money to certain anti-trafficking organizations, but I think for most individuals, it ends there."

Peter nodded in agreement.

Ryan looked down at the table, noticing the wood grain and the feel of varnish on his fingertips. After a second, he said, "Do you remember the law enforcement seminar we went to in high school, the one where Tyler Ruger's dad was a keynote speaker?" They'd both known the Ruger family since elementary school.

Peter nodded slowly. "Yeah, I remember."

Ryan could see the searching look behind Peter's eyes, and he knew what they were both thinking about. And he didn't want the conversation going in that direction. Instead, he grinned and continued, "So you remember how cool we all thought he was?"

"Tyler's dad? Yeah, I mean just his name alone — *Jack Ruger*." With a laugh, Peter added, "I remember the time Tyler brought him in for career show-and-tell. Every kid in our school wanted to be an undercover agent afterward, I swear."

Ryan grinned and continued, "At the seminar Jack talked about a trip he made to Thailand. I think it was part of a church mission trip or something. I remember he said a few pastors went with him."

"Yeah, he was fairly active in our church," Peter responded. "I don't recall him ever telling that story though."

"It was intriguing to me, and it left an impression." He hunched forward and continued, "While they were there, his group worked with the local police to identify sex sellers in red-light districts. They posed as johns then reported their information back to law enforcement." He glanced absently down at the table. "I just remember listening to his story and thinking that someday..." He looked back at Peter. "I thought I might want to do something like that."

Both were silent for a moment.

Finally, Ryan concluded, "If I were to decide to do this, I'd be all in. You know I don't half-ass anything."

"No, you never have," Peter grinned. "I'm glad you'll consider it. I really do think this is a unique opportunity. You could make a big difference in a lot of lives." His face clouded over suddenly, and his smile faded. "There's something else I have to tell you though." He took a deep breath, then with furrowed brows continued, "There's another reason for why I volunteered your name." He hesitated, and his eyes darted to the table momentarily. Looking up, he finished quietly, "Ryan, the FBI have reason to believe that one of the women being trafficked is Tara Hayes."

Riding the 'L' back to the airport two hours later, Ryan was still having difficulty processing Peter's revelation. There must have been some sort of mix-up. Tara simply could not be one of the victims. It was just too bazaar. He'd find out for sure once he could connect with the FBI agent, but there was no longer any question in his mind as to whether he would take on the assignment.

He arrived at the airport later than he'd planned and barely made his flight; by the time he landed in Seattle, he was exhausted.

"They have reason to believe that one of the women being trafficked is Tara Hayes."

The sentence kept repeating itself in his mind like a broken record.

3

The following morning, Ryan awakened to the sound of a boat motor and the chirping of birds. Sitting up with a yawn, he barely registered the soft morning sunlight seeping in through the thin curtains of his bedroom window. He felt hungover, despite not having consumed any alcoholic beverages in weeks, and like a wrecking ball, his conversation with Peter came back to him. He ran his hand through his hair, processing everything all over again, trying to remember each detail. Finally, he glanced at his phone lying on his nightstand. *Fuck.* It was almost 9:30. Fortunately, he didn't have any meetings on his agenda that day, and he'd already planned to work from home. He glanced around his room then rose and walked over to the chair where he'd tossed his jeans and T-shirt the night before. He retrieved his wallet from his jeans pocket and took out the business card Peter had given him. After staring at it for a few seconds, he grabbed his phone and dialed the FBI agent's number. Almost immediately, his call went to voicemail. He left a brief message then tossed the phone on the bed, frustrated. He knew he wouldn't be at ease until he could speak with the agent.

His stomach was growling, and he groaned as he suddenly remembered that his housekeeper was away on vacation until the end of the week; she would have had breakfast all set and waiting for him. However, on the other hand, he was grateful for the alone time as he needed space to think through everything. He walked to the kitchen and started a pot of coffee then put a slice of bread in the toaster. Ten minutes later, with toast and coffee in hand, he seated himself at the breakfast table. After scooting his chair forward a few inches, he opened his laptop. In the search bar, he typed "tara hayes berkeley college." Peter had said she'd attended for a few years. The top three results were generic links to the college, followed by a LinkedIn profile belonging to a "Tara Richardson." The link directly underneath that one was for an obituary. After verifying that Tara was not the same person as Tara Richardson, he clicked on the images tab at the top of the search bar. None of the resulting photos looked anything like her. He thought for a moment, then typed "tara hayes highland school district." That line of inquiry eventually led him to a second-grade photo of her, looking almost like he remembered her from the last time he'd seen her. He tried a few more generic searches, skimming through the resulting links as he went along, but didn't find any additional information or photographs. She didn't appear to be on any social media.

He took a sip of his coffee and tried to recall the first names of her parents. He'd always referred to them as Mr. and Mrs. Hayes, so it took a while for him to remember her mother's first name: Diana. She'd been an art teacher at one of the local elementary schools. He still couldn't recall her father's name, but he knew that he'd been an architect.

Frowning, he set his mug down and was just about to try a different search when he heard his phone vibrate against the hard surface of the granite kitchen counter behind him. Leaning back in his chair, he grabbed it and saw that it was his sister.

"Hey," he said, taking the call. "Happy Birthday."

"You, too!" she replied brightly. "Are you doing anything special? You are planning on going over to mom and dad's tonight, right? To celebrate?"

"Yeah, I'll be there." He figured he didn't have much of a choice, and it wasn't worth the effort to explain to his twin sister that he wasn't really in the mood to celebrate their thirtieth birthday. "When is Andrew getting in?" His brother had been out of town competing in a Taekwondo championship.

"He got back late last night," she replied. "I picked him up at the airport."

"Did he tell you how it went?"

"Kind of. He seemed pretty tired, and we didn't talk much, but he was in a good mood." She smiled and added, "I'm sure the two of you will enjoy picking apart the details of the match tonight."

He took a sip of coffee and glanced at his laptop, scanning the list of search results again, looking for anything pertinent to Tara.

"So," Rachel continued, "You have any plans, other than dinner tonight?"

"No, not really, just working. You?"

"I'm getting a manicure, then coffee with a friend. We might go shopping for a birthday dinner outfit."

His phone started vibrating once more, and his heartrate sped up; he was quickly disappointed however when he saw that it was just his business partner calling, and not Agent Mitchell. "Hey Rach – sorry to cut things short. I've got another call coming in. I'll see you later tonight, okay?"

"Alright, no worries. See you then."

He quickly accepted the incoming call.

"Hey Sean. I'm guessing you got that CoStar report from the broker yesterday." Ryan could hear traffic in the background, and he assumed Sean was driving.

"Yes," Sean replied. "You're going to have to explain those graphs he put in. They don't make any sense to me."

Half an hour later, they were still going over some of the analytics when Ryan's phone began to vibrate yet again. This time, the caller ID displayed an unknown number. After assuring Sean that he'd send a follow up email, he quickly hung up and accepted the call.

"This is Ryan."

"Hi Ryan, Agent Mitchell here....I got your voicemail. I'd like to talk to you in person if you have some time."

"Sure," he responded. "When were you thinking? I have some free time today if that works for you." He would clear his schedule if need be.

"That'd be great. How about 2:00?"

Ryan glanced at the clock. "Yeah, that works."

"Okay, my office is on the second floor. Someone will escort you up when you get here. You know where the building is?"

"It's a couple of blocks down from the art museum, right?" He'd already Googled the location but thought it wise to double check.

"Correct – right on 3rd, next to the library."

"Okay, got it."

He hung up then headed to the bathroom for a shower. The hot water running down his back felt good, and he was tempted to linger; however, if he wanted to catch the 1:10 ferry to the downtown district, he'd need to leave soon. He shut the water off and grabbed a towel. After a quick look in the mirror, he headed to his room and threw on a pair of jeans and an old Manchester United T-shirt. He glanced at his phone: 12:15. Plenty of time to walk to the ferry terminal. He hated driving around Bainbridge Island if he didn't have to, and he wouldn't be needing his car since the FBI building wasn't far from the wharf front. He walked briskly to the kitchen and gave it a brief scan before grabbing his keys and wallet.

Twenty minutes later found him standing at the back of the ferry, watching as the island shrank behind him. Resting his forearms on top of the side railing, he listened to the sound of the motor as it churned the water, tossing spray and foam into its wake. He shifted his gaze forward, his thoughts turning to Tara. Just thinking her name in his head brought on a rush of dark memories associated with the night her brother and sister had died in a tragic car accident. He shook his head and pushed away the mental images, focusing instead on what he remembered of the Hayes family. They'd moved into the neighborhood the summer that he'd turned twelve. The house they'd bought was just around the corner from his and Peter's. It hadn't taken long for him, Andrew, and Peter to become fast friends with Tara's brother, Preston, especially since they were all around the same age. They'd quickly absorbed Preston into their pack, and the two summers that followed had been full of backyard campouts, late-night football scrimmages, and mini expeditions into the woods surrounding their neighborhood.

Preston was fifteen at the time of the accident, which meant Tara must have been about eight or nine. She'd been the typical little sister, always trying to tag along. He suddenly felt guilty thinking about all the times they'd told her to leave them alone. She didn't have any siblings near her in age since both Preston and her sister, Brittany, were much older; it made sense that she was constantly shadowing them. Ryan and Andrew would never have admitted it to Preston, but they'd both had a crush on Brittany, even though – or because – she was roughly four years older. She was nineteen when the accident happened.

With a sigh, he moved on from his memories of that night and went back to focusing on what else he could remember about the Hayes. They'd been the typical suburban family. Mr. Hayes worked long hours and was often absent. Even when he was around, he was withdrawn and emotionally distant – characteristics exhibited by Ryan's own father. Mrs. Hayes, on the other hand, was warm and caring. She filled in the gaps left by Mr. Hayes and was always present at sporting events, recitals, and school plays. She took the kids to the catholic church down the road every Sunday, but he wouldn't have described her as staunchly religious.

That summed up what he knew about the Hayes. His family had moved to Seattle a few weeks after the funeral service, due to his father's prior acceptance of a job offer. He could still hear the rigidity in his father's voice as he explained why they weren't postponing the move. *"Ryan, I've already accepted the job. It's unfortunate timing, but we're not changing our plans now."*

And that was the only comfort he'd received over the loss of his best friend.

Once more, his thoughts turned back to the night of the car accident, but this time he couldn't distract himself; his mind was magnetically drawn back to the memory. The edges of it were vague, but the center of it was clear and bright, as if it had suddenly been placed under a blinding surgeon's light. It came back to him in a rush as he observed his fifteen-year-old-self sitting next to Preston's hospital bed in the intensive care unit. The scent of disinfectant pervaded his senses, and he could hear hushed, tired voices just outside the door. Mr. Hayes had tossed his jacket over the back of a vinyl armchair before exiting, leaving him and Preston alone in the dimly lit room, cast in shadow. All he could do was sit there, his eyes on the floor, listening to the sound of his friend's shallow breathing through his oxygen mask.

After a few minutes, Preston turned his head towards him. "Ryan," he whispered. There was a slight quiver in his voice. "I don't know what's going on and no one's telling me anything." His voice faltered. "I...I can't feel my legs."

Ryan couldn't think of a response, and he was desperately trying to hold back tears of his own. If there was ever a time to put on a brave front, this was it.

Preston attempted to slide his body closer in his direction, but Ryan could tell he was fighting against layers of sedation. "Hey," he said quietly, "don't try to move. I'm right here. I can hear you."

Preston ceased his effort. "Please, Ryan..." He paused to inhale. "I want you to promise me you'll look after Tara." His voice broke again as he exhaled and finished weakly, "you know, in case I..."

"No." Ryan swallowed the growing lump in his throat. "You're gonna be alright. The reason you can't feel anything is...it's just because they gave you a lot of pain killers and stuff." He could feel stinging tears gathering in the corners of his eyes, and his mind felt numb. Words weren't coming together properly in his head, so he just repeated, "You're fine, okay. Everything's fine." But he knew it wasn't. The doctors were all saying there was too much internal bleeding.

Preston laughed weakly. "Whatever makes you feel better." Silence filled the space between them for a moment then he added quietly, "Look, I already know that Brittany didn't..." His voice broke. "They wouldn't say anything when I asked...and that's how I know." His voice broke again. "I just don't want Tara to be all alone. I need to know that you'll look after her."

Ryan jerked himself out of the memory, but another one quickly took its place. Two caskets, sitting side by side, next to two freshly dug graves. Everyone wearing black. Black everywhere, in different shades and textures. His black wool sweater was itchy, and when he looked across from him, he saw Peter wearing a stiff black suit. If he looked down, he saw Andrew's black, scuffed up church shoes standing next to his. And if he looked up, he saw the black, glossy caskets. He couldn't escape the blackness, even when he closed his eyes. There was just an empty, black void behind his eyelids.

Another memory slowly began to emerge, one with Tara. It was the day after the funeral. He was knocking on the Hayes's front door, with a gift for her. Her father opened it and asked what he wanted; he couldn't think of anything to say, but then Tara had appeared in the doorway.

"Hi," she said softly, giving him a shy smile.

Her father went back inside, leaving them alone on the porch.

He handed Tara a stuffed animal, a small rabbit named Hoppity that had belonged to Rachel – she had planned to come with him to deliver it but had bailed at the last minute, overcome by tears.

Tara took the rabbit and hugged it tightly.

"Rachel wanted you to have it," he said. "She thought you'd like it."

Ryan sighed and let the memory slip away, but the twinge of guilt remained. He tried to convince himself that he'd done everything that a fifteen-year-old boy could have done to follow through on a promise like the one he'd made Preston. After all, he'd moved away, and it wasn't like he could have prevented this from happening to her. Even God didn't hinder the hand of tragedy – or just pure evil, for that matter. He suddenly felt angry at everything in general.

Still hunched over the railing, he watched the churning water and tried to calculate how old Tara would be now. She couldn't have been much older than nine at the time of the accident, and he was fifteen when it happened. They were six years apart....so she had to be about twenty-four now. He rubbed his jaw thoughtfully, trying to remember what had happened after he last saw her, but he was unable to recall anything else. After they'd moved, his parents hadn't stayed in touch with the family – a fact that heightened his feeling of anger. However, he acknowledged that at the end of the day, it'd been his responsibility to stay in contact.

As he continued reflecting, an image of a nine-year-old girl came into focus. Dark brown hair, pulled back in a stringy, disheveled ponytail. Wide, brown eyes, bright and full of innocence. He could feel his fist clenching around the railing as he thought about where she might be now. The sudden guilt punched him in the gut. *What if he was too late?*

As the ferry chugged steadily onward, he continued to think back over the two years that he'd known the Hayes family, grasping at his memories for the smallest details. He was finally pulled from his musings by the splattering sound of a seagull's droppings landing on the railing next to his forearm. He inched away, still leaning on the railing, and glanced towards the front of the ferry. The downtown skyline was closer than he'd expected it to be.

4

When he entered the FBI office on the fifth floor, the receptionist pointed to a seat positioned directly across from the agent's
door; it was closed, but Ryan could hear muffled conversation
behind it. After a few minutes of pretending not to listen, he
guessed the agent was on the phone with someone. To distract
himself, he casually looked around the room. There were some
large scuff marks just above the molding on the wall next to
the agent's door; a layer of dust rested along the top edge of the
molding. He looked to his left and noticed that a dull-colored
path had formed between the front entrance and the agent's
door, which he surmised was the result of years of footsteps
packing down the burgundy carpet fibers.

He pulled out his phone and began to skim through the
news headlines. Gradually, he became aware that the skin on
the underside of his left forearm was becoming irritated; the
chair in which he was seated was upholstered in some type of
rough, nubby fabric. He leaned forward, resting his elbows on
his knees, and continued reading.

Suddenly, the door in front of him opened and the agent
emerged. He was tall and slim, with dark blond hair and a
matching mustache; Ryan estimated him to be in his early for-

ties. Despite his lack of bulk, his presence seemed to fill the room, and an energetic aura radiated outward as he stepped forward with a smile.

"You must be Ryan Harker."

Ryan rose from his seat and found that they were almost eye level, with himself being the taller one. After exchanging a quick handshake, the agent moved aside so Ryan could enter his office first then he closed the door behind them. After gesturing toward a seat, Mitchell walked behind his desk, pulled his office chair out, and swiveled it around. Once he was seated, he wheeled it forward with his feet, the wheels squeaking.

"So, you know Peter Dalh," he said, raising an eyebrow.

"Yes," Ryan answered. "We grew up together."

"Whereabouts?"

"The Midwest. A small town, about an hour east of St. Louis."

The agent nodded. "I have some family out that way." He rested his elbows on his desk and clasped his hands together in front of him. "So you talked to Peter yesterday?"

Ryan nodded. "He told me about the case and said I might be useful to you guys."

"Right," Mitchell responded. "From what he's told me about you, it sounds like you're in a good position to help us with an aspect of the case, namely getting an 'in' with the guy who's running the club." He paused and glanced at Ryan. "The case is confidential, so if you decide to help us there'll be several waivers and other forms we'll need you to sign."

"Understood," he replied. "I want to help, but first can you tell me for certain that Tara Hayes is one of the victims?"

Slowly, the agent nodded. "I'm afraid she is." He paused then continued, "Peter told me that you both know her. Did he give you any other details about the case?"

"Just a brief overview." He cringed inwardly as waves of guilt and anger suddenly pounded him in the chest.

"Did he tell you about Kristen?" Mitchell continued. "The victim that got away?"

"Yeah. She jumped off the yacht and swam out to an island. Two men from the yacht followed her and started to attack her but were interrupted by some campers."

The agent nodded. "She was in rough shape by the time they got her to a hospital." He reached for a mug on his desk and paused to take a sip. "We had to wait until she was released before we could do any interviews, but since then, we've had three with her. We can listen to some of the audio from yesterday's in a minute – you can hear the details in her own words."

Since the agent still hadn't explained how they had proof of Tara's involvement, Ryan asked again, "But how do you guys know for certain that Tara's one of the victims?"

Without responding, Mitchell swiveled his chair to the right and reached for a thin manila file lying near his desk phone. "Here." He handed it to Ryan. "That's a copy of her missing person's report from the Portland PD. When we reviewed other recently filed missing person's reports filed in Portland and Seattle, and showed them to Kristen, she was able to ID her."

Ryan looked at the folder in his hand, unable to think of a response. All he could feel was the sinking of his heart as the last ray of hope he'd been holding onto was quickly extinguished. He slowly opened the folder and glanced at the contents.

The agent gave Ryan a few minutes to peruse the file then said quietly, "I know you were probably hoping it wasn't her. Can you tell me what you know about her?"

"I really don't know that much." His jaw clenched. "She was the little sister of my best friend...he died in a car accident when he was fifteen." He swallowed then quickly finished, "My family moved out of the area a few weeks after the funeral."

The agent reached for his mug again. "Sorry to hear that." He took another sip then placed it back on his desk.

Ryan stared vacantly at an empty wastebasket tucked away in the corner behind the agent's chair. "His older sister died in the accident too, so Tara was the only child they had left." He ran a hand through his hair and pushed on. "I think she was about nine at the time. I saw her at the funeral, and then it was kind of a blur from there. We moved to Seattle and that was that. I have no idea what Tara looks like now except for this photo." He glanced down at the folder the agent had given him. She was very attractive, with a few features that linked her to the girl he remembered, mostly her dark hair, wide brown eyes, and pointed chin. He closed it and handed it back to the agent. "She doesn't have any social media accounts, at least none that I could find."

"That's right." Mitchell took the folder and set it aside. "I'll have my staff assistant make a copy of that for you. So far, Portland PD hasn't picked up any leads as to the night of her disappearance so there's not much in the file." He leaned back in his chair and gave Ryan a sideways look. "Do you think she'd recognize you, if she were to see you?"

Ryan shook his head. "I don't think so. I was fifteen the last time I saw her. I doubt she'd recognize me now."

Mitchell nodded firmly. "That's good."

Frowning, Ryan responded, "How exactly is that a good thing?"

"Well, for starters, it would add another layer of complexity if she were to recognize you – assuming you'd even cross paths. And just for arguments sake, let's say that you do." He squared his shoulders. "If you tell her who you are, it'll raise more questions than we'd be willing to answer, since this is an on-going investigation with multiple victims. For now, we just need you to gain access to the organization." He took a quick sip from his mug then added, "It would undoubtedly draw the trafficker's attention to you if she were to recognize you." He gave Ryan a cautious look. "On a positive note, if we could manage to get her away, you have a better chance of gaining her trust over time, along with her cooperation in the investigation."

"You don't think she'd cooperate?" He couldn't imagine why she wouldn't, once she was rescued from the situation.

"It depends. A lot of trafficking victims are afraid of talking to law enforcement. They think they'll be charged with a crime. And often, that's what traffickers tell them, as a way to manipulate and coerce." He took another quick sip from his mug. "Traffickers can be ruthless in the misinformation and lies they tell these women once they have them under their control. And initially, many sex trafficking survivors won't even see themselves as a victim at all, depending on how long they've been with a trafficker. In most cases, the longer the time, the deeper the attachment. It usually takes multiple interviews with law enforcement to get to the bottom of the narrative. And the type of interview that we do is going to be different than the type of interview that, say, a therapist would do." He gave Ryan a quick glance. "If you do come across Tara, it'd be helpful for us to get a sense of just how deep she's in with the traffickers. If you can establish a degree of trust, that's probably when I'd say, 'Sure, go ahead and tell her who you are.' At that point, if she's willing to talk, it'll go a long way for her to have someone who's working with law enforcement, someone who's on her side, advocating for her. You might be the perfect person, if we make it to that stage."

"Okay." He reflected for a moment then asked, "So can you give me more details about the case?'

Mitchell set his mug down then leaned back in his chair, lifting one leg over the other so that his ankle rested on the opposite knee, and placed his hands behind his head. As the agent directed his gaze towards the ceiling, Ryan hunched forward in anticipation.

"Let's start with the night Kristen was abducted," Mitchel began. "She'd met a guy earlier that day at a college job fair in Portland, her city of residence. He told her he was a recruiter. He was attractive and well spoken, and she thinks he's of Arab descent. She remembers he wore a Rolex, but that's all the description we have on him thus far. They went out for dinner. Kristen's pretty sure he slipped something in her drink. She doesn't remember much after that, just brief snapshots. She thinks she might have been taken to a warehouse at some point, but her memories are vague during the time she was drugged." He lowered his hands, resting one elbow on the arm of his chair. "When she fully awoke, she was alone in a bedroom with no sense of her location or what day it was." The agent glanced at a nearby pad of paper, refreshing his memory. "Next, she went through what she described as 'orientation'."

He gave Ryan a sideways glance. "Apparently, these traffickers have a systematic process for brainwashing their victims – she describes all this in her interview. But basically, these guys target their victims ahead of time, enticing them with offers of employment in the modeling industry, and other similar, high-paying jobs. Once they get these women to the complex, they're kept in isolation for a few weeks to establish complete dependency on the traffickers for everything. Food, clothing, etc. The traffickers exercise total control, down to when they can use the bathroom. After that, they're assigned to a 'handler' who supervises them and is responsible for their wellbeing. It's all part of their process for forming an attachment." He lifted his hands and merged his fingers together, conveying synergy. "With any type of trafficking, the goal is to form a strong emotional bond. A lot of times it becomes romantic on the part of the victim. Kristen said that the women move in with their handler who then trains them, sexually, so that they'll perform well when they're with a client." The agent cleared his throat and continued, "She's had a hard time talking about the sexual elements of the case, but she verified that the handlers sleep with their 'trainees' on a regular basis. Part of forming an attachment."

With each new detail, Ryan's anger and frustration mounted. He clenched his fists, struggling to keep his emotions detached.

Mitchell seemed to think he might need a break because he asked, "Would you like some coffee? I forgot to ask before we sat down."

"No, thanks." Right now, he just wanted all of his questions answered. "Going back to the complex...do you guys have any clues as to where it is? Or any information about the yacht?"

"We're working on both those angles. Nothing yet on the yacht, but it shouldn't be that difficult. However, with that said, there are quite a handful of superyachts in the northwest area that could fit with Kristen's description." Mitchell set his mug down. "But once we identify it, we can track it to the complex using a GPS device." His forehead creased and in a grim tone, he added, "They may have multiple complexes and routes, but I strongly suspect that they dock somewhere near Seattle or Vancouver, based on where Kristen was found. We'll know more if we can get someone into the club to pose as a client and hopefully get some insider information on how the club operates their business." He gave Ryan a pointed look. "That's where you come in."

He nodded. "Do you think Tara will be on the yacht?"

"There's no guarantee. Kristen said that Tara hadn't completed her orientation yet. She only recognized her as a new face and said she'd shown up at the compound a few weekends ago. Kristen also said that none of the women go on the yacht until they're deemed ready, so it's possible Tara hasn't been approved yet." He gently rocked his chair back and forth with his foot. "Apparently all the sexual activity – with clients – takes place on the yacht."

"So she's been there for almost four weeks now?" Ryan asked, crossing his arms. "And this coming weekend will be her fifth weekend with them?" He'd already started tracking the dates, based on the information Peter had shared, but he wanted an official confirmation.

Mitchell nodded. "The missing person's report was filed on April 9th." He turned toward his computer, rolling his chair with him. "Let me pull up the audio from Kristen's interview. Just a sec."

Ryan watched as Mitchell refreshed his screen and clicked into a folder on his desktop. It took a moment for the media player to pull up on the screen, but once it was open Mitchell moved the time bar forward on the clip, stopping it near the two-minute mark. "Detective Bennett did the interview. She's great with these types of cases." He hit the play button then quickly adjusted the volume of the speakers. "This is the part where Kristen's talking about what happened on the yacht."

"....if we weren't with a client we were expected to help with hospitality duties, or whatever other areas needed coverage."

"Okay Kristen, that's helpful information." The detective's voice was calm and reassuring. *"Can you give me a little more specifics about what the expectations were when you were with clients?"* There was silence for a minute or so, and he heard muffled crying. *"I know this is hard for you,"* the detective continued. There was a slight pause, and he heard what sounded like someone blowing their nose. *"We want to help you all we can, and we're almost done. Then we'll take a break – we can pick this up again later, okay?"*

He heard ragged breathing for a moment or two then, *"Okay."* Kristen's voice was higher pitched now, and it broke as she asked, *"But what if they find me? What if they find out I've talked about all of this?"*

"We're doing everything we can to make sure that won't happen, and I want you to know that you're safe here. We're arranging a safe

place for you and your family, and you'll be able to see them soon. The more details you can give us, the faster we can get these guys." After a moment of silence, the agent continued, *"Let's focus on the yacht. You mentioned that it was used as a sort of floating playboy mansion....can you tell me how big it was?"*

"Yes," Kristen sounded calmer now as she continued, *"There's six decks. I can draw a picture of the layout for you."* He heard her take another deep breath. *"It's really nice, like staying at an expensive hotel. There's a pool, and a spa, a theater for performances, several lounges and bar areas, and a casino. The staterooms are all very luxurious, with lots of amenities. There're also a few VIP suites for clients who have medallion status. Those are larger and come with a view."*

"What does medallion status mean exactly?"

"It's the highest level of membership, but that's really all I know. I wasn't there long enough to figure out all the ins and outs of how the club membership worked. And we weren't supposed to ask questions. That was kind of a given."

"Can you tell me a little bit about the clients? How old they were?"

"Yeah, a lot of them were older. But I saw some younger guys too, mid-thirties maybe. I think the oldest guy I saw was in his seventies. I'd say most of the clients were in their late forties to early sixties."

"And how about the ages of the women?"

"I don't know for sure, but some were definitely high school age. We were told to lie about our age if we were ever asked."

"Can you tell me how many women were on the boat, at any given time?"

"About fifty, maybe. It was hard to tell. Each time I was on board, I saw different women. They came from somewhere else, I believe." There was a moment's pause. *"I think we were rotated around. I*

never got a chance to ask though, and like I said, asking questions was strongly discouraged."

"There would be consequences?"

There was another pause, and Ryan assumed she nodded yes because the agent continued, *"What kind of consequences?"*

" I don't know, just...." This time, there was a much longer pause.

"Did you ever get in trouble?"

"No, not really. I mean..."

Ryan heard several seconds of crying before she finished, *"It was really bad, okay? I never wanted any of those things to happen to me and so I just...."* More crying. *"When I jumped off the yacht, I was willing to take the risk. I couldn't take another night."*

"You did a very brave thing, Kristen." There was slight pause, and he heard Kristen blow her nose again before the detective continued, *"Do you think these other women, the ones you didn't recognize, were being held against their will, like yourself?"*

"Yeah, I don't think any of us were free to leave, except maybe Charlotte. She was in charge of us, mostly. She had her own room, and she didn't have to stick to a schedule, like we did. It seemed like she could do whatever, whenever."

"She was able to come and go freely?"

"Yeah, I think so. At least, that's what it seemed like. It felt like they trusted her more. She's the one that oversees the orientation process for new girls."

"Was there anyone else in charge?"

"Well, there were always security guards around, and then two guys who seemed to alternate the day-to-day management, from one week to the next. One was Joe and the other one was Zach. I don't know if those were their real names or not."

There was another pause, and it sounded like the detective was taking some notes. *"Okay, you've already given us their physical descriptions. Anything else you can remember about them?"*

"No, I think that's it."

"Okay, and how many women lived with you at the complex?"

"Usually about twenty-five. But the numbers fluctuated sometimes. There was a core group of us, but every now and then some of the women would be missing, then I'd see them again a couple weeks later. And that's what makes me think there's some sort of rotation going on, with the ones that have been there longer."

"Right. And you think there's more than one complex?"

"Yes. I overheard one of the women say something about how she'd been to both complexes and then something about Vancouver. But that's all I know."

"Okay. And what about the ethnicities of the other women? Did there seem to be a lot of diversity?"

"Yes, there was. I think they try to do that on purpose, to offer more choices."

"How many male clients do you think there were? Did you see the same men every time when you were on board?"

There was a pause before she answered, *"On board, I think there were about twenty or so at any given time. Maybe a little more. I saw some of the same guys, but every now and then there'd be a few new ones. Or ones that I hadn't seen in a while would show up."*

"Okay, and how much time did you spend on the yacht each weekend?"

"Well, we would leave the complex Friday morning and then sail back Sunday night. So three days, I guess."

"Did the yacht stop anywhere along the way, either going to the client pickup location or coming back to the complex?"

"No. Well not exactly.... I mean, when we had clients, there'd be stops during the day for stuff like sports fishing and jet skiing. But we never docked anywhere."

"Okay." She cleared her throat and continued, "So you and the others would board the boat Friday mornings from the complex, then sail to a port somewhere to pick up clients, and then you would sail around for a few days before coming back to the same dock to drop the clients off?"

"Yes...at least I think so. We never left the yacht once we were on it, so I guess it's the same dock. But I can't be sure."

"Okay, and you don't remember seeing the name of the boat anywhere? You're sure it wasn't on the linens or dinner menu, or anything like that?"

"No, I don't think so." Her voice sounded deflated. "I tried to keep my eyes open for stuff like that, but I didn't see anything on board. And I didn't want to ask any of the clients I was with what they knew. We weren't ever supposed to ask the clients questions."

"That's okay. You've already given us a lot of information, and it shouldn't take long before some leads develop." There was a slight pause then she continued, "There's one thing I want to confirm. Were you ever offered payment or told you would receive payment of any kind?"

"No, I was never paid anything. None of us were, as far as I could tell. At least not money. I mean, they fed us and we had a bed to sleep in. But we didn't have any phones or computers or anything like that." There was another pause, then she added, "On the boat, we got to wear expensive clothes. Evening dresses, lingerie, designer jeans...stuff like that. Very upscale. I think they wanted to make it look like we were paid well or something. But we were only allowed to wear the clothing when we were around clients, on the yacht. The rest of the time, at the compound, we all wore the same thing – exercise leggings and plain T-shirts." She paused for a second then added, *"We were checked weekly for STDs, and we had physical screenings when we came back from the yacht, to check for injuries or whatever, so I guess they kind of cared about our health."*

"Can you tell me what you mean by 'injuries'?"

There was a long pause. *"Well, um, you know, like from rough sex, I guess."*

"You mentioned earlier that there were special rooms on board, on the lower deck – used for BDSM. Were you ever in one of those?"

Another long moment of silence, and he could hear muf-fled crying again. Then she said, *"No, but one of the other girls had been."* This was followed by more crying. *"I'd only been there for about a week, and I hadn't been on the yacht yet. I didn't even know it existed. I was still in the orientation process. Anyway, the girl came back that night with all these bruises on her legs. And her...her back."* More crying.

Ryan clenched his fists tighter.

"She told me later that it was, you know... that the guy had just done whatever he felt like to her in there." Her voice broke, and Ryan could hear all-out sobbing. *"I just never wanted that to happen to me."*

"You're doing great, Kristen. This is all very helpful, and I know this is difficult for you to talk about. We're almost done." There was a long pause, filled with Kristen's crying, before the agent continued, *"The next questions should be easier, okay? Let's go back to the complex. You said earlier that all of you were kept pretty active?"*

Kristen cleared her throat. *"Yeah. We had lots of exercise. There was a small track, with a weight room off to the side, and personal trainers. They also doubled as security guards."* A moment's pause, then she added, *"We had weekly weigh-ins, and there was a lot of pressure to stay thin. Everything was very regulated and scheduled."*

"Were you or any of the other women given drugs?"

"No, that was a rule. No drug use." She paused then said, *"Except, I remember that some of the girls had prescriptions for stuff for anxiety and depression."*

"Do you know how they were getting those kinds of medications? If they were prescribed?"

"I don't really know. I never saw them come in with the supply deliveries. We just put away what was brought into the complex, but I don't know how they got it there."

"So you had tasks assigned to you?"

"Yes. Stocking the supplies was part of our chores. We all had duties throughout the week, like cleaning and working in the kitchen, food prep and laundry. Whatever was needed. We had a rotating schedule." There was a slight pause then she added, *"Not everyone went on the yacht on the weekends. Some of us stayed behind to keep things running at the complex."*

Agent Mitchell reached towards the computer and hit the pause button. "There's some more audio we can listen to later, but that's about the gist of it."

Ryan leaned back in his chair, sinking into it as he folded his arms over his chest. "I wonder what their profit margins are like," he mused. "Must be lucrative enough to outweigh the risk."

Mitchell nodded. "I'm not so sure that the clients fully grasp what they're into. Kristen said the girls were all instructed to tell anyone who asked that they work under a contractual agreement, in which they're paid directly by their employer." The agent reached for his mug but set it back down with a grimace. "I've reached the dregs." He swiveled his chair around and stood. "Do you want any?"

"Yeah, that'd be great," Ryan responded. "Thanks."

"Cream...sugar?"

"Black is good." He'd found that most people had a different interpretation than he did as to what "a little" cream meant.

"I'll be right back," Mitchell stated. "Hold tight."

Ryan took out his wallet and removed a small, neatly folded piece of paper. Opening it, he looked at the bulleted list of questions he'd written down while on the ferry. Mitchell had answered most of them. He stared absently in the direction of the window that loomed over the agent's desk; there wasn't much daylight coming in. He hoped it was just because the building was built up against the side of another one, blocking the sunlight, and that it didn't mean the weather had changed for the worse.

A moment later, the agent returned, enveloped in the rich scent of coffee. He handed a plain white mug to Ryan and sat down. "Any questions?" he asked, leaning slowly back in his chair, careful to keep his coffee from spilling over the brim.

Ryan took a small sip, testing the heat level. It was hot, but it was clear that it hadn't been poured from a fresh brew. He peered over the mug's brim, noticing for the first time a small stain on the agent's cream-colored shirt, peeking out from underneath his tie. He took another sip then asked, "Did Kristen describe the complex in more detail?"

"Yes. When we asked her about it, she described it as an underground compound, one level, about the size of a college dormitory. She mentioned the running track, but there's also a kitchen and dining area. She said the women always enter and exit the compound from an entrance next to the kitchen. There's a stairwell that goes up to what she described as a very small warehouse; the doors open out onto the pier and from there, they're ferried to and from the yacht on a speedboat. She said that on one occasion, she was able to catch a brief glimpse of the grounds and a private residence; she thinks the complex is probably underneath it."

The cellphone on the agent's desk began to vibrate. He leaned over, glanced at it, then shifted his attention back to Ryan. "Any more questions?" He began to slowly rock his chair back and forth with one foot.

"Kristen said something about BDSM rooms on board?"

He nodded. "There are two of them, designed for all of that. Both are tucked away on one of the lower decks, fore and aft."

"Hmm." Ryan looked at the floor for a second then back at the agent. "How exactly does a woman, or anybody for that matter, get into a position where they could become a victim in the first place? Peter explained somewhat, but I want to hear it from you."

Mitchell relaxed back into his seat. "Well, for under-aged youth, the vulnerability is usually created by a dysfunctional, turbulent home life. Drug use, mental health issues, foster homes. That kind of vulnerability is what traffickers look for. In terms of older teens and young adults, they are often able to run away from that kind of environment, but they have no real place to call home." He reached for his coffee. "Victims who have never been around people who care about them, or provide for their basic needs, are automatically vulnerable and susceptible, and women in particular. It's very easy for a woman to mistake attention for affection, and sex for love." He paused to take a sip then continued, "And an absence of good male figures in a woman's life plays a big role. When you really think about it, you can begin to understand how a young girl could find herself manipulated to stay in a toxic relationship." He paused for a second, reflecting. "Oftentimes, a victim will have arrived at a point of desperation in their life – they don't have the financial means or education to be functionally independent on their own. And this is where traffickers come into the picture. They'll pose as a caring adult, as 'the only one who truly loves and understands them.' They'll establish the concept of 'we're a family'." He set his mug down and shook his head. "Pimps will provide security and a place to stay with no strings attached – at first. Once they've hooked their victims, traffickers find ways to keep them by offering incentives, like giving them nice clothes and promising luxurious vacations, fancy dinners, etc. But they have to earn it. Or they'll hold something over their head, like taking away their passport or driver's license. In most cases, they'll try to isolate them from family and friends, or any other outside influences."

"And you said they're unlikely to go to law enforcement?"

"Pimps will tell their victims that they're doing something illegal – 'prostitution's a crime', etc. – and that they'll get into just as much trouble as themselves." He leaned back in his chair. "Then there's the element of shame. That's one of the hardest things we have to overcome when interviewing victims and getting them to talk. There's just so much shame and humiliation. Not to mention fear. It usually takes a handful of interviews to get through all the layers."

Ryan leaned back with a heavy sigh. There were no words to express what he was feeling.

Mitchell continued, "It's sad how easy it is for a pimp to gain trust just by assuming the role of a boyfriend or a father figure. At that point, a victim can be so drawn in, with such a deep attachment formed, that they'll usually do anything to receive favor, praise, or attention. The Stockholm Syndrome can even begin to take effect. It can take a while for victims to let go of their sense of loyalty to the trafficker. And you must remember that in some cases, these women have really fallen for their abuser, romantically."

"So do pimps even have to resort to violence? Is it all just emotional manipulation?"

"Depends. Sex trafficking really runs the gambit. Anything from 'Taken' to 'Pretty Woman.' Most cases fall somewhere in between those two." He tilted his head to the side. "A lot of pimps are what we call 'finesse pimps.' Meaning they don't want a damaged product, so they use more subtle tactics, along the lines of what I described earlier. But if they have to, they'll use force. Their bottom line is always to control and dominate in order to get what they want."

"Okay, so going back to our case. Peter said that the traffickers are looking for smart, refined, educated women. That doesn't seem to fit the victim profile you've been describing, unless I'm missing something?"

"No, you're right. These traffickers aren't typical. We asked Kristen if she knew how the other women came to be at the complex, but she only had a few stories to share – you have to keep in mind that she was only with the traffickers for a few months. One of the girls told her she was approached at a college admissions event – Kristen thinks she's sixteen. Another girl told Kristen she met her abductor while she was hanging out with friends at a bar, close to a college campus." He shrugged his shoulders. "I think these guys are recruiters of some sort, and their job is to look for women that fit the desired profile, wherever they may be. Sounds like some locations are targeted, like the admissions fair, while others might be chance encounters." He leaned back in his seat and glanced at his phone. "Have I answered most of your questions?"

"I think so." Ryan rubbed the back of his neck and looked vaguely at the floor. "I've heard that in some countries, in the impoverished places, parents will sell their kids into the sex trade. I guess the traffickers tell them that their kids are doing honest work and will send money home or something like that. Do you see the same kind of thing happening here in the U.S.?"

"Here it's largely sex-based, but we get forced labor cases as well. Massage parlors are a big one, especially with the Asian demographic. Traffickers will take advantage of the language barrier, making it very difficult for the workers to communicate with law enforcement. Those types of cases fall into the international trafficking category." He leaned forward. "And there's a whole thing now called 'trafficking tourism.' Government representatives, such as ambassadors, public affairs officials, etc., will transport their victims into foreign countries using their positions of trust to hide their activity and evade suspicion."

"Hmm." Ryan could hear the faint sounds of traffic outside the window as he leaned forward and set his mug on the agent's desk. "So where does Tara fall in all this? How do you think she got involved?"

"Not sure. We only have Kristen's information to go on, and she said she didn't interact with Tara. Only saw her a handful of times. But it's helpful to know what kind of women they're targeting. Kristen was pursuing a degree in physics. And if you look at Tara's file, you can tell she's driven and smart. She went to Berkeley on a dance scholarship, so she's also talented."

Careful to keep his tone even, Ryan casually asked, "What else do you know about her that I wouldn't be able to find in a basic Google search?"

"It's all there in her file, including a domestic violence altercation. Her boyfriend was convicted on a misdemeanor assault charge. The police report's in there if you want to read it."

"Great," he replied sarcastically with a sigh, trying to suppress his anger at this newest piece of information. "Sorry," he apologized. "This is just so....I just didn't think anything like this could happen to someone I know."

Mitchell nodded. "It's a lot of information to process."

Ryan rested his elbows on his knees and glanced at the agent. "Peter said you could use me to make some connections. Can you explain that a little more?"

"We think the traffickers are running their operation in the guise of a gentlemen's club. An exclusive one. Sounds like clients have to be invited to become members or are sponsored, maybe. Not sure on that end of things. You'll need to make a connection to someone who's already in."

"Do you have anywhere I can start? A lead to somebody? I'm not sure what I'm looking for here. How am I supposed to know if I've found the right place, or people?"

Mitchell quickly opened the top drawer of his desk and pulled out what looked like a business card. He handed it to Ryan. "I'd start with that. Kristen managed to nab it from a client. She had it with her when she escaped. She even put it in a plastic bag so it wouldn't get wet. We got a partial fingerprint from it, but not enough to give us an identity."

Ryan took the card, noticing that it felt heavier than most. It was dark grey and simple: the only thing on the front was a symbol embossed in glossy black ink that vaguely resembled a wolf's face. He couldn't resist running his finger over it. The overall simplicity of the design gave the card a sleek and sophisticated feel. Intrigued, he flipped it over

Durnhardt Holdings
Darin Robson, Asset Manager
Email: drobson@durnhardt.com

Ryan raised an eyebrow and glanced at Mitchell. "No phone number?"

"Just the email. We have someone working on finding out who the service provider is." The agent scratched his chin. "We did pose as a potential client and emailed this 'drobson' person, but all we received back was a 'failed to deliver' response." He smiled and gave Ryan a pointed look. "So there's your starting point. Make as many connections as you can. And keep an eye out for a card that looks like that one. Or something that matches that symbol." He leaned toward his desk and scribbled something on a sticky note. "I'm going to have you meet up with another agent assigned to this task force. His name's Ethan Bridger. He'll coordinate your training and take you under his wing, so to speak. The two of you will be working closely together on this." He handed the note to Ryan. "I'll have him reach out to you, but there's his contact info for future reference."

Ryan pulled out his wallet and stuck the sticky note inside, then slid one of his business cards out and handed it to Mitchell. "You already have my cell number, but that has my work email and the phone number for my secretary." He stood up to go. "Thanks for meeting with me. I'm looking forward to working with you."

"Likewise, Ryan." The agent smiled as he rose from his chair. "Ethan should be calling you later today – I want you in for an initial assessment as soon as possible. And you need to meet with someone from our human resources department to go through the hiring process and discuss a salary."

"I'm not interested in compensation."

"Peter thought you'd say that," Mitchell smiled. "But legally, we have to pay you. Besides, you're bringing a lot to the table. You're in the perfect position to help us, especially with your business credentials and established network." He stepped to the door. "So don't sell yourself short just because you happen to be in the right place at the right time." He turned the knob, thrust the door open, and added wryly, "You can donate your pay to an anti-trafficking organization."

5

The following morning, Ryan awoke a full hour before his alarm was set to go off. Knowing it would be futile to attempt to fall asleep again, he got up and dressed for his usual morning run. He headed quickly out the door and into the brisk morning air. For twenty minutes, he tried to keep his mind off of everything Agent Mitchell had disclosed the day before. However, his anger and frustration gradually took over, fueling his energy as he continued to run and reflect. He'd already outlined a plan and made a list of practical steps he needed to take to locate Tara, which was his overarching goal. Additionally, he'd put himself on a timeline, starting with the date that Tara had been reported missing. Since this Saturday would mark her fifth weekend with the traffickers, he had only three days to accomplish the first few steps of his plan if he didn't want to let another weekend slip by. But it was doable.

Returning home a half hour later, he took a quick shower then proceeded to select a charcoal grey Armani suit to wear to his downtown office, which was a half-hour ferry ride from the island. He arrived at the dock fifteen minutes before the ferry's departure and pulled into one of the car lanes. When the gate dropped, he slowly drove his Audi onto the car deck and parked in his assigned spot. He then grabbed his briefcase, locked the car, and strode towards the upper deck stairwell. Upon reaching the top, he scanned the main seating area and spotted a row of empty seats toward the front of the ferry. He headed in that direction and selected one at the end of the row. Once he was settled, he pulled out his cell and called Anna, his secretary. She answered on the second ring.

"Good morning, Ryan."

"Hey, I'm on my way in. I should be there in a half hour or so. Can you pull the Eastcott file for me? And clear my schedule for today and tomorrow."

"I'll put the file on your desk, and I'll let you know when I've updated your calendar."

"Perfect, thanks."

"Anything else?"

"Yes, can you make a list of all my past and present business associates? I think there's a spreadsheet or something somewhere, but I don't know if it's up to date."

"Yes, we have one. Julie and I both use it regularly. There are phone numbers and emails for each contact on it. It should be up to date, but I'll double check."

"Thanks. Can you print it out for me?"

"I'll have it on your desk before you get here. Anything else?"

"That's it for now. See you in a bit."

As soon as the ferry docked at the wharf, he headed back down to the car deck to retrieve his Audi. Upon disembarking, he drove the short distance to his office building, parked in the underground garage, and made his way to the bank of elevators. His ride to the 38th floor went uninterrupted, and the doors eventually opened into the sleek, wood-paneled lobby of his office suite. He gave his receptionist a passing "good morning" as he headed in the direction of Anna's office. A light rap of his knuckle on her door was sufficient to get her attention, and she looked up quickly from her desk, smiling. She had a youthful essence about her despite her greying hair, which was pulled back into a neat bun at the nape of her neck, and she wore a navy suit paired with gold earrings; the hand holding her coffee cup sported perfectly manicured nails, painted in a mauve shade.

"How was Chicago?" she asked.

"It was good. I think Howard will be in touch sometime this week. Any messages while I was out?"

"A few. I put the details on a sticky note for you, and the Eastcott binder is on your desk."

"Thanks." He stepped out and walked briskly into his office. After setting his coffee cup and briefcase on his desk, he sat down and opened the binder containing the details of his latest residential development, a high rise named Eastcott Place that was just a few blocks away. He pulled out his phone and dialed the number for his commercial broker, Heather.

"Hi, Ryan," she answered promptly. "What's up?"

"I want to talk to you about Eastcott. I'm interested in taking the top unit."

There was a slight pause then she asked, "When do you want to meet up?"

"Today would be great, if you have time." He was eager to get a place downtown as soon as possible so he didn't have to waste time taking the ferry in case anything urgent came up regarding the investigation; additionally, he needed to be closer to Seattle's night life and the adult entertainment scene.

"I have a few showings over at Ridgemont this afternoon," she continued, "but I'll be free after that."

"Does 5:00 sound good?

"Yes, that'll work."

"I know the listings aren't live yet," Ryan stated, "but the last time I checked in, the contractors were finished with all the units on the upper floors."

"Yes, those are all move-in ready."

"Do you think we can get the deal closed by the end of the week? It'll just be a matter of moving some money around on my end."

"I'll do my best." She hesitated then added, "I didn't realize you had a personal interest in Eastcott."

"I need a place downtown, closer to the office." He sensed that she was waiting for a more elaborate explanation, one that he wasn't planning on providing. "So, I'll see you at five?"

"Yes, see you then."

Hanging up, he reached for the spreadsheet that Anna had printed out. The next task was to call around and see if Darin Robson's name struck a bell with any of his contacts. He glanced at the first name on the list then reached for his phone.

An hour and a half later, he hadn't made much headway. A small portion of his calls had gone to voicemail, but for the ones that were answered, he'd had to hedge his way around small talk before he could get to the point. So far, no one recognized the name.

Frustrated, he shoved the list aside and leaned back in his chair. He spent a few minutes in quiet contemplation before picking up the spreadsheet again, ready to return to his pursuit. Just as he reached for his phone, it began to vibrate. He glanced at the caller ID and saw that it was Sean.

"Hey, what's up?"

"I was just wondering if you're in town this weekend," Sean responded. "I'm flying in. Thought we could meet up for drinks or something."

"Sure."

"Are you planning on going to Ed's retirement party?"

"When is it?" He pulled up his Outlook calendar on his desktop.

"This Sunday."

"Oh, right..." He'd completely forgotten about it.

"Do you think you'll make it?"

He hesitated. "I'm not sure yet what my plans are for the weekend." He was very much hoping that he'd be busy moving into his new place.

"A lot of the guys will be there," Sean pressed. "It'd be a good time to touch base about phase three."

"I'll think about it. It's probably too late for me to RSVP though."

"Oh come on, you know Ed won't care."

Ryan sighed, raking a hand through his hair, unable to think of another excuse. He glanced absently at the long list of names he had yet to call. "Hey, I have a question for you. Have you ever heard of anyone by the name of Darin Robson?"

There was a moment's pause on the other end. "I'm not sure, it sounds kinda familiar. Why?"

"Looks like he's the manager for a holding firm. Durnhardt Holdings." He paused then gave the same vague reason he'd been giving everyone else that he'd called thus far. "A friend recommended I get in touch with him regarding some asset acquisition questions I have."

"Durnhardt...yeah, I've heard of them. Actually, you should talk to Ed. I think he's done some work with one of their corporations. He might know the guy."

An hour later, Ryan entered FBI headquarters once more to meet with Ethan Bridger, the FBI agent that Mitchell had set him up with. His wait was much longer than his initial visit to the bureau, but eventually the office door next to Mitchell's opened, and a tall, muscular figure emerged. Although he was wearing jeans and a plain black T-shirt, there was a professional air about the agent; he was clean shaven, his haircut was close-cropped and trim, and his T-shirt was tucked in. There was a slight swagger to his walk as he approached.

"You're Ryan Harker?" The agent crossed his arms over his chest and gave Ryan a blank stare.

He nodded, rising from his seat, and upon standing found himself to be slightly taller than the agent. They appeared to be similar in age.

Bridger jerked his head in the direction of his office then turned around and walked toward it, not waiting to see if Ryan was following.

Deciding not to take offense, Ryan trailed behind him and stepped into his office. He took the only empty seat facing the agent's desk – the one next to it bore a stack of files – and waited for the agent to sit down.

Bridger settled into his chair, leaning back in it with his arms crossed, and stated flatly, "I've been told that you'll be joining our operation." He raised an eyebrow, and with a hint of sarcasm, added, "As a playboy socialite."

Ryan merely nodded, not quite sure how to respond. He couldn't blame the agent for his less than welcoming attitude. He got it – he was an outsider. Unfazed, he added, "I'm here to help in whatever capacity I can."

"I want to get one thing straight," said the agent, leaning forward, his eyes narrowing. "You're here to help us find someone who's connected to the club we're looking for – and that's it. Once you've made the connection, we'll take it from there. And if I'm being honest, I really don't think you'll accomplish anything, but Mitchell seems to think otherwise." He shrugged his shoulders. "I guess we'll see."

Ryan nodded. He could play along with the agent's wishes – for now.

Bridger reached for a legal pad on his desk. "I have some standard interview questions to go over with you, about your background and any other skills you might have. When we're through with that, I'll take you downstairs for a physical assessment." He flipped through the pad of paper, looking for a blank page. "After that, you'll be meeting with a psychologist for a behavioral analysis." He jotted the date down on his pad then gave Ryan a pointed look. "I'll be reviewing my notes with Agent Mitchell at the end of the day."

Ryan felt a surge of adrenaline. He'd always enjoyed taking tests, and he was ready to meet head on whatever challenges the agent was planning to throw his way.

A half hour later, upon completion of the interview, Bridger took him down to the basement level for the physical evaluation. They passed a workout area then a sparring ring, and wishing to prove his worth, Ryan disclosed his martial arts training. Bridger had no comment as he ushered him into a locker room off to the side. Ryan quickly changed into the sweatpants and T-shirt he'd brought with him then stepped out to find Bridger waiting by the sparring ring.

"It just so happens that our top training instructor is here today," Bridger stated, glancing from him to a lithe older gentlemen standing at attention a few feet away. He was bald, with a black, scruffy goatee on his chin. One ear bore a small diamond earring.

"He'd like to test your capabilities," Bridger continued with a smirk. He stepped out of the way and waved Ryan forward. "I'll be around."

From the corner of his eye, Ryan watched Bridger take a seat on a nearby bench, his pad of paper in hand and his pen poised. He was still smirking.

Ignoring him, Ryan shifted his attention to the task at hand and introduced himself to the instructor.

The match turned out to be lengthy, as their skill level was equal, but in the end, Ryan decided he didn't want to give Bridger another reason to resent him so he deliberately took a misstep that resulted in a win for the instructor.

Bridger had no comment.

Next, he was evaluated on his firearms skills where he once more proved his worth – almost all of his shots were bullseyes, and the ones that weren't were close. *You really are an egotistical bastard* he thought, grinning to himself as he was escorted down the hall to his next assessment. He couldn't help it that one of his best friends was a gun collector, or that they met regularly at a nearby shooting range for fun.

His meeting with the psychologist, a stout middle-aged woman, consisted of a series of differing mental assessments. When she released him an hour later, he was feeling drained but gave no indication outwardly; he was certain that Bridger was looking for any signs of weakness.

Next, he was escorted to Mitchell's office. After giving Ryan's assessment forms a brief perusal, the agent glanced at him and wryly stated, "You didn't mention your martial arts training the other day."

Ryan tried to keep the corner of his mouth from tilting up into a grin. "It slipped my mind."

Mitchell set the paperwork on his desk. "Everything's in order to move forward. I need you to stop by HR before you leave today. You'll be onboarding with us as an independent contractor, which means you'll have to sign a waiver of liability releasing the agency from any responsibility regarding your wellbeing."

"Understood."

The agent dismissed him with the further understanding that all their future meetings would be held elsewhere and that he was to pick up a burner phone as his final step on the way out.

Ryan left FBI headquarters feeling completely spent, but he didn't want to call off his meeting with Heather at Eastcott Place. He phoned her to let her know he was on his way. When he arrived, they walked through the unit thoroughly, taking notes of some minor changes that were needed. Afterward, they went to a nearby bar for a drink, where they discussed the rest of the details and completed all the necessary paperwork. By the time they were finished, the deal was mostly done, and apart from a few signatures from his attorney, he was set to move in. Satisfied yet exhausted, he walked back to his office building, retrieved his car, and caught the late-night ferry back to Bainbridge Island.

6

Despite his best efforts to speed things along, Ryan ended up having to wait until Saturday morning before he could move in. But the wait was worth it. As he approached Eastcott Place, driving his newly acquired Bugatti, his gaze swept quickly upward to the top of the building where his penthouse suite was located. He continued to take in the building's towering height until the car behind him honked, alerting him that the light had turned green. He pulled forward and turned left, heading in the direction of the underground parking garage just around the corner. Upon reaching it, he stopped at the gate, punched in the keycode Heather had given him, and proceeded to locate his assigned spot. Once he'd parked, he cut the engine then sat for a moment, reflecting. The hushed silence of the garage enveloped him, and he rested his head against the back of the seat, lingering in the solitude. Agent Mitchell had given him a training schedule, and the last few days had been fast and furious. He'd poured himself into the long list of webinars and online modules, all of which provided an overview on investigative procedures, surveillance techniques, cybercrimes, and sex trafficking. Completing ten of the webinars had taken up most of his Wednesday and Thursday, and yesterday he'd participated in a tactical operations simulation with some other agents-in-training. He'd done alright, all things considered. After the simulation, he'd gone home and picked up where he'd left off on the modules, pouring over the content until two in the morning.

He kept his eyes closed as he continued to sit and reflect in the stillness of the garage. He'd already decided to cut back on work for the next few weeks so he could devote himself fully to training. But for now, he just needed to focus on today, which would be spent on moving in. And then there was the retirement party for Ed Fincher the following evening.

If it weren't for Karen, his housekeeper, he'd undoubtedly be feeling in over his head. She'd returned from her vacation on Thursday and had since taken over the coordination of the move, discharging him of all responsibilities in that regard. He trusted her completely, having known her for years prior to her acceptance of the position. His family had moved into the same neighborhood that she and her husband had resided in, and they had both played a significant role in his adolescent life, helping to mold him into the man he now was (or at least the man he tried to be). She was practically a grandmother to him, and she knew it. He smiled to himself, grateful that he still had someone to keep him in line every now and then.

Along with her exemplary skillset, Karen was also a great conversationalist – something he had grown to value in his solitary bachelorhood. Open minded and nonjudgmental, she still held to her own moral values and was not afraid to express her opinions. He couldn't help but laugh to himself, remembering the narrow look she'd given him when he'd picked her up at the ferry terminal upon her return to the island. She hadn't refrained from commenting on his haggard appearance. *"You look as if you're hung over."* Her eyes had squinted in suspicion, and despite her thin frame and grandmotherly appearance, a chord of fear had run through him. *"That's not like you,"* she had continued. *"What have you been up to?"* She'd stopped him from responding with a wave of her hand. *"Never mind. I'll find out later."*

So far, he'd been able to dodge her questions, but it was only a matter of time before he'd have to provide some sort of reasonable explanation for his hasty move-in. He ran his hand through his hair and allowed himself one final moment of solitude before stepping out of the car and removing a large suitcase from the trunk. Wheeling it behind him, he entered the garage's lobby where the elevators were located. He pushed the button for the 62nd floor, the highest level of the building; since his penthouse occupied the entire floor, he was the only one with access to that level.

When he reached the top and entered the door to his unit, he was greeted by the cheerful cacophony of female voices: his mother, Karen, and definitely Rachel. He'd recognize her laugh anywhere.

He said a quick hello, setting his phone and keys on the kitchen counter, then headed to the master bedroom. When he reached the threshold, he gave the empty space a quick perusal then set his suitcase by the door and headed back to the kitchen to join the ladies.

Glancing at Karen, he gave her a teasing grin and said, "Didn't I tell you not to let them in until I got here?" He gave her shoulder a quick squeeze.

"We're here to help you with the move," Rachel stated, her voice firm but her eyes playful.

"No you're not." He grinned, tilting his head to the side. "You plan on decorating."

"I don't decorate," she responded, narrowing her eyes.

"I know, I know," he grinned. "You're a designer."

She jabbed him quickly in the chest. "What I do involves a lot more than just hanging up some curtains."

"Hey," he laughed, taking a step back. "You know I'm just messing with you."

"Well...good." She crossed her arms over her chest and smiled surreptitiously. "Because I'm making this place my next project."

He held up his hands in mock protest. "I'm guessing I don't have much say in the matter."

"Nope." She gave him a serene smile.

He turned his attention to the conversation Karen was having with his mom. So far, it didn't sound like Karen had hinted at any concerns regarding himself, but he wasn't going to give her an opportunity to do so if he could help it.

"Hey mom," he cut in. "How much time do you and Rachel have today?"

"I don't know about Rachel, but I'm free all day." His mother opened one of the kitchen drawers then glanced at Ryan. "Andrew said he'd be coming by later to help with a few furniture deliveries." She surveyed the sparse kitchen and empty living room. "He told me you aren't planning on bringing anything over from Bainbridge. You're keeping both places?"

"For now. All I brought with me is my suitcase. How do you feel about doing some shopping today?"

"I'd be happy to." She glanced in Rachel's direction and added with a smile, "And I'm pretty sure Rachel came with that in mind."

"She informed me that she's making this a personal project." Ryan gave his sister a wry look, but she wasn't paying any attention; she was hunched over the counter sketching out a floor plan on a notepad that he assumed she'd brought with her. It was obvious that she couldn't wait to get her hands on the blank canvas surrounding her.

He pulled out his wallet and handed a credit card to his mom then glanced at Karen. "Do you want to go with them? I thought you might like to pick out the kitchen ware since you'll be the one using it."

Karen nodded. "You don't mind if I come, Maggie?"

"Not at all," his mother responded. "I was just going to ask if you'd like to join us." She turned her attention back to Ryan. "Do you have a list? Should we pick up some groceries on our way back?"

"No list," he called over his shoulder as he headed down the hallway towards the bathroom. "Get whatever you think I'll need. Just don't give the credit card to Rach. And Karen's already taken care of the groceries. The pantry's fully stocked."

"Hey," Rachel called after him. "You can trust me you know."

"Your apartment says otherwise," he yelled back, loud enough for his voice to carry down the hallway.

He reappeared a few minutes later, after using the bathroom.

"I have a mattress and a sofa that are supposed to be delivered sometime this afternoon," he said, glancing at the time on his phone. "Andrew should be here any minute."

"Okay," Rachel responded. "What are you doing about all the other furniture? Are we eating dinner on the floor when we get back?"

"That's part of the moving-in tradition," he grinned. "You have to eat at least one meal on the floor." He gave her a sideways glance, a smirk on his face. "But we'll have designer plates and silverware when you come back, right?"

"Sure," she smiled archly. "I guess that just means you're planning on cooking for all of us."

"As long as the ingredients are limited to Cheerios and milk."

She quirked an eyebrow. "Don't you mean Lucky Charms?"

"That was in high school," he responded flatly.

They both glanced furtively towards the walk-in pantry. Before he could grab her, Rachel scampered gleefully in that direction, certain of what she would find there. It only took a few minutes before he heard the inevitable "I knew it!" exclaimed from deep within the cloistered space. He could even hear her shaking the box. Ignoring her, he turned his attention back to his mother. "I'll take you all out for dinner when you guys get back."

Maggie smiled at him. "Do you want me to look at some furniture too while we're at it? I have a few accent chairs and some side tables on hand at the boutique, but we'll have to shop around for some of the other items you'll need."

"That'd be great," he replied, feeling both relieved and grateful. His mother owned and operated an upscale home decor store. "If you and Rachel want to take on a project, I'll be glad to pay you."

"You know you don't have to do that," she responded warmly. "At least not for me." Her forehead creased slightly as she added, "But if you want to work out something with Rachel..." she trailed off then said, "The last time we talked, she told me she was 'in between clients.'"

"Okay, I'll ask her about it later. For now, just use my card to order the rest of the furniture and whatever else you need for decor. If you can set up deliveries for today and tomorrow, Andrew and I can help move things into place." He glanced at Karen. "You'll come with us for dinner?" He thought she might like to have her husband come too so he added, "See if Bob can join us."

She smiled and said, "I'll give him a call."

A few minutes later, he followed the three women to the foyer and waited as they gathered their purses. Once they were through the door, he stepped into the hallway after them.

"Have fun," he said. "And take as long as you need." As he watched them leave, he added, "And keep an eye on Rachel."

Faint laughter drifted from the elevator as the door started to close on the trio.

"Mom!" he called out, "I trust your judgment!"

He stepped back inside, smiling to himself. His mother's taste usually aligned with mainstream trends, but Rachel was known to deviate; if left solely to her own whims, he could only guess at what her eclectic leanings might yield. He was thinking specifically of the pink, zebra-striped pillow he'd seen on her sofa the last time he was at her place.

Hands in his pockets, he walked leisurely over to one of the floor-to-ceiling windows in the living room and leaned against the frame. The cityscape sprawled beneath him, extending from his firmly planted feet all the way to Puget Sound. In between the neighboring skyscrapers, he glimpsed bits of the wharf district, bustling with a medley of miniaturized traffic and people. After a minute or two, his gaze swept over the sound towards Bainbridge Island. The view at night would be spectacular.

He turned away from the window and slowly scanned the living room, trying to decide where to put the piano. If the delivery guys came when they were supposed to, it would be set up before the women returned. He hadn't mentioned it to his mom as he was hoping to surprise her. She'd taught all of them how to play, and he wanted her to be the first to break it in. He'd chosen a 1921, walnut stained, baby grand, similar to the one that his nana had passed down to his mother as a wedding gift. It would need to be tuned, and there were a few areas that needed some restoration; but overall, it was in beautiful shape, with a varnish that had mellowed into a lovely patina over the years.

He heard his phone ring in the kitchen, and after taking several lengthy strides, he was able to pick it up before it went to voicemail. "Hey, Andrew. Are you here?"

"Yeah, pulling up now. Have they delivered the piano yet? And where should I park?"

"Park in the spot next to mine – the code's 9871. I'll come down and meet you in the lobby."

7

Ryan reached for his phone on the bedside table, rubbing the sleep from his eyes, and glanced at the time: 9:28am. He slowly sat up, feeling groggy and slightly disoriented after yesterday's move in. They'd managed to get a lot done, but it would take some time before the place began to feel like home. He stretched his arms up over his head then let them fall loosely to his side before pushing himself to his feet. The smell of fresh coffee had an invigorating effect on him. He walked briskly towards the suitcase in the corner that he had yet to unpack and retrieved a T-shirt and sweatpants. He hastily threw them on then headed for the kitchen where he found Karen making breakfast.

She gave him a sideways glance. "I was just beginning to think that you'd snuck off to your office without saying anything."

"On a Sunday?"

"That's never stopped you before," she responded wryly.

Giving her a brief smile, he took a seat at the kitchen counter and said, "I'm heading to Bainbridge in a few hours. I need to pack up some things from my office to bring here."

She handed him a cup of coffee, eying him carefully. "I hope you're not stretching yourself too thin." She rested one hand on her hip. Her other hand held a spatula, which she pointed at him like a laser pen and continued, "Can I ask what prompted this whole move?"

He rubbed his jawline, thinking. He'd known she would start asking questions as soon as she got a chance. After taking a sip of coffee, he answered casually, "I'm doing more business downtown now, and it makes sense. I've been thinking it over for a while." He shrugged his shoulders and tried to give her what he thought was a winning smile. "And I wanted to grab this unit before the listings went live, so I just thought 'why not.'"

After giving him a calculating look, she turned back to the stove with a simple "hmm." A moment later, she slid an omelet onto his plate and asked, "And what are you planning on doing with your house on Bainbridge?"

"I'm not sure yet," he replied, taking the plate she handed him. "I have a few ideas, but my more pressing concern is Ed's party tonight. I still need to get a gift."

She quirked an eyebrow. "Do you want some help with that?"

"Please." He smiled then took a bite of his omelet. "You don't mind?"

"No, it's no trouble." She rinsed the skillet with some hot water then placed it in the dishwasher. "I'll call you when I find something." She closed the dishwasher door and added, "As much as I like Bainbridge, it'll be nice to have more shopping options close by. And I do love the market."

"I know the decision was sudden," he said. "And I didn't mean to spring it on you..." He trailed off and took another bite of his omelet.

"I won't deny that I was surprised; however, it really doesn't affect me all that much, whether it's here or Bainbridge. And I don't mind keeping an eye on both places."

Karen's adaptability and willingness to help filled him with a deep sense of appreciation. "I hope you know you're one-in-a-million," he stated sincerely.

She harrumphed, but he saw the corner of her mouth tilt up in a smile just before she turned away.

An hour later, he drove to the wharf and boarded the ferry to Bainbridge, where he spent the rest of the morning and afternoon packing up his office. By the time he was finished and on his way back to Seattle, it was close to 4:00. He had hoped that packing would've distracted him from his anxiety about the evening ahead, but it hadn't worked. All he could think about was the possibility of finding Darin Robson – the one man who might be his only link to Tara.

8

Ryan glanced at his watch again then back towards the large double glass doors that marked the front entrance of Eastcott Place. The escort he'd hired for the evening was running late. Irritated, he scanned the empty lobby, looking for something to distract himself. His eyes lingered on a large, colorful mural positioned on the wall opposite him, but it failed to hold his attention. He turned his focus back to the entrance, and with folded arms, continued to stare out the long glass windows, waiting impatiently for her arrival.

He'd decided to hire an escort for two reasons: first, it would help him build his playboy socialite persona – a role that he needed to establish quickly to solidify the kind of reputation that would draw the attention of someone from the mysterious club he was looking for. And secondly, he was hoping that she – and other escorts in the future – might already know of the club or be able to connect him to someone who did.

A second later, his phone began to vibrate. He promptly removed it from his dinner jacket and answered it.

"Hi, I'm so sorry." The female voice on the other end was breathless. "I'm on my way. I should be there in about five minutes. This is Kat by the way."

"Alright, I'll meet you out front."

Perhaps it was better to arrive late to Ed's party after all, if he wanted to be seen as carefree and above-the-rules. He exited the building and waited impatiently for a few more minutes before Kat pulled up to the curb in a silver BMW.

She rolled down the passenger window then leaned over the seat and said, "I'm so sorry. I couldn't find my keys."

"Don't worry about it."

He walked around to the driver side, opened her door, and in a tone that left no room for argument, stated, "I'm driving."

Without protest, she stepped out onto the pavement, all legs and cleavage in a tight black dress. She gave him a coy smile as she handed him the keys then skirted past him toward the passenger side.

He ducked into the driver's seat and waited for her to get in. Once she was settled, he pulled away from the curb then drove around the corner to the entrance of the parking garage.

"We're taking my car," he stated, punching in the code.

After quickly trading her BMW for his Bugatti, to which she had no objection, he exited the garage and merged into the flow of traffic.

Kat was the first to break the silence. "So," she gave him a quick glance. "I'm curious as to why you hired me. You don't exactly fit the mold for my typical clientele."

"Oh?" He raised an eyebrow.

"I mean, you're not old – or unattractive." The color in her cheeks heightened as she continued, "I have a hard time believing you couldn't find someone else to go with you tonight."

"Not anyone as attractive as you," he grinned. "And I certainly wasn't going to chance it with a dating app."

She laughed then in a suggestive tone asked, "What are you looking to get out of tonight?" She gave him an inviting smile.

He hesitated then replied, "Let's see where the night takes us."

"Sounds good to me," she responded pleasantly, her tone light and carefree.

He glanced at her again then turned his eyes back to the road; unless she proved to be useful, he had no intention of seeing her after tonight. He maneuvered into the left lane and accelerated. "How long have you been an escort?"

"About six months now."

"Do you like it?"

There was a slight pause before she answered tightly, "Yes, I do. I enjoy making good money."

"Tell me if I'm prying," he responded.

"No, it's fine," she sighed. "I don't mind." She looked down at her hands. "It's a good side gig for now."

He glanced at her once more then turned his full attention to the road, wishing her cleavage wasn't so distracting. After a few minutes, he asked, "Are you familiar with any of the clubs around here?"

"Night clubs?"

"Yes. I have a wedding coming up soon, and I'm the best man."

"Oh," she smiled. "You're looking for a strip club then."

"Well, not exactly. I was thinking more like a gentleman's club. Something exclusive and not well known."

"Hmm, I don't think I know of anything that could be described as exclusive, but I can ask around." She hesitated then added, "I can call you if I find something?"

"Sure." He merged onto the highway, and intent on fast-tracking the formation of his new persona, increased his speed to well over the speed limit.

Twenty minutes later, he pulled up to the entrance of the Brazilian steakhouse in Bellevue that Ed's wife had rented out for the occasion. After handing the car off to a valet, he escorted Kat to the front door. Placing his hand on the small of her back, he guided her into the lobby. They were greeted by the low hum of conversation, gently mingled with the sound of a jazz quartet. A moment later, he spotted Sean leaning against the bar. He headed in that direction with Kat following close behind.

Sean looked up from his drink as they approached.

"Hey," he said, giving Ryan a brief glance before shifting his eyes to Kat.

Ryan quickly introduced her then asked, "Did I miss anything important?"

"No, not yet. I think Marcia's about to make an announcement."

Ryan scanned the area and spotted Ed's wife moving toward a large table at the front of the room where several gifts had been neatly arranged. She raised the glass she was holding in her hand and clinked it with her spoon until she had everyone's attention.

"I want to thank all of you for coming out tonight to celebrate Ed," she began. "Each of you has had an impact on both of our lives over the years, and we're so grateful for you." She looked around the room, then continued, "Before we sit down to eat, I want to set aside a few minutes for anyone who'd like to come up and say something. Ed will close it out after that."

A round of clapping ensued as she made her way back to her table. A moment later, an older gentleman from across the room stepped forward and launched into a heartfelt speech, highlighting Ed's business success and their personal friendship over the years.

Once more, Ryan swept his gaze over the room, looking for any unfamiliar faces; there were quite a few.

Eventually, a waiter bearing a silver platter of wine glasses slowly approached and paused in front of him. Ryan quickly selected a glass of white wine and nodded a silent "thank you." He continued to stand on the fringe of the circle of guests gathered around the front table, casually sipping his wine and doing his best to pay attention to the speeches. Most were quick and to the point. Some were funny. One tried to be but failed. An awkward silence ensued, and seizing the opportunity, he stepped forward, his glass raised.

"I just want to say how much I've valued your mentorship over the years, Ed. You've helped me to avoid mistakes that I otherwise would have made, and you've encouraged me to take risks when I wouldn't have. I appreciate all the sound advice you've given me, and your common-sense approach to business." He looked around the room. "And I think we can all say that no matter the circumstance, your dry sense of humor always came through." There were a few scattered laughs as he lifted his glass in the air. "Here's to a long and happy retirement."

A chorus of cheers broke out as Ed rose from his chair. Ignoring the applause, he smiled and said, "I wouldn't be where I am today without your friendships and partnerships. I've learned so much from each of you, through the most challenging projects right down to the seemingly insignificant conversations." He looked around the room and Ryan could see that he was getting misty-eyed. "I appreciate each of you, and I'm so grateful to have worked alongside you. Your spirit and individual effort are evident in each collective success we've experienced together." He paused and cleared his throat. "Thanks again for coming tonight, and I just want to close by thanking my lovely wife Marcia who has stood by my side all these years and faithfully supported me with her presence, wisdom, and guidance. I wouldn't be the man I am without her." He pulled her close and gave her a peck on the cheek as the room swelled with applause.

The quartet began to play again as Ryan scanned the vicinity once more, weighing his options for where to sit. There was an empty table close to where Ed and his wife were sitting. With a quick nod in Kat's direction, he motioned for her to follow him. They reached the table a moment later, and he wasn't surprised when Sean chose to take the seat next to Kat's. Under normal circumstances, Sean's hedging himself in on his date might have rattled him, but tonight his mind was solely focused on finding out more about Darin Robson.

Ryan sat quietly throughout the meal, vaguely listening to the conversation around him, occasionally making a comment or responding to a question. Eventually, he saw Ed rise from his chair. He watched him make his way to the men's room then, excusing himself from the table, he headed in the same direction. Just as he drew near, he was abruptly interrupted by a touch on his shoulder.

"Hey, Ryan."

He turned around to find an old colleague of his. "Dan," he responded slowly, masking his impatience. He glanced at the other two men standing next to his friend.

"This is John Downing," Dan stated, introducing the older gentlemen first. "And his son, Cullen."

Ryan eyed the older man, giving him a quick assessment. He seemed to be the type of person that was thoroughly prepared to step into the spotlight without needing a moment's notice; he also looked vaguely familiar.

"Have we met before?" Ryan asked him, shaking his hand.

"I don't believe so." John's voice was a smooth baritone. "However, I'm running for senate so you might have seen my face on one of the campaign billboards."

"That explains it then," Ryan nodded.

He shifted his attention to Downing junior who appeared to be in his early twenties. The navy suit he was wearing hung stiffly from his shoulders, making it appear boxy on him. His hair was slicked back with an overabundance of styling gel. On one cheek, several deep pit marks formed a trail down to his jawline; his dark, chunky eyebrows and prominent nose didn't help to tip the scale of attraction in his favor; however, there was an air of confidence and ease about him, which made up for some of the latter.

"Are you helping your dad with the campaign?" Ryan asked him, throwing a sideways glance in the direction of the restrooms. He didn't see Ed anywhere in the vicinity.

"Not really. I'm working on some projects of my own."

Disinterested, but wanting to be polite, Ryan asked, "What is it you do?" He glanced at the restrooms again.

"Asset management, mostly." Cullen took a sip of wine from the glass he was holding.

Ryan turned his full attention to the young man, and in a tone that he hoped conveyed nonchalance, he asked, "Are you working with a firm?"

"I did, up until a few months ago. I still do some consulting for them though."

Ryan maintained a casual air despite the sudden pounding in his chest. "Which firm?"

"Durnhardt Holdings."

He stifled the sudden feeling of elation thrumming through his veins and in a smooth, even tone, he said, "I've heard the name. Are you familiar with Darin Robson?"

"Yeah, he's one of the senior managers," Cullen replied. "You know him?"

"Not personally. But a friend handed me his card recently and recommended I get in touch." Ryan shrugged his shoulders. "I've been meaning to contact him but haven't had time." His mind was racing as he strategized how to maneuver the conversation.

"I can introduce you, if you like. His daughter's band is playing next weekend at The Crocodile. He'll be there." Cullen took another sip of wine then reached into his pocket and pulled out his wallet. He slid out a business card. "There's my contact info. Text me if you plan to go to the concert on Friday. Darin usually throws a VIP party for the band after the show. He won't mind if I bring a friend."

"Thanks," Ryan replied, tucking the card into his suit pocket. "How long have you known Darin?"

"About a year or so." Cullen set his empty wine glass on a nearby high top then said, "I should get back to my table. It was nice meeting you."

"Likewise," Ryan nodded. "And I might just take you up on your offer."

"Yeah, just text me if you're planning on coming."

From the corner of his eye, Ryan watched as Cullen headed for one of the tables near the front. He quickly scanned the faces of those seated but didn't recognize anyone. Turning away, he walked briskly in the direction of the restrooms, his heart still pounding. When he entered, he saw that it was empty. Ed must have slipped by without his notice. He quickly used the restroom then headed back to his table.

Gliding into his seat, he languidly draped his arm along the back of Kat's chair and asked, "Are you having a good time?"

"I am," she smiled. "Your friends are all very nice." Her eyes flickered across the room then she added hesitantly, "I'm not so sure about your father though."

"My father?" His heart rate spiked, and he quickly removed his arm from Kat's chair. Glancing in the direction she'd indicated, he spotted him at Ed's table. Their eyes met for a moment, and despite the distance between them, Ryan could sense his disapproval. *Great.* What had he done wrong this time? There was always something.

He turned back to Kat. "He came over and talked to you? What did he say?"

"Not much. He must have seen us come in together. I think he assumed I was your girlfriend or something." She blushed. "He came over and talked with Sean then he asked how you and I had met. I didn't know what to say, so I just said that we met at a bar."

Ryan inhaled sharply. His father was stanchly against alcohol of any kind, and the story Kat had given him was the worst one she could have invented, although she did so unknowingly. He slumped back into his seat, his prior elation quickly ebbing away. He didn't have to use his imagination to envisage the kinds of assumptions and conclusions his father had most likely already formed based on what Kat had said. And her low cut, skintight dress didn't help matters.

"What happened after that?" he asked, doing his best to keep his deflation concealed.

"He didn't really say anything else," she replied. "Just kinda walked away."

"Typical," he sighed.

He tried in vain to focus on the dinner conversation buzzing around them, but after a few minutes he fell into his own self-absorbed thoughts. Slowly, he began to realize the full depth of what his mission was going to cost him. He didn't care much about what his friends or business associates would think about his new persona, not when he had a chance at finding Tara. But his family? And their opinion of him? His heart began to sink. This was going to cost him something that might be difficult to recover again. And it didn't just involve his reputation – this could affect relationships that he genuinely cared about. *Well*, he thought bitterly, *at least I won't have to worry anymore about trying to live up to everything he expects me to be*. Ready to leave, he reached for his drink, downed it, then glanced at his father's table. He knew he'd have to say something to him before making an exit; it would only complicate matters if he avoided him.

He leaned toward Kat. "You ready to head out?"

"Yes, if you are," she nodded.

They both scooted their chairs away from the table. He glanced at his father then turned back to Kat. "I need to say goodbye to him first."

"I'll wait for you here."

He laughed quietly and reached for her hand. "I don't want to leave you alone with Sean." In reality, he felt he needed a little moral support. He tugged her to him, and she giggled lightly with a humor he wasn't feeling.

They began to weave their way around the other tables toward his father's. Halfway there, he was tempted to turn around and leave; he'd done it before. But it was too late now.

At their approach, his father rose slowly to his feet and placed his napkin on the table. His face remained expressionless.

Ryan cleared his throat. "I didn't think you'd be here. I thought you were out of town."

"I got back yesterday," he replied in a clipped monotone.

There was an awkward pause as Ryan searched for something more to say.

There wasn't.

"Well, I'm glad you made it back okay."

His father merely nodded.

Kat gave Ryan a quick glance then said, "It was lovely to meet you, Mr. Harker." She smiled warmly and continued, "I hope you don't mind, but we have to run."

His father nodded again, then without a word, turned on his heel and walked away.

Ryan watched him go then said, "Well, that's my dad for you. The man of few words. Or no words at all." He rubbed the back of his neck, feeling a little embarrassed but not surprised. "I never quite know what he's thinking."

"It's okay," Kat smiled. "Maybe he was just in a bad mood."

"Yeah, maybe." If that were true, then the man had been in a bad mood his entire life. He looked around for Ed and spotted him at the bar, near the main entrance. He put his hand on the small of Kat's back and guided her in that direction.

"Ryan." Ed stood up with a smile as they approached. "I'm so glad you could make it tonight." He clasped Ryan's hand warmly. "We'll have to arrange a poker night soon." He glanced vaguely at Kat.

"Yes, we should," Ryan replied. "Let me know when you're free." Now was not the time to ask Ed about Darin Robson; it would have to wait. And since he had no desire to continue the ruse that Kat was his girlfriend, he didn't introduce her. He said a quick goodbye then steered Kat toward the entrance, taking her arm and gently tugging her along behind him. They walked silently back to his car, the parking lot still full. He opened her door and quickly helped her in.

Traffic was heavy as Ryan shifted gears and merged on to the highway a few minutes later.

Ge glanced at Kat. "Sorry if my father made you feel uncomfortable."

"No need to apologize," she replied kindly. "He really didn't bother me that much."

He gave her a wry smile. "If you say so." Keeping one eye on the road, he turned the audio on and found a classical music station.

She glanced at him. "You like classical music?"

"When I want something that doesn't have any lyrics." *And when I don't feel like talking,* he wanted to add.

"This is peaceful," she nodded. "What song is it?"

"Clair de Lune." He didn't feel like elaborating further.

The rest of the drive was quiet, and Ryan appreciated that she didn't attempt to make conversation. Twenty minutes later, he pulled into the Eastcott's parking garage. He cut the engine then walked around to Kat's door and helped her out.

He walked her to her car, and not wishing to linger over a goodbye, simply said, "I had a great time tonight. Thanks for being so understanding about my father." He pulled out his wallet and took out the remaining amount he'd agreed to pay her once the night had concluded. "Perhaps I'll see you again."

She took the money and placed it discreetly in her purse. "You can call me anytime." She gave him an arched smile as she turned to go.

He waited until she was in her car before heading towards the lobby.

When he reached his unit, he quickly punched in the keycode, entered, and went straight to his office where he retrieved the burner phone from his desk.

The phone rang a few times before Agent Mitchell answered. "Ryan. What's up?"

"I found him," he replied. "Darin Robson."

There was a moment's pause before Mitchell responded, "Quick work."

"Don't get too excited. I haven't met him in person yet, but I know where he'll be on Friday: at The Crocodile, for a concert."

"I want you to take Agent Bridger with you."

Ryan hesitated. "I'm not so sure if that's a good idea. I need to get a sense of who Darin is, business-wise, before we pull someone else into the picture. If Ethan's going to be interacting with him, we have to have a plan beforehand. He's going to need an identity, some kind of business profile."

There was a long pause before the agent responded, "Alright. I'll make sure you have a recording device beforehand."

"You're making me wear a wire?"

Mitchell laughed. "No, we don't do it that way anymore, for the most part. What I'll give you is about the size of a thumb drive and looks like a key fob."

"Okay." That sounded easy enough.

"On second thought," Mitchell continued, "we should probably give you something with audio and video capabilities, in one device. Maybe a watch. I'll talk to our tech guy."

"Okay, so what's next for my training?" Ryan asked. "I should probably put in an appearance at my office tomorrow morning, and let my staff know that I'll be working from home this week."

"Good idea. I'm meeting with Ethan today, and we'll put together a more robust training schedule for you. Have you ever taken a defensive driving course?"

Ryan could almost hear the grin in the agent's voice.

9

Scowling, Ryan flopped Tara's file on his desk then glanced around his new home office at all the cardboard moving boxes that had yet to be unpacked. Karen had offered to help, but he'd declined; everything had to be organized in his own way. It would take at least a few days to sort through the files, paperwork, and books the boxes contained, and the fast-approaching weekend wouldn't afford him the opportunity to do so.

With a sigh, he leaned back in his seat and swiveled his chair around to face the window. Clouds tinged with pink and orange hues hovered loftily above the glass skyscrapers, and he could hear the quiet, rhythmic hum of traffic in the street below. He'd always loved the sights and sounds of downtown Seattle as it awakened to meet the night, but in his current frame of mind he wasn't feeling it. Every time he thought about tomorrow night's concert, knots formed in his stomach. It might be his only chance at establishing a connection with Darin Robson, and there was no room for error.

He turned back around and glanced at the thin manila folder lying next to his keyboard. Reading through Tara's file had only added to the depression that had settled on him after the encounter with his father. The dip in his mood hadn't surprised or alarmed him as it would have in the past; he was almost expecting it. Stress and change had always been precursors to his bouts of depression. Additionally, he'd been on a little bit of a high with all the FBI training that week; it seemed natural to now be experiencing the feeling of "coming down." But like the turning of the tide, he knew his mood would shift eventually; it was just a part of a natural ebb and flow. What goes up must come down. Unfortunately, his "down" descended a little farther than the average person's, and earlier that week, he'd briefly considered calling his former therapist but had decided against it. He was managing the situation okay on his own, and he'd been able to distract himself the past few days by showing up at the office and attending some meetings. The rest of his time had been spent in following Agent Mitchell's training schedule and, despite the knots in his stomach, he felt that he was prepared for whatever lay ahead.

He reached for Tara's file again and opened it, this time lingering on her photo. The dark brown eyes staring back at him held his gaze for several minutes. He studied her facial features carefully, trying to visualize what she might look like in person. Would he be able to recognize her at first glance? His eyes skimmed over the personal identifier information listed under her photo – full name, date of birth, and social security number – then landed on the next line:

Marital status: Single

Moving on, he skimmed through the missing person's report again, looking for something he might have missed from his initial reading:

Last seen Friday, April 8ᵗʰ, around 8:00pm at her father's house in the North Beach district...wearing jeans and a black sweater.....in Portland to visit her father....left house after argument.....no personal vehicle....reported missing April 9ᵗʰ by her father.

He moved on to the brief narrative that Agent Mitchell had typed up regarding her background. Apparently, her family had moved to San Francisco a year after her siblings' car accident. A few years after that, her parents divorced. She was fifteen at the time. Her dad had moved to Portland shortly after the divorce, and Tara had chosen to live with her mother full time in San Francisco. According to Mitchell's narrative, Tara's current address was that of her mother's who was still residing in San Francisco.

Next, he turned to the domestic violence report that had been filed on February 14, 2020. For the second time, he read through the officer's affidavit:

Officer Dayton and myself responded to a call regarding 110 RIDGEWAY. Upon arrival, we spoke with the complainant who identified the apartment unit she had called about. Complainant reported that she heard what sounded like a fight between the two occupants, TARA HAYES and JUSTIN SLADE. She reported that she could hear yelling and what sounded like items being thrown. She then observed SLADE exit the apartment and drive away in a black Dodge Ram.

Officer Dayton knocked on the unit's door, and we were both admitted by a female who identified herself as TARA HAYES. I observed that she had bruising and swelling around her right eye.

She was visibly crying and appeared shaken. From my position, I could see broken plates on the kitchen floor. HAYES showed me her cracked cellphone screen which she said SLADE had thrown at her but missed and it had hit the wall. I asked if anyone else was in the apartment. She confirmed that she was alone. I then asked about her swollen eye, and she said her boyfriend, whom she identified as JUSTIN SLADE, had struck her while they were arguing. I then asked what the argument had been about. She stated that she had started the argument but she declined to say more. I asked about the broken plates on the floor, and she stated that both she and SLADE had been upset during the argument. I asked how the plates had broken and she said that he had thrown them at her. I asked if SLADE had made her afraid that he would hurt her, and she said yes. I asked her if this type of argument had happened before and she said yes, but that this was the first time he had struck her. At that point, Officer Dayton explained to her the elements of domestic abuse and that the altercation between her and SLADE aligned with state criminal statutes and that a report would have to be filed. I asked if there was somewhere else she could stay that night, and she said she would go to her mother's house. I asked if she would feel safe there and she replied yes. Officer Dayton handed her his card and we both vacated the premises.

The D.A.'s office had prosecuted the case, and Justin had pled guilty to a misdemeanor charge. Supervised release, no jail time.

Ryan glanced at the date on the report again: February 14th. That must have been a real shitty Valentine's. What had happened to her after that night? Had she stayed in the relationship? Another thought suddenly occurred to him: what if she was still with this guy? Or if she wasn't, did she have a current boyfriend? Wouldn't he have stepped forward regarding her missing person's report? So far, a significant other had not been mentioned in any of the paperwork that he had read.

He shrugged his shoulders. It shouldn't make a difference to him whether she had a boyfriend, just as long as it was someone better than this Justin guy. Someone much better.

Before he closed the file, he skimmed through a grainy copy of Agent Mitchell's handwritten note to himself regarding Tara. It was dated a week ago:

No updates from Portland PD regarding night of disappearance. Conference call scheduled for Friday.

He glanced at her photo one more time. There was no denying that she'd grown into an attractive woman. The smile that played around the corner of her mouth held his attention for several moments before he caught himself. This was Preston's sister. There was no way he could see her in any other light than that. And besides, it was his fault that she was where she was.

He snapped the file shut.

10

Situated on the corner of 2nd and Blanchard, in the heart of Belltown, The Crocodile wasn't much to look at from the outside; however, it was considered one of Seattle's better music venues. Despite its small capacity, it had hosted several legendary bands since its founding; simultaneously, it was recognized as a haven for independent artists, and any band that got the chance to play at the iconic venue could consider themselves "made."

As Ryan stepped across the threshold of the main entrance, two newly hired escorts on each arm, he was confident that the evening's show would be good, although it didn't matter one way or the other to him. He wasn't there for the music.

While his eyes adjusted to the dim lighting, he scanned the crowded bar area for Cullen. After a few seconds with no result, he decided it'd be better to let Cullen come to him. He guided the women to a couple of empty seats near the end of the counter and stood between them while they ordered drinks. He glanced at his designer wristwatch, the one that he'd given to Mitchell to have surveillance mechanisms installed. It was eight o'clock, and the opening band was set to play in a half hour. He glanced casually at the two escorts he'd brought with him: one blonde, the other brunette, both from a different online source. Unfortunately, neither of them had heard of a club that fit the specifications he'd given them.

The brunette, Amber, leaned closer, placing her hand on his forearm. "What are you doing after the concert?"

"Not sure yet" he responded. "There's supposed to be some kind of VIP party later."

The bartender placed Amber's cocktail in front of her. She took a sip then asked, "You're planning on going?"

"Yes, if I can meet up with my friend. He has the access. I don't know how many people arc allowed in." He smiled and added, "I guess we'll find out."

The blonde, Shelby, nudged his shoulder and asked him roughly the same question that Amber had. The place was getting more crowded by the minute. He leaned toward her and replied loudly, "Just going with the flow tonight."

He anxiously scanned the area again, hoping to catch a glimpse of Cullen. This time he spotted him, standing about ten yards, looking like he'd just stepped out of an Abercrombie & Fitch display. He was conversing with an older man who was clean-shaven and dressed in casual attire that subtly indicated affluence; he appeared to be in his mid-to-late fifties.

Ryan angled his body toward them and leaned against the counter, waiting to see if Cullen would notice him. He took a sip of his beer and continued to engage the women in light conversation, all the while keeping an eye on the two men. He lifted his arm to check the time again, adjusting his wrist so that his watch aligned directly with Cullen and the other man. The tech guys at the agency had placed a miniscule camera lens on the side of the watch, designed to look like the winding knob.

Eventually, Cullen turned towards them, his eyes lingering on Amber before they flicked to Ryan. Recognition slowly lit his face, and he smiled. Motioning for the older gentleman to follow him, Cullen made his way in their direction.

"Ryan," he said, shaking his hand. "Good to see you." He turned to the man beside him. "This is Darin Robson. His daughter is the bass player in tonight's headliner."

Ryan shook Darin's hand and said, "Looking forward to hearing the band."

"They've got real talent," Darin nodded. He glanced at the two women seated beside him. "Looks like you brought some friends with you." He smiled broadly, revealing cosmetically perfect teeth. Amber and Shelby didn't hesitate to introduce themselves.

"Nice to meet you both," Darin responded smoothly. "We're having a party in the back afterwards; you're certainly invited." He looked at Ryan and added with a wink, "You can come too."

Ryan took it good humoredly and laughed.

"Sounds like the first band has started to play," Darin stated. "I'll find you later." He turned and walked casually in the direction of the darkened entryway that led to the main stage.

Out of the corner of his eye, Ryan watched him fade into the crowd, wondering what he knew about the yacht, the gentleman's club, and the people running it. Darin fit the physical description that Kristen had given to the FBI of the man from whom she'd stolen the business card – the same card that was now in the FBI's possession, with Darin's name written across the back in bold lettering.

Cullen took a sip of his Heineken then looked at Ryan. "You ready to go in?"

"Sure. Let me grab another beer first."

Two hours later, the band Nowhere House finally took the stage.

Cullen leaned towards Ryan and pointed out Darin's daughter. In an undertone, he said, "Even from here, you can tell she's pretty hot."

Ryan didn't offer a response. He tapped his foot impatiently, willing time to speed up, then glanced at his watch: 9:47. It was going to be a long night.

The band's first song ended, and Shelby leaned into him, wrapping her arm around his. "What do you think of them?" she asked, almost shouting to be heard over the noise, her words slightly slurred.

"Too soon to say," he yelled back.

It took another hour and a half for the band to get through their set, and just when he thought there wouldn't be an encore, the band came back onto the stage. He anxiously made it through another two songs, unable to keep his mind off Tara and what might be happening to her as he stood there, waiting for the concert to end.

Raucous applause broke out as the band finally wrapped it up for the night. Cullen motioned for Ryan and the women to follow him. They threaded their way through the thick crowd and ended up in a dimly lit hallway near the back of the stage. Ryan could hear laughter as they approached an open door off to their right. Darin welcomed them in and proceeded to make introductions.

"And this," he finished, sidling up to a tall, thin girl with long black hair and fringed bangs, "is my daughter, Emmy." He gave her a quick side hug, which she ignored.

Looking at Ryan, Emmy asked in a bored tone, "Want a drink?"

Before he could respond, she handed him a shot glass of what he guessed was tequila, judging from the bottle on the speaker beside her. He downed it and set it on a side table with some other empty glasses. "You guys were good. How long have you been playing together?"

"This is our second year," she replied. "We're finally starting to get some momentum." She picked up his empty glass, filled it with more tequila, and handed it to him. This time he hesitated briefly before throwing it back. He'd already had four beers, and his thinking was starting to get foggy. He wasn't sure what his plan was for getting home if he couldn't drive, but if he wanted to find out how Darin was connected to the sex trafficker's "club," he had to play his part, which meant giving off a carefree air while keeping it together. He glanced around the room for Darin and spied him huddled in a back corner with Cullen. Simultaneously, their eyes shifted to him, and he got the sense they'd been talking about him. Darin motioned him over.

When he reached them, Darin stated, "Cullen was just telling me you might be in the market for an asset manager."

"Right now," Ryan grinned, "I'm in the market for a good time." He looked around the room then back at Darin and teased, "Don't worry, I'll stay away from your daughter."

Darin simply smiled and replied, "She prefers that I not stick around once the party's going – and the feeling's mutual."

109

He finished what remained of his drink then set the empty glass on a nearby amp. "We're going to head over to a more adult-themed place." He gave Ryan a subtle smile. "You'll like it."

****

"I think he meets the criterion, Darin." Cullen slammed on the brakes as the car in front of him suddenly turned into a parking lot without signaling. "Sorry," he muttered as he hit the gas again. They still had a few blocks to go before reaching the nightclub, where they planned to meet Ryan.

Darin glanced at him. "What did you find out about him?" He had tasked his young mentee with doing the research ahead of the concert even though he himself had already done an exhaustive investigation into Harker's background – financials, work history, education, known associates, current and previous addresses. It was his job to ensure that potential clients were fully vetted before making a recommendation to Jai for club membership. If Cullen were to take on a bigger role in the enterprise, he needed to be sure that his mentee knew how to be thorough.

"I'm almost finished putting his file together for you, but I can give you the highlights. He's the CEO of Environ Corporation. He's also one of the main investors behind that residential high rise that just went up: Eastcott Place. His net-worth is in the billions." He looked in his side mirror then swerved into the left lane. "He's the perfect target."

Darin stroked his chin thoughtfully. "If tonight shows some potential, we'll go from there." He pulled out his cellphone and pressed the number for his right-hand man. His call was answered almost immediately.

"Hey, boss."

"Marcus, I need you to head over to GLAM tonight."

"I'm already here. I'm working the bar."

"Good. I'm coming in with a cold client."

"You want me to engage?"

"Just watch how he interacts and keep an eye on his tab. I want to know how much he spends tonight."

"You got it."

Cullen waited to be sure Darin had ended the call then he asked, "So what's my role tonight?" He knew that Darin used the nightclub as a sifting ground for potential clients, but he didn't know much beyond that. He figured it was intentional until he earned more trust.

"Just make sure our investment gets home safely."

"And then?"

Darin slowly drummed his fingers on the leather armrest. "We'll see. Don't contact him unless I tell you to."

****

Ryan followed Cullen's Porsche into an underground parking garage located beneath a tall brick building fronting on Pioneer Square. He parked next to Cullen then helped Amber and Shelby out. As they fell in step behind the two men, Ryan gave the parking garage a sweeping glance. Almost every space was filled. He looked up to see several security cameras peering down at him from strategic perches, and he quickly shifted his eyes forward. A moment later, the group came to a halt in front of an elevator, which appeared to be guarded by a bouncer. Darrin gave him a solemn nod, and the bouncer hit the down button. It was a quick ride to the basement level. When the doors opened, they were met with heart-pounding, body-vibrating club music. Red light fell in a hazy glow around them as they entered. Ryan scanned the area and quickly located the exit points. He wasn't anticipating any trouble, but he was learning to be more aware of his surroundings.

He leaned toward Cullen. "You know where the restrooms are?"

Cullen pointed to his left, and Ryan began to push his way forward in that direction. He entered the restroom and relieved himself. After washing his hands, he gave himself a hard look in the mirror. *Get drunk just enough to come across as irresponsible and carefree, but not enough to become incapacitated. Assume that people may be watching you, but don't look alert. Find out more about Darin without asking too many questions.*

Shelby greeted him as he emerged from the doorway. "There you are," she giggled. The alcohol in her glass swished from side to side, spilling over the rim.

Amber stepped beside her and glanced at Ryan. "Hey, do you need me to be the designated driver?"

He'd just been thinking the same thing. "Yes, that'd be great. Thanks."

"Let's grab one of those booths in the corner." Amber took his hand and tugged him gently along behind her as she maneuvered her way through the crowded dance floor. She slid gracefully into the booth, and he followed suit, with Shelby close behind. The set up was ideal: he was now sitting between two very attractive women.

Cullen joined them in the booth just as they were placing a drink order.

Ryan glanced at him. "You want anything? I opened a tab. Get whatever you want." He leaned back in the seat, stretching his arms behind Shelby and Amber. "Everything's on me."

While they waited for their order, Ryan scanned the crowd but didn't see Darin.

A moment later, Amber leaned toward him. "Well, that didn't take long." He felt her hand on his knee as she nodded in Shelby's direction. Excruciatingly aware of Amber's touch, he glanced to his left and saw that Shelby and Cullen were engaged in a heavy make-out session. He turned back to Amber, her body now pressed against his, and his thinking started to blur. Her hand hadn't left his knee. Something inside him began to loosen. *This was okay, right? He needed to solidify his new identity...*

He bent his head toward hers and kissed her gently.

Heated passion hit him like lightning. He kissed her again, rougher this time. As his last shred of resolve dissipated, he had an odd feeling that he was cheating on someone.

11

Karen set another pot of coffee to brew then glanced at the clock and wondered when Ryan was going to make his morning appearance for breakfast. It was almost nine o'clock, and it was highly unusual for him to sleep in that late, even on a Saturday. After a moment's contemplation, she filled a teapot with hot water for herself and gently placed it on the stove then slipped a small pouch of Twining's Earl Grey into a mug. A few minutes later, the kettle began to hiss. While she waited for her tea to steep, she walked toward the end of the butler-style kitchen and pulled down three cookbooks from an open shelf. After stacking them tidily on the breakfast table, she walked back down the length of the kitchen to retrieve her tea. She stirred in a few drops of honey and was just about to head back to the breakfast nook when she heard a door open, followed by the sound of heavy footsteps. A moment later, Ryan rounded the corner.

"Hey." A sheepish grin escaped him as he ran a hand through his hair. His head was pounding, his throat sore from talking over all the noise of the club the night before.

Karen remained stoic, eyeing him critically for moment, before crisply stating, "You seem to be in a slightly better state than the last time I saw you." She reached for the mug that she'd set aside for him and poured him a cup of coffee.

He hung his head, rubbing the back of his neck as he tried to remember the details of the night before. He took the mug she handed him and warily asked, "Did I text you last night?"

She nodded. "Except it wasn't last night. It was three o'clock this morning. And you were quite drunk when I arrived."

"Arrived?" His thoughts were completely muddled. "Arrived where?"

"Here, of course," she stated wryly. "You forgot the code to your unit and couldn't get inside."

He stared down at the counter, cringing inwardly. "Thanks for coming. I..." He didn't know what to say. "You didn't have to."

"I was worried." She folded her hands around her mug and took a sip. "Who was that woman with you?"

Stifling a wave of panic, he quickly sorted through his scrambled memories. He vaguely recalled Amber and someone else helping him into a car, but that was it.

"I don't remember," he sighed, slowly massaging his temples in an attempt to alleviate his throbbing headache.

"She was sitting with you in the hallway when I got here," Karen remarked. She took a sip of her tea. "I told her I was your mother."

He almost spewed his coffee but managed to hold it in, along with his desire to laugh. From her facial expression, he could tell Karen was not amused.

"I'm sorry," he said. "For the whole situation. I never meant to put you in that kind of position."

115

She acknowledged his apology with a curt nod, then took another sip.

"So what's really going on with you?" she asked, her tone concerned.

He grimaced, knowing that he really did owe her some sort of explanation, but also wishing that she would just let it go. He slid a bagel into the toaster and waited as the seconds ticked by. Finally, he glanced at her and, resigned, said, "Let's sit down."

He grabbed a plate, buttered his bagel, and walked over to the breakfast nook.

Karen took a seat across from him, pushing aside her small stack of cookbooks, ready to hear his explanation for his atypical behavior over the past few weeks.

He took a bite of his bagel first, followed by a quick sip of coffee, then asked, "What happened to the woman who was with me?" From his faint recollection, he guessed that the woman who'd come home with him was Amber, but he couldn't be sure.

"She helped me get you to your room. Then she left."

"She just left?"

Karen harrumphed. "Oh she certainly expressed an interest in staying. That was when I told her I was your mother."

"I see," he replied, hiding his grin behind his mug of coffee.

"Yes." She waved her hand dismissively. "Tell me what happened last night."

"I don't know exactly. I went to the concert and had a few drinks." He shrugged his shoulders. "Guess I lost track of how many I had."

She eyed him suspiciously. "What's really going on, Ryan? You haven't been yourself lately. You've been preoccupied and

116

stressed, and then this sudden move – and now this." She thrust her hand in his direction and made a circular motion, indicating his overall hungover state of being. "Are you having a pre-midlife crisis?"

He laughed shortly. "I hope not."

He continued to stare down at the dark swirling liquid in his mug, wishing he could tell her everything. But since he couldn't, he simply said, "I've taken on a side project. There's been a little bit of a learning curve, more than I expected, I guess. It's been stressful."

She crossed her arms and leaned back in her seat, her expression doubtful. "Is this project why you needed to move downtown?"

He nodded. "Being here makes things much easier for me. It's going to be a lengthy endeavor, and the guy I'm working with has a firm just a few blocks from here. It'll save me a lot of time if I don't have to take the ferry every day." He wasn't exactly lying; the FBI could be called a "firm," of sorts. As she still looked skeptical, he added, "Things just got a little crazy last night. I was at the concert and then there was a party afterward, and –" He paused, searching for the right words. "I'm truly sorry you had to come over and let me in. I can assure you it won't happen again."

And that was the truth. He'd lost too much control over himself and the situation last night. Something suddenly itched at the back of his mind.

The watch.

He pushed himself out of the booth, assured Karen that he'd be right back, and headed for his room, trying to keep himself from running. Upon entering, he did a quick scan. His clothing from last night had been neatly folded and placed on a side chair, with his shoes aligned perfectly underneath. He spotted the watch on his nightstand and with a sigh of relief, picked it up and looked it over, making sure it hadn't been damaged.

He strode quickly back toward the breakfast nook and grabbed his coffee from the table, ignoring the quizzical look that Karen gave him.

"I have to take care of a few things," he explained hastily. "If you need anything, I'll be in my office."

He headed in that direction, and after taking a seat behind his desk, took out the burner phone he'd been given. Five missed calls. *Fuck*. He assumed they were all from Agent Bridger since that's who he'd been told to report to at the end of last night's outing.

Pushing his coffee aside, he dialed the agent's number.

"It's about time," Bridger answered sharply. "Why didn't you pick up last night?"

"I was occupied with our target." He was not in the mood to deal with Bridger. "I didn't get back to my place until 3:00 this morning. Sorry I didn't check in."

"We need to meet up," Bridger stated, ignoring his apology. "I'll be on the 4:45 ferry to Bainbridge this afternoon. Meet me on the upper deck. And drop off the watch before then. I want to review everything before we meet. You can put it in an envelope and leave it in the drop box. I'll give you an hour."

Ryan hung up and tossed the phone on his desk. He'd set up a drop box in the lobby of his office building for the sole purpose of making exchanges; anything small enough to fit through the slot on the exterior of the building could later be retrieved by unlocking the box from within the lobby. He'd given a set of keys to both agents – one for the box and one that gave them access to the lobby through a discreet side entrance – in the event that the building was closed.

He glanced at his phone and saw that it was almost ten. If he hurried, he could review the recording to make sure he hadn't let anything slip the night before in his drunken state. He picked up the watch and grabbed a USB cord from one of the desk drawers. Next, he plugged one end into the narrow slit on the watch, then inserted the other into the USB port of his desktop.

After listening intently to the conversational parts – he'd paused the recording during the concert to save space – he felt confident that he hadn't given himself away or put the mission at risk. On the other hand, the device had run out of recording space around midnight so he couldn't be sure that he hadn't let something slip.

Frustrated with himself, he set the watch aside and was just about to head for his room to take a quick shower when his phone rang. He glanced at the screen and saw that the caller ID was blocked.

"This is Ryan," he answered.

"Hi Ryan, it's Darin. Just wanted to make sure you made it home okay last night."

"Yeah, I did. Thanks for checking up."

"Did you have a good time?"

"I did," he replied, trying to add some enthusiasm into his voice. "It was great. I didn't know that club existed until last night."

Darin laughed smoothly. "That's the way I like it. I'm very particular about who I let in."

"You own it?" he asked, his heart rate picking up. Maybe this was the club they were looking for.

"I do. And you're welcome back anytime. All you have to do is call. You have my number?"

"No, I don't believe so."

"I'll text it to you." There was an infinitesimal pause then Darin added, "If you like my place, you might be interested in something similar. This one's rather unique. An associate of mine owns it."

"Oh?" Ryan glanced around his desk for something to write with in case he needed it.

"He runs it on a 'members only' business model – and he only entertains serious applicants." He paused then added, "Actually, he really only entertains the applicants that I recommend."

Ryan's hear rate sped up again. "So you're calling to see if I might be interested?"

"Yes. But I'm not saying that I'd recommend you for membership just yet. We'd need to have a discussion first. Maybe over drinks."

"Sure," he replied. "When do you want to meet?"

"Monday evening would be good. Six o'clock. At the club. Just call me when you get here, and I'll let you into the garage."

"Okay." Ryan jotted down the day and time on a sticky note.

As he hung up, he saw that Amber had texted him. Again. She'd texted him first thing in the morning while he was still asleep then again during his conversation with Karen. He wasn't planning on responding. From the tone of her texts, it seemed obvious that she wasn't viewing him as just another client, and he didn't have time to address that. Right now, he just needed to take a shower, drop off the watch, and then find some mental space to prepare for his meeting with Agent Bridger, who he was certain would spare him no criticism over last night.

12

Ryan had no trouble locating Ethan on the ferry later that afternoon; he was standing near the back, where the sound of the ferry's motor would cover their conversation.

"Darin called me a few hours ago," Ryan stated, stepping next to him.

Ethan remained hunched over the railing, his gaze on the water, only turning his head slightly to acknowledge Ryan's presence.

"He wanted to follow up with me about my experience at his club last night," Ryan continued, leaning casually against the railing. "Apparently he owns it."

"What's the name of it?" Ethan asked, his eyes still on the water.

"GLAM. He said he wants to meet with me to see if I'd be interested in a place that a friend of his owns."

Ethan gave him a sideways glance.

"It requires a membership," Ryan continued. "I'm supposed to meet with him on Monday for further discussion." A gust of wind almost knocked his ball cap off, but he managed to keep it in place. "It sounds like Darin's supplying the clients for his friend's business, and probably getting some kind of commission for doing it."

"I'm assuming you said yes to meeting him?" Ethan quirked an eyebrow.

"Yeah, at his nightclub. Six o'clock on Monday."

"Okay, we'll do the same thing we did last night with the watch."

"Right." He cleared his throat then nonchalantly asked, "Was there anything useful on it?"

"Not much to go off of for the audio, and you only took a few photos."

Before the agent could comment as to why that was, Ryan explained, "The lighting was dim at the club, and Darin disappeared once we'd arrived." Something prompted his memory suddenly, and he pulled out his phone. He scrolled through the string of text messages that Amber had sent him. A few of them had photos.

"Here." He handed the phone to Ethan then watched as the agent slowly swiped through the images. The first two were photos of the band. The next one was a selfie that Amber had taken of herself and Shelby at The Crocodile; they were each holding a cocktail. The last photo depicted Amber standing between Cullen and Darin, their arms around her.

"There." Ryan pointed to the man on her left. "That's Darin." He moved his finger to the side. "And that's Cullen. Cullen Downing. He's the son of John Downing, who's running for senate. And you should have the image I took with the watch – the one of Darin and Cullen together, before the concert started."

Ethan stared for a few seconds at the photo then handed the phone back to Ryan. "Go ahead and put that last one on a flash drive for me."

Ryan nodded, sliding his phone back into his pocket, and adjusted his ball cap.

"We also need to get a trap-and-trace on your phone."

"A what?"

"For your cell," Ethan clarified. "It'll allow your cellphone carrier to capture the phone numbers of any incoming calls, along with signaling information, routing details, and physical locations of placed calls. We can eventually ask a judge to sign off on a wiretap order for any targeted phone numbers, but those orders are typically harder to get. We need to build a strong case first."

Ryan shifted his gaze to the horizon. "So I just use my phone like I normally would?"

"Yes," Ethan replied. "You don't have to do anything on your end." Changing the subject, he asked, "You said you're meeting Darin on Monday?"

"Yes," Ryan confirmed.

"Where's it located? We need to start surveillance."

"It's right on the corner of Pioneer Square." He pulled out his phone again and showed Ethan the exact location on his map app.

"Okay." The agent took out his phone and pinned the location. "We'll get a pole cam set up outside."

The sound of the ferry's motor ceased as it slowly began to ease up to the dock. Ethan stepped away from the railing. "Between now and then I expect you to have the training modules completed. And," he continued edgily, "you need to figure out a way for both of us to get a membership into that club, if it ends up being a lead."

Choosing to ignore the agent's tone, Ryan simply replied, "I'll work on it."

13

Monday morning, Ryan ate a quick breakfast then shut himself in his office. After attending to all the emails that had accumulated in his inbox since he'd last checked it, he moved on to the voicemails that had been left on his work phone. He started with the first one and worked his way down. When he got to the fourth, he paused. It had been left by his father. With some trepidation, he hit play:

"I saw the photo in the paper, Ryan. Call me back."

What the hell? He glared at his phone then did a quick Google search. His name was tagged in a link that led to a social column in *The Seattle Times*. He clicked on it. A photo of himself kissing Amber leered at him from the screen. His shirt was half unbuttoned, and Amber's leg was draped across his lap; her exposed upper thigh, of which he was gripping, was clearly visible. A table in the background held a copious amount of empty cocktail glasses and beer bottles. The caption underneath the photo read, *"Ryan Harker, CEO of Environ Corporation, enjoying one of Seattle's private nightclubs."* Photo submitted by Amber Teaton.

God dammit, Amber.

He closed the laptop then sank back into his chair. If it weren't for his father, he wouldn't have cared about the photo, especially since he was trying to build his playboy reputation as quickly as possible. He glanced at Tara's file sitting on his desk, and his jaw tightened. This was about doing everything he could to get to her. And if he had to choose between her and his father's opinion of him, he would choose her every time. He reached for his phone, deleted the voicemail, and turned his attention to Amber's string of text messages. He was curious to see if she had posted the photo out of spite or for attention. Probably both. Her last text message read: *Don't bother responding to these. And please don't contact me. I have more important clients, and I don't need your business.*

He didn't text back.

As the afternoon wore on, it became more difficult to stay focused on the menial tasks he had set his mind to, and he found himself wishing that Karen was around to distract him with conversation; however, she only worked Thursday through Sunday. With a sigh, he turned to the tax documents and quarterly marketing reports spread across his desk. There was also a pile of proposals that he'd been meaning to go through, but since he had zero desire to sort through any of the documents, he swept everything into one bundle and set it on the windowsill behind him. He turned back around and surveyed the messy landscape of his office. After a moment's reflection, he came to a conclusion: he needed an office assistant – someone who could come for just a few weeks to work alongside him; he could hand off all the simple and mundane tasks that he'd been putting off, thereby freeing up his time to give his undivided attention to the investigation. With that in mind, he typed an email to Anna asking her to reach out to a temp agency. He included a brief job description then hit send. Hopefully, it wouldn't take long for her to find someone. Swiveling his chair around, he slowly stood up, stretched his arms above his head, and stared vacantly out his office window. It had been two weeks since his conversation with Peter in Chicago, and he hadn't allowed himself a single moment of downtime since then.

As he continued to stare at the cityscape, thoughts about his impending meeting with Darin later that night kept spinning around in his head. He ran his hand through his hair and decided there was only one thing that would take his mind off of everything. He grabbed his phone, scrolling through his favorites list until he reached Andrew's number. His call was answered a few rings later.

"Hey, bro. What's up?"

"I wanted to see if you're free to spar this afternoon." Andrew trained at a place in the Northgate area, and since he also taught there throughout the week, he'd been given free access to come and go as he pleased.

"Sure. We don't open until six tonight, so if you can make it by four we can have the place to ourselves for a while."

Ryan glanced at his watch. "Yeah, that's perfect. See you in a few."

Two hours later, Ryan stepped off the black rubber sparring floor, breathing hard. He braced himself against a padded wall, taking a moment to catch his breath before turning toward his brother.

"Thanks, I needed that."

"Yeah," Andrew laughed. "You're not as rusty as I thought you'd be; you're still pretty good for someone who doesn't practice on the regular."

"I had you a couple of times." With a grin, Ryan stepped off the mat and headed toward the nearby locker area where he'd left his gym bag on one of the benches. Unzipping it, he took out a towel and wiped the sweat from his forehead.

Andrew came alongside him, opened one of the lockers, and removed a pair of shoes. He set them on the bench then turned to Ryan. "It's obvious you're stressed about something. You weren't fully present on the mat."

Ryan glanced at him then shrugged his shoulders. "I have a lot of different projects going on with work. Nothing too crazy." He wiped the towel over his face again, tasting salt along the corner of his mouth. "This really helped though."

Andrew eyed him carefully for a moment then said, "How's your sustainable water project thing going?"

He could tell Andrew was trying to get him to open up. "It's coming along," he replied. "We're still working on getting some government contracts in place for some of the equipment we need." He made a point of glancing at his watch then said, "I wish I had a little more time to catch up, but I have a meeting in about an hour."

Andrew nodded. "I'm glad we could do this. You know I'm around if you ever feel like you need to decompress."

"I know you are, and I appreciate it." He reached for his gym bag. "We'll do this again." He slung the bag over his shoulder, gave Andrew a quick thump on the back as a goodbye, and headed for the door.

Returning home, he took a quick shower then headed toward his enormous walk-in closet. After a brief perusal of his wardrobe, he decided to go for a more laidback affect and selected a casual T-shirt, a pair of faded black jeans, and a blazer. He made sure to grab his IWC Schaffhausen watch, the one the agency had converted for surveillance.

He arrived at GLAM approximately seven minutes late so as not to appear overeager. As he approached the parking garage, he called Darin's cellphone to let him know he'd arrived, and a few minutes later, the wide, metal door to the underground garage slowly glided sideways. Once parked, Ryan activated the watch then headed for the elevator. There was no attendant this time, and when he pressed the down button, the doors opened automatically. Stepping inside, he felt a slight jolt of fear run up his spine; he didn't know for sure if Darin was involved in anything nefarious, but he nonetheless had the vague sense that he was walking into a lion's den.

Upon emerging, he spotted Darin sitting casually at the bar watching a Mariner's game. He was clean-shaven, his silver hair slicked back and trimmed around the edges, indicating a fresh cut. He wore khaki slacks and a navy polo.

Behind the bar, a tall black male, with a handsome face and a confident air, was hand-drying glassware.

Darin tore his eyes away from the game, but remained seated. "You want a drink?" he asked, by way of a greeting. He jerked his chin toward the bartender.

"Sure," Ryan responded. "I'll have an old fashioned if it's not too much trouble. On the rocks."

"Did you catch that, Marcus?" Darin glanced over his shoulder.

The bartender nodded. "I got you." He slung his dish towel over his shoulder and reached under the counter.

"I'll have the same," Darin stated, dismounting his barstool. "And we'll take our drinks over at the table." He motioned for Ryan to follow him as he began to amble toward a recessed booth in the corner. Ryan managed to snap a quick photo of Marcus with his watch before he turned and followed Darin.

The lighting was dim, and the club was eerily quiet. Aside from Marcus, it appeared that he and Darin were alone.

When they were both comfortably seated, Ryan asked, "So how long have you owned the club?"

"About two years now, but only in business for one. Had to do a lot of renovations before I could open it."

Ryan looked around. "Seems like the work paid off – the place was completely packed on Friday."

Darin nodded. "I attribute the success to more than just the atmosphere. Exclusivity seems to be the key. It creates demand, as I'm sure you know." He leaned back in his seat as Marcus set their drinks on the table then left.

"So," Darin continued, taking a sip, "tell me more about what you do. I know you're the main investor behind Eastcott Place. And you're the CEO of Environ." He stretched his arm languidly along the back of the booth and eyed him.

"You've done some research." Ryan thought he sensed a predatory glint in Darin's eyes. "Now that Eastcott is in the final stages," he said, "I plan to focus more on expanding what I'm doing with Environ. Growing the company. Branching into other markets, that sort of thing." He reached for his drink. "Do you plan on establishing more of a presence in the hospitality industry?"

"Perhaps." Darin took a swig from his glass then pushed it aside. "I'm assuming you're still interested in the club I told you about the other night?"

"Yes, I'm still interested." He leaned forward.

"Well, like I told you earlier, it operates on a members-only basis." Darin folded his hands in front of him, clearly getting down to business. "What really makes it unique though is its location."

"Oh?" Ryan's heartrate quickened.

"Yes." There was subtle gleam in Darin's eyes as he paused for effect before stating, "It's on a yacht."

Ryan raised an eyebrow, casually taking a sip from his glass and ignoring his racing pulse as he waited for Darin to continue.

"Members board the yacht at the start of the weekend then embark on a cruise, returning Sunday. To put it in simple terms."

Ryan stroked his jawline thoughtfully. "What are the perks?"

Darin's eyes gleamed even brighter, and his smile was smug as he settled back into his seat. "Whatever you want, you can have."

"Really." Ryan set his glass down. "Anything?"

"Anything," Darin nodded. "There's live entertainment, a casino, a pool. Michelin star chefs. Luxury staterooms. And of course..." He lifted his glass as if for a toast. "There's the women."

"Hmm." Ryan took a long swig, finishing his drink, then set his glass to the side.

Darin gave him a wide smile, displaying his unnaturally white teeth, and continued, "We provide our members with the widest selection, both in age and ethnicity."

"I don't want to seem," Ryan traced a circle along the edge of his glass, "unappreciative of the opportunity, but to be blunt, I can generally get whatever I want. Including women." He grinned. "I can buy my own yacht. What would your friend's club be able to offer me, personally?"

"Anonymity, for one." Darin smiled, obviously prepared to answer such questions. "The owner ensures that members remain clear of any possible entanglements or liabilities." He paused then slowly said, "I saw your photo in the paper, the one taken at the club on Friday. Privacy is something that the owner takes very seriously, both for himself and his clients. We go through great lengths to ensure it. You would never have to worry about a photo like that getting leaked. I can guarantee it."

"Go on," Ryan responded.

"You made a good point about being able to buy your own yacht, but trust me, what we provide is a curated *experience*." Darin leaned casually back into his seat again. "In conclusion, and if your membership is approved, you'd be accepted into an exclusive 'league'." He cleared his throat. "I submitted roughly thirty applications over the past six months; only two were accepted, and they had to be added to a waiting list. All the other applications were denied."

Ryan studied his drink for a second, rubbing the stubble along his jawline. "So even if I'm approved, I'd be waitlisted?"

Darin adjusted the ring on his finger, the gleam still in his eyes, and smiled.

"Exceptions have been made."

14

Ryan tried to ignore the aching pain in his right knee as he finished typing out an email. He'd taken a bad fall in yesterday's field training, much to his embarrassment, and it was now swollen. He sent the email then leaned back in his office chair, adjusting the ice pack before swiveling around to gaze languidly out the window.

He'd met up with Mitchell and Bridger Monday night, after he'd left Darin's club, and was instructed to do nothing but wait. It was now Wednesday morning, and he was still waiting for something to develop. He'd been very tempted to call Darin back yesterday to ask for an update regarding his possible membership, but the field exercise had provided the distraction he needed. The exercise had taken place at an off-site training location, a repurposed warehouse designed to give agents experience working with different types of case scenarios. In the training, his group had been presented with a simulated sting operation. They'd been more or less successful in completing the scenario, despite the few mistakes he'd made. As he recalled the details in his mind, thinking about what he could have done better, his phone rang. He picked it up and glanced at it. No caller ID. He let it ring one more time before answering.

"This is Ryan."

"Hello," the caller responded. "Ryan Harker?"

"Yes," he replied, reaching for a pen and paper. The voice on the other end belonged to a male, with a heavy Indian accent.

"Hello," the man repeated. "My name is Jai Kumar. Your number was given to me by your friend, Darin Robson. I'm calling to set up an appointment for you to meet with me in person, regarding your interest in a client membership."

"Oh....yes," Ryan responded, keeping his tone vague. "When would you like to meet?"

"This morning, if possible. I have several other matters to attend to this afternoon, and my schedule is quite full for the rest of the week. If you're not available..."

"I can be free around eleven," he responded.

"Excellent. I'll send my driver to pick you up. Where should I direct him?"

"Eastcott Place. He can pull up to the front entrance, and I'll come out and meet him."

"It's arranged then."

With that, the call ended.

Ryan promptly removed the burner phone from his desk and dialed Mitchell's number.

"Hey," Ryan said, skipping over a greeting when Mitchell picked up. "I just got off the phone with the club's owner. His name is Jai Kumar, and he wants me to meet him in an hour."

There was a brief pause then Mitchell asked, "Where does he want to meet you?"

"He didn't say, and I didn't get a chance to ask. It was a very brief phone call. He's sending a chauffeur to pick me up."

"From Eastcott?"

"Yes."

"Okay, I'm going to have Bridger tail you. Give me a call after the meeting, and we can debrief."

"Got it."

He hung up then sank down into his office chair, pivoting to look out the window. Leaning back, he placed his hands behind his head and took a deep breath. This was it.

Approximately one hour later, a black Rolls Royce Phantom pulled up to the front of his building and parked. Ryan watched from the lobby as the driver emerged. Given that he was wearing a clean-cut black suit with a matching tie and cap, Ryan assumed he was Kumar's driver. Without hesitating, he stepped briskly from the lobby to meet him. After a minimal introduction, the driver opened the side door for him and motioned him forward.

"Where are we headed?" Ryan asked once they'd pulled away from the curb. "I've never met with Jai before."

"I'm taking you to the White Heron Country Club," the chauffer responded, checking his side mirror before switching lanes. "I'll drop you off at the front entrance. Mr. Kumar will be waiting for you at the bar, just inside."

Thirty minutes later, the driver, who had introduced himself simply as Sam, exited the highway and turned left onto a narrow side road that meandered through an affluent neighborhood. Eventually, they came to a stop at an ornamental wrought iron gate, which slowly swung open after Sam entered a set of numbers on a keypad.

The road continued up a hill then came to a stop in front of what looked like a plantation estate. A freshly cut lawn surrounded the club, every shrub trimmed to perfection, with a terraced rose garden lining the front steps. Ryan emerged from the car, thanked the driver, and headed straight for the entrance, discreetly setting the watch to record as he mounted the steps. He entered through the set of wide, double doors then paused to gather his bearings. Above him, a large, domed fixture lit the entrance, its light reflected in the gleaming paneling and polished wood floor. A quiet lull filled the space, broken only by the sound of faint footsteps and hushed voices coming from another quarter. He glanced at the bar area where a row of leather bar chairs, neatly spaced, lined the length of the counter. Shaped like armchairs and mounted on swiveling bases, each one had a high back and winged sides, perfect for enclosing their respective occupants.

A chair near the end slowly turned towards him, revealing a figure in a khaki suit with a pinstriped tie. The gentleman eyed him for a moment, then reached for a briefcase on the counter and gracefully vacated his seat. Without hesitation, he made his approach. Ryan wasn't surprised to see that his guess about Kumar's nationality had been correct. The man walking towards him had sleek black hair and toffee colored skin. Despite the grey around his temples, and the pair of wire-framed gold glasses perched on the bridge of his nose, there was a youthful aura about him.

"Hello, Ryan," he stated, his voice low and smooth. "I recognized you from your online presence. I'm Jai Kumar."

"Pleasure to meet you." Ryan stepped forward and shook his hand.

"Likewise." Jai's tone was friendly, although slightly austere. He nodded over his shoulder. "Come this way."

Ryan followed him to a booth near the back of the bar and took a seat.

Once Jai was seated, Ryan watched him open the briefcase and remove a leatherbound portfolio from it, after which he promptly snapped the briefcase closed and set it to the side.

"Before we start, Mr. Harker, do you wish to order anything?"

"Only if you'd like to. Otherwise, I'm fine."

"As am I." Jai briskly opened the portfolio and removed a single sheet of paper. As he did so, Ryan's eye was drawn to a large ring encircling Jai's index finger. It was made of jade and ornamented with gold filigree. Ryan raised his wrist to his chin, making a pretense of rubbing his jawline, and used the watch to snap a quick photo of Jai's face.

"I'll need you to sign this NDA before we can go forward." Jai slid the piece of paper across the table.

"Naturally," he replied. After taking a few minutes to read it over, he signed his name and handed it back.

"Thank you," Jai responded crisply. He turned the paper over and placed it face down on the other side of the portfolio. Next, he pulled out a brochure and gently slid it across the polished surface. He kept his index finger on it, tapping it lightly. "This is a description of what my establishment has to offer you, Mr. Harker." He paused, looking him directly in the eye. "You will find that it is very detailed, and in some sections, explicitly so." He kept his finger on it. "I imagine you wouldn't be meeting with me if you were interested in something less, but if this isn't what you're looking for, then we'll simply go our separate ways."

Ryan nodded unaffectedly. "I'm still interested."

"Good." Jai pushed the brochure forward about an inch then withdrew his hand. "For the sake of discretion, I can't allow you to take this, or any of the other documents, home with you, so please read it thoroughly and ask me any questions you may have along the way."

Ryan opened the brochure and examined the first page, which featured a photo of a superyacht, similar to some of the ones he'd seen in the sound, but longer in length. Below the image, there was a mission statement along with a brief, non-descript history of the club's origins and its founders, all of which Ryan imagined were mostly fabricated. He turned to the second page, making sure to take his time. The page described what kind of experience clients could expect. Photos featuring scantily clad women accompanied the sections on accommodations, food, and entertainment. As he continued to skim over the page, a heading under the entertainment category caught his eye:

AUCTION

Clients are invited to participate in a live auction in which erotic dancers are up for bid. The minimum bid is $100,000. Clients are instructed to refer to the bidding roster they will receive upon boarding. Bidding instructions and profiles of each woman are listed. Aside from those featured on the bidding roster, all women on board are available at any time, with pre-established, fixed rates.

Ryan looked up. "Bidding?"

"Yes," Jai smiled. "It's part of the fun and adds a competitive element. Our erotic dancers are auctioned off at the end of the Friday night performance. At its conclusion, clients are free to depart with their 'prize'."

"I see." He faked a grin then went on to the next section which went over the general fee structure for all the women on board. He noted that the "cheapest" option would be a non-dancing, not-featured-on-the-roster woman, with the cost being $8,000 for one hour. An eight-hour day package would cost him $50,000, and an evening package, which started at 8:00pm and ended at noon the next day, was $80,000. Lastly, if he wanted to spend the entire trip with one woman, the cost would be $200,000, which he noted was double the minimum bid to participate in the auction. He wondered if the same fee structure was applied to any of the women who were auctioned off, in addition to the bidding price, but since the cost was of no concern to him, he simply moved on to the next section.

HEALTH AND SAFETY PRECAUTIONS

To ensure the health of all parties, one of our health service professionals will collect a small blood sample from each client to check for any possible concerns before boarding. Once cleared, clients are required to leave all electronic devices in assigned safes, which are located in a secure room. Before boarding, clients must step through a body scanner to check for any firearms or other weapons. These items are not permitted on board. We care at all times about the safety and overall health of our clients, service professionals, and staff members.

He glanced at Jai. "The screenings are for STDs, I'm assuming?"

Jai nodded, without offering any further explanation.

Ryan leaned back in his seat and closed the brochure. "This seems fairly straightforward. What are the membership fees?"

Jai smiled. "I like to discuss that directly with potential clients, apart from the brochure. Memberships last for three months, with three different pricing tiers. The tiers determine the nature of accommodations. Our base level membership is $50,000. At this level, the staterooms are slightly smaller and are located on the lower deck levels. Our signature membership cost is $70,000. At that level, the staterooms are larger and come with additional amenities. And lastly, we offer medallion membership for $90,000. Our premier staterooms are reserved for these members, and the membership renewal fee is waived. Any questions regarding membership?"

"No, not at the moment."

"Good." Jai adjusted his glasses and continued, "The club operates every other weekend, with some exclusions. We do have another location near Vancouver that follows the off-weekend schedule of our location here, thus making it possible for clients to be at one of our locations every weekend, if so desired. Apart from that, there are no alternate arrangements or refunds if a member is a no-show at the time of departure." Jai rested his elbows on the table and clasped his hands together. "And we do depart promptly at seven o'clock on Fridays."

Ryan nodded. "I have another question about your no-electronics policy. Does that include computers?"

"Yes. Since most computers have cameras, we can't allow it. There is no video recording or photography of any kind allowed. This is to protect your own privacy, as well as the privacy of our other clients and staff members."

"Good to know," Ryan replied. "What happens if there's an emergency? Or if a client simply needs to leave? Do staff members have a means of communicating with the outside world?"

"Yes," Jai smiled reassuringly. "A few members of our security team are assigned phones, and all members of our staff are certified in CPR and first aid. In the event of a life-threatening emergency, the necessary actions would be taken, of course." His smile widened as he continued, "We rarely deal with the issue of anyone wanting to leave prematurely, but there have been a few instances here and there. In that event, we are able to take clients back to shore by motorboat – for a fee, of course."

He nodded. "Is there anything else I should be aware of? Any additional costs for anything on board?"

"Accommodations, meals, and entertainment are covered by the membership fee. Drinks are open bar. The auction bidding and poker buy-ins are the only additional costs you would incur. Do you have any more questions?" He glanced at his watch.

Ryan took the subtle movement to indicate that the meeting was drawing to a close. "No, I don't believe so. When's the soonest my application could be processed?"

"If you can complete it now, I'll process it later tonight. Otherwise, we'll have to arrange another meeting to do the paperwork. And we do run a background check as well. Should I anticipate any issues?"

"No, nothing should come up."

"Excellent." He removed another thin folder from the portfolio and handed it to him. "This is the application. Take your time."

He opened the folder and started filling out the paperwork. There was a form for the background check and another regarding the policy on electronics and firearms. The application itself asked for standard information: name, address, contact information, emergency contacts, health and allergy questions, and payment information. There was a section that asked for the names of three references, followed by a section asking if the applicant were a party to any legal actions. The packet ended with a financial agreement form and a final signature page.

He signed his name and handed the packet back to Jai. "I would like to join as a medallion client, if possible."

"That shouldn't be a problem, Mr. Harker. I'll have one of my staff run your background check this afternoon. If I approve your application, you'll get a confirmation call." He smiled. "You may even be able to join us on board Friday evening if everything is in order." With that, he closed the portfolio and reached for his briefcase. "I'll see you out."

15

Ryan arrived back at Eastcott Place the same way he'd been taken. As the driver pulled away from the curb, he attempted to memorize the license plate then realized Bridger most likely already had it, if he'd been following them. He turned away and headed for the lobby. After entering his unit, he strode directly to his office. He then took out the burner phone from the back of his desk drawer and called Mitchell who answered promptly. He proceeded to give him a brief rundown of his meeting with Jai, making sure to mention the second club location near Vancouver.

"So," Mitchell asked, "do you think you have a shot at getting on board the yacht on Friday?"

"I think the possibility is high. He said he'll have someone contact me once my background check clears, which it will."

"And you're sure you're not able to bring Bridger?"

"I'm fairly certain this is not a 'plus one' situation." He raked his hand through his hair and pressed the burner phone closer to his ear. "I've been working on a business persona for him, but it's going to take some time to solidify all the angles before we're ready to 'introduce him to society'." Attempting to release some of the tension he was feeling, he began to pace back and forth. He was looking forward to a good, long run as soon as he was off the phone.

"Alright, do you think you can handle this weekend on your own then?"

"Yes, without a doubt." He was relieved he didn't have to deal with Bridger's ego. That was the last thing he needed.

"And how do you plan on navigating the sexual component of everything once you're on board?" Mitchell asked.

He slowly ceased his pacing. That element wasn't something he had considered. He thought for a moment then replied, "I'll have to react and adjust to what I encounter, but that's why you guys recruited me. I know how to maneuver my way around delicate situations with subtlety and – "

"Yes, but you're not quite answering my question," Mitchell cut in. "The other club members are there for sex. And you are not. How do you plan to decline that aspect of the club without causing suspicion?"

He sighed. "I don't really know yet. Do you have something in mind?"

"Not in that regard. I just wanted to make sure you've considered all the angles and implications. I trust you'll exercise good judgment."

"Sounds like we're on the same page."

"Good. Did you happen to ask where the yacht docks?"

"No...I didn't think to." He mentally kicked himself.

"Don't worry about it. I'm more concerned with how we're going to stay in communication once you're on board. It doesn't sound like you'll have a phone."

"No, I won't. And what should I do about recording? Use the watch?"

"Yes," Mitchell replied. "It shouldn't be a problem going through their security scanner. We also have a pair of sunglasses with audio and video capability that I can get to you, just for backup. And the button cams we ordered came in the other day. You can affix one to a dress shirt, and I'll give you some extras in case you run out of recording room. Each one has the capacity for about six hours. So that should cover us. We can meet briefly before Friday, and I'll show you how to use everything."

"Sounds good," he replied, looking forward to practicing with the surveillance gear.

"There's one more thing I need you to do while you're on board," Mitchell stated. "Get the hull identification number. It should be affixed to the rear of the transom. If you can get it without drawing attention to yourself that'll help us with obtaining warrants later."

"Search warrants?"

"Yes, and seizure warrants when the time comes. But for now, I want to get a tracking warrant so we can install a GPS device on the yacht, so focus on getting the hull number and any other intel you can without getting into trouble. We'll plan to debrief Sunday evening when you get back. And put your watch in the drop-box today. I'll have Bridger pick it up later tonight to review what you recorded during your meeting with Jai. I'm assuming you got some photos as well. And one or two of the chauffeur?"

"Yes, to both."

"Good. We followed you to the White Heron, and we'll establish surveillance there as soon as we can. And I'm meeting with Kristen tomorrow to see if she can ID anyone you've photographed thus far."

"Kristen – the victim that escaped, right?"

"Correct."

He took a moment to make sure there wasn't anything further he wanted to ask, then said, "I'll call you when I hear back from Kumar."

They hung up, and he carefully placed the phone back in the far corner of the desk drawer from which he'd taken it. There were a million things running through his head, but his foremost thought was what he would do if he found Tara on board the yacht. He began to pace again, mentally rehearsing a range of differing scenarios and planning what his reactions would be to each. Eventually, he glanced out the window and noticed that the sun was starting to set. He could feel the pressure begin to build in his chest, his body tense with pent-up energy that needed release.

Twenty minutes later he was outside, jogging at a fast clip in the direction of Centennial Park. He glanced at his watch then increased his speed to race pace. He continued to focus on his run, but thoughts about Tara kept edging into his head. Her missing person's photo still haunted him, and no matter how hard he tried to shake it from his memory, the image always came through crystal clear. He could see her long, brunette hair framing the delicate features of her face, the color matching her eyes; high cheekbones swept up towards elf-like ears, and she had a slightly heart-shaped hairline. One arched eyebrow was lifted slightly more than the other, giving her expression a mysterious quality. But it was her half smile that truly held his attention, captivating him and haunting him at the same time, endlessly fueling his guilt.

An hour later, as he stood in front of his usual park bench stretching, his phone began to vibrate. Disregarding his sweaty palms, he scooped it up from the bench.

"This is Ryan."

"Hello." The voice was female. "I hope I'm catching you at a good time, Mr. Harker."

"Yes, I'm free." He took a deep breath and tried to slow his breathing down.

"My name is Charlotte," she continued. "Jai Kumar instructed me to call you regarding Friday night. I can schedule a chauffeur to pick you up, if you're available this weekend."

"I'd rather drive myself, if that's an option."

"I'm sorry, Mr. Harker, but parking is very limited. And there's also liability issues for us when cars are left unattended over the weekend. I hope you understand."

"Yes, that makes sense. A chauffeur is fine."

"Perfect. We stagger our clients' arrival times in order to accommodate a brief overview of the yacht, along with a Q&A session, before departure. You'll be assigned to one of three groups, depending on your arrival time. Our medallion clients are given preference on arrival times. You may select 5:00, 5:30, or 6:00. Do you have a preference for when you'd like to arrive?"

"Six would be preferrable, thank you." He wanted to make sure he had time to thoroughly prepare before being picked up, and he needed to ensure that all his personal business matters were settled beforehand, completely freeing his mental space.

"Okay, I'll put you down for that time. The drive is roughly an hour from your residence so I'll arrange for the chauffeur to pick you up at five on Friday night. His name is Jin."

"Is there anything specific I need to bring with me, or anything else I need to be aware of?"

"No, I don't believe so. Unless you have any questions for me?"

"I can use my phone in the car, right?"

"Yes, of course. You'll just have to leave it, and any other electronics, in the safe we have reserved for you. Mr. Kumar went over all of that with you?"

"Yes, he did."

"Alright, if you have any other questions between now and Friday, don't hesitate to call."

"This number?"

"Yes," she responded pleasantly. "One of our member representatives will answer."

"Got it, thanks."

"We look forward to seeing you, Mr. Harker."

He hung up and quickly finished stretching before heading back home at a light jog. As soon as he arrived, he went straight to his office and dialed Mitchell's number on the burner phone. His call was answered mid-ring.

"Ryan. What's up?"

"I'm in. We're officially a go for Friday night."

16

Ryan was on his last conference call of the day. Once he hung up, the weekend would officially commence. He tried to keep his focus on the person speaking instead of wishing that he could speed up time. Finally, the last agenda item had been discussed and the call ended. He placed his hands behind his head and leaned back in his chair, relieved that he had the rest of the afternoon to relax before Kumar's driver came to fetch him. His carry-on was packed and ready to go, with the button cameras and sunglasses safely concealed within.

He glanced at his wristwatch then reached for his phone again and dialed Anna's number. He figured he should check in with her before signing off for the weekend, and hopefully she'd found an office assistant for him.

"Hello, Ryan," she answered cheerily.

"Hey, Anna, just checking in...any updates?"

"It's been quiet this week," she responded. "Did you see that your meeting with Mr. Romero got moved to next Monday?"

"Yes, I saw that. How's the job search going for the office assistant?"

"I have several interviews lined up for Monday and Tuesday. I haven't added them to your calendar yet. Would you like me to?"

"No, that's alright. You can conduct the interviews without me; I trust you to determine the right candidate. I'll most likely be working from home next week, but I'll try to stop by the office."

"Alright," she replied.

"Thanks for the update," he said, closing his laptop. "Enjoy your weekend."

"You too."

He left his office and headed for his bedroom, passing one of the guest rooms along the way. He paused to glance inside. It was empty, except for an antique bedframe that Rachel had found at an estate sale. He had to admit it was kind of unique looking – in a good way. It featured a high headboard, upholstered in a floral-patterned fabric. Even though she'd completely ignored his request not to get anything feminine, he had to admit he liked it – as long as she followed through on her promise to get it reupholstered. He smiled ruefully, doubtful as to whether she'd change anything about it. According to her, it was a one-of-a-kind find. At any rate, he could easily buy another if necessary and give her the beloved headboard as a Christmas present. He laughed to himself and continued down the hall. He did want to talk to Rachel's art dealer to see about acquiring a few pieces, but other than that, he felt settled in. Both his mother and Rachel had chosen items that aligned with his tastes, making the place feel warm and welcoming while maintaining an air of masculinity.

He quickly changed into a pair of shorts, slipped on his running shoes, and headed out. A few minutes later, the elevator landed him in the main lobby, which turned out to be empty. He breathed a quick sigh of relief, grateful that there was no one to sidetrack him with idle chitchat. He hit the sidewalk and jogged at an even pace to the square a few blocks down. After pausing at a bench for some light stretching, he set out briskly for Centennial Park.

An hour later, feeling refreshed after the run and a hot shower, he began to prepare for the evening. He threw on some slacks and a matching navy blazer then quickly chose a tie with a paisley pattern, the hues muted and understated. After a glance in the mirror, he left his room and made his way to the kitchen where he found Karen unloading the dishwasher.

"Do you mind helping me with these cufflinks?" he asked. "This pair always takes me twice as long when I do them myself."

She turned around, briefly assessed him, and after nodding her approval, held out her palm for the cufflinks. "I must admit," she said as he handed them over, "you do look rather dashing. Do you have a date tonight?"

"No," he laughed quickly. "Just meeting a potential investor."

"I see." The disbelieving look that accompanied her reply made him wonder exactly what it was that she saw, but in a matter of seconds she had inserted the cufflinks into the buttonholes of his sleeves and stepped away. "There, all set."

"Thanks." He grabbed his keys and phone then turned hesitantly towards her. "I won't be back tonight. I'm leaving for a conference directly after my meeting." He saw her eyes dart towards his carry-on. "I'll be back by Sunday. Feel free to text me if you need anything." He gave her a quick smile then hurried to the door.

As he waited in the lobby for the chauffeur, he alternated between reading the news and checking his email, glancing up every now and then. The feeling of having to wait didn't help the pulsing energy coursing through his veins. Eventually, a gleaming black Maybach Benz pulled up to the front and parked at the curb. He lowered his phone and watched as a young Asian male in a sharp black suit exited the driver's side.

Ryan stepped through the revolving door and walked in his direction.

"Mr. Harker?" the young man asked, coming around to the other side of the car.

"Yes," he responded. "You're the chauffeur I'm assuming?"

"That's right. Nice to meet you. My name's Jin." He smiled broadly then reached for Ryan's carry-on and set it to the side as he opened the rear passenger door for him.

Ryan ducked his head inside and lowered himself onto a sleek leather seat; the door closed with a gentle, metallic click, and a moment later the Maybach pulled away from the curb.

A few intersections went by before Jin initiated a conversation. "Is this your first time on the yacht?" he asked.

Ryan saw his eyes in the rearview mirror, peering back at him. "Yes," he replied. "I'm not exactly sure what to expect. Have you worked for Jai long?"

"Not really. I just started a few months ago." He put his turn signal on before gliding smoothly into the right lane.

"You mostly chauffeur then?"

"Kind of. I'm also part of the yacht crew."

"Sounds like a fun job. What do you do on board?"

"I'm one of the deckhands. But technically, I'm still in training."

"There must be a lot to learn."

"Yeah," Jin replied quickly, seemingly distracted by the car in front of them which had suddenly switched lanes without signaling.

"I'm curious," Ryan said, leaning forward. "What else does Jai do, besides operate the club?" If there was a possibility that Jai was laundering a portion of the club's profits, he wanted to know what the means might be.

"I'm not sure exactly, but I know he owns a few hotels."

"Are they local?"

"One's on an island in the sound somewhere. It's some kind of private resort or something. I don't really know. And then he has a hotel in Japan."

"Interesting. Do you like working for him?" It sounded like tracking the money would be quite a project for the FBI's financial analysts. There were multiple avenues to funnel the money, and in addition to having the ability to set up shell companies, Kumar could have legitimate subsidiary companies for cleaners, caterers, hotel staffing...event planning.

"Yeah, it's been good so far," Jin replied. "I don't really work directly with him though."

Ryan leaned back in his seat, reigning in his urge to ask more questions. Probably best not to appear overly curious. He switched his focus to asking Jin more personal questions, and during the next half hour, he learned that he loved coffee, had a twin, was dating a musician, and had grown up in the

Seattle area. He also had plans to run his own brewery after he graduated college.

"So is this just a summer job for you?" he asked.

"For now. Not quite sure about my fall semester yet, but Mr. Kumar said he might have some other positions open that would fit with my school schedule."

He was just about to ask a follow-up question when he felt his phone vibrate. He removed it swiftly from the inside pocket of his jacket and saw that it was one of his business partners.

"Hey, Sean. What's up?"

"I hope I'm not catching you at a bad time, but I just found out my dad's had a stroke."

"Oh," he responded, concerned. "Is he alright?"

"Yeah, he's doing okay, but he'll be in the hospital for a few days. He asked me to take his place at the board meeting on Monday. He said you could catch me up to speed?"

"Of course. I'm glad your dad's alright."

"Me too," Sean responded hurriedly. "Can we meet tomorrow night, so we can go over the presentation before Monday?" He sounded anxious.

"Hmm," he replied, stalling as he thought how to best formulate a response. "I'm out of town tomorrow, but I can meet with you Sunday night. Around eight or so?"

"Can we do a phone call tomorrow? Just to go over a few things before we meet on Sunday. I want to be prepared."

Dammit. He glanced quickly at his wristwatch. In roughly half an hour, his only means of communication would be locked up inside a safe. He had to decide now. If it were any other business deal, he would have simply thrown it to the wind and picked up the pieces later, but this was about acquiring the equipment they'd need to complete the first stage of the rainwater project. Since the equipment was being held by a government-owned agency, they'd already had to go through multiple layers of red tape just to set up the meeting.

"I know this is sudden," Sean added heavily. "And I hate to put you out. It's just that dad compiled so much information on this – there's like twenty different binders just for the proposal, and I'm not sure what's relevant to the meeting and what's not." He sighed. "Maybe we should just try to postpone it entirely?"

"No," Ryan replied, shaking his head. "We can't do that. It's too short notice for everyone, especially since we have people flying in." He had no idea if he could make a phone call happen or not, but since he was sure he could work something out with Kumar, he went ahead and said, "I'll give you a call tomorrow night around seven. Does that work?"

"Yes, I really appreciate it. Thanks."

He ended the call and glanced at his watch again.

Jin must have noticed because he said, "We should be there in about fifteen minutes."

By this time, they'd left the freeway behind and were now traveling down a minimally trafficked road on the outskirts of Seattle. The occasional glimpses of water told him they were still close to the sound. Eventually, they passed by a cluster of buildings and quaint houses that made up the main street of a small seaside town. After passing an old library, a well-groomed park, and "Annie's Ice Cream Parlor," Jin turned left onto a side street and drove another ten minutes before pulling up to the front of a two-story brick building. He parked the car along the edge of the sidewalk, and a moment later

Ryan emerged from the vehicle to find himself standing on a cobbled walkway. A damp evening breeze, smelling of saltwater, swept over him. A sign on the front of the building, which resembled a warehouse, read: "Harry's Feed and Grain." A moment later, he heard the rattle of his carryon as it rolled over the cobblestones.

Jin pulled up beside him and nodded toward the front of the building. "This used to be an old mill, but it was retrofitted to serve as a cocktail lounge. The main level isn't used for much, but underneath it, there's a speakeasy." He smiled and added, "Mr. Kumar has a flair for the dramatic; I think you'll find it has an authentic feel." He turned to his left and motioned for Ryan to follow him. "The entrance is around the back."

As he fell in step behind Jin, Ryan noticed that a small parking lot to their right was nearly full. "Is this place open to the public?" he asked.

"Kind of, but Mr. Kumar's picky about who goes in and out, and there's a capacity limit."

The cobbled path took them around the side of the building, to a stone stairwell. He followed Jin down the winding steps, which led to a small, enclosed portico near the back of the building. A lantern with a green bulb was suspended above the door; it diffused the stoop with an eerie light. Jin lifted a circular brass ring that was bolted to the center of the steel door and rapped it firmly against the metal three times, evenly.

Ryan watched as a panel in the door, directly above the knocker, suddenly slid sideways with a rusty screech.

"Password," demanded a deep voice on the other side.

"Ulysses," Jin replied stoically.

The door opened, and they were ushered into a dimly lit room where a thick stratosphere of cigar smoke hovered above its occupants' heads. A sultry rendition of "I've Got You Under My Skin" pulsated gently from the overhead speakers. Ryan took a seat at the bar, half-expecting Frank Sinatra's ghost to walk up at any moment to claim the empty seat beside him; George Clooney in a tux wouldn't have surprised him either. Instead, he saw Jai advancing towards him from a hazy, shadowy corner of the room. He was dressed in a black tuxedo, the pair of glasses he'd worn at their meeting absent.

"Hello again, Mr. Harker." His voice was deep, silky, and vaguely hypnotic. "It's a pleasure to see you here."

He motioned for Ryan to follow him through a set of service doors to the right of the bar then into a dimly lit hallway. They descended a short set of stairs, turned a corner, and walked until Jai stopped in front of what appeared to be a dead end; however, after applying pressure to a specific spot on the molding, the narrow wall in front of them slid silently to the left, revealing a metal door behind it. Jai pressed his thumb on a security touch screen that was mounted above the handle, causing the door to swing inward.

As he ushered Ryan into the room beyond, Jai stated, "This is our screening area." He then gestured to an attractive woman seated behind a reception counter. "And this is Charlotte. She'll take you through the steps."

Charlotte glanced up and smiled at them. She was thinly-boned, with long blonde hair and a model's face.

Jai turned to leave. "I'll see you on board, Mr. Harker."

Ryan watched him disappear into the hallway, the door clicking quietly into place as it closed behind him. He then turned his attention back to Charlotte, briefly scanning the room as he did so. The upper halves of each wall were painted navy, the lower halves covered in wood paneling; to his right, hung a large painting of an old wooden ship cresting a wave. A decorative rug stretched over the hardwood floor, and given that the seating was limited to a set of brown, leather, wing-back chairs in the corner, Ryan assumed clients were processed one or two at a time.

Charlotte cleared her throat and said, "Let me show you where you can store your electronics, Mr. Harker, along with anything else you'd like to leave behind for safekeeping."

She stepped away from the counter and motioned for him to follow her through a large, open doorway that served as a segue between the reception area and a small lobby containing an elevator bank and several doors. Charlotte turned to the door on her left and punched in a code. It swung inward, revealing the interior of a long, narrow room filled with old-fashioned black safes, each with gold handles and gilt engravings. The safes were mounted in rows, set into the wall so that only their metal door fronts and gold hinges were visible.

Charlotte walked towards the end of the room and pointed to one of the safes. "This one is yours. Number 107. Once I process your thumbprints, you'll be able to access your safe biometrically."

Turning around, she led him back into the reception room and over to a door situated next to the reception counter. Opening it, she announced in a professional tone, "This is the exam room."

After ushering him inside, she pointed to a vinyl chair next to a desk. "You can have a seat there. I'll need to do a quick blood draw, then get your thumbprints. After that, you're all set. It'll just take a few minutes to get the results of the draw."

She turned around and removed a thin folder from a metal filing cabinet. "I'll need you to fill these out. The first one is a HIPPA form; the other ones are for your emergency contact information and medical history."

Ryan took the folder, along with the pen she offered, and asked, "What happens when we're done with this?"

She smiled and replied, "Once we're done with this part, I'll take you through our security corridor, which is located on the ground level. You'll be asked to step through a body scanner, and after that you're ready to board."

He nodded and commenced filling out the paperwork.

Approximately twenty minutes later, he had completed the intake process and passed through the scanner without incident. He now found himself standing in a large atrium with exposed brick walls and floor-to-ceiling windows. The latter provided a view of what looked to be a small, three-tiered, cruise ship christened "Valmera," moored at the end of a long wooden pier. Circular tables with wicker chairs had been neatly arranged around the room. A bar at the back of the atrium took up the entire wall, spanning from one end to the other. Clear halogen bulbs dangled overhead, suspended from a maze of exposed pipes and ventilation ducts. Throughout the atrium, there were small groupings of well-dressed men engaged in conversation; a few individuals were standing near the windows, drinks in hand, enjoying the view.

As Ryan continued to scan the room, he didn't see anyone familiar until his eyes landed on Cullen Downing who was talking with another gentleman at the bar. Although he hadn't expected to see him, Ryan wasn't altogether surprised; he was curious, however, as to whether Downing senior was aware of his son's spending habits.

Eventually, he caught Cullen's eye, and he was beckoned over. With a few swift strides, he reached him and was introduced to his companion, a high-profile commercial real estate agent from Los Angeles.

After some brief conversation, Ryan glanced around the room and asked, "Is this everyone?"

"No," Cullen responded. "They boarded the two groups before ours." He took a sip from his wine glass. "What do you think so far?"

"As of now," Ryan replied. "I'm quite impressed."

Cullen grinned. "Wait until you're on board."

17

Tara stood on the upper deck observing the last group of men about to board; thus far, none of them had proved capable of holding her attention. She shifted her gaze upward to the twilight sky. High above the horizon, a sprinkling of stars sparkled brilliantly against a dark velvet background, placed there as if a magician had just brushed some flecks of silver glitter from his sleeve. She spared one more downward glance at the group of men below her then leaned away from the railing, ready to head back to the room adjacent to the dining hall where the other women were preparing for the grand entrance. Just before she turned away, however, one of the men arrested her attention; she wondered how she hadn't noticed him before, standing casually in the lamplight, one arm across his chest and the other lifted so his chin was resting in his hand as he conversed with another client. His frame was tall and lean, but not what she'd consider lanky, and he had broad shoulders. The navy suit he wore, which was accompanied by a white shirt and patterned tie, was perfectly tailored to his body. His hair was dark, with a matching five o'clock shadow that covered his angular jaw and cheekbones. From what she could see of his face underneath the lamplight, he seemed to have a handsome one: thin lips coupled with a straight, narrow nose and a firm chin. He laughed suddenly, and there was something about his crooked, youthful grin that continued to hold her captive; it seemed familiar, as if she had somehow seen it before. His stance as he listened attentively to his companion's monologue was confident and self-assured, and she saw him give an assertive nod every now and then. Given the coloring of his hair, his eyes could be any hue. She hoped they were green or hazel, although brown would be alright too. Just anything but blue. She halted her thoughts, frowning to herself. It shouldn't matter what color his eyes were. To him, she'd be just another body – one of many in a long line, no doubt. And that was assuming he would even choose her.

Suddenly, he gazed in her direction, directly at her, almost as if he had seen her watching him. With a sharp inhale, she glided swiftly back into the shadows, her heart racing and her face flushed. Quickly, she turned and headed in the direction of the dinner hall, composing herself as she walked.

Throughout dinner, she was determined to pay him no attention, unless it was required of her, and instead poured herself into the conversation at her table, loosely flirting with the man seated to her left. Despite her best effort not to, she couldn't resist a quick glance every now and then; but each time she did so, she found that he was already staring at her with an intensity that both unnerved her and made her blush. After meeting his gaze for the fourth time, she decided to position her chair so that her face was no longer visible to him.

At eight o'clock, all the women were dismissed to prepare for the evening's performance. Tara followed the others to the backstage changing room where she proceeded to slip out of her floor-length, velvet green evening gown and into her dance attire. What she would be wearing for the show was scanty and risqué, while still leaving room for imagination, and it would remain on throughout the entirety of the performance, a regulation that she was more than happy to follow; apparently, not stripping attracted higher bids from the clients during the auction that followed the performance.

While Tara had been told what to expect, tonight was her fist time on the yacht and she wasn't sure that she was prepared for what might happen after the performance, given that her "training" had been somewhat different from that of the other women due to the circumstances of her arrival at the complex. Since she'd been in a state of mental duress, they'd helped to stabilize her by telling her she was at a clinic for treatment; it had been a rude and frightening awakening when she'd put two and two together and realized the true nature of her circumstances. Fortunately, the handler she was assigned to was kinder and more personable than the others. He had even attempted to stall her from going on the yacht tonight by saying she wasn't quite ready, but Charlotte had been persuaded otherwise, and she'd been cleared.

The door to the dressing room suddenly flew open, cutting off her reflection, and her eyes darted to the doorway. She relaxed when she recognized the woman walking through it.

"Hi, Nicole," she said, giving the young woman a brief smile before attempting to lace up the back of her corset.

"Do you want some help with that?" Nicole asked, eyeing her.

"Yes, if you don't mind," she replied.

"Not at all. Just come over here in the light so I can see better."

Tara obliged then stood facing the mirror, with her back to Nicole.

She sucked in her breath as she felt the laces tighten.

18

Ryan leaned in to take a closer look at the poster mounted to the wall just outside the performance hall.

It was her. The woman he'd seen at dinner was Tara.

He hadn't been completely certain, especially after she'd turned her chair away, but the woman in the poster he was now examining looked almost identical to the missing person's photo he kept tucked away in the back corner of his desk. The poster featured the performers for the weekend, and the woman front and center was Tara. Her name, however – according to the poster – was "Stacie." If he was remembering the membership documents correctly, her status as a performer meant that she would be up for bid at the end of the show. And he was determined to win.

His attention had been drawn to Tara almost immediately upon his entrance to the dining hall. Her eyes had swept to his, and for a moment everything had faded into the background. Conversation had dulled to a hum; the sound of clinking dinnerware had disappeared; even the lights seemed to have grown dimmer behind her. He had attempted to hold her gaze, but she'd quickly turned her attention back to the gentleman seated next to her. The side of her face, however, still exposed to him, had provided evidence of his effect on her, as her cheeks had undeniably heightened in color. It was this, and the smile she had tried to hide, that had awakened some primal instinct in him to hunt and pursue, an instinct he knew he should suppress; but in that moment, the pull to her had felt like that of a moth to the light, and he'd found it difficult to concentrate on anything else.

Throughout the meal, he'd made a point of conveying his interest, his gaze already on her whenever she nonchalantly glanced in his direction; but eventually, and with a somewhat haughty air, she had angled her chair away from him, twisting her body so that he could no longer see her face. He hadn't paid any attention to the two women seated on either side of him, although they had both tried hard to keep him engaged, and as soon as he'd finished eating, he had politely excused himself, intent on retiring to his stateroom to freshen up before the performance; however, the poster had brought him to an abrupt halt.

He lingered on it now, gazing at her image a second longer than he should have, then abruptly turned away and proceeded toward his stateroom, which he'd been told was located just below the main deck. He found it without any difficulty, and after punching in the code he'd been given, opened the door and entered. The room was larger than he expected it to be, considering the yacht's size and all that it accommodated. A floor-to-ceiling window, offering a private view of the water, drew his attention first. He walked over and took in the vista for a moment then continued to peruse the room, which was painted dark grey and reflected a neutral palette in its decor. The most noticeable furnishing was a king-sized bed, with a matching set of wall sconces on either side; from its perch above the headboard, a large, rectangular, abstract painting overlooked the room. A leather chair had been positioned in the corner nearest to the bathroom, and directly to his right, a built-in wardrobe extended from the floor to the ceiling; his carryon had been placed neatly beside it. He turned to face the other side of the room then cocked his head, intrigued. There was something off about the wall that bordered the left side of the bed. It was partitioned into two paneled sections, with a pair of grooves in the middle that looked like handles. With a few lengthy strides, he crossed the room to stand in front of it, assuming he'd find a flat-screen TV behind it. He opened one of the panels, then the other, and stepped back to observe the long, mirrored wall he had just created. He could see the bed reflected behind him...and then it made sense. Smiling to himself, he gazed in the mirror and straightened his tie, glancing at the button camera on his dress shirt. It was indistinguishable from the other buttons running down the front, and the palm-sized rectangular box that the camera was attached to hung weightlessly on the inside of his shirt, the configuration wireless.

He closed the panels and glanced at his watch. It was almost 8:30, leaving him with just enough time to unpack before the performance. He hoisted the small suitcase onto the bed and unzipped it. As he transferred his clothes to the wardrobe, he ruminated on his plans for how he would be spending his time on the voyage. He was certain of two things: he would win the bid for Tara that night, and he wasn't leaving the yacht without her. Both would test his powers of negotiation, but the latter would require subtlety. In her interviews, Kristen had revealed that all of them worked under a "contractual" agreement, so he figured it would come down to bartering with Jai over how much it would cost for him to buy Tara – or Stacie, rather – out of the fake contract. He just hoped that money would be the only factor standing between him and his goal.

Continuing to unpack his carryon, he removed a small leather bag containing his toiletries and walked toward the bathroom. He set the bag on a shelf above the sink and thought about what would happen when he brought Tara to his room later that night. To avoid sleeping with her, he decided, he'd have to convincingly play the role of an inebriated and thoroughly exhausted man. Perhaps he could add in a touch of motion sickness as well. He had to know the extent of her loyalty to Jai and his illegal activities before he could disclose who he was and what he was really doing, and tonight would not be the night for that disclosure. Mitchell had advised him that any one of the women could have formed a trauma bond with their handler. If that were the case with Tara, he'd have to determine how strong the bond was before he even came close to telling her the truth. Bottom line, it was crucial that he win her trust as the first step.

He splashed some water on his face and ran a hand through his hair before exiting the bathroom. After tucking away his empty carryon, he gave the room a brief scan. Satisfied, he reached into his shirt, turned on the recording device, and stepped into the hallway, closing the door behind him with a soft click. A handful of men were making their way up the main stairwell, and he quickly fell in behind them. A pulsating club-beat greeted them at the top of the stairs, the music beckoning them into the darkened performance hall. After breaking away from the others, Ryan secured a seat at the end of a side row, about halfway between the entrance and the stage. Overhead, purple and blue lights bounced off the walls and ceiling, making it difficult to recognize anyone in the shifting shadows. Relaxing into his seat, he noticed that the stage was separated from the audience by a thick wall of plexiglass, keeping the dancers sealed behind it.

Cullen Downing suddenly slid into his row, brushing his legs as he scooted past. He plopped himself down in the seat next to his, an excited grin on his face, and said, "Trust me, this is better than anything I've seen in Vegas."

Ryan simply nodded, keeping his eyes focused on the stage.

"Are you going to participate in the auction later?" Cullen asked, leaning towards him.

"I haven't given it too much thought," he replied smoothly, with an air of indifference. "Probably."

The conversational din began to blend with the music as more men entered and took their seats. Ten minutes later, the lights flickered briefly then dimmed as the volume of the music was amped up. The room was plunged into total darkness as a quarter-note beat began to thump from every speaker. Eventually, a sensuous melody began to thread itself around the heavy base. A sudden flash of light revealed a curvaceous silhouette, center stage. From that point on, Ryan did his best not to watch; the entire thing made him feel sick to his stomach, knowing what he knew about the true nature of the club.

After what seemed an eternity, the show ended, and Jai appeared from the wings to stand before them in front of the plexiglass. He waited for the applause to subside then announced in his deep, hypnotic voice, "Gentleman, I hope you enjoyed the performance. The auction that you've all been waiting for will commence in exactly twenty minutes." He gave them all a broad smile, his white teeth flashing in the spotlight. "Please feel free to grab a drink at the bar while you wait." With that, he stepped back into the wings.

Knowing that he would need to appear drunk later that night, Ryan decided to get a drink. He stepped out of the row and made his way to the exit, emerging from the auditorium a few minutes later. He proceeded directly to the cocktail lounge just around the corner and ordered an old fashioned. As he waited for his drink, he leaned casually against the bar top, taking in a few deep breaths to calm the angst he was feeling. He still needed to figure out how to get the hull number of the yacht, which would require that he find the transom. He assumed it would be on the main deck.

"Greetings," said a deep, familiar voice behind him, interrupting his thoughts. "How did you like the show, Mr. Harker?"

Ryan set his drink down and turned to face Jai. "It was quite the production. I'm thoroughly impressed, and I'm looking forward to the auction."

"I'm delighted to hear that," Jai responded. He glanced at his watch then said, "I must return to the auditorium, but I wanted to make sure everything has exceeded the expectations of our newest medallion client."

"It has, thank you."

"Excellent. I'll leave you to your drink. Please don't hesitate to ask if you need anything." Jai stepped away, pressing his hands together in a prayerful manner and giving him a slight bow before pivoting gracefully on his heel and walking away.

Ryan left the bar a few minutes later and found his seat again. He hadn't been lying to Jai when he'd said he was looking forward to the auction. The competitive nature of the event energized him, flooding him with adrenaline; it was the thrill of the chase, and all his senses were heightened.

Eventually, the room was full again, with Cullen once more seated by his side; a moment later, Jai stepped into the spotlight, microphone in hand, causing the room to erupt with applause.

Jai's eyes gleamed brightly in the spotlight, and with a wide smile, he announced, "Good evening gentlemen, and welcome back!"

The room filled again with applause, and Jai waited for the tumultuous sound to diminish before continuing, "Each of you should have been handed a bidding paddle with your client number on it." He briefly paused as the last bit of noise faded away then continued, "For the benefit of our newer members, I'll explain how this works. Our lovely performers will be presented in sets of three, but will be bid on sequentially, one at a time. Bidding begins at $100,000. Please raise your number up high so our auctioneer can see it." Another spotlight suddenly flicked on to reveal a man in a black tuxedo standing behind a podium to the right of the stage. "Each round has a time limit of three minutes," Jai continued. "The man with the highest bid when the clock stops will be declared the winner. The beautiful young lady will then be his for the rest of the voyage. She will exit the stage and meet you over there." Another spotlight clicked on to illuminate a wide, open doorway at the top of a set of steps. "At that point, you are welcome to leave or stay." He briefly cleared his throat then continued, "Now, for any of you who find yourselves outbid, please be a good sport and remember that all of the women on this yacht are available to you." Laughter followed as he paused for dramatic flair. "And now," he gestured towards the wings, the spotlight following, "I present our first round of women."

This time, the noise from the audience rose to an intense crescendo as a sensuous song began to play. A moment later, three women in evening gowns emerged from the left wing. The first one walked smoothly to the center of the stage, the plexiglass still in place, and stepped up onto a red-carpeted platform. She looked like a living mannequin in a storefront window. The auctioneer began his chant, and Ryan silently watched the proceedings, paying attention to the names of the women and the winning bid amounts. A half hour passed, and he surmised they were getting close to the end of the auction since there were only two more sets of women left. So far, Tara hadn't appeared. Glancing around the room, Ryan observed that it was still quite full; it seemed that some of the men had exited with their female companions, but most of the paired duos had stayed to watch the finale. Ryan glanced to his left and noticed Cullen standing at his side.

The current round of bidding came to a close, and the auctioneer announced the final round. Two women stepped from the wings, a different song playing. Ryan's body tensed when Tara didn't join them, and he was left to hope that they were saving her for the very last since she was the featured performer.

The two women proceeded through the rounds of bidding then made their respective exits down the stairs upon completion. The tension was palpable now, with everyone collectively holding their breath in anticipation. The room dimmed and the spotlight moved to the left wing. A new song started, and Tara emerged at last.

Ryan's heart almost stopped when he saw her.

Her gown was silver, fashioned out of a material that sparkled and glimmered underneath the spotlight. It had thin halter straps holding up the outer edges of a gaping V-neckline. The dress clung tightly to her waist and hips, but then fell in loose folds to the floor. One long leg emerged repeatedly from a lengthy slit up the side as she glided to center stage. From his vantage point, Ryan had a partial view of her exposed back, the material stopping just above her tailbone. Her voluminous, brunette hair trailed over her shoulder in luscious curls that fell to her waist.

If he thought the whistling and catcalling had stopped for the evening, he was proven wrong as the room erupted once more. Thus far, the highest bid had fallen just shy of $350,000. The auctioneer began his chant, and Ryan waited silently as the remaining group of men placed their initial bids. By this point, no one was using the numbered paddles anymore as the bids were now being shouted out. With twenty seconds remaining, there were two bidders left: Cullen and a tall, lanky older gentleman with a potbelly that extended over his large, western-style belt buckle, studded with rhinestones; his silver-white hair was slicked back into a short ponytail at the nape of his neck, and he wore a small diamond earring in his left ear. Overall, he had the air of a Texas oil magnate. Ryan had been seated next to him at the dinner table, and he'd introduced himself as Raymond Colt.

Now, at the ten second mark, the bid had reached $450,000.

Ryan finally stepped forward and called out calmly and clearly, "$600,000."

Both Raymond and Cullen turned toward him. In the dead silence that followed, he could almost smell Raymond's perspiration. A vein on his forehead stood out, pulsing.

Cullen took a seat.

Five seconds to go.

Raymond looked him cooly in the eye. "$650,000."

Giving him a lighthearted grin, Ryan glanced at the clock. Three seconds remaining. He locked his gaze on Raymond's face. "One million."

Raymond turned frantically towards the podium, then back to Ryan. He opened his mouth, but nothing came out.

The buzzer sounded loudly, and the auctioneer boomed, "Gone. For one million."

Fierce clapping and rowdy cheering ensued.

Raymond's jaw clenched, his face purpling as he inhaled sharply. With a light shove of his shoulder, he brushed past Ryan and retreated angrily down the aisle.

Ignoring him, Ryan kept his gaze on Tara, watching breathlessly as she disappeared into the wings. A moment later, she reappeared at the top of the steps near the front of the stage. Her dress glittered, casting flecks of light all around her, making her seem other-worldly. When she looked at him, his breath caught in his chest. She held his gaze briefly then began to descend the steps. Swiftly, he moved toward the end of his row and out into the aisle. He reached her just as she was nearing the bottom of the stairs. Offering his arm to her, he guided her down the last two steps then pulled her gently to him.

19

"Where do you keep your things while you're onboard?" Ryan asked, leading Tara down a small corridor.

"We have rooms on one of the lower decks." She anxiously ran her fingers through a strand of her hair then stopped when she realized what she was doing. Since this would be her first time with a client, she wasn't exactly sure how to maneuver smoothly to whatever came next. "I can bring my things up to your stateroom if you'd like. I don't have very much, but it's up to you." Despite the price he'd paid for her, and that he had reserved her for the entire weekend, Tara wasn't sure if he'd want some space. She wouldn't be surprised if, after having sex, he wanted his bed to himself.

"Sure," Ryan replied. "I'll help carry your things up."

"You don't have to do that," she stated, keeping her tone even-keeled and polite. "I can manage on my own." Doing what she could for herself was now the only way that she ever felt some small degree of control. "I'll only be a minute," she continued. "What's your room number?"

"107. What if you give me a tour on the way down?" Ryan asked, careful not to sound pushy. "I can wait outside your door when we reach your room."

"Alright." She really could have used a moment to herself to process the situation and calm her nerves; it didn't help that she felt butterflies in her stomach whenever he looked at her. "Would you like to start with the cabana lounge?" she asked. "It's on the uppermost deck. We could start there and work our way down."

"Lead the way," Ryan replied. As he followed behind her, he attempted to focus on the back of her head instead of her backless dress but only managed to sustain the effort for a few seconds.

Tara turned left at the end of the hallway then slowly ascended a winding set of stairs that led to the upper deck. As they crested the last step, a rectangular pool came into view. No one was in it, but the area wasn't entirely deserted. Ryan could hear the soft whisper of conversation near a series of small enclosures.

He nodded toward them. "What are those?"

"Private lounge areas for couples to use."

Ryan noticed that the color of her cheeks had heightened. Without commenting, he continued to trail along behind her. A moment later, they ascended another short flight of stairs that led to the open-aired cabana. As they neared the top, Ryan turned to look back at the shimmering pool water below him and pushed away thoughts of what Tara might look like in a bikini. He quickly regained his focus, just as she was pointing out a cocktail bar near the back of the lounge. He moved in that direction, keeping in mind his ploy to appear drunk later that night. When they reached the bar, he asked for a beer. He then glanced at Tara.

"Do you want anything?"

She nodded. "I'll have a vodka cranberry."

A few minutes later, drinks in hand, they emerged from underneath the roof of the cabana and moved toward a set of empty lounge chairs. Rather than sit, Ryan chose to lean against the deck railing. Tara did the same. A gentle breeze swept her hair away from her face, and Ryan forgot what he was going to ask her. He took a sip of his beer and looked around. So far, the yacht was quite something.

"How long have you been working for Jai?" he asked eventually, his eyes flicking to Tara's face.

She took a quick sip of her cocktail then replied simply, "A few months or so." She leaned away from the railing. "Are you ready to go down to the second deck?"

"Sure." Ryan noticed the way she quickly averted her eyes back to her drink, and he realized he was making her nervous. Part of him enjoyed it – it was a boost to his ego to think she might be attracted to him – but the other part of him wondered if she was nervous because she was genuinely afraid of him. He'd seen her hand shake slightly as she drank her cocktail.

"Right then." Tara nodded in the direction of an elevator, with stainless-steel doors, situated across from them. "Elevator or stairs?"

"I'd rather take the stairs if you don't mind. I could use the exercise." In truth, Ryan didn't wish to be alone in an elevator with her, especially one that was probably made to fit only two people. Staying at a distance was already hard enough.

"I'll just carry these then," Tara stated with a smile, handing him her drink and removing her stilettos. "They're killing my feet."

"In that case," Ryan replied, "let's take the elevator."

"No, it's alright. I'm with you on taking the stairs." There was a playfulness in her tone as she tossed her head and offered him the stilettos. "Here – you can carry these if it makes you feel better."

He grinned at her. "You really want to go barefoot?" He set their drinks down on a nearby table and accepted the heels.

"Yes. I can't wear them one minute more. I'll grab a pair of shoes from my room when we get there." She glided past him then looked beckoningly over her shoulder.

Ryan followed her back down to the main deck then around a corner to another set of stairs that descended to the deck below. The staircase was wide and grand, the steps covered in a burgundy carpet runner that was held in place with gold rods; every spindle of the railing was elegantly carved with etchings of flowers and cherubs. Upon descending it, Ryan found himself standing in the middle of the casino, which was quite busy. At first glance, it reminded him of one he'd seen on a Natchez riverboat in New Orleans. Extravagant chandeliers dangled over the gaming tables, casting little diamond-shaped spheres of light over each one, and the walls had been plastered in a fleur de lis print and hung with gilt mirrors. Oriental rugs and Tiffany lamps rounded out the décor.

Tara nodded in the direction of what looked like an old western saloon. "Do you want to stay for a bit or keep moving?"

"Let's keep moving.," Ryan replied. "I'm eager to see what else is on this yacht."

They exited the casino through one of the side doors and stepped outside into the night air. As he followed Tara along the deck's outer corridor, an invigorating breeze swept over him, filling him with renewed energy. He continued to follow her until she came to an abrupt halt in front of a panel in the wall to their right. He watched as she tapped a code into a keypad, which caused a large pocket door to slide to the side. He followed her through the opening then came to an abrupt halt behind her. The space they were in was no bigger than a walk-in closet and was dimly lit. The door closed with a soft click behind him, and he wondered whether he should be nervous.

Tara turned to her left, and in the dim lighting, entered a code on another keypad mounted to the wall. "This is just a barrier entrance," she explained.

"A barrier entrance?" he replied warily, quirking an eyebrow.

She glanced at him with gleaming eyes and simply said, "You'll see."

The mischievous smile playing around the corners of her mouth held him captive, and he was quite certain he would follow her anywhere without question.

A second later, the door whooshed sideways, and the sound of chirping birds quickly surrounded them. Ryan stepped through the opening and found himself standing in a replicated rainforest.

"It's a menagerie," Tara said, smiling.

"A menagerie," he echoed. He stood in silent amazement, listening to the sound of trickling water and the differing melodies of the birds. The air was misty and smelled like rain. "This is..."

"Unexpected?" she suggested, tilting her head to look up at him.

"Yes," he replied softly, watching as a small, colorful bird alighted on the tree limb directly above him.

"It's not very big," she remarked in a hushed tone. "There are some exotic birds. Rare butterflies. A few monkeys." She paused then added, "Oh, and a python."

"That's all?" he responded, a smile tugging at the corner of his mouth.

Tara laughed quietly and began to move forward along a winding path, which appeared to be part of a small loop. Brightly colored butterflies flitted all around them, perching every so often on tropical fauna or soaring higher to alight on the thick, leafy greenery hovering above their heads. Ryan focused his gaze on a tiny, cerulean one as it flew gracefully upward towards the domed roof.

"What kind of birds are those?" he asked, pointing up to a mural that covered most of the dome's surface. It featured a stunning creature, frozen in flight, with long, beautiful tail feathers that trailed gracefully behind its body. Its head was divided lengthwise into two colors: emerald green around the eyes and bright yellow at the back. The yellow color extended along its body until it reached the wings, which were light brown. The long tail feathers were ruby red except for the very ends, which looked like they had been lightly dipped in white paint. Finally, two razor-thin black feathers, whip-like in nature, extended beyond the white tips of the tail feathers and dangled below its body for several feet. The bird hovered above a smaller one, perched on a branch. They appeared to be a pair, but the smaller one was much plainer and lacked most of the fanciful plumage of the larger one. It was also missing the two distinctive black feathers that were present in its counterpart.

Tara followed his gaze upward to the mural. "Those are Red Birds of Paradise," she replied. "The smaller one, sitting on the branch, is Valmera. She's the female."

Ryan raised an eyebrow. "The ship's named after her?"

"Yes. They both represent real birds. The one flying above her is the male, Rama." She lowered her head and crossed her arms loosely in front of her. "The menagerie was originally built for them. They were a mated couple."

He looked around him. "Are they in here somewhere?"

"No," she responded softly. "Not anymore."

Her melancholy tone piqued his curiosity. "What happened to them?"

"It's kind of a sad story, really. I heard it from one of the women who..." She hesitated then quickly continued, "She worked for Jai longer than I have. Apparently, Valmera – the female – had been suffering for a while before Jai decided to put her down." Lowering her gaze, she turned and slowly continued along the path. "Her wings had been clipped when she was younger, to keep her from flying. They were meant to grow back, but it seems the clipping had been done carelessly and the ends were too damaged." She stopped to take a closer look at one of the exotic flowers. "Do you know much about them? Birds of Paradise?"

"No, not really," he replied.

"I wrote a paper on them in high school," Tara continued. "There are about forty different species, all uniquely different from one another. The males perform these elaborate courting rituals to attract their mates, changing the colors and shapes of their bodies and feathers to attract attention." She turned her head slightly in his direction then shifted her gaze to another flower, touching its purple petals lightly. The melody of the birds mingled with the sound of spraying mist. "But back to Valmera. When a bird's flight feathers are clipped, they tend to pluck at the ends – it's called feather picking. Sometimes, they'll end up plucking most of the feathers out, right down to the skin in the worst cases."

"I'm guessing Valmera was one of those cases." He tried not to grimace.

Tara gave him a small nod. "I saw a photo of her, taken near the end. She looked horrific." She paused then added tonelessly, her shoulders slumping, "No one would have ever guessed that she was a Bird of Paradise. I don't even know who would take a photo of an animal in such a state." She stopped suddenly and her gaze shifted to her forearm where a small purple butterfly had alighted. The winged creature crept daintily down to her wrist then took flight, spiraling freely upward.

They both stood still and watched as the butterfly was joined by several others; they darted in and out among the treetops, alighting, then taking flight again.

Watching them suddenly caused Ryan's chest to tighten with anger, as he thought about what Tara must be suffering through, trapped, like the animals in Kumar's menagerie. He took a small step toward her, leaning in. "I'm sorry about Valmera. That sounds horrible." He felt her body shudder, almost imperceptibly, before she quickly stepped away from him. As she stopped to examine another flower, her back to him now, he saw her quickly lift a hand to her face and brush her cheek. A moment later, she turned and looked over her shoulder. "I'll show you the python."

"Tell me it's behind glass," he stated humorously, attempting to lighten the mood.

Her laughter drew the attention of two small birds, hiding in the undergrowth. They emerged from the dark recess and, in a chipper manner, skittered across their path. They looked like quail, but their upper plumage was a soft merlot color that paired nicely with their maroon side feathers.

"What were those?" Ryan asked, as he watched them disappear underneath a low-lying palm leaf.

"I'm not really sure," she replied. "I think they help to keep the insects under control."

"How environmentally friendly," he murmured, mostly to himself.

They continued forward along the path until Tara stopped in front of a large glass enclosure, its occupant a bright yellow python, coiled on top of a branch.

Ryan stepped beside her, acutely aware of the fragrant scent of her hair, and asked, "What happened to Rama, the other bird?"

A moment of silence passed before Tara responded, "I heard he got progressively worse after she died, but he wasn't put down. Apparently, he suffered right up until the end." She stared vacantly through the glass. "I mean, she did too. Just not as long."

Ryan's jaw tightened. "It seems Kumar's reluctant to part with anything he prizes." If Kumar had difficulty letting go of a pair of birds, it might be harder than he thought to get Tara away from him.

She merely nodded, her gaze remaining on the coiled, listless python. Without looking away, she asked, "Do you have any pets?"

"Hmm?" The fragrant smell of her hair was still invading his senses, causing his thoughts to scatter.

"Pets. I was just curious if you have any."

"Oh, right. Pets." He shook his head. "No, I don't have any."

"Is there a reason why?" she asked, quirking an eyebrow.

"I don't have the time, mostly. That, and I like to come and go as I please without having extra responsibilities."

"That makes sense."

"What about you?" he asked.

"No. I don't have any either." She tilted her head up and gave him a quick glance. "Ready to head back?"

"I haven't seen any monkeys yet," he replied jokingly.

"Oh, right." She turned and stepped around him, peering up through the leafy branches. "There's two of them in here somewhere. Let me see..." She walked a few more feet in the direction they had come from then stopped suddenly. "There –" She pointed upward, at a tree branch a few feet beyond them, near the inner wall of the enclosure. "He's a capuchin, I think."

The monkey stared at them curiously, cocking its head to the side before jumping to a neighboring tree, farther away.

"Well," Ryan stated, "I guess I'm satisfied now."

Smiling, Tara led him back through the barrier entryway then out into the main corridor. "One more thing to show you." She gave him a quick glance then nodded towards the elevator to her left.

Before making their advance, the doors suddenly opened, and a couple emerged.

Ryan inhaled sharply when he saw it was Colt. He'd really been hoping to avoid him.

Raymond gave him an icy glare then shifted his eyes to Tara.

"Next time," he said quietly, giving her a thin smile before continuing down the corridor.

Ryan turned and looked at Tara. Her face had grown pale and taut, her eyes worried.

"You alright?" he asked, concerned.

"Yes," she replied hastily. "I'm fine. Let's continue." She brushed past him and hit the down button.

He wasn't reassured that she was "fine," but he refrained from further comment as he followed her into the elevator. He leaned into the corner, attempting to put a few extra inches between them, hoping it would ease the sudden sexual tension; judging from her flushed face and averted eyes, he knew she felt it too. A few seconds later, the doors opened, and he fell in step behind her as she led him down another short corridor. She stopped abruptly in front of another black keypad on the wall that looked exactly like the ones he'd seen her use previously. He noted that the code was identical to the one for the menagerie.

Upon entering the room, he stood, silent, and gazed across the room to a roughly 20 x 20 foot, floor-to-ceiling viewing window that was completely submersed underwater, making him feel like he'd just stepped into an aquarium. A strip of light extending along the bottom of the window dimly lit the entire room. Above him, additional light streamed softly from recessed fixtures. Long, semi-circular sofas were arranged in tiered rows, creating a small amphitheater. Glimmering streaks of light rippled along the walls and interior surfaces of the room, reflecting the movement of the water. He took the few steps down to the window and stood, peering into the depths, which were lit by a beam of light mounted to the outside of the yacht. He watched as several medium-sized fish darted into view before disappearing into the darkness.

Tara stepped beside him. "I take it you're impressed, thus far?"

He nodded then gave her a pointed look. "With everything."

She quickly turned her face away, hoping he hadn't seen her blush.

They both continued to stare out the window, watching the fish periodically appear then disappear. Eventually, he gave her arm a light touch. "Are you ready to get your things and go up?"

She nodded, and they proceeded out into the corridor where they caught the elevator and rode it down to the crew quarters. After exiting, Ryan followed her until she stopped at an orange door, one of many lining the narrow hallway.

She gave it a light rap then said with a smile, "I have a few roommates."

They waited for a moment or two, but after no response, she opened the door.

"You can come in if you want," she said. "It's a little cramped though."

Ryan nodded and continued leaning against the doorframe. "Cramped" was an understatement. There were two sets of bunk beds and a tall, narrow dresser in between. He watched Tara open the door to a small closet and remove a garment bag from its interior. Stepping just inside the room, he offered to take it from her. After handing it to him, she pulled a duffle bag from underneath one of the beds and removed a pair of Adidas from it. Taking a seat on the bed, she slipped them on then reached for the garment bag and unzipped the bottom portion.

"The heels can go in here," she said, taking them from Ryan and placing them inside the pocket. She glanced around the room then said, "That's everything I think. I just have a few toiletries in the bathroom across the hallway."

Several minutes later, with all of Tara's belongings collected, they stood in front of the elevator once more, waiting in silence. With a sudden "ding," the doors smoothly parted, and Ryan moved to his left so Tara could enter first. As the doors closed shut, Ryan realized that the duffle bag at his side was the only thing keeping their bodies from touching.

20

An hour had passed since Ryan had left her in his room, and Tara was struggling to decide whether she should go and look for him. With a sigh, she put down her book and reluctantly rose from the comfort of the king-sized bed where she'd been reposing for the past forty-five minutes in her black negligee, reading the novel she'd found in the nightstand.

The awkwardness that had suddenly arisen between them, right after he'd ushered her inside his room, was a surprise to Tara. She certainly hadn't expected him to leave so he could grab a drink. *What could he possibly be doing*, she wondered. Considering the energy that seemed to have sparked between them earlier, she'd been expecting him to reach for her as soon as the door was closed. Instead, he'd asked her if she wanted him to bring something back for her from the bar; when she'd declined, he'd told her to make herself comfortable, which she had then proceeded to do.

She'd been "comfortable" for the first twenty minutes of his disappearance, but now she was starting to feel uncomfortably annoyed with his desertion; however, what was of more concern to her, was the fact that she wasn't just annoyed. She felt hurt too. And this, more than anything else, angered her. Why did she care where he was or what he was doing?

A thought suddenly occurred to her, something she hadn't considered. What if some other woman had captivated his attention? It was certainly possible. But then he'd paid such an extravagant amount of money to have her. None of it made any sense.

Exasperated, she rose from the bed and walked to the bathroom to check her make-up. She stared at herself for a moment, pleased to find that she looked better than she'd expected. A confident glow swept over her face as she realized that she actually wanted to sleep with him, a desire that she hadn't felt for a man in quite some time. She'd been imagining the worst-case scenario: Raymond Colt winning the bid for her. Several of the women had identified him as one of the worst clients to get; he almost always reserved one of the playrooms, and the stories she'd been told about what happened to the women he brought in there –

She abruptly stopped herself from thinking about it and returned her attention to her reflection in the mirror, feeling incredibly grateful that Ryan had won the bid. And she was to be with him for the entire weekend. At the end of the day, that was really all that mattered.

After pinning up her hair in a bun, Tara flicked off the light and left the bathroom. She'd never been good at waiting. Sighing, she flopped herself down on the bed again, lounging on her stomach, and reached for the book, which was some sort of action thriller by Tom Clancy and not something she normally would have read, given a choice. After a quick glance at the clock on the bedside table, she flipped to the last page she'd read and picked up where she left off.

Another half hour passed slowly by, and her heart began to sink. Maybe someone else had stolen him away after all. She turned the next page a little too viciously, causing it to partially tear from the binding.

"Fine," she muttered under her breath, closing the book. She'd done her part. It was 1:17 in the morning, and she could barely keep her eyes open. Setting the book aside, she headed into the bathroom once more where she washed off her make-up, brushed her teeth, and took her medications: 25 milligrams of Seroquel and 200 milligrams of Lamotrigine – the same prescription she'd been on for the last few years and taken every night without fail. Well, almost without fail.

She made sure to leave a lamp on for Ryan before sliding under the covers. As she drew the edges of the comforter around her, something gnawed at the back of her mind. She sat up suddenly, wide awake as she realized what she'd forgotten. Tossing the covers aside, she sprinted into the bathroom. *How could she have forgotten?* She scooped up the two pill bottles that were lying on the counter and quickly shoved them into her cosmetic bag. She zipped it closed and placed it in one of the bottom drawers of the sink cabinet. She couldn't believe that she'd left them in plain sight. That was absolutely the last thing she wanted him to know about her.

21

Ryan had no intention of returning to his room anytime soon. He figured Tara would get tired of waiting and simply go to bed, or at least that was his hope. If not, if she came looking for him – well, he'd deal with it. The most pressing matter now was finding Jai and convincing him to relinquish her. Ryan took the elevator up to the casino, making sure that the button cam was recording before stepping out. After taking a moment to gather his bearings, he headed straight toward the saloon.

The bartender standing behind the varnished countertop looked as if he'd just stepped off the set of an old western film. He was wearing a cream-colored dress shirt, with a pair of elastic armbands twisted around the sleeves just above his elbow. The ends of a black necktie, loosely knotted in a bow, dangled over a pinstriped vest. Judging from the lack of hair on his head and the whitish–grey mustache, the ends of which were neatly curled upwards, Ryan guessed that he was in his mid to late sixties. Using his watch, he snapped a quick photo then took a seat on one of the barstools.

The gentleman turned to him and gruffly asked, "What'll it be?"

"Bourbon – neat," he replied, casually leaning against the counter. He perused the casino floor, and his eyes came to rest on a small cluster of men and women huddled around one of the blackjack tables. After staring for a moment, he turned his attention to the center of the room where another group was carrying on a game of craps. Most of the women in the group were wearing old-timey dresses, with corsets and gaping cleavage. Their high-spirited laughter echoed throughout the casino. Ryan cast a glance to the six-handed poker tables near the back and was relieved to see that his white-tuxedoed target was sitting in one of the chairs, his back turned partially away from him. One of the casino girls, sporting the barmaid getup, flirtatiously hovered behind the gentleman seated to Jai's left.

Drink in hand, Ryan leisurely began his approach. As he drew near, Jai turned in his seat.

"Ah, Mr. Harker," he said with an amused smile, "I didn't think I'd be seeing you until the better part of tomorrow." He pulled an empty seat away from the table and motioned for him to sit down.

"Just needed a quick breather," Ryan responded, faking a grin, "before I go back." He placed his glass on the table and took the empty seat next to Jai. "What's the game?"

The dealer responded in rote fashion, "Texas hold'em. No limit. Ten's the minimum, twenty is usual, thirty for a big stack. Blinds are one and two."

Ryan rested two fingers on the felt table and pointed towards the dealer, indicating he was buying in for $20,000.

"Seat two, twenty behind," the dealer responded, "Action is on you. $1,000 to call."

"Call," he stated quickly, without looking at his cards. It didn't matter what they were. His only agenda for the hand was to determine how his opponents played. Pretty tight, he noted, as each player in turn folded their hands to the small blind, who chose to call. The last action went to Jai as the big blind. He checked.

The gentleman to his left set his drink down next to his stack of chips and extended his hand toward him. "Gary," he said, by way of introduction, giving him a quick handshake.

"Nice to meet you," Ryan responded affably.

The other two men at the table didn't bother to introduce themselves.

The dealer pushed Ryan $20,000 worth of chips, minus the $1,000 he had used to call, and laid out the first three cards.

Ryan glanced at the flop. A nine of hearts, a two of spades, and a Queen of clubs. He picked up the two cards he'd been dealt: a deuce and a seven of hearts – the two worst cards you could be dealt in the game. But the deuce meant he had the low pair, and there was the possibility of making a flush depending on the remaining two cards still to be dealt. With just the small and big blind in his hand, he had the advantage as the last action would be his.

Both players checked, so he bet $2,000 into the $3,000 pot. The small blind folded and Jai called, an action which indicated that Jai liked his cards. It also meant that Jai was likely holding a much better hand than he was.

The dealer placed the turn card, an eight of hearts, alongside the other three. Jai checked, so he decided to bet $3,500 – roughly half the pot. The action went back to Jai who check-raised $1,500 – a show of strength, but a smallish raise.

Ryan decided to call, with the knowledge that he'd have to fold if Jai bet into him on the river.

After discarding the top card from the deck, the dealer turned up the river card, a two of diamonds, and placed it next to the eight of hearts. Ryan now had trip deuces, the one in his hand pairing with the two on the board. He needed to size his bet so that Jai would call with what was surely a pair of nines or Queens.

"$5,500," Ryan stated firmly, which was roughly one third of the pot. High enough to represent a good hand but low enough to ensure a call.

Jai looked at the five cards trailing the deck in a neat row then folded. He glanced at Ryan and made a point of briefly showing his Queen of Hearts as he folded.

Ryan was surprised. Most players would have called, lacking the willpower to fold a top pair. He knew it wasn't an accident that Jai had showed his Queen. It was both a notice and a warning that he was a skilled and disciplined player, capable of getting out of a tight spot.

Ryan removed his tie and loosened his collar. For the next two hours, the two men sparred, neither one gaining a clear advantage. The other four players seemed oblivious to the real game being played before their eyes. Eventually, Ryan lost a nice-sized pot to Jai with A-Q, Jai calling every bet to the river with A-K, Big Slick. Neither one had made a pair, and both had played their hands perfectly. Ryan looked at his chips and saw that he'd just about broken even; he mused as to whether Jai had learned more about him than he had of Jai, and the thought troubled him.

Jai rose and scooted his chair under the table, seemingly content with his sizable winnings and ready to leave the game. "Gentleman, it's been a pleasure."

Ryan nodded, also rising from his chair. He glanced at Gary. "It was nice to meet you."

"Same." Gary stood to shake Ryan's hand. "See you tomorrow," he said, putting his arm around one of the casino girls who'd been hovering nearby.

Leaving the table behind him, Ryan hastily made his way in the direction that Jai was headed. With a few swift strides, he caught up to him in front of the elevator.

"Heading down?" Jai asked, giving him a sideways glance.

"Yes, but I was hoping you'd have a drink with me first. I'd like to run something by you, if you have a minute or two."

Jai glanced at his watch. "I'd be happy to meet with you in the morning."

"My proposition has an effect on tomorrow," Ryan stated firmly, keeping his tone even-keeled.

Jai took a moment before responding, his eyebrow raised, then nodded curtly toward the bar. "One drink."

Ryan followed behind him, taking a seat on one of the stools as Jai ordered his drink.

"And you?" the bartender asked, glancing in his direction a moment later.

"Bourbon," Ryan replied. "On the rocks."

Once Jai had his drink in his hand, he swiveled his bar stool around so they were facing one another.

"So what's this proposition of yours, Mr. Harker?"

Ryan took a sip of his bourbon, reminding himself to use Tara's stage name, and replied, "I'd like to take Stacie with me when we disembark."

For a moment, Jai's face went blank then he broke into a broad smile. Chuckling, he responded, "Do you think you're the first man who's wanted to take one of my women home with him?" He swirled the bourbon around in his glass and added, "I'll give you credit though for not beating around the bush." He looked at Ryan intently before tossing his head back and downing the rest of his bourbon. "They are all under contracts, and there are heavy penalties for breaching them, I'm afraid." He set his glass down on the bar top, his air dismissive. "Come back around in another six months or so."

Ryan leaned unconcernedly against the edge of the counter, resting his elbow on top of the varnished surface. "I took Cullen Downing up on a bet," he lied with ease. "He said I wouldn't be able to convince you to let me take Stacie with me when I depart." He grinned and took a quick swig from his glass. "Naturally, I accepted the challenge."

"I'm sure he'll be pleased then when you tell him he's won the bet, Mr. Harker."

"Losing goes against my nature. My real question is how much money will it take to sway you?" Ryan leaned forward. "If I paid $1,000,000 for a weekend, then I'll pay triple that amount for a week." He reached for his drink and took another swig. He was almost certain that Jai was lying about there being any sort of contract, but if indeed everything was above board, then what reason could he give to refuse his offer?

Jai stroked his chin thoughtfully for a moment then replied, "She's one of my top performers, Mr. Harker. And additionally, she does all the choreography. I'm afraid I can't spare her."

"Not even for a week?"

Jai gave him a calculating look then took another sip from his glass. He continued to mull for a moment more. Finally he stated, "You'll bring her back with you next weekend."

Ryan gave him a firm nod.

"We'll be operating out of our Vancouver location." Jai pushed his glass aside and stood to go. "You'll have to meet me there – with her of course."

"Agreed." Ryan rose from his seat.

"It seems the deal is done then." Jai turned to the bartender. "You can close down for the night." He slid his empty glass across the bar top. "I'll see you in the morning, Mr. Harker."

"One more thing." Ryan registered a look of annoyance on Jai's face, but he pressed on. "I'm afraid I have to leave the voyage earlier than planned. I received a call just before I arrived at the dock today. One of my business partners had a stroke." He felt it best to elaborate. "We have an important board meeting first thing Monday morning, and his son will take his place. I'll have to catch him up to speed on several matters. You mentioned in our initial conversation that members could be taken to shore, for a fee?"

Jai's facial expression relaxed. "I'm sorry to hear you'll have to go." With a smile, he added, "I'd be happy to arrange for someone to bring you back to Seattle in the morning. I usually take my breakfast in the cabana lounge. Come find me there at nine."

22

Ryan quietly opened the door to his stateroom. The talk with Kumar had gone much better than he'd expected. Maybe that should worry him, but for now, he didn't care. He closed the door behind him with a quiet click then turned to scan the room. One of the lamps by the bed was on, and his eyes were immediately drawn to Tara who appeared to be asleep; her long, tousled hair obscured her face so he couldn't be sure. He moved closer, waiting to see if she would stir. She was lying on her stomach, with her right arm tucked underneath the pillow. One long, slender leg, exposed up to her thigh, was twisted around a corner of the blanket. The rest of her body was hidden from view, and he wondered if she was wearing anything. He took a step closer and saw the sleeve of a T-shirt. Relieved, he turned toward the wardrobe with the intention of changing his clothes, but then thought better of it. If his ruse for not sleeping with her was that he'd been too drunk to do so, then he'd have to remain dressed. Removing the button camera from his dress shirt, he slipped it into the interior pocket of his dinner jacket then shrugged his arms out of it and hung it on a hanger. After kicking off his shoes, he walked to the bed and laid down atop the covers, face-up, leaving plenty of space between Tara's body and his.

Watching the slight movement of her back as she quietly breathed, he wanted nothing more than to roll over, circle his arms around her waist, and pull her tightly against his chest. He quickly willed himself to think about something else, anything else. He had to remember that he'd utterly failed to keep his promise to her brother; it was his fault that she was here. He thought again of that night in the hospital, sitting by Preston's bed, watching helplessly as he slipped away. It would've been so easy to keep the promise he'd made. *So why hadn't he?* A wave of guilt hit him hard in the chest. Would Preston have forgiven him if he knew he'd failed? What if the situation were reversed, if it was Rachel in Tara's shoes?

The heavy guilt remained as he reached to turn off the lamp. Preston aside, he couldn't imagine Tara ever forgiving him if she were to find out about the promise that he'd ignored. Folding his hands behind his head, he stared vacantly up at the ceiling, brooding, until the steady rhythm of Tara's breathing lulled him to sleep.

A few hours later, something nudged him in the chest, and he jerked awake, ready to take action. Upon seeing that it had merely been Tara's elbow, his heart rate returned to normal; however, it spiked again as he realized her body was pressed tightly against his. Sometime in the night, he must have rolled over and reached for her. His right leg was now draped over her lower hip, pinning her against him. He was lying on top of the covers still fully clothed, one arm tucked around her waist.

He remained motionless, loath to let her go and knowing that he must. He breathed in the scent of her hair for a moment longer than he should have then carefully shifted his body away from hers. He could only assume she was a heavy sleeper, as his movements didn't seem to affect her.

Soft morning light was streaming through the window, falling in patterns across the room, and since he was now fully awake, he decided there was no use staying in bed. He glanced at the clock on the nightstand; it was 8:12am. A rough plan for the day began to take shape in his mind. He strode toward a small desk in the corner, opened the top drawer, and discovered a pen and a pad of paper. After scribbling a quick note, he walked over to Tara's side of the bed and placed it on the nightstand. Next, he grabbed a change of clothes and proceeded to take a quick shower. After dressing hastily, he stepped back to look at himself in the mirror. Considering his lack of sleep, he didn't look half bad. He ran his hand through his hair, left the bathroom, and quietly made his way to the door. Just before stepping out into the hall, he took one last look at Tara lying in much the same position as he'd found her earlier; this time, however, her dark brown hair was swept back from her face. The light from the desk lamp softly illuminated her features, and for a moment she reminded him of an illustration he'd seen somewhere in a book...the sleeping figure of the goddess Aphrodite. He gently closed the door then turned and walked toward the elevator that would take him up to the cabana lounge. He wouldn't be able to rest easy about the situation until Tara was off the yacht and as far away from it as he could reasonably manage. He'd already thrown Mitchell's instructions out the window, as his mission had merely been to observe and gather information. However, he'd already set his own agenda from the moment he'd first learned that Tara was tied to the case.

He took the elevator to the upper deck and eventually found Jai in the cabana lounge, sitting at one of the outdoor, café-style tables.

"Hello again, Mr. Harker." Jai set his newspaper down and offered him a stiff smile. "I take it you have everything arranged with Stacie?"

"Yes," he lied. He obviously hadn't had a chance to talk with her yet, but he saw no reason why she would refuse to go with him.

Jai stood and motioned for Ryan to follow him over to the railing. With a downward glance, he stated, "A speedboat should be arriving any moment now." He pointed to the main deck below them. "Head down to the stern when you're ready. He'll dock there and wait for you."

23

With a start, Tara awoke and slowly opened her eyes. Rolling over, she glanced at the crumpled covers and tried to orient herself to her surroundings. She leaned across to what she had expected to be Ryan's side of the bed and looked at the floor. No clothes. No shoes. If he had crawled into bed with her, she certainly had no memory of it. Sitting up, she rubbed the sleep from her eyes then looked at the bedside clock. Almost 9:20. *Where was he?* Had he simply forgotten about her? Her heart clenched tightly in her chest, like a rag being wrung out, but the emotional tension quickly faded as she pushed the thought to the back of her mind. It didn't matter. She didn't care who he'd spent the night with. Nonetheless, her shoulders slumped as she sat on the edge of the bed and put her feet on the floor. It was then that she noticed the note resting on top of the Tom Clancy novel.

I ordered breakfast for us. Don't go anywhere.

Her heart fluttered involuntarily as she re-read his clipped message to her. He hadn't forgotten about her. She quickly tucked the note in between the pages of the book then walked to the bathroom and removed her cosmetic bag from one of the drawers. Sweeping her hair into a tight bun, she proceeded to take a shower. Ten minutes later, she stepped out and hastily donned one of the white Versace bathrobes hanging beside the door. She stood still for a moment, listening for any sounds of movement, then peeked out into the room. It appeared to be empty. Hunger pains twisted her stomach, so to distract herself she decided to start getting ready for the day. She was just about to rub some moisturizer on her face when a light rap on the door suddenly interrupted her preparations. Still in her bathrobe, she darted to the door and attempted to control the fluttering of her heartbeat as she opened it. Relief and disappointment filled her when she saw that it was only Jerry, the easygoing, rotund sous chef; however, any disappointment she felt quickly dissolved at the sight of the breakfast tray he was holding.

"Mr. Harker sent me down with this and told me to say that he'd be back momentarily, and that you're not to wait for him to eat."

"Thanks, Jerry. I'm starving."

He carefully handed her the tray, and with a smile, turned to go.

"Jerry...." she paused, searching for the right phrasing. "I fell asleep before he came back to the room last night....do you know where he might have been?" Attempting to sound aloof, she added, "I'm just curious."

"I believe I saw him playing poker with Jai."

"Oh," she stated, surprised. She cleared her throat and said, "Well, this was very thoughtful of him. Thank you for bringing it down."

He nodded. "My pleasure. Take it easy now. I'll see you around."

"You too," she smiled. "See you later."

Holding the tray with both hands, she carefully backed into the room then tapped the door lightly with her foot to close it. After setting the tray on top of the bed covers, she lifted one of the domed lids to reveal toast, scrambled eggs, and a large blueberry muffin. She wondered if Ryan had specifically requested the muffin, as there was a limit to how much sugar they were allowed to have. She doubted that Jerry would have added it of his own accord. To the left of her plate, there was a slender coffee carafe and a small bowl of fruit. She quickly ate a few bites of toast, then tried the eggs; they were a little undercooked for her taste, but she ate them anyway. She poured some of the steaming coffee into one of the mugs, reveling in the rich scent as she watched the liquid rise to the brim. After a few slow sips, she took another bite of toast then glanced at the second mug. Hoping that Ryan would appear soon, she took her time eating, lingering on each bite. The thought of having breakfast with him had excited her. He was obviously attractive, but it was more than that. He was her kind of attractive, and it went beyond just looks. There was something about the way he had grinned at her the night before. She recognized his smile because it was exactly the way she smiled. They had the same smile. She felt an inner glow at the thought, as if someone had lit a small candle in one of the many hidden recesses of her heart. She allowed herself to revel in the glow for a moment before she snuffed out the flame and shoved her feelings back where they belonged. She recited the mental script she'd written for herself. *He didn't want her. He would never want her.*

There was somebody else already in his life. He was taken, or he was just killing time while he waited for someone better to come along. He was married – yes, that was the one to use. The line that would keep her from being pulled under, that would turn any romantic feelings to ice. She repeated it to herself one more time. He's married. And that made him a cheater and a liar. She would never trust him. This was simply a fun fling for him, despite how much he'd paid for her. It didn't mean anything.

A light knock on the door startled her, and she quickly rose from the bed, her heart racing. She went to the door, took a deep breath, and opened it a crack. This time it was him.

Ryan leaned casually against the doorframe and smiled. "Good morning."

"Good morning," she replied, hating herself for the slight breathiness in her tone. She could feel herself blushing as she turned and walked back towards the bed. "Thank you for this." She gestured at the breakfast tray.

"Sorry I couldn't join you until now. Did you sleep well?" Ryan closed the door behind him.

"Um, yes, I did...thanks." Her thoughts were jumbled. "Did you? I must have fallen asleep before you came back." She walked slowly over to the bed and sat down, careful not to disrupt the breakfast tray.

"I noticed." He tossed her a grin as he sat down on the opposite side of the tray, facing her. She blushed again, suddenly aware that she was still wearing the bathrobe. And only the bathrobe. She reached for her mug, contemplating her next move. She couldn't think of anything else to say. His presence, his nearness – it was a little overwhelming. She took another bite of toast. What was he expecting? Was he wanting sex now?

Was he just waiting for her to finish eating? Her heart was still beating fast, and she could sense her body tensing. Shifting her position, she glanced out the wide window across from them and took in the view. The morning light shimmered on the surface of the water, and she watched a few seagulls fly by before turning back around. Determined to start some sort of conversation, she opened her mouth, but Ryan spoke before she could say anything.

"I want to ask you something," he said, looking at her intently. "I'm not sure if it's…" he paused for a moment. "Something you'd consider."

Tara glanced at him – at his jawline, rather – and nodded for him to continue.

"I wanted to see how you might feel about spending more time with me." He cleared his throat. "Just me." He paused to gauge her reaction; receiving no response, he continued, "Just for a week. I'd bring you back next weekend to Vancouver."

"To Vancouver?" she quirked an eyebrow.

"Yes, to the club's other location."

"Right," she nodded slowly. "Vancouver." She paused then said, "Jai is very strict about our contracts. I doubt he'd entertain the idea of me leaving with you."

Ryan smiled. "I've already spoken with him. The choice is entirely up to you. I would take care of the financial end of everything, so you don't need to worry about your contract." He reached for the empty mug and poured himself a cup of coffee. "Or anything else."

She could feel his gaze on her, waiting to see what she would say. Would Jai actually let her go with him? A flower of hope began to bloom in her chest, as thoughts of escaping sprang to the forefront of her mind. This might be her only chance, but it seemed too good to be true....which meant it must somehow be a very bad idea. What would Ryan do with her? He seemed nice enough, but he was still a stranger, and there was no one to vouch for his character. However, if she wanted a way out, wasn't this an opportunity? She brushed away the troubling thoughts, deciding she could figure it all out later. Right now, she desperately wanted to say yes, to leave with him, to give in to her feelings that he might want her for more than just sex....perhaps companionship too? She cleared her throat and in a slow, even tone, replied, "Yes, I'm amenable to that."

"Good." He took a sip of coffee. "Of course, you'd be free to go at any time if you felt like it wasn't working for you."

She nodded, staring at his jawline again, wishing she could look him in the eye. It was frustrating, the way he made her heart race. He was close enough now that she could smell the light scent of his cologne, masculine and heady.

"We have to leave soon," he continued, "as I need to be back in Seattle tonight for a meeting. Kumar's arranged a ride for us."

"Oh." She couldn't think of anything else to say, hardly able to contain herself at the thought of not returning to the complex, if only for a week. She looked up at him for a second then quickly shifted her gaze back to the breakfast tray lying between them. Crossing her legs, she straightened her spine so that she wasn't slouching then reached for her coffee and took a sip. She made no attempt to reposition her robe over the leg that was now exposed to his view, and out of the corner of her eye, she saw him take a look before shifting his gaze elsewhere.

A moment of silence ensued as they both took a sip from their mugs then he lowered his and asked, "How long do you need to get ready?"

"Not long," Tara replied. "Maybe a half hour or so?'

"You don't have much on the yacht, do you? Only what you brought with you?"

"Yes, that's right."

Ryan tilted his head, giving her a sideways glance. "Do you live in Seattle?"

"No," she replied hesitantly. Before he could prod further, she said, "It's probably easier for me to just buy some things in Seattle, when we get there." She rose from the bed and lifted the empty breakfast tray from it, hoping this would signal her desire to be done with the conversation.

He stood as well, taking the tray from her and walking the few feet to the desk where he set it down before turning to her. "I'll cover the cost of whatever you need to buy while you're with me."

He crossed his arms over his chest, and she got the impression that this wasn't up for discussion.

24

Wishing to give Tara some time to herself, Ryan took the elevator up to the main deck, his carryon in tow. After Tara had assured him she'd meet him at the stern in twenty minutes, he'd felt better about heading up without her. As the elevator doors opened, the sounds of laughter and splashing water drew his attention. He rolled his carryon over to the railing and glanced across at the pool area. A young woman in a string bikini was flirting with Raymond Colt, who seemed to be in a better mood this morning. The sight of his sagging chest and hairy potbelly hanging over his swim shorts was jarring, especially juxtaposed against the youthful body of the woman beside him; she couldn't be much older than eighteen, but that was being generous. Ryan snapped a few photos with his wristwatch.

Turning his gaze away, he looked out over the deck railing at the horizon, watching the sun shimmer on the gentle waves while he thought about his next steps. The original plan had been to debrief with Mitchell first thing Monday morning. He knew he'd have a lot of explaining to do regarding his deviation from the agent's instructions, but his more pressing concern was what to do with Tara now that he had her in his keeping.

How would he explain to her that he had no plans to use her sexually, when that was essentially the very thing they'd just agreed to? The simplest solution would be to just tell her the truth. However, if he did tell her who he was and what he was doing, would she go back and tell Jai? What was the nature of Jai's control over her? He sighed heavily. The answer to his question about whether to tell Tara the truth had to be a decisive "no." There was just too much he didn't know about her yet. The way he saw it, he had one week to figure it out. He just needed to walk a fine line between distance and intimacy. Keep her at arm's length romantically while purposefully drawing her closer. Make her like him just enough to win her trust, but not enough to form an attachment. How hard could it be?

He continued to the stern, where he found a few crew members performing odd jobs. He adjusted his sunglasses, which he'd put in video mode, and scanned their faces while he thought of a way to get close enough to the transom without looking conspicuous. If he could get the hull ID number for Mitchell, he might be granted some partial redemption for his decision to alter the plan. He scanned the deck again and his eyes landed on Jin, the chauffeur from the other day. He was standing right next to the transom. Perfect. Ryan glanced over his shoulder. No sign of Tara yet. Hands in his pockets, he made his approach.

"Good morning," he said. "I wasn't sure if I'd see you again or not."

Jin looked up. "Oh, hey," he said, continuing to coil the rope he was holding. "How are you liking it so far?"

"It's been quite a trip. I'm impressed." Ryan took a step closer to the transom and spotted the hull number. "I don't know much about these types of yachts," he continued, keeping his gaze on the number for a moment, recording it with the sunglasses. He turned his attention back to Jin. "How many crew members does it take to man this?"

"I don't really keep track of everyone," Jin replied. "but there are ten deckhands, including myself."

Ryan leaned casually against the transom. "If I were to buy one, could I convince you to come work for me?"

"I don't know," Jin responded, laughing. "Will it be as nice as this one?"

"I'd make sure of it," he smiled, glancing toward the outer deck corridor where he spotted Tara heading his way. Any thoughts that had been in his head vanished. With a sharp inhale, he watched as she continued toward him wearing black denim shorts, the front pockets stylishly shredded and frayed, and a simple white tank top, with a bit of the hem tucked into the front of her shorts. Her dark brown hair, long and wavy, trailed over her shoulder, the wind blowing it behind her like a model on a runway. He swept his gaze to her face, refusing to take a second look at her long, slender legs, and met her as she reached the stern. He took her duffle bag, which he noticed was quite light, slung it over his shoulder, and guided her over to the waiting speedboat. As they approached, the man at the helm jumped deftly onto the deck to take their luggage. He was middle-aged, short, and swarthy, with a bald head and muscled arms. With a nod of acknowledgment and a brief thank you, Ryan handed over their luggage. As he turned to help Tara into the boat, he spied Jai walking toward them.

"I thought I would see the two of you off," he stated as he approached, smiling broadly.

213

"Thank you," Ryan nodded. "I look forward to seeing you again next weekend."

Jai turned to Tara and handed her something. "I believe you forgot this."

"Oh...yes." Her eyes flickered to Jai's, then she quickly slipped it into her purse. "Thank you."

The exchange happened too fast for Ryan to see exactly what it was that Jai had handed her, but it looked like a small box.

As they pulled away from the yacht and picked up speed, Ryan kept a subtle eye on Tara, watching her as she looked out over the water, seemingly unaware of his gaze. She appeared to be enjoying the experience; her manner was now more at ease, almost carefree. Her long hair whipped across her face, and as she angled her body into the wind, he glimpsed an excited smile. Eventually, she turned her body to him, relaxing into their shared seat. He couldn't resist stretching his arm lightly along the transom, just behind her shoulders, but he was careful not to touch her; his precaution, however, didn't prevent a spark of electricity from jolting through his body. She glanced quickly up at him, and he wondered if she felt it too. Her head turned forward to face the bow of the boat, and he contented himself with the smell of her perfume which was an intoxicating blend of flowers and citrus.

When the boat docked two hours later, Ryan carefully stepped onto the pier then turned to help Tara out.

The driver jerked his head in the direction of the old brick building from whence they'd departed the previous evening and said, "Just go back through the same entrance, and Charlotte will meet you. I'll take care of your luggage."

Ryan led Tara down the pier and into the atrium where Charlotte greeted them with an enthused smile that quickly faded when she saw Tara standing behind him. She gave her a cool, sideways glance, but otherwise didn't acknowledge her presence, which irritated him slightly.

"I need to get my things from the safe," he stated. "We're in a bit of a hurry." He made a point of looking at Tara. "We have a dinner engagement that I'd prefer not to miss." He grinned as Tara glanced up at him, and he could see that he'd made her blush; she looked away with a quiet smile.

Charlotte nodded and responded in a polite tone, "Of course. Follow me."

After retrieving his personal effects, they followed Charlotte through a series of hallways which led back to the bar area where he'd met Jai the night before.

"Enjoy the rest of your day, Mr. Harker. We hope to see you again soon." Charlotte threw Tara a parting glare then disappeared back down the hallway. The bar was empty, except for a lone figure leaning against the counter near the exit. As Ryan approached, the man straightened and asked, "Mr. Harker?"

He nodded.

"I'm your driver, Marvin. I'll be taking you back to Seattle."

"Great," Ryan replied. This wasn't a chauffeur he'd seen before. "I just need to make a quick phone call."

The driver nodded and said, "I'll be waiting at the car."

Ryan turned to Tara. "This'll just take a sec." He waited until after she'd left with the chauffeur before taking a seat at the bar. His first call was to Sean, letting him know that he could meet with him later that night in person to go over everything for their Monday meeting. Next, he dialed Karen's number.

This should be interesting, he thought as he took a deep breath, preparing to deliver his ruse.

"Hello, Ryan."

"Hey, I was just calling to let you know I have a friend who'll be staying with me this week. She's the niece of one of my business partners. She just moved to the area, and I'm helping her out until she finds an apartment." Satisfied with the story, he continued, "Can you get one of the guest rooms ready for her? We should be arriving later this afternoon. Sorry for the short notice."

If he'd caught Karen off guard, she didn't show it. "I can put her in the guest room down the hall from yours," she responded.

"That should work. Did Rachel finish up in there?" Now that he thought about it, he seemed to recall that his sister had told him she'd be swinging by to do that very thing over the weekend. He hoped she'd done something with the headboard, as she'd promised.

"Yes, but let me double check while she's still here."

God, no. But it was too late to stop her. He could tell Karen had already set the phone down. He sighed, knowing Rachel was certain to make something of the information he'd just given Karen. And sure enough, it was Rachel who picked up the phone again a few minutes later.

"Ryan!" she gasped. "You have a guest coming? A woman!?"

He wasn't surprised at her enthusiasm, given that he hadn't dated anyone in years. "Yes," he replied hurriedly. "And I'd prefer it if you weren't there when we arrive. She doesn't need to be peppered with questions."

"Okay, but at least tell me who she is."

Rachel's voice had risen to the next octave, and it made him wince slightly. Perfect. Now he'd piqued her interest. "She's just a friend." He paused then added, "I'm simply doing her uncle a favor. She just moved here, and she needed somewhere to stay for the week. It's nothing more than that. Don't let your imagination run away with you."

"My imagination has a mind of its own." This was followed by an innocent laugh then a dramatic pause. "So...is she pretty?"

"Goodbye, Rachel." He hung up, frowning. It was only a matter of minutes before the rest of his family knew about the "mystery woman." He suddenly wondered if there was a possibility that any of his family would recognize Tara. He rubbed his jawline, thinking for a moment. If he hadn't recognized her, he didn't see why anyone else would either. Tara had been nine when they'd moved out of the neighborhood – fifteen years ago. As far as he knew, none of his family had kept in touch with the Hayes. Besides, he didn't plan on Tara meeting any of his family anyway, so really the whole thing was a non-issue. He pondered for a moment more then, satisfied, rose from his seat and headed for the door.

25

As he sat next to Tara in the backseat of the Maybach Benz, he commented, "I got the sense that Charlotte doesn't like you very much. Unless I read that wrong?"

"No, I agree with you," Tara replied.

"Is there a reason?"

Tara stared vacantly at the top of Ryan's knee, next to hers. "Maybe she was just jealous."

"Jealous?"

"I mean..." she paused then said hurriedly, "Obviously, you're attractive."

He raised an eyebrow. "So you think she's jealous that you're with me....or jealous because she could tell that I obviously prefer you over her?" He looked at her pointedly and grinned, beginning to enjoy the effect that seemed to have on her. And he wasn't disappointed. She blushed deeply and looked down at her hands.

With a subtle laugh, he replied, "I'm positive it's both." It frustrated him slightly, the way she avoided direct eye contact; it was making it difficult for him to read her, and he'd always been good at reading people. However, on the other hand, he was beginning to enjoy the challenge.

Changing the subject, he asked, "So where are you from?"

With some hesitance, Tara replied, "San Francisco." She tilted her head to the side. "I've never been to Seattle."

"I think you'll like it," Ryan said. "I'll show you around." *What was he saying?* He was supposed to be keeping his distance, not indicating that he'd be spending substantial time with her. "Do you have family in San Francisco?"

She hesitated again, and he deduced she was struggling with how much information she should reveal about herself and her past. "Yes, mostly," she replied simply, "but my dad lives in Portland. What about you? How long have you lived in Seattle?"

He wasn't surprised that she was deflecting. "Since high school." He realized then that he couldn't share much about his past either, especially the part where they'd both lived in the same small town for most of her early childhood. "So," he said, changing the topic, "Kumar mentioned you create the choreography for the performances. I'm guessing that means you're an experienced dancer?"

"Yes. I've been dancing my whole life, for the most part. I studied at Berkeley for a bit, before this."

"You must really enjoy it."

"I do," she smiled. "What about you? What did you study in college?"

"I started out with the intention of going on to law school, but I decided on a business track instead and switched to economics and finance. Did you minor in anything?"

"Yes, psychology."

"Really?" That wouldn't have been his first guess. "I suppose mind and body is a pretty good combination."

219

She smiled and replied, "I would have to agree."

He decided to ease the conversation towards a topic that might be more sustainable and less revealing about either of their pasts. "Do you like to read? I saw the Tom Clancy novel on your nightstand."

"It's not mine," she replied with a little laugh. "I found it in the drawer. I was just reading the start of it while I was..." she was going to say *while I was waiting for you,* but finished instead with, "It helped me fall asleep."

"Action novels aren't really your thing then?"

"No, not really. The last book I read was non-fiction. One of Eckhart Tolle's books."

"The name sounds familiar," Ryan replied. "He's a sort of spiritual guru, right? Mindfulness and all of that?"

She nodded. "The Power of Now is probably his most popular book. It's about staying actively in the present moment, being fully aware of it, and keeping your thoughts centered as you experience it, instead of dwelling on past memories or future worries." She tilted her head to the side. "Without purposely drawing awareness to the present, we tend to passively succumb to our daily experiences, barely noticing what's around us, or in us." After a moment's reflection, she added, "He typically writes about the inner spirit and healing the soul. He references a lot of different psychological concepts to show how mental and emotional processing feeds into our spiritual lives and how to re-interpret our past so that it's useful to us in the present."

"Sounds like one I should read," Ryan replied thoughtfully. "I've done a little bit of work with mindfulness and found that it's much harder to practice than one would think."

Their conversation continued to ebb and flow throughout the drive, and Ryan was pleased to find that Tara was knowledgeable on a wide range of topics. After an eventual lull in their dialogue, he looked out the window then glanced at his watch. It was almost 3:30. He could see the familiar outline of skyscrapers in the distance.

Thirty minutes later, their chauffeur pulled up to the front of Eastcott Place and parked. They waited on the sidewalk while their luggage was unloaded then, several minutes later, watched as the Benz pulled away from the curb and disappeared around a corner.

Before heading into the lobby, Ryan pulled Tara aside and said, "I'd prefer that my housekeeper not know about our arrangement. She's a little old-fashioned."

"Of course," she responded, feeling slightly hurt but masking it with a smile.

Reassured by her positive reaction, Ryan continued, "How do you feel about being the niece of one of my business partners?"

Tara quirked an eyebrow then in a conspiratorial tone said, "Go on."

"You just moved here, and I graciously told him you could stay with me while you're searching for an apartment." With a roguish grin, he added, "I told him I'd look after you."

"And has my 'uncle' met you in person?" She gave him a playful laugh. "Because if he has, I doubt he would trust me to your care."

"You think he'd see me as a wolf in sheep's clothing?"

"Undoubtedly." Tara tossed her head to the side and swept her hair over her shoulder. "I'll be sure to use my imagination if your housekeeper asks for any details."

Ryan grinned again as they entered the lobby and walked to the elevator. "I hope you're not afraid of heights," he said, pressing the up button.

Tara glanced at him as they stepped inside then watched anxiously as he hit the button for the 62nd floor. Despite the dropping sensation in the pit of her stomach, she forced a smile and tried to concentrate on taking slow, even breaths. At least the elevator was enclosed; if there were windows, she'd be on the floor right now, huddled in a corner. She smiled wryly to herself. *That wouldn't be embarrassing at all.*

Finally, the elevator came to a halt and the doors parted. She followed Ryan out into the foyer and glanced around. A few feet away, there was a set of double doors, sleek and black. No other doors lined the small foyer.

As Ryan entered a code on a keypad positioned off to the side, she asked, "Is your residence the only one on the floor?"

The keypad beeped, and he reached for one of the door handles, nodding his confirmation to her question. He ushered her inside, and a moment later, they were greeted by a thin, older woman wearing a pale-yellow gingham dress with a white cooking apron that was spotless. Her thick, silver-grey hair was curly and cut stylishly short, just above her ears, of which each bore a pearl earring. On her feet, were a pair of clean, thick, white sneakers, accompanied by tan stockings that were a little darker than her natural skin tone. Overall, she conveyed a sense of efficiency and neatness.

"This must be your guest." The woman gave her a kind smile, the wrinkles around her blue eyes crinkling. "Come in, come in."

Ryan wheeled his carryon behind him then closed the door. "This is T –" He caught himself just in time. "Stacie." He cleared his throat. "Stacie, this is Karen, my housekeeper."

Tara took a step forward. "Lovely to meet you." She tried to decide if a handshake would be awkward or not, but before she could think any further, another figure entered the scene and rushed toward them. Her hair was pulled back into a ponytail, and she was dressed casually in jeans and a loose-fitting, hot-pink T-shirt.

"I'm Rachel, Ryan's sister," she said, stepping next to Karen. "It's so nice to meet you!" The young woman smiled enthusiastically as she reached for Tara's duffle bag and stated, without pausing for breath, "I just finished getting your room ready. Come on, I'll show you. It's just down the hall." She threw Ryan a mischievous grin.

Tara found it hard not to catch Rachel's contagious excitement, and with a parting glance at Ryan, she turned to follow the sprightly figure in front of her.

Rachel led her past the galley-style kitchen then turned down a corridor to her left. "I made this room my pet project." She opened the door and set Tara's bag next to the bed. "I'm an interior designer, mostly." Her entire figure seemed to be vibrating with an underlying happiness. "What do you think?"

Tara stepped inside and swept her eyes over the room. "This looks just like a magazine photo. It's so...perfect." Her swift appraisal elicited a delighted squeal from her companion.

Clapping her hands, Rachel exclaimed, "I'm so glad you like it!"

Tara walked slowly to the bed, glancing around her at the furniture and decor. Pale blue walls peeked out from behind a variety of artwork, in mixed styles. A plush armchair, bathed in a ray of late afternoon sunshine, sat nestled in a corner. She moved towards the set of floor-to-ceiling windows next to the armchair. "The view must be beautiful at night, with all the lights." She kept a good distance between herself and the windows.

"It really is," Rachel responded. "You'll love it!"

Next, Tara's eyes were drawn to an elegantly framed painting hanging above the armchair. It was a landscape, featuring a field, a house, and some trees – all of which were minimally conveyed. The style reminded her of one of her favorite artists, Fairfield Porter. "Who's the artist?" she asked, turning her head over her shoulder to glance at Rachel.

"A friend of mine painted it. I bought it from her a while ago, but I wasn't quite sure where to put it at the time." Facing the painting, she gave it a satisfied nod and said, "I always knew I'd find a place for you one day."

Tara continued to walk around, examining a few of the other pieces on the wall. Eventually, her eyes landed on the bed's headboard, and she slowly ran her hand along the top of it. "This is so unique. Where did you find it?"

"An estate sale," Rachel responded proudly, with a wide grin on her face. "I couldn't resist when I saw it."

"The fabric has a nice patina to it."

Rachel beamed at her. "You can see that, too? That's what sold me on it – it's faded in just the right spots."

Tara glanced at the bed and idly wondered how much she'd be sleeping in it. She just assumed that Ryan would want her in his. The thought set off a tingly sensation that spread through her entire body. She could feel her cheeks flush.

Karen's appearance at the door quickly brought her back to reality. The housekeeper gave her a warm smile. "Will this do?" she asked, giving the room a quick look-over.

"It's perfect, thank you." She still felt slightly shocked over the sudden change in her circumstances. It all seemed too good to be true, and of course it was, because at the end of the day, no matter what happened in the next week, she'd be leaving it all behind.

"Well," Rachel said with a contented sigh, "I was supposed to have left before you got here, so I should probably leave before I get into any more trouble than I'm already in. It was lovely to meet you." She leaned toward Tara and gave her a quick hug before bouncing back into the hall.

Tara turned to Karen and remarked with a smile, "She seems nice. And she's Ryan's sister?" It seemed strange to say his name out loud; it sounded too intimate, too familiar.

"Yes, his twin," Karen responded. She glanced briefly around the room then back to Tara. "Can I get you anything? Are you hungry?"

"I'm fine for now," Tara replied. "Thanks."

"Alright, I'll let you unpack. Just let me know if there's anything you need."

She waited until the sound of Karen's footsteps faded down the hall then she took a seat on the bed. Feeling relieved to have some time to herself, she let her eyes roam freely over the room, assessing it subjectively. It really did look like something from a magazine. A large door next to a mahogany highboy caught her eye, and she walked over to it, picking up her duffle bag on the way. What she assumed to be a closet door opened instead into an opulent, ensuite bathroom. The grandeur took her breath away. Her eyes were immediately drawn to a set of tiled steps in the corner under a window; they led to a recessed spa bathtub, and her jaw dropped even further. She stared for a few moments then let out a sigh. A long time ago, she would have felt as if she'd just stepped into a fairy tale. But now she knew better. It had gotten easier over the years to recognize when a story was meant for someone else. She turned off the light and turned around, leaving the door ajar behind her as she walked briskly toward the only other door in the room. After examining the spacious walk-in closet, which was almost as big as the bathroom, she decided not to unpack anything yet. She left the duffle bag next to the closet door then slipped her purse from her shoulder. Remembering the box that Jai had given her, she unzipped the purse and removed it. She was almost afraid to open it; if it was from Jai it couldn't be anything good. She unsealed the edges and lifted one of the flaps. It was a phone – a bare-minimum, black Nokia flip phone. There was a note tucked underneath it, handwritten in elegant cursive. She took it out and read:

Call me when you open this.

Her hands began to tremble as she turned the phone on. There was no doubt as to who'd written the note. She walked numbly towards the bedroom door, and after closing it, sank to the floor. Any thoughts of escaping slowly faded away. She sat for a few minutes, staring at the phone and feeling sick to her stomach. Best to get it over with. She opened the contacts and saw one number saved under favorites. Anxiety filled her as she tapped on the number and waited. Her call was answered mid-ring.

"Tara?"

A jolt of fear zipped through her at the sound of Jai's voice. "Yes...I...."

"I expect you to call me before you go to bed each night," he cut her off curtly. "If I don't hear from you, I can assure you that you won't like the consequences. Am I clear?

"Yes." Her hands were shaking.

"Good. You will leave it on at all times so I know where you are."

With that, the call ended. Tears that had begun to pool at the corners of her eyes now spilled over. She allowed herself to cry quietly for a few minutes then she picked herself up from the floor and washed her face in the bathroom. That was really all she could do.

Ryan closed the door to his office and frowned. Rachel was not supposed to be here, and Karen's sympathetic smile had done little to alleviate his annoyance. As he stood behind his desk, he reflected long and hard on what he would say before dialing Mitchell's number on the burner phone. It rang a few times before the agent answered.

"Mitchell here."

"Hey." He took a second to clear his throat. "It's Ryan."

"Is everything okay?" Mitchell responded. "I wasn't expecting to hear from you until tomorrow night."

He took a deep breath. "Yes, everything's fine. I came back early." He squared his shoulders then added matter-of-factly, "I have Tara with me." He figured it was best to confront the issue head on.

There was a long pause before the agent sighed and said, "Please tell me you didn't do something that's going to jeopardize the investigation."

"I worked out a deal with Jai. It was a simple business transaction; just a matter of price, and I paid it." He switched the phone to his other ear and continued in an undertone, "We altered the terms of her 'contract.' She's allowed to be my companion for the week then I'll take her back with me next weekend to the Vancouver location. That should give us another opportunity to get more information."

"Okay, so you're saying that you are to go back next Friday, to Vancouver, with Tara?"

"That's what Jai's expecting."

"We need to fully debrief before I can make any decisions as to how to proceed now. She doesn't know anything about you yet, I'm assuming?"

"No, I haven't said anything to her." He began to pace back and forth.

"Okay then, "Mitchell sighed. "It sounds like you have a week to gain her trust."

Ryan nodded. "We're tracking."

"Good. Let's meet first thing tomorrow morning – early."

"Where?"

"You're at your place downtown?"

"Yes," Ryan answered.

"Okay, meet me at seven. There's a church on 6th and Boniface – First Presbyterian. It'll be open. I'll meet you in the foyer."

"I'll be there." Ryan rubbed his jawline then said hesitantly, "The only thing I'm worried about is..." he trailed off then finished, "I need to figure out how to tell her I don't want to have sex with her."

The agent laughed wryly. "Yeah, I think you'll have to figure that one out on your own." He was silent for a moment then with a sigh he said, "Look, I can understand why you wanted her off the yacht. But this isn't just about her."

"You don't have to remind me," Ryan replied, trying to hide his frustration. "I think about it every day."

Neither of them spoke for several seconds. Finally, Mitchell said, "Best case scenario, she wants to help us. Worst case scenario, she goes back to Kumar and hands him any suspicions about you."

"Yeah." He ran a hand through his hair. "I'll guess we'll find out at the end of the week which one it is."

26

As Ryan made his way back to the kitchen, he pushed aside his worried thoughts and directed his attention to the present moment. He really wanted to take Tara out somewhere expensive for dinner, but he wasn't sure whether she had the appropriate attire, judging from the size of her duffle bag. He'd have to take her shopping first thing in the morning.

He walked into the kitchen where he found Karen unloading the dishwasher; Rachel was nowhere to be seen, and he breathed a sigh of relief.

"I was thinking about taking Stacie out for dinner," he stated, glancing at Karen. "I hope you don't mind. I know you had dinner planned already." Under normal circumstances, he'd have stayed in; however, the less time Tara spent interacting with anyone the better. He had no desire to keep track of a web of made-up stories and half-truths.

"It's no trouble," Karen responded. "I haven't started anything yet."

"Okay," he smiled. "You can leave whenever you want to."

She nodded, taking off her apron. "I'll head out in about a half hour or so."

"Where's Stacie?" he asked, glancing around.

"I believe she's in her room, unpacking."

Just then, Tara rounded the corner, a shy smile on her face.

"Are you all set?" Ryan asked, shifting his attention to her. "Is there anything you need?"

"Not right away," Tara responded. "We can wait until tomorrow to go shopping, if that's alright with you."

"Of course," he replied. "Are you hungry? I was thinking we could go out for dinner." He noticed Karen had left. "There's a nice place just around the corner that we can walk to. Does that sound good?"

"Sure," Tara replied. "Should I change?"

"You look great just the way you are, but I'm going to. I'll be right back."

Tara attempted not to watch him leave, but the way his muscles moved under his polo shirt as he walked away made it hard not to stare. As soon as he'd disappeared around the corner, she commenced a brief survey of her surroundings. The kitchen stretched out, galley style, in front of her. The navy blue, lacquered cabinets spanned the walls on either side creating a wide passageway. Following her line of sight down to the end of the marble counter, she could see part of a breakfast nook hiding just beyond the corner. She turned her head to the side and glanced at the spacious living room, which was surrounded by floor-to-ceiling windows on two sides. The walls were painted a muted cream color, with a balanced blend of traditional and contemporary artwork adorning them. A beautiful grand piano stood in the corner, and she rested her eyes on it, admiring it from a distance.

Karen entered the kitchen again and, seeing where Tara's attention was directed, asked, "Do you play?"

"A little," she replied, turning toward her. "Does Ryan?"

"Yes," Karen nodded. "Quite well, too."

Unable to think of anything else to fill the silence, Tara simply said, "This is a very nice place." She quickly added with a little laugh, "*Nice* is an understatement."

Karen smiled and responded, "It's bigger than it looks too. There's a library down that way," she gestured towards the opposite end of the kitchen, "along with Ryan's office and another guest room." She shifted her gaze back to Tara and continued, "If you walk past your room, there's two more – a media room and the master bedroom."

Tara was about to ask a question concerning the library when Karen added, "Oh, and the laundry room is back over that way." She tilted her head sideways toward the end of the kitchen, near the breakfast nook. "Speaking of which, do you have anything that needs to be washed?"

"No" she replied. "I don't have anything." Which was quite literal.

"Well, when you need your laundry done, you can just leave your basket near your door, and I'll know to grab it."

Ryan suddenly reappeared wearing jeans and a Mariner's T-shirt. Tara tried not to blush when he smiled at her, but she could feel the heated flush spreading along her cheekbones. She pressed her back against the counter as he stepped closer and reached his arm around her to grab his keys and phone. The heat from his body as he leaned toward her, his arm almost touching hers, made her heart beat faster. She swallowed and tried to steady her breathing.

He took a step back, grinning. "Ready?"

She nodded then proceeded to follow him into the foyer.

Throughout their dinner, the conversation between them remained informal and spontaneous. He made her laugh outright a couple of times, much to her chagrin, as several heads turned in their direction. He didn't seem to mind the attention, merely appearing amused. By the time they were through eating, she felt slightly more relaxed around him but not enough to stop analyzing her thoughts and words. And he still caused her thinking abilities to dissolve entirely whenever she felt his eyes on her.

As they drove back to Eastcott Place, she realized just how much she was looking forward to sharing his bed that night. And she was confident that she wanted nothing more than that. She could do a no-strings-attached arrangement without any feelings getting in the way. But there was a tiny voice somewhere deep inside that told her she was lying to herself. She hated that voice. Her feelings didn't matter anyway, she argued with herself. What was happening was happening – she couldn't prevent it. There couldn't be anything wrong with letting herself enjoy it while it lasted. She pushed her thoughts to the back of her mind as Ryan drove into the garage and parked.

For some reason, their ride down in the elevator a few hours prior hadn't felt as electrically charged as it did now, and with forty floors still to go she could feel the sexual tension pulsing throughout the small interior. She risked a glance at his face, hoping to a get a read on his thoughts, but he was staring at the elevator buttons.

He crossed his arms in front of his chest and leaned away, slouching against the elevator wall, then said, "I really enjoyed our dinner."

She tried not to stammer as she responded, "I also had a great time. Thank you." *Keep it together.*

He glanced at her. "You must be pretty tired after today."

"No, not really," she replied. "I actually feel kind of energized." She looked up at him briefly. "Are you? I mean, tired?"

"Yes. I didn't get much sleep last night." He gave the elevator doors a vacant glance then looked down at his folded arms.

His response and distant manner were starting to puzzle her. She'd been expecting him to take some sort of action now that they were alone, but he stayed where he was, with no indication of getting any closer to her. The elevator dinged and slowed to a stop. He motioned for her to exit first then she followed behind him to the front door.

As he opened it for her, he said, "I have a business associate coming over for a meeting." He looked at his watch. "In about ten minutes. We might be a while." His phone buzzed, and he gave it a quick glance then said hurriedly, "He's here early. I have to go down to the lobby to let him in. I'll be right back."

"Oh, okay." Quickly gathering her thoughts, she added, "I guess I'll see you when you're done?"

He raised an eyebrow. "We'll probably be a while. You don't have to wait up if you don't want to." He gave her a brief smile then walked back toward the elevator.

Unsure of what to do with herself, she closed the door behind her then headed down the hallway and entered her room. Leaving the door ajar, she slowly looked around. She should probably call Jai. With that in mind, she removed her phone and dialed the number, then listened and waited as the phone rang several times, without answer. After leaving a short message, she set the phone down where she could see it in case he called back. After another glance around the room, she decided to curl up in the armchair. She was feeling pleasantly satisfied from the pizza she'd ordered for dinner; it seemed like forever since she'd eaten anything close to unhealthy, and nothing had ever tasted so good. As she settled into the chair, she thought about Jai and Ryan, juxtaposing them in her mind. While she wanted to believe that Ryan was an entirely different sort of man than Jai Kumar, Ryan's true nature had yet to reveal itself; and despite all his charm, he was still a complete stranger. Additionally, he was a businessman. Maybe he had his own plans for making money off her. The thought suddenly made her angry. She was completely powerless over the entire situation.

Or was she? She slowly straightened herself in the chair, thinking. Maybe it wasn't such a bad idea to make some sort of plan for getting away from Jai if she could work up the courage. After all, this might be her only real opportunity. She should at least entertain the idea. Maybe at the end of the week, she could trust Ryan enough to confide in him and tell him what was really going on? Maybe. Would he even believe her? Or care? If she were to attempt to get away without any help, she'd need money. But where would she go? Returning to San Francisco was too risky if there was a chance that Jai knew where her family lived. Could she go to the police, without repercussions? She didn't even have any real evidence to provide. But surely one of her parents had filed a missing person's report – she'd been gone for six weeks. A new thought slowly formed in her mind. What if Jai had somehow forged a note or, more probable, a text message saying that she was fine? He had her phone after all. The more she thought about it, the more depressed she became. Even if she managed to somehow escape, Jai wouldn't stop searching for her until he found her. No matter what angle she looked at the situation, that would be the end result. She was trapped. At best, even if she confided in Ryan and he believed her, he'd just encourage her to go to the police. And if she went to the police, and they believed her, what would they do? *No*, she decided. There were just too many unknowns, and she had no real proof to offer. She couldn't even remember who had abducted her, or how she'd been brought to the complex. The only thing that she had any real control over was her own person – keeping herself safe and her head above water. It suddenly occurred to her that it might be wise to be prepared in the event she might need to defend herself. For all she knew, Jai could send someone in the middle of the night to bring her back then make it look like she'd left on her own. She'd never thought about the possibility of having to kill someone before; however, if she had to defend herself, she didn't think she'd hesitate.

She pushed herself out of the chair. At any rate, she didn't intend to be found helpless if things started to go south – more south than they already were. She strode towards the bathroom and flicked on the light. Perhaps she could find some sort of weapon – something sharp. She began to go through the drawers of the sink cabinet. The top one held hand towels and washcloths, while the second contained an assortment of luxury body washes, lotions, creams, and a few bath bombs. She took one out and inhaled the lavender scent then set it on the counter. She really wanted to examine all the drawer's contents, but she forced herself to move on. The next drawer held an assortment of odds and ends: Band-aids, cotton balls, nail polish remover, disposable razors, and a pair of scissors.

Elated, she removed the scissors and held them in her hand for a moment before parting the blades. She ran her finger along the edge of one and found that it was quite sharp. She closed the blades then used her fingertip to feel the end point. Satisfied that they would get the job done if necessary, she left the bathroom. After scanning the bedroom for a hiding place, she walked to her nightstand and, feeling slightly more empowered, placed the scissors at the very back of the drawer then closed it shut.

Now that her mission had been accomplished, she looked for something else to do. Her eyes landed on a small stack of books that had been placed on top of her dresser. She didn't remember seeing them earlier that afternoon. She picked the top one up then laughed. It was the exact same Tom Clancy novel she'd been reading on the yacht. Ryan must have taken it when she wasn't looking. There was a note tucked inside:

Just in case you change your mind and want to finish it. But if not, I selected a few others. One is a personal favorite of mine, and the others are some I thought you might like. And of course, you have free use of the library. Just ask Karen, and she'll show you around if I'm not available. Please make yourself at home.

Why did he have to be funny and thoughtful? She sighed and glanced at the other three books: The Collected Works of George Bernard Shaw, Modern Man in Search of a Soul by Carl Jung, and a memoir titled, Taking Flight: From War Orphan to Star Ballerina by Michaela DePrince.

She picked up the memoir and thumbed through it, then decided on the Tom Clancy instead. She couldn't resist the urge to finish what she'd started. And she'd already read the one by Carl Jung.

Settling back in the armchair, she picked up where she'd last left off and allowed herself to become engrossed. After what seemed like a lengthy amount of time, she glanced at the clock and saw that it was almost 10:30. Surely he must be done with his meeting by now; however, she hadn't heard his footsteps in the hall, and he would have had to pass by her room to reach his. Maybe she should be ready for him? He had to be wrapping things up soon.

To that end, she stepped toward the spacious walk-in closet and opened her bag. After sorting through her array of lingerie, she chose a light blue baby doll. It was simple and feminine; innocent yet revealing, with lacey trim covering strategic areas to add mystery. She quickly donned it then went to the bathroom to check her hair and make-up. Satisfied with her reflection, she flicked the light off and made her way to the bed, book in hand. When she opened it, the note he'd left her earlier that morning fluttered out. Fondly, she picked it up and read it once more:

I ordered breakfast for us – don't go anywhere.

Us. She hadn't been part of an "us" in a long time. She thought back to their very first interaction, right after he'd won the bid for her, when he'd taken her hand and gently placed it on his arm to help her down the last few steps leading from the stage. She'd been so relieved as she'd watched him make his way to her from across the room. But it wasn't just relief that had flooded through her. She'd felt wanted in a way she never had before. Maybe it was because of the amount he'd paid to have her; or maybe it was that he'd chosen her above all the others when he clearly had his pick; or perhaps it was simply the way he'd kept his eyes fixed only on her, even though the room was crowded with beautiful women. And now she was here, in his home, holding his handwritten note to her. She knew she should throw it away, knew that she was giving in to some girlish, immature longing by keeping it. What had made him choose her? What appeal did she have to him that the others didn't? There wasn't anything remarkable about her aside from her looks, at least not that she could see. With a heavy sigh, she tucked the note between the pages and went back to reading.

A few minutes later, she heard the faint sounds of his footsteps on the hardwood floor. Her heart rate immediately spiked. Tossing the book aside, she rose quickly and walked to the door, peering through the crack. She could see the outline of his shadow as he approached down the darkened hallway. She opened the door wider and leaned provocatively against the doorframe, knowing that the light behind her was silhouetting her figure perfectly. He drew closer then stopped short when he saw her. She glanced up at him, and despite the dim lighting, his facial expression was plain to see – he looked as if she'd just splashed him with a glass of cold water.

He inhaled sharply and took a step backward, gazing at her with an unreadable expression.

"Fuck," he said, low and breathless, his tone strained, with no hint of a smile. But he didn't look away.

If she'd been at a loss as to what to do before, she was completely clueless now. Words failed her. Coherent thoughts failed her.

He raked his hand through his hair. "I thought you'd be asleep." He swallowed and his voice was tight as he added, "I figured you were probably too tired. I was just planning on calling it a night."

"Oh," she managed, after scrambling to find something to say, to no avail.

She felt like she'd done something wrong, assumed something she shouldn't have.

"I'm sorry," she said quickly, feeling completely embarrassed. "I should have known that you weren't expecting me to still be up." Trying to conceal her rising emotions, she rushed on, "I wasn't feeling tired, so I just thought.....I mean, I didn't have anything else to do."

She heard him take a deep breath, and when she glanced up, he was staring intently past her, as if someone were standing behind her.

"Look," he said rigidly, "I don't mean to be short, but it's late, and I'm exhausted. The meeting lasted a lot longer than I wanted it to." His voice remained rigid and strained, as if his teeth were clenched. "I'm sorry if you were expecting something."

"I...I wasn't." She self-consciously moved one arm across her chest to cover her bare skin, suddenly feeling horribly exposed. Forcing a smile and hoping her voice sounded steady, she replied coolly, "I understand completely."

She watched as his eyes, burning wild with feral intensity, swept quickly over her body, then to her face. He gave her a piercing yet indecipherable look before he pushed brusquely past her, throwing a quick "goodnight" over his shoulder.

Stepping back inside her room, she tried to ignore the deep sense of rejection that had been surfacing in the pit of her stomach. Tears pricked her eyes. She silently closed the door then rushed to the closet. The one thing she wanted more than anything else now was to cover up, as quickly as she could. She felt angry at herself, at him, and at the situation. The thought of grabbing her things and leaving briefly crossed her mind. It'd be so simple to just walk out the door – except that it wasn't. Hot tears began to spill over her lower lashes, despite her best efforts to hold them at bay. How could she have been so stupid? She slumped to the floor with her back against the wall of the closet and quickly stretched her hand up to pull the door closed. In the darkness, she hugged her knees to her chest and let the tears flow freely. With each ragged breath, her heart clenched tightly. All day, she'd been looking forward to more than just sex. All she wanted was to just feel his arms around her. To be held. It was something she hadn't experienced for some time. She'd felt numb for so long that she didn't ever think she would fully awaken again to any feelings; and now that a small flame was making her feel alive again, she didn't know how to put out the kindling.

But she would have to find a way. The pleasure of a moment spent with him would never outweigh the painful train wreck of emotions sure to follow. She would simply have to ignore the intense longing she'd seen briefly in his eyes before he'd shrugged her off.

She attempted to dry her eyes but more tears rose to the surface. She could think of only one reason that made any sense to her for his rejection: he'd gotten his needs met elsewhere. A work meeting? *Please.* She should have seen this coming. He probably had a girlfriend, or a wife. She clenched her fist tightly. From here on out, he would have to beg her if he wanted anything, agreement or no agreement.

27

Ryan tossed and turned, unable to fall asleep. The pained look on Tara's face when he'd refused her advance kept burning in his mind – that, and the sight of her with almost nothing on, bare to his perusal. It'd taken every ounce of self-control not to reach for her and pin her against the wall with his body. He'd desperately wanted to feel the touch of her skin against his, to feel what it was like to kiss her, to hear her whisper his name as his hands explored her body. He honestly couldn't remember a time in which he'd wanted to have his way with a woman as much as he did in that moment, nor had he ever been so freely offered the opportunity to do so; but if he'd acted on his instincts, he clearly would have been taking advantage of her. And that was something he would never do to her.

He glanced at the clock – 2:32am. With a sigh, he rolled onto his back, staring up at the ceiling. What was he supposed to do now? He had to figure this out before he screwed it all up. The turbulent storm of his thoughts continued to rage until he finally drifted off into a fitful sleep only to be jolted awake by the sound of his alarm a few hours later.

He sat up and put his feet on the floor, taking a moment to rub his temples before slowly rising to a standing position. He quickly dressed in jeans and a T-shirt then threw on a baseball cap. On his way out, he grabbed a bagel from the kitchen.

Since he was familiar with the location of the church where he was to meet Mitchell, he stopped briefly for coffee at the first Starbucks that came his way. Ten minutes later, coffee cup drained, he turned into the church's parking lot and pulled up next to an old, beat-up suburban. Taking the church's stone steps two at a time, he reached the entryway and opened the front door. As soon as he entered, he saw Mitchell conversing with a bearded gentleman dressed in a black, ecclesiastical garment. The agent turned in his direction and waved him over.

"This is Brian Hennings," Mitchell said. "He's a close friend of mine."

"Hi," Ryan responded, shaking the clergyman's hand.

Mitchell turned back to the minister. "Thanks, Brian, for letting us meet here. We won't be long."

"Anytime, Tom. The service won't be starting for another hour or so." With a parting smile, the minister turned and walked towards the rectory.

Ryan followed Mitchell down a short flight of steps leading to the church's basement then into a small office to the left of the stairwell. Closing the door behind them, Mitchell quickly scooted two plastic chairs out from under a table. The metal rings covering the bottom of each leg jingled as he dragged one of the chairs along the carpeted floor, positioning it so that they would be facing each other. Sitting down, he nudged the other chair towards Ryan then placed a pad of paper, along with an iPad, on the table next to him.

"So how did last night go?" Mitchell grunted, reaching into his shirt pocket for a pen.

"Everything was fine until the end of the night," Ryan replied heavily, taking a seat. "We went out for dinner then went back to my place. I had already arranged for one of my business partners to come over for a late-night meeting, so I figured I had it all worked out. I made sure to draw the meeting out longer than it needed to be, and I assumed Tara had gone to bed." He leaned back in his seat and rested his arm on the table, lightly drumming the surface with his fingers. "She was waiting up for me." A vivid image of her from the previous night instantly sprang to the forefront of his mind; her body leaning against the doorframe. Gorgeous. Sexy. And dressed in *that*. He quickly pushed the finely de-tailed picture from his mind and added, "She caught me by surprise, and I think I came off as a huge jerk when I told her I didn't want anything." He glanced at a particularly gruesome crucifixion painting hanging on the wall to their left then added absently, "I didn't know what else to say."

"Well, I can't help you there." Mitchell crossed his ankle over his knee and grabbed his pad of paper. "Tell me what's gone down so far, starting from when the chauffeur picked you up Friday evening."

Ryan proceeded to relate everything he could remember while Mitchell took notes. Every now and then, the agent stopped him to clarify a detail or ask a question. Half an hour later, he'd caught Mitchell up to the present day. Mitchell set the legal pad down on the table and rubbed his chin thoughtfully for a moment.

"When you go to Vancouver for your next yacht outing," he said, "see if you can find out more about the hotels that Jai is operating."

Ryan nodded. "Seems like the perfect avenue for money laundering."

"Which is another thread we'll follow when we get to that point," responded Mitchell.

Ryan hunched forward, resting his elbows on his knees. "How's the investigation coming along?"

"We've been surveilling Darin's nightclub for the last week or so. And we've found Jai's residence."

"Really?"

"Yes. Bridger followed you on Wednesday when you were taken to the White Heron. He stayed behind after the meeting and tailed Jai back to Broadmoor. The whole thing's pretty much a gated area, so he only made it to the main entrance. We put up a pole cam though." Mitchell glanced at his notes and read, "Around 9:00am on Friday, Bridger followed Marcus from GLAM." He looked up. "He's the bartender, right?"

Ryan nodded and the agent continued,

"He followed him to a warehouse in Renton and watched as he loaded up a white delivery van, unmarked, with what we're guessing were supplies for the yacht, based on the labeling of some of the boxes. When he was done loading the van, Bridger followed him to what you just described as the speakeasy that you were taken to later that night. The yacht was there at the dock when Marcus arrived, with Bridger close behind. He watched Marcus drive the van into the old millhouse, then approximately ten minutes later, he saw three guys go in but no activity after that. The millhouse is multi-level, and we're guessing they were taking the supplies down to the ground level and out to the yacht, in preparation for its departure later that night."

The agent reached for his tablet. "Bridger got photos of the three men before they went inside the millhouse. Any of them look familiar?"

Ryan scrolled through the handful of snapshots. "Yeah, that one is Jin." He pointed to the young man standing near the van. "And I saw the other two on board, as deckhands. Didn't get their names though."

Mitchell set the tablet aside and continued, "A few hours later, Bridger followed Marcus – who was driving the van again – back to GLAM. We set up video surveillance at the millhouse and the warehouse in Renton later that night, once the yacht had departed." The agent smiled thinly. "I'm hoping that either of those is where Kristen remembers being taken the night she was kidnapped."

"Hmm." Ryan rubbed his knuckle along his unshaven jawline. "So Jai's house is in the Broadmoor neighborhood?"

"Yes. We put trackers on Jai's car and the chauffeurs' and found out which house is his. We looked up the deed later and confirmed that Jai's the owner."

"Okay, so there are four places under surveillance now, if I'm keeping track: GLAM, the millhouse, the warehouse in Renton, and Jai's residence?"

"Yes," Mitchell nodded.

"And the speakeasy underneath the millhouse?"

"We couldn't get access to the inside of the speakeasy, but we've got surveillance set up to cover the entire grounds, including the parking lot and the dock area. We also have cameras inside both the millhouse and the Renton warehouse, so if they're taking victims there in the van, we'll see it."

Ryan adjusted his ballcap, leaned back in his seat, and asked, "So how many agents are working on the case?"

"The task force consists of six agents, including myself. And you."

Ryan was pleased to be considered part of the operation, at least to Mitchell anyway. "What happens next?" he asked.

"We need to get the tracking warrant for the yacht. If I can get it today, we can install a device before it leaves the dock tonight. You got the hull number?"

"Yeah, I made sure to capture it. Speaking of which..."

He leaned forward and handed Mitchell the sunglasses that he'd hooked over the crew-cut collar of his T-shirt just before leaving; he then removed the button camera from his jeans pocket and set it on the table; lastly, he unclasped the watch from his wrist and placed it next to the other items.

"Okay, I'll download everything you got," Mitchell responded. "I have my affidavit prepped so I should be able to submit the tracking application to the judge when we're done here." He crossed his arms and leaned back in his chair, tilting it so the front legs were off the ground.

"You think there's a chance of finding the complex this week?" Ryan asked, removing his ballcap and quickly running his hand through his hair before replacing it.

"I'd say we have a decent shot. There's a good possibility though that the yacht might go directly to Vancouver after the clients get off tonight." He shrugged his shoulders. "We'll have to wait and see. If there are two complexes like Kristen thinks, maybe it'll stop at one or the other to switch out the women before heading to Vancouver."

A moment of silence passed between them then Ryan said, "Anything else? Other lines of investigation?"

Mitchell lowered his chair back to the ground, causing the metal rings on the legs to jingle again. "I met with Kristen this past Thursday and showed her the photos you've taken so far. She was able to ID Jai and Marcus right away – she saw Jai at the complex once, then a handful of times on the yacht; he wasn't on it the night she escaped. She's only seen Marcus twice, handling some supplies on the yacht. Never saw him at the compound. It seems that Marcus manages the day-to-day operations landside, at the speakeasy and GLAM." Mitchell straightened in his chair, twisting his torso from side to side for a quick stretch. "I looked up the registration information for the van and confirmed it belongs to him. We also got his cellphone number from the trap-and-trace on your phone, along with some other numbers. We'll be getting wiretap orders for all of them."

"Do you know who the numbers belong to yet?" Ryan asked.

"We know a few of them." Using his fingers, Mitchell began to list them off. "The number Cullen used to text you about the concert; Darin's number from when he called to arrange the meeting with you at GLAM; and Jai's number from your meeting with him at the country club. And then the number Charlotte used to confirm your booking on the yacht."

"Sounds like we're getting somewhere." He felt some relief at the thought.

Mitchell nodded. "You've done good work. Just handle this situation with Tara now."

"Right," he sighed. "I'll manage it." His feeling of relief quickly clouded over.

"Good." The agent set his pad of paper next to the surveillance equipment and rose from his seat. "Keep me posted."

28

Tara awoke with a start, the embarrassing incident from the night before still fresh in her mind. She looked over at the clock on the bedside table. It was rare for her to sleep in so late, even with the drowsiness caused by her medications. She rolled back over and pulled the comforter around her, reluctant to start the day. She was very much dreading her next encounter with *him*. It would inevitably be awkward.

Eventually, the faint smell of bacon beckoned her from the bed. She made her way to the bathroom where she proceeded to sweep her hair into a loose bun and wash her face. She stared at the bags under her eyes, the result of her fitful night. Feeling slightly depressed, she left the bathroom and threw on a pair of running shorts, a sports bra, and yesterday's tank top then quickly glanced at her phone to make sure Jai hadn't called or texted her.

So far, nothing.

Bracing herself, she cautiously opened the bedroom door and peeked out into the hallway. The faint sounds of sizzling bacon and running water were the only noises she could make out. Slowly, she looked down to the end of the hallway and saw that the door to the master bedroom was slightly ajar, which did not give her much information as to whether the room was occupied or not. She took a deep breath, squared her shoulders, and emerged from her room, hoping she would appear calm and collected when she saw Ryan. She walked down the hallway, rounded the corner of the kitchen, and found Karen, alone, rinsing some silverware at the sink.

"Hi," she said politely, relieved but still feeling out of place in her new surroundings.

Karen looked over her shoulder. "Good morning." She nodded towards the stove. "I've made some bacon. I wanted to wait until you were awake before making anything else. Are you hungry?"

"I am," she nodded.

Karen reached for a towel and quickly dried her hands. "What're you in the mood for?"

"I usually just have some eggs and toast." With the exception of her breakfast on the yacht, she hadn't had toast for breakfast since her arrival at the complex, and she quickly decided that she would eat whatever she wanted, within reason, during her stay; if she kept up her exercise routine, it'd be easy to shed whatever weight she might gain in the span of a week. For today, she wasn't going to worry about her caloric intake – she would have her toast and eat it too.

Karen stepped towards the refrigerator, took out a carton of eggs, and placed it on the gleaming, granite countertop. She then removed a wire whisk from a drawer and set it next to the carton.

"I can make them," Tara offered. "I'd actually love to, if you don't mind." She paused for a second then added, "It's been a little while since I've cooked anything."

"Sure," Karen responded kindly. She stooped and grabbed a mixing bowl from one of the lower cabinets and set it on the counter next to Tara. Pointing to some drawers on her left, she said, "Silverware and utensils are in there." She then turned in the direction of the stove and showed her where the pots and pans were. Finally, gesturing up to a cabinet near the sink, she said, "Most of the plates, bowls, and cups are in that one." She turned off the burner beneath the pan of bacon and smiled. "Stove's all yours." She looked around for a moment, giving the kitchen a sweeping glance, then added, "Don't worry about any of the dishes you use – I'll take care of those later. Just enjoy your breakfast."

"Alright, thanks." She hesitated then nervously asked, "Did Ryan eat already?" She was naturally curious, but she also wanted to ease her mind as to where he was. Breakfast was usually her favorite meal of the day, and she wanted peace of mind to enjoy it.

"I'm not sure," Karen replied. "But I do know that he went out early this morning." She turned around, took a step toward the refrigerator, and removed a sticky note. Handing it to Tara, she said, "I almost forgot to give this to you. He wanted me to make sure you saw it. I'm guessing he wrote it before he left."

"Oh," Tara replied, taking it from her. She glanced at it for a second then tucked it into the front pocket of her shorts and reached for the mixing bowl. "Well, I guess I'll get started then."

"I'll be in the breakfast nook if you need anything – it's just around the corner." Karen gestured to the other end of the long stretch of kitchen countertop. "I have to put together this week's menu. Do you have any preferences, or allergies?"

"No allergies," she smiled. "And I'm not a picky eater. I'm sure I'll love whatever you make."

"Okay then," Karen replied. "Just let me know if you need anything." She lifted a stack of cookbooks off the counter and walked in the direction of the nook.

As soon as she was out of sight, Tara removed the note from her pocket and read:

I'll be back around noon. If you want to use the gym or pool, the code is 17830. It's on the same level as the parking garage. The number to get back into my unit is 14568. I'm sorry about last night.

He'd scribbled his phone number down as well, and underneath it he'd written, *"text if you need anything."*

"Yeah right," she muttered under her breath, shoving the note back into her pocket. She wouldn't be reaching out to him for anything. Not after last night.

When she brought her plate over to the breakfast nook, Karen was absent and, happy to have the table to herself, she ate slowly, savoring each bite. She thought about the gym and decided she'd check it out once she'd finished eating.

Approximately twenty minutes later, she took her plate to the sink and, ignoring Karen's directive to leave her dishes on the counter, proceeded to rinse off everything she'd used. Once her task was completed, she walked to her room and retrieved the one other pair of shoes she'd brought with her, the pair of Adidas sneakers she'd changed into Friday night after giving Ryan the tour of the yacht.

Riding the elevator down to the garage level several minutes later, she wondered how busy the gym would be mid-morning on a Sunday. Upon exiting, she followed the signs that pointed to the fitness area and easily located it. After inputting the code Ryan had given her, she stepped through the doorway and stopped in front of a sleek placard that listed the club's amenities and provided further directions. The yoga room, Pilates' studio, and co-ed gym area were listed underneath the arrow pointing to her left, while the sauna, pool, and women's locker room were to be found in the opposite direction. She smiled to herself and headed to the yoga room, hoping that it had mirrors and wasn't occupied. She had one objective in mind and that was to dance. It was the one thing that would give her emotional release, apart from crying, and it would also help her forget all about her current situation since it required a level of focus and intensity that left room for nothing else. A careful glance inside the yoga room revealed that it was indeed empty. Smiling to herself, she set her bag down and started her warmup routine, which mostly involved a lot of stretching. The only thing missing was her music, but she could make do without it.

An hour and a half later, she glanced at the clock on the wall and began the cool-down part of her dance session. She spent ten minutes longer than she normally did on stretching, making sure she was aware of her breathing patterns and listening to her body. The room must have been soundproof or the gym mostly empty because she didn't hear any outer noises, and by the time she packed up to leave, both her mind and body felt completely relaxed.

Ten minutes later, she emerged from the elevator and entered Ryan's unit, using the code he'd given her.

She went directly to her room where she took a quick shower, knowing that it was drawing close to noon, and he would be returning any minute. Upon emerging, she swaddled herself in the luxurious towel she found hanging next to the shower and exited the bathroom, heading straight for the walk-in closet. After donning the denim shorts she'd worn the day before, along with the only clean T-shirt she had left, she stepped back into the bathroom, towel dried her hair, put on a minimal amount of makeup, gathered her dirty work-out clothing, and dumped the wad into the laundry basket just outside the bathroom.

With nothing more to do, she walked to the bedroom door where she remained rooted in place, listening for any sign that he might have returned. Once more, she peered down to the end of the hallway; it didn't look like his door had been touched, as it was still ajar, exactly as she had seen it earlier that morning. Taking a deep breath, she glided out into the hall and quietly made her way to the kitchen, which was empty. Bored and not sure what to do with herself, she decided to seek out Karen to see if there was anything she could help with. Not entirely confident that Ryan hadn't returned yet, she proceeded cautiously through the kitchen and over to the breakfast nook; a glance at the open cookbooks strewn across the table gave her the impression that they'd only been temporarily abandoned. She wondered if perhaps Karen might be doing laundry so she headed warily down the hallway to her left toward the laundry room, listening all the while for any sounds that might indicate someone was in the penthouse. Upon finding the laundry room to be empty, she stepped back into the hallway, wondering where she should go next. She glanced to her right and saw a line of doors, all ajar, their doorways darkened. Curiosity got the better of her, and she walked the few feet to the first door and peeked inside the room. Although it was shrouded in shadow, it was clearly the library. She stood in amazement, peering from the doorway at the book-lined walls and fine furnishings that filled the room. In front of a large fireplace, two plaid armchairs sat facing each other; there was a small stack of books on one. Her eyes were drawn upward to the stained-glass window at the back of the room, which was positioned directly above a cushioned window seat. The paned glass cast a faint, colored pattern of light onto a nearby Oriental rug. Her eyes roamed freely over the room for a few more minutes before she slowly pulled the door back to the semi-open position in which she'd found it.

Of their own accord, her eyes wandered to the next open doorway. The floor creaked beneath her feet as she quietly stepped towards it. An initial glance into the dimly lit interior revealed what could only be Ryan's office. However, its state of disarray seemed at odds with the man who, two nights ago, had worn carefully pressed, hand-tailored suits. It awakened a strong desire to see if his bedroom was in a similar state, but she'd already promised herself to never see the inside of it unless he was forcefully carrying her over the threshold, a vision that instantly caused her body to tense with sudden desire. The thought of him taking off his shirt, his dark eyes burning with need as he towered over her...

She quickly shut the door and headed back down the hallway to the kitchen, hesitating when she reached the breakfast table. The nook was hemmed in by walls that extended all the way to the ceiling, preventing her from seeing clearly what lay beyond it, aside from the start of another hallway. After casting a quick glance behind her, then sideways to the kitchen, she decided to follow it. Light streamed across her path as she rounded the nook and found herself in a medium sized area that served as a sort of pass-through lounge. To her left, a wide, floor-to-ceiling window loomed over her, and the sudden view of the skyscrapers caught her off guard, instantly causing her head to spin. She carefully took a seat on the light grey, L-shaped sectional to her right and took a moment to adjust her skewed sense of depth perception.

She ran her hand over the plush velvet fabric as she sank into a large, olive-colored throw pillow. The sectional was fitted perfectly to the corner, with built-in bookshelves rising above the top edge of the sectional and extending all the way to the ceiling. The hallway, which had led her from the kitchen area to her present location, continued beyond her into what appeared to be a large dining room. Across from her, she saw that a fireplace had been built into the back wall of the breakfast nook. She imagined herself sitting comfortably on a cold wintery day, next to a warm fire, reading one of her favorite novels. Scanning the books above her, she noticed that many of them were thick and wide, like coffee table books, and most appeared to be art related.

She turned her attention back to the window, staring at the skyscrapers until curiosity nudged her to continue exploring. She rose and followed the hallway into the formal dining area where she found a large rectangular table, lined with plush, taupe-colored chairs. Another pair of floor-to-ceiling windows, spanning the length of the table, served to solidify her notion that she was staying in a palace made of glass. The room was quite expansive and not entirely closed off from the living room beyond it, giving it an airy feel. As she glided alongside the table, she ran her hand along the top of each chair, watching her reflection in the table's polished surface until she reached the end of it and stepped through the broad opening to find herself in the largest of all the rooms she had seen thus far, the living room. This one was bounded by more floor-to-ceiling windows, on two sides. A large, L-shaped beige sectional took up a good amount of the room. It faced a fireplace, which was set into the wall that she could now tell backed against the kitchen. Lastly, the walnut-stained, baby grand piano that she'd glimpsed earlier sat in the corner, flanked by two large windows on either side. She stared at the beckoning instrument for a minute then continued around the corner of the sofa, back into the kitchen where she found Karen peeling potatoes at the kitchen sink. It looked like she had just started.

"I was wondering where you might be," Karen said cheerily as she entered. "I had to run out to get Ryan's dry cleaning." She set aside the peeled potato and reached for another.

"I decided to check out the gym," Tara responded, smiling. "It's very nice."

"Was it quiet?" Karen asked. "It usually is on Sunday mornings."

Suddenly, everything faded into the background as Tara heard the front door open. With a sharp inhale, she scanned the kitchen for something to focus on, something she could do to make herself look occupied. She stepped around Karen, using her as a shield, and grabbed a potato; she then stole the peeler that Karen had just set down and quickly began to shave the potato's skin into the bottom of the sink.

"Hey," Ryan called from the foyer.

At the sound of his voice, a nervous shiver ran through her body, and her heart started beating faster. A moment later, she heard his footsteps coming their way.

"Hey," he said again, briskly walking around Karen and over to the cupboard containing glasses and plates, which happened to be right next to her. She kept her eyes on the potato, ignoring him as he reached above her head. The scent of his bodywash suddenly enveloped her, and she could feel the warmth of his skin as he stood beside her.

He eyed her cautiously, lowering a glass from the shelf, then asked, "How're you?"

The memory of the night before lingered awkwardly between them.

"Good," she replied tensely, not looking up.

He moved toward the refrigerator, filled his glass with water, and returned to her side. With his back to the counter, he casually leaned against it and took a long swig.

Out of the corner of her eye, Tara watched his Adam's apple move up and down.

Ryan set the glass aside and asked, "Have you had lunch yet?"

"No, not yet." She picked up another potato and began peeling it viciously. Karen hadn't seemed to mind that she'd taken over the task.

"I was thinking we could head down to Pike's Place," Ryan said.

Tara turned the potato over and started on the other side. "Um, sure. Where is it?"

"It's close to the wharf front," he answered. "We can walk there if you're up for it. It's not that far."

"Alright," she agreed nonchalantly. Against her wishes, a quick spark of excitement zinged through her at the thought of going somewhere with him.

"Okay then," he smiled. "I'm ready when you are."

Tara set the peeled potato next to the others on the cutting board then rinsed her hands off and reached for a dishtowel. "I'm ready."

29

Ryan kept his hands in his pockets as they walked down the overcast sidewalk, neither of them saying much; at the light, he switched places with Tara so that she was walking on the inside of the sidewalk, thereby placing himself as a buffer between her and the busy street. He glanced down at her and noticed that her arms were folded across her stomach, which caused him to wonder if she was purposefully closing herself off.

How was he supposed to find the right words to explain what their relationship was going to look like going forward, without pushing her away?

"So," he started slowly, "I'm sorry for my reaction last night. It was very rude of me to be so short with you...I was just surprised –"

"It's fine," she smiled, cutting him off with a wave of her hand. "Don't worry about it."

He glanced at her, knowing enough about women to know that "fine" almost always meant the opposite. Unable to think of something better, he simply repeated, "I truly am sorry, and I feel bad."

"Don't worry about it," she replied evenly, keeping her eyes on the sidewalk.

They continued onward in an awkward silence that he attempted to fill by commenting intermittently on the various restaurants, coffee shops, and landmarks they passed along the way. She responded with polite smiles and occasional remarks, which did nothing to make him feel better; he knew she was concealing a layer of resentment underneath her outwardly pleasant manner. And he didn't blame her.

When the sidewalk started to get busier and more congested, he moved in front of her, shielding her from the oncoming pedestrian traffic. As they approached the wharf area, the smell of fish intensified. He breathed it in, appreciating the pungent odor. It always stirred a longing in his chest to be out on the open water, with the *'wheel's kick and the wind's song and the white sail's shaking.'*

Once they neared the entrance to the market, he looked over his shoulder and asked, "Do you like clam chowder?"

"Yes," Tara replied loudly, trying to be heard over the bustling crowd.

"Alright then, let's head this way."

He angled his body sideways to avoid a collision with a pair of running kids. The jerky movement made her stumble against him, and she loosely grabbed at his shirt to stop herself from tripping. He reached for her arm to steady her, but a heavyset woman shoved past him, throwing him slightly off-balance. Tara collided fully into his body, and he slid his arm around her waist to keep her from falling. For one fleeting moment, they stood twisted together, frozen in place, the sounds around them fading into the background.

His eyes met hers then he took a step backward and muttered, "Sorry."

Turning around, he pushed through the oncoming pedestrians, looking over his shoulder to make sure Tara was following. The feeling of her body pressed against his slowly began to fade, leaving him wishing that the moment had lasted longer. They continued to thread their way through the noisy, colorful throng of shoppers and vendors and eventually stopped behind a dense cluster of people standing underneath a sign that read, "Market Grill." As they waited in line, he glanced at the nearby merchant stalls fronting the covered boardwalk. The one next to them displayed an array of seafood placed on a bed of ice: shrimp of varying sizes, fish with missing heads, and lobsters fully intact; lemon slices were arranged neatly alongside the chilled, lifeless specimens.

A few minutes later, chowder in hand, he led Tara down a set of stairs, below street level. As they reached the bottom, the din of the crowd faded. He looked around then headed in the direction of a small table across from a boutique book shop.

He set his bowl down and pulled out a chair for her. "What do you think so far?"

"About what?" Tara asked, glancing at him as she took a seat.

"This." He glanced around them. "Seattle, in general. I know you haven't seen much of it, but do you like it so far?"

"Yes." She smiled across the table at him. "So far." She lifted a spoonful of chowder and hovered it over her bowl. "I like the ocean and being near water."

He nodded and took a bite, watching her as she looked across the boardwalk to the book shop. Her comment reminded him of the poem he'd thought of earlier. "Have you ever read any of John Masefield's poetry?" He lifted his spoon and clarified, "Talking about the ocean made me think of one of his. 'Sea Fever'."

"You like poetry?" she asked, lifting an eyebrow.

"I do, although I don't read it very often."

"I've read some," she responded." I don't know anything by Masefield though."

"Alright then," he grinned. "I feel obligated to quote a stanza for you. I'll most likely butcher the delivery, so be prepared for that."

She laughed quietly, and he caught a spark of levity in her eyes before she looked back down at her chowder.

"Alright, here it goes." He took a quick breath then began, "I must go down to the seas again, to the lonely sea and the sky. And all I ask is a tall ship and a star to steer her by. And the wheel's kick and the wind's song and the white sail's shaking. And a grey mist on the sea's face, and a grey dawn breaking."

She glanced up with a humorous smile when he paused. "Lovely. Do you know the rest?"

"I do," he grinned. "There's only two more stanzas." He cleared his throat dramatically, and she laughed.

In an even tone, he continued, "I must go down to the seas again, for the call of the running tide is a wild call and a clear call that may not be denied; and all I ask is a windy day with the white clouds flying. And the flung spray and the blown spume, and the seagulls crying." He tilted his head, glancing toward the wharf, and finished, "I must go down to the seas again, to the vagrant gypsy life. To the gull's way and the whale's way where the wind's like a whetted knife; and all I ask is a merry yarn from a laughing fellow-rover, and quiet sleep and a sweet dream when the long trick's over.'"

He took a bite of his chowder. "My mom made us memorize poetry, as a supplement to our schoolwork."

"Interesting," Tara replied. "She sounds like a wise woman."

"I didn't think so at the time," he laughed. "But I appreciate it now."

"You seemed to enjoy reciting it," she said dryly.

He laughed and took another bite, relieved that she seemed to have forgiven him for last night. They ate in silence for a few minutes then he set his bowl aside and gathered his thoughts.

"So," he began, "going back to last night."

Her face suddenly tensed with apprehension.

"You deserve more than just a simple apology," he said quickly, hoping to put her at ease. He rubbed the back of his neck. "I've just given it some thought, and...I really like you, as a person."

"Good to know," she replied with a tight laugh. A fly landed on her napkin, and she waved it away.

Ryan stared down at the table for a moment then glanced at her. "What I mean is that I don't want to use you."

Tara kept her eyes on her bowl, her expression clouded. She set her spoon down and quietly said, "I don't know what you want from me." She swallowed nervously. "I mean, am I still attractive to you?"

Completely surprised that she would even think such a thought, Ryan replied, "Of course, you're attractive to me – that's not it at all." A frustrated sigh escaped him before he could help it. "I've just been..."

He stared vacantly at the table, trying to find the right words. After a second, he said, "I've been reflecting over the direction of my life, and the way I've been doing things. And our arrangement doesn't feel right to me. I have too much respect for you." He glanced at her anxiously, trying to gauge her reaction. "I don't want to keep making the same mistakes I've made in the past, regarding women."

He ran his knuckles along his jawline, the stubble rough beneath his fingertips, and watched Tara take another bite; he didn't have high hopes that everything was coming across better than he was making it sound. "I guess what I'm really trying to say is that it's not my intention to pursue anything sexual with you." He exhaled and finished, "So there's no pressure on you now."

Tara's eyelashes fluttered slightly as she stared at her soup, not meeting his gaze. "So you want us to be...friends?"

"Yes. I absolutely want us to be that." A fly buzzed by and alighted on the rim of his bowl; he quickly flicked it away.

"Okay." She gave him a darting glance before returning her attention back to her chowder. She took another bite then asked, "What's your plan for the rest of the week then? We're just going to hang out until we go to Vancouver next weekend?"

"Yes – if that's what you want of course."

"That's fine with me," she replied evenly, "but won't I be getting in the way of your work?"

"I don't have much on my plate this week," Ryan responded. "Just a few things I'll have to attend to."

Tara kept her eyes on the table and tried to pay attention as Ryan went into more detail about his work plans for the week, but she was still struggling to process the sting of his

"I don't intend to pursue anything with you" statement. Of course he didn't want a relationship with her. He thought she legitimately worked for Jai – as a sex worker. He would never consider her to be the kind of girl he could take home to meet his mother. She scooted her bowl to the side and clasped her hands together, wondering just how she would make it through the rest of the week with him. She focused on a seagull that had landed nearby and forced her tears to stay at bay. Well, she didn't want him either. So there. Regaining her composure, she folded her hands and returned her full attention to what he was saying.

"I have a meeting tomorrow morning," he continued, "and then I need to stop in at my office to meet with my secretary. She's been trying to find me a temporary office assistant who can help me out while I'm working from home."

Her ears pricked, and she cautiously asked, "How temporary?"

A brief silence ensued then he slowly replied, "Maybe a week." He quirked an eyebrow. "Or two."

"Hmm." She gave him a subtle smile. "I think I may know of someone, and she just so happens to have moved to the area recently."

Not skipping a beat, he grinned and replied, "You think she might be interested in working a couple of hours a day until she finds a real job?"

She tossed her head playfully. "It can't hurt to ask."

"Are we thinking along the same line...."

She could tell he wanted a little reassurance that he wasn't making a gross assumption, so she simply replied, "Yes, I'll accept the position."

He laughed then asked, "Are you sure? You haven't seen the state of my office yet."

"It would give me something to do while you're working."

"True," he nodded.

"And," she smiled, "we can keep up our ruse."

"Yes, that's right. I'd almost forgotten about that." He stood and gathered their empty bowls, then walked a few paces to the nearest trashcan. Returning, he sat back down and placed his elbows on the table. "So we continue to tell anyone who asks that you're the niece of one of my business associates. You're staying with me until you find a place of your own. Additionally, you've accepted a legitimate temp position assisting me with my business affairs – your virtuosity remains intact and my reputation..."

He grinned at her. "I was going to say 'remains reputable' but I think I'll have to work toward that."

She nodded, crossing her legs under the table. After a second, she asked, "What exactly do you do?"

"I'm an investor, for the most part."

"An investor in what?" She looked across the table at his crumpled napkin then raised her gaze to his chest. It was as close as she could get to looking at him whenever they spoke. She'd have to work on that.

"Renewable energy, biotech, emerging sectors....that kind of thing. I also like to support entrepreneurial start-ups."

"That sounds interesting," she replied, brushing a strand of hair from her cheek.

"Unless you're really into engineering and science, it's probably not." He smiled ruefully and continued, "I have a board meeting tomorrow morning that I'm hoping will be fruitful.

We should be able to secure some government contracts that will allow us to move forward with a project that's been several years in the making."

A group of teenagers suddenly darted past their table, their rowdy laughter breaking up the conversation. Tara watched as one of the girls pulled on the arm of the guy in front of her. Grinning, the boy stooped down to lift her onto his back. With a squeal of laughter, she threw her arms around his neck. He grabbed her legs and pulled them around his torso, then stood up straight. "Wait up!" he shouted after their friends. He started jogging, and the sight of the girl bouncing up and down on his back made Tara laugh.

Ryan followed the scene with an amused expression. "Teenagers," he commented, rising from the table. "You ready to go?" He cocked his head in the direction of the stairwell. "I want to show you something."

She fell in step behind him, keeping her eyes on the back of his T-shirt, and the broad shoulders underneath it, as they took the stairs up to the street level. After leading her along the crowded boardwalk then down a few streets and around a corner, he slowed to a halt in front of the infamous gum wall. She smiled when she saw its rainbow-colored surface, and they both spent a few moments examining the wide variety of thoroughly chewed gum wads that had been thumb-printed into place.

Two small boys, one a toddler and the other a few years older, stepped next to them. Tara gave them a sideways glance, noticing that the older boy had a worried expression on his face.

He gave Tara a furtive look then said hesitantly, "Have you seen a woman wearing a red dress?"

She bent down and replied, "We haven't. Are you lost?" She could tell that the boy, who she guessed was around six or seven, was holding back tears now.

"Maybe," he replied, his voice quivering. "I don't know."

"Don't worry," she responded reassuringly. "I'm sure she's close by. We'll help you find her." She turned to Ryan. "Why don't I stay here with them while you look around?"

He nodded. "Don't go anywhere. I won't be long."

"Alright," she replied. "We'll be right here."

Ryan turned and headed in the direction they'd come from. His eyes were alert but his thoughts were on Tara. He couldn't keep himself from smiling at her eagerness to help the lost boys find their mother. He supposed anyone would have stopped to help, but the way that Tara had stooped down so that she was eye-level with the boy had pulled at his heartstrings. Not only had she been reassuring, but she had conveyed genuine concern and empathy.

He continued on his way, glancing to the left and right, his eyes scanning for a woman in a red dress. After walking quite a ways with no result, he turned around and headed back to the gum wall, hoping that the mother had since been reunited with her children. A few minutes later, he rounded the corner and was relieved to find that this was the case.

"Thank you," the woman stated as he approached the group. "You have no idea how relieved I am. I turned my back for a minute, and they were both gone."

"They didn't get too far," Tara replied reassuringly. "I'm sure you would have found them within a few minutes."

"I'm just glad you told them to stay in one place," she responded, her relief evident. "Thank you again." She smiled at both of them then took each boys' hand and walked away.

Ryan watched as they retreated towards the pier then he turned to Tara. "I'm glad that worked itself out."

"Me too. She showed up right after you left, but she wanted to wait until you got back before leaving me on my own."

"A good call," he replied, slipping his hands in his pockets. "Ready to head back?"

By the time they reached Pioneer Park, the clouds had parted. Late afternoon sunlight filtered through the trees as they made their way along the sidewalk. Birds chirped and hummed in the branches above, and Ryan watched as a sudden breeze played with Tara's hair, sweeping it over her shoulder.

Eventually, they came to a crosswalk. While they waited for the light to turn, he looked to his right and noticed the entrance to the mall. Leaning toward her, he said, "You still need to go shopping, don't you?"

She nodded then replied tentatively, "I mean, it's not anything urgent."

He angled his body so he could see her face. "Of course it is. You have, like what, two T-shirts? I feel terrible for not remembering until now." He paused for a second then said with a grin, "Come on," and nodded for her to follow him. Normally, he would have suggested that Karen go shopping with her, but he had no intention of letting Tara out of his sight, as much as he could help it. He opened the door to the mall and waited for her to walk through. "Where do you want to go first?" he asked, smiling as her eyes lit up. "And remember I'm paying for everything, so don't just think about what you need, okay? Get whatever you want." He glanced down at her. "I don't want you feeling shy about money around me." He grinned and added, "Or resisting me on this."

"I guess I'll have to allow it then." She gave him a small smile.

"I'm glad that's settled." Grinning, he waved her forward and said, "Lead the way."

30

Four hours later, they returned to the penthouse, weighed down with shopping bags. Once they'd set everything on Tara's bed, Ryan turned to her and said, "I'm going down to the gym for a bit. Do you need anything before I go?"

"No, I should be fine," she replied. "Thanks."

"Okay." He glanced at his watch. "Karen said dinner should be ready in about an hour."

Tara waited until his footsteps had faded down the hall before surveying the array of bags. She reached for the one closest to her and smiled as she removed a pale-yellow sundress, remembering Ryan's admiring gaze when she'd stepped from the fitting room wearing it. The memory, however, quickly frosted over when she thought about the remark he'd made earlier, during their lunch. *"I have no intention of pursuing anything with you."* The sting of the statement hadn't lessened any, despite the multitude of times it echoed in her mind. Swallowing the lump in her throat, she continued to sort through the bags, pulling out the items and placing them in organized piles on the bed.

Roughly an hour later, she entered the dining room wearing a new pair of jeans, a white blouse, and a set of pearl earrings.

She'd swept her hair into a bun, deciding it would add a layer of sophistication to her overall appearance. Ryan was standing at the head of the table wearing a crisp black polo shirt, his five o'clock shadow neatly trimmed. His dark brown eyes were on his phone, but he glanced up as soon as she entered. He set his phone on the table and pulled out a chair for her, directly to his right. As she walked toward him, she thought she could feel his eyes lingering on her, but she was determined not to make more of what she was sure was just her imagination. A moment later, she took her seat, and he followed suit, sitting at the head of the table so that they were at right angles to one another.

The scent of his cologne made it difficult for her to center her thoughts, and she found it necessary to concentrate her full attention on the meal spread before them: chicken marsala, mixed vegetables, a salad, and a small basket of warm dinner rolls.

"Will Karen be joining us?" she asked.

"Not tonight." He poured them each a glass of red wine. "She usually stays until after dinner on most evenings when she's here, but I told her she could go home early."

"I see," she remarked, placing her napkin on her lap and taking the basket of rolls he handed her.

He gave her a sideways glance as he reached for the salad. "You look nice."

"Thank you." As she couldn't think of something better to say than *so do you*, which she was *not* going to say – even though it was true – she instead took a sip of wine, watching as he served her some of the salad. "I really enjoyed today," she remarked, smiling. "Especially the market. It was so vibrant, and I liked how busy it was. It felt good to be part of it all."

"Do you enjoy crowds?" he asked, serving them each a piece of chicken, followed by some vegetables.

"I do," she nodded. "Especially outdoors. Festivals and fairs, that sort of thing. What about you?"

"It depends on the event I suppose, but in general I don't mind them." He settled into his seat then picked up his knife and began to butter his roll. "I'm guessing you enjoy going to concerts?"

"Yes," she nodded, cutting into her chicken.

"What's the most memorable concert you've been to? And clearly, I'm asking because I have one in mind."

Laughing, she replied, "You should tell me yours first then while I think of one."

"Alright," he grinned. "It was a Blink-182 concert that I went to with my brother, when we were both teenagers. We had to sneak out of the house because our parents highly disapproved of the band." As an aside, he added, "They're very religious, my mother in particular when it comes to music." He leaned back in his chair. "If I'm remembering correctly, she once said something along the lines of 'That band is of the devil'."

Tara laughed then waited for him to continue.

"The concert was great, and everything was going fine until we got home and realized that the house was locked. Andrew had forgotten to grab a spare key." He pressed his lips together in a thin line. "He had one job."

His facial expression made her laugh, and it took a moment before she regained her composure.

"There was no way we were ringing the doorbell," he continued, "so we had to figure something out. We tried the main floor windows, but they were all locked. And we were trying to avoid setting off the motion detector above the garage, so we were stumbling around in the dark."

"What did you end up doing?"

"Andrew finally remembered that my dad had been using a ladder in the backyard earlier that day. And I knew my bedroom window was unlocked. So problem solved." He took a sip of wine and smiled.

"I'm guessing it wasn't?"

He nodded and with a grin continued, "Andrew was almost to the top when a rung gave out; he managed to grab the gutter, but of course it broke and everything came crashing down – the ladder, the gutter, and Andrew. Along with our plan for quietly sneaking back into the house."

"Was he hurt?"

"No," he laughed. "He was fine."

"Did your parents find you?"

The corner of his mouth tilted up and his eyes gleamed mischievously. "Not exactly. We heard my dad come out the front door, apparently armed with something, based on what he was yelling. We could tell he was heading our way so we ran around the opposite side of the house, back to the front, and dashed through the door that he'd left wide open. We both made it to my room without being seen."

"Sounds like you got lucky."

"It gets better," he grinned. "Andrew decided it'd be funny if we changed into our pajamas then went back outside to help dad with the 'robbers'."

"You didn't!" She covered her mouth with her hand, laughing.

"We did," he responded, still grinning. "And we got away with it too. To this day, my dad still thinks it was his fault for leaving the ladder out where it could have been used for nefarious purposes."

"You never told your parents?" Her eyes were tearing up from laughing.

"No, we never have." He took a bite of salad, followed by a sip of wine, then said, "Your turn."

"I don't have anything nearly as humorous as that." She reflected for a moment. "I'd probably have to say my most memorable concert experience was going with my mom to see Taylor Swift. I think it was 2014." She tilted her head to the side, thinking. "She'd just made her big switch from country to pop. The concert was amazing, and we had a really great time together. My mom and I have always been close."

"That's good," he smiled, taking a bite of his chicken.

She thought he might add something regarding his own relationship with his parents, but he took another bite instead. After a moment, she deduced that he wasn't planning to expound so she decided to concentrate more on her food and less on making conversation; he must have thought similarly, because they lapsed into a comfortable silence.

Eventually, Tara asked, "So when do I start my new 'job'? Tomorrow morning?"

He nodded. "I was thinking we could both work until lunch then wrap up for the day."

"Sounds good to me," she replied, taking another sip of wine.

"We need to discuss compensation," he continued, "since you'll officially be my employee. And there's some documents I'll need you to sign. Tax forms, etc."

278

"Alright," she responded slowly. "But you really don't have to pay me."

"I'm legally obligated to, but I would insist despite that."

"Of course you would." She rolled her eyes and asked anxiously, "How much?"

"Well, the more I pay you, the more I can write off on my taxes." He laughed then said offhandedly, "How does $20,000 sound?"

She set her fork down. "For one week? That's a ridiculous amount. I'd be the highest paid office assistant ever."

He grinned. "It's decided then."

"I don't get a say?"

"No." He smiled and set his napkin on the table.

"Fine." As bad as she felt at the thought of being grossly overpaid, she had to admit that she needed a decent amount of money in order to execute a successful escape plan...if she went that route. "When do you want me to start in the morning?"

"I'm usually up around six." He laughed when he saw her eyes widen. "Don't worry, I'm not expecting you to be up that early. How does eight sound? We can eat breakfast together, and I should have plenty of time to show you around my office before I need to leave for my board meeting."

"Okay, so I'll just meet you in the kitchen at eight?"

He nodded, finishing off his wine and setting the glass down; he rose from his chair and since her plate was empty, offered to take it.

She handed it to him then scooted her chair away from the table.

After helping to clear the table and load the dishwasher, Tara excused herself to finish putting away the items on her bed; her task, however, was interrupted a few minutes later by a light knock on her door, which she'd left ajar.

"Come in," she stated, giving Ryan a quick smile.

"I just wanted to ask you something." He leaned casually against the doorframe.

The sound of his voice, deep and resonant, caused her heart to skip a beat. "Yes?" she responded, turning to face him, willing her expression to remain neutral. She watched as a playful smile started to form at one corner of his mouth. Her heart fluttered violently, and she reached for one of the hangers that she'd left on the armchair next to her.

"I was just curious what your real name is. I'm pretty sure it's not Stacie." He paused, his tilted smile still in place. "But maybe I'm wrong?"

"Oh," she responded, thinking fast. It made sense to just tell him her name. Would she get in trouble with Jai if she did? A deep part of herself longed for Ryan to know who she really was, and what was happening to her, but obviously that wasn't something she could divulge. Maybe someday ....or maybe never. However, her desire for him to know at least one true thing about herself momentarily outweighed her fear. She glanced his way again then picked up one of the blouses and hung it on the hanger she was holding. "It's Tara."

"Alright," he responded with a firm nod. "Tara. I'll make sure to let Karen know that you're no longer 'Stacie.'" He paused, thinking, then added, "I'll just say that I misremembered your name or something."

"Okay," she replied with a grin. "You might have to make it a little more believable than that. She seems pretty sharp."

"You're not wrong about that," he laughed. "I'll work on my lines." He continued to linger in the doorway, leaning against the frame as his eyes roamed over the room. "So this is what my sister's been up to. Do you like it?"

"I think she did a lovely job," Tara replied, "right down to the paint she chose for the walls." Smiling, she added "Blue is my favorite color." She turned and looked briefly over her shoulder at him. His nonchalant stance in the doorway gave her the impression that he was reluctant to leave. And she didn't want him to. She moved a stack of folded clothes out of the way and sat down on the edge of the bed. Glancing at the array of empty paper bags, stamped with logos and brand names, she asked, "Where should I put these?"

"There's a recycling bin in the pantry," he answered. "Did Karen show you around?"

She shook her head. "I don't think she had a chance to." She decided not to mention that she'd went on a self-guided tour earlier that day.

He nodded behind him toward the hallway and said, "Come on, I'll show you around."

Leaving her pile of clothing behind, she followed him through the door.

"You know where my room is," he stated, gesturing toward the end of the hallway. "Feel free to knock if you need anything."

She nodded then turned her head in the opposite direction. She couldn't think of any scenario that would give her cause to do so – it would most assuredly take a catastrophic event of some kind.

Continuing down the hallway, he said, "The main bathroom is over here, as I'm sure you've seen." He waved his hand vaguely toward one of the open doorways that she had passed regularly on her way to the kitchen. The next room they came to, which was the last one before coming to the kitchen, she had passed as well but had never peeked inside. He opened the door and slowly slid the dimmer switch up to reveal an expansive, maroon-colored sofa, some plush swivel armchairs, and a giant TV screen, which took up most of the space on the wall directly across from the sofa. The walls themselves were painted dark grey.

"I'm not in here that much," he commented. "Feel free to use it whenever you like."

"This has a cozy feel," she said, glancing around, "but not cramped."

"I agree. Although, I'll have to invite some people over to test that out." He rubbed his jawline thoughtfully. "I should probably get some friends together for a Mariner's game. I haven't had anyone over yet."

"Really?"

"Yeah, I moved in about a month ago after I decided I needed to be closer to my office building."

He flicked off the light and they moved on, rounding the corner to the kitchen then passing through it; when they reached the breakfast nook, he turned left and entered the next hallway.

He quickly pointed out the laundry room and said, "Just set your basket outside your door when its full, and Karen will grab it."

Next, he showed her the library and after assuring her that she was free to take any of the books, they moved on to the room that she already knew was his office.

Opening the door, he remarked, "And here's where you can probably tell why I need some assistance. I haven't managed to find the time to really unpack everything in here."

She looked around at the general disarray, and said, "Well, I'm good at organizing things."

He gestured her inside then stepped around a pile of books. "I can set up a desk for you over there." He indicated a spot next to a filing cabinet.

She nodded, pleasantly imagining herself working alongside him, taming the chaos around them. She hid her smile by turning to examine a row of textbooks that filled one of the shelves of the many built-in bookcases. A neon-colored spine caught her eye, and she pulled the book from the shelf.

He looked over her shoulder and gave the title a quick glance. "Keen to learn statistics?" he asked playfully.

From the corner of her eye, she saw him rest his forearm on the shelf above her shoulder. Knowing that he was observing her made her cheeks suddenly feel warm.

"Maybe," she replied humorously, "but I'd rather discover the artist behind this little sketch of woodland creatures—here, at the bottom of page eighty-eight." She grinned. "Looks like he forgot to sign it."

He reached for the book and stated, "I think that's enough statistics for one day." Grinning, he dramatically snapped it shut and placed it back on the shelf.

Laughing, she turned toward the door and was just about to step in that direction when he nudged her elbow and said offhandedly, "I've been thinking about visiting a friend I haven't seen in a while. He has a ranch, and I've got a couple of handguns he's been wanting to see. Thought I might go out there sometime this week." He paused then asked, "Is that something you'd like to do?"

She glanced up at him, surprised to find that he was standing closer than she thought. Lowering her gaze to his chest, she replied, "Sure. I'm not really into guns though."

"I can assume you've never shot one then?"

"Or held one," she replied, grimacing. "I guess they kind of scare me."

"I'll have to rectify that then. I think every woman should feel comfortable with at least holding one." He smiled and added quickly, "That's just my opinion."

"I suppose." She eyed him skeptically. "I just feel like guns are a last resort. I'd prefer to know enough self-defense to disarm someone instead."

He quirked an eyebrow. "And do you?"

"Well...no." Her forehead wrinkled, and she crossed her arms. "Not at the moment," she added defiantly.

He laughed abruptly then said, "I think I'm going to make it a condition of employment."

"You mean you want me to learn self-defense?" she asked. "How exactly am I supposed to do that?"

"I've had some training myself." He gave her a subtle smile. "I'll show you some moves."

"That should be interesting," she replied doubtfully. An image of him wrestling her to the ground and holding her in place filled her mind. She quickly willed it away and took a step backward, only to trip over a pile of books directly behind her.

She felt his hand slide around her back as he caught her from falling, then he quickly released his hold.

"This place is officially a mess," he stated. "Are you okay?"

"Yes, I'm fine," she smiled, turning away from him so she could regain her focus. "Do you want to finish giving me the tour?"

"Right." He walked to the doorway, waiting to turn off the light until she was out of the room.

She hadn't finished her exploration of the hallway that morning, afraid she'd run out of time; she was curious now as to what else lay ahead of her.

"There's two more guest rooms," he stated, pointing to two doorways on opposing sides of the hallway as they passed by them. "And another bathroom."

This brought them to the end of the hall, and he opened the final door. As soon as he'd switched the light on, he moved out of the way to let her enter first.

The room was completely empty.

"I haven't decided yet what to do with this one," he explained. "I think it's meant to be another bedroom, but I'm pretty sure I have enough of those. Any suggestions?"

She surveyed the room and said, "Well, if I were you – or rather, if you were me – I'd use it as a dance studio. It's the perfect space for it." She glanced at the floor-to-ceiling windows and imagined early morning sunlight streaming through them.

"Hmm," he grinned. "That might not be a bad idea. I could put in a wet bar and a dance floor."

"I'm sure you'd have some very entertaining parties." She tilted her head to the side. "Do you mind dimming the lights?

I want to see what it looks like in the dark, with all the city lights."

She heard him take a few steps back and the room slowly grew darker.

A spell-like silence fell over the room, broken only by the muffled sounds of the city just beyond the thick windowpanes. His footsteps echoed softly as he came toward her.

Without turning her head to look at him, she said in a hushed voice, "This space has a lot of energy. It's rhythmic."

"Hmm," he replied, pondering.

His rich baritone hum echoed close to her ear.

"I'm afraid of heights," she said offhandedly, keeping her eyes fixed on the window in front of her as she slowly inched away from him. "I've always dreamed about dancing in a loft studio, but I don't know if I actually could."

He angled his body between her and the window then grinned. "Okay, what about now?"

"What do you mean?"

"Do you feel better? If I'm standing here, like this." He planted his feet a little wider.

"Maybe." She wasn't sure which scared her more at this point – him, or the ten-foot window looming behind his silhouette. They both carried an association with free falling.

He looked at her for a second. "You want to try?"

The hopeful expression on his face made her smile. "You mean dancing?"

He nodded affirmatively.

"Right now?" She wasn't sure how she felt about dancing in front of him. It reminded her too much of being on the yacht, on display.

"Sure," he replied. "But only if you want to."

She hesitated for a second, then smiled. Tilting her head, she asked, "Have you ever done any ballroom dancing?"

"No," he replied. "I can definitely say that's not in my skill set."

"Okay then. I'm going to teach you the waltz."

"Oh?" He quirked an eyebrow, grinning.

"Yes. The steps are easy." She motioned him forward.

"Oh, you're serious," he laughed.

"Yes," she stated, giving him an arched smile. "If you're going to teach me self-defense, I think it only fair you take a dance lesson from me."

"When you put it that way...."

He watched as she proceeded to show him the basic step: one foot forward, a glide to the side, then another step backward, then to the side again, ending with both feet together. After she'd repeated the pattern a few times, he asked, "So I step forward with my left?"

"Yes," she replied over her shoulder, giving him an encouraging smile. "I'm showing you your part. When we put it together, you'll step forward on your left, while I step back on my right. We're essentially making a box together as we move." She stood with her back to him, showing him his part of the pattern again; he followed along, tracing her footsteps with his.

After a few minutes, she turned around. "You think you've got it?"

He nodded. "This is the basic step?"

"Yes. Not too complicated, right?" Without waiting for a response, she continued, "Now we'll do it together. Put your arm here." She guided his arm around her back to her upper shoulder blade, ignoring the thrilling sensation that zipped down her spine when she felt his touch. She then placed her right hand in his left to establish their frame, her heart skipping a beat as she slipped her hand in his. "Keep your elbows level with the floor," she instructed, her voice sounding breathy.

"Right." He inhaled then took a step forward, glancing down at their feet.

The next few steps were smooth, but he fumbled the footwork at the end of the pattern.

"That's okay," she said. "Let's start over. Slower. And don't look at your feet."

"Okay," he grinned. "Noted."

The next go around went better as he began to grasp it. They repeated the steps a handful of times then she said, "Let's try turning now, so we're not just staying in one place. We'll maintain the pattern, but this time when you step, you'll pivot just a little instead of stepping directly forward. Just angle the steps a little more and turn your body, if that makes sense."

He nodded. "I'll do my best."

She peered up at him and smiled. "You're doing great. I'll find us some music in a minute so you can feel the rhythm." She glanced anxiously toward the windows. "You'll make sure we don't get too close?"

"You have my word." He smiled reassuringly then cleared his throat. "Ready?"

"Yes." She waited for him to step towards her, allowing him to lead.

They started off perfectly, but angling the footwork proved to be slightly more difficult and it took several tries; however, once he got it down, she could tell that maintaining the pattern was starting to feel more natural to him.

"Alright, let's try it with music," she said a few minutes later, dropping her hand from his.

He pulled out his phone. "You have a song in mind?"

She gazed at the ceiling for a moment, pondering, then answered, "'Come Away With Me' by Norah Jones." She watched him as he made a scrolling motion on his phone. The glow from the screen highlighted his facial features, and she allowed herself to stare openly at his chiseled jaw, a boyish grin tugging at one of the corners of his mouth. Gritty stubble. Perfect nose. His brows were furrowed slightly as he continued searching.

"Okay, found it." He hit play then offered his hand to her.

They both held their breaths in anticipation.

As the song began, she said, "Wait until you feel the beat, then start when you're ready."

"Can you count us off?" he said, his voice sounding slightly anxious. "I think that will help."

"Right. I'll give us a few measures then we'll start on 'One'." She began counting a series of "one, two, three," nodding her head to the rhythm with each count. When she sensed he was feeling it, she gave him a small tug forward then let him take the lead. He followed through with the step, and they easily fell into the rhythm of the dance. She had to adjust her stride to match his, which was quite a bit longer since he was taller.

They continued around the room, and Tara could feel his confidence increasing with every turn; she was surprised at the natural grace he demonstrated. When the song ended, silence filled the room as they both lowered their arms. She felt a slight reluctance on his part as he slowly released her hand and took a step back.

She glanced at him, smiling. "That was fun, right?"

He nodded. "Maybe you can teach me more sometime."

"I'd like that. And you did great for your first time." She paused then added, "Then again, you strike me as one of those people who's good at everything."

He grinned. "I think so far, you've only seen me drive a car and walk down a sidewalk. But I admit, those are two things I do very well."

Her laughter echoed quietly throughout the empty space as she shifted her gaze to the twinkling glow of the cityscape. He stepped toward the window, gazing out at the scene.

After a moment's hesitation, she decided to join him; however, she stopped just behind him, unable to go any further.

He turned towards her and offered his arm. "Here, hold on to me."

Her mind was telling her to step away, but his imploring eyes had already cast a hypnotic spell over her; she wanted to feel him again, smell the subtle hint of his cologne.

He was standing about three feet away from the window. Too close. Her heart started to pound. With a shaky hand, she reached for his forearm and grasped it firmly. An electrical charge swept through her body.

"All good?" he asked gently, glancing at her.

"I don't know yet," she answered breathlessly. "Don't. Move."

"I won't," he whispered in her ear.

They stood for a moment, both silent, appreciating the dazzling view. Eventually, he tilted his head in her direction and softly said, "Come on, I'll finish showing you around. And I'll make it quick. I'm sure you want to finish putting your things away."

She let go of his arm, her heart sinking a little as she did so. It'd felt so reassuring standing at his side, like he could protect her from anything. Every part of him was so thoroughly masculine – the sound of his voice, the gritty stubble along his jawline. His broad chest and shoulders. The color of his hair, almost as black as the night. His hands, strong and sure. The way he moved with complete confidence. His essence...his touch. Everything. It left her feeling empty when he stepped away.

He led her back down the hallway then through the rest of the circular layout until they ended up next to the kitchen.

"Well, that's everything." He lingered for a moment in front of the hallway leading to their bedrooms. "You good for the night?"

"Yes," she replied. "Thanks."

"Okay then," he flashed her a quick smile. "I'll see you in the morning."

She watched him walk down the hall, knowing he was headed to the one room she would never see because he didn't want her like that. As she walked to her own room and closed the door behind her, she tried to ignore the sinking of her heart.

"I have no intention of pursuing anything with you."

31

The following morning, Ryan awoke at his usual time, ready to start the week. After making his bed, he walked to the bathroom and turned on the faucet. He splashed some cold water on his face then stared at his reflection in the mirror, allowing the water to run for another second or two before shutting it off. Placing his hands on the edge of the marble counter, he leaned forward and looked himself in the eye. By the end of the week, he'd have to tell Tara the truth. Would she be angry? Hurt? Would she understand his reasons for not telling her who he was from the start? And just how much of the truth should he tell her? The promise he'd made to her brother all those years ago echoed in his mind as he stared down at the sink drain. When the time came, he would have to be honest about all of it, including that night in the hospital with Preston; she would have to know everything before he could truly attempt to forgive himself.

He turned away from the mirror and reached for the toothpaste. As he brushed his teeth, the memory from the night before flooded his mind. He hadn't been able to take his eyes off her, the way her face had lit up when they began to dance;

he could still feel the shape of her hand in his, and the song had continued to play in his head long after he'd said goodnight.

Setting the toothbrush down, he ran a hand through his hair and sighed. The way she constantly turned him on was frustrating, but even more so because he couldn't take any action. It was obvious that he made her nervous, but he knew it didn't necessarily mean she was attracted to him. Given her experience with Jai, most men probably made her nervous at this point. His fist clenched around the towel in his hand, and he gritted his teeth. The swell of anger pushing against his chest was almost overpowering; he wanted to punch a wall or hear something shatter, like the sound of a jaw breaking. Taking a few deep breaths, he attempted to let go of his pent-up frustrations. He couldn't change Tara's past, but there was the future to consider, and he could think of a few less violent ways to achieve justice, especially in the financial sector.

After taking a quick, rejuvenating shower, he walked towards his closet and selected a white dress shirt, navy slacks, and a tie with a pinstripe pattern. Once dressed, he grabbed a blazer and his watch then left his room and headed down the hallway. He paused when he got to Tara's door, which was ajar; since the light was on, he decided to knock.

"Come in," she called from somewhere inside the room.

He opened the door to find her sitting in the armchair by the window, wearing athletic shorts and an oversized graphic T-shirt. Her hair was pulled back in a high ponytail, Ariana Grande style.

"Good morning," she smiled, setting aside the book she'd been reading. "I woke up early and couldn't go back to sleep."

"Were you comfortable enough?" he asked, prepared to make whatever adjustments she might need.

"Yes," she nodded. "I slept wonderfully. What about you?"

"I slept well, thanks. Are you ready for breakfast? We'll have to make it ourselves since Karen's off today. She's only here Thursday through Sunday."

"I'm ready," Tara replied, rising from her chair.

She followed him to the kitchen and watched as he set his phone down on the counter, next to a small Bose speaker.

"You like Citizen Cope?" he asked, leaning over his phone as he searched through his music.

"Yes – especially his first album." Tara walked toward the cabinet that contained the mixing bowls and stooped down to retrieve one. A moment later, she heard the familiar melody of the first song on the album, "Night Becomes Day." Standing, she said, "I usually eat scrambled eggs and toast for breakfast. Would you like me to make you some as well?"

"That'd be great, thanks." He made a pretense of scrolling through the news as he subtly watched her remove a carton of eggs from the refrigerator. His eyes darted to her slender, lightly tanned legs extending below the hem of her shorts before naturally being drawn to her shapely derriere; this particular feature was especially hard not to notice when she bent over to grab a potholder from one of middle drawers.

Clearing his throat, he asked, "Would you like some coffee?" He stepped over to the coffee maker, knowing that Karen had prepped it the night before, so all he had to do was press the brew button.

"Yes, thanks," Tara responded, cracking an egg into the bowl.

Ryan reached above him and grabbed two plates from the cabinet, along with a pair of mugs. As the coffee began to brew, he walked toward the pantry and emerged a moment later with a loaf of bread. He set it down on the counter next to her and grabbed a cutting board.

"That doesn't look like it came from a grocery store," Tara remarked, glancing at the bread, which was sealed in a Ziplock bag.

"Karen makes a fresh loaf every Thursday morning. I try to make it last the whole week, but so far I've never been successful."

"I don't think I'd be either," she said with a smile.

After inserting two slices of bread in the toaster, Ryan leaned against the counter and casually asked, "Do you run?" His eyes darted to her shorts, which appeared to be the running type, before moving to her face.

She looked up quickly. "Yes. Not fast or anything." She smiled and added, "But I do enjoy running."

"Would you want to join me later? For a run? Once we're done for the day."

"Sure." She gave him a sideways glance, then reached for a spatula.

After breakfast, they quickly did the dishes then headed to his office.

"I'm going to let you unpack the boxes with the books," he said, following her into the room. "I'll sort through the others. I just need to go through some emails first."

She nodded, stepping toward the first box full of books. "Which shelves do you want me to use?"

"I'll leave that up to you," he replied, taking a seat at his desk. "I trust your organizational abilities."

"Alright." She scooted the box over to a row of empty shelves. After glancing at the titles, she determined they were all college textbooks. As she shelved them, she listened to the steady rhythm of his typing.

After a few minutes, he glanced her way. "I'm going to print off those forms for you to sign."

"Okay," she nodded, keeping her focus on the books. She heard the printer come to life with a gentle hum.

A moment later, he retrieved the documents and motioned her over. "Read through these carefully," he stated, pulling over a chair for her. "Ask me if you have any questions along the way."

She took a seat and began to peruse the forms, tuning out the sound of his typing as she read. Eventually, she reached for a pen and signed the ones requiring a signature. She handed them back to him.

"Any questions?" he asked, taking them from her.

"No, everything seems pretty straightforward." She tried to ignore the sudden thrill she felt as their hands accidentally touched, and she wondered if he felt it too.

He cleared his throat. "I'll need to make a copy of your driver's license to go with the W-9."

Hesitating, she asked, "Can we do that later?" How was she supposed to explain that she had no ID? Her license, and any other identifying information, had been taken from her and confiscated.

"Sure." He turned and reached for a laptop next to a stack of files and placed it on the desk. "I got you set up with an administrative email. This is an old laptop I haven't used in a while, but it's good to go. I just need to change a few settings."

She watched in fascination as his masculine fingers flew over the keys. A few minutes later, he turned the laptop around so it was facing her. "Mind if I lean over you?"

Her pulse quickened as she breathed in the familiar scent of his bodywash, and she wondered if he was feeling the same sexual tension that she was. "Go ahead," she stammered, blushing. "I don't mind."

As he moved the curser to open the Outlook application, his shoulder brushed hers lightly, causing her breath to hitch. A second later, he pushed his chair away and swiveled around to his desk, leaving her to bask in the lingering scent of sandalwood and leather.

"I'm going to email you some spreadsheets in just a sec." He clicked into a folder on his desktop and dragged some items into an email. He hit "send" then wheeled his chair next to hers once more.

While he proceeded through the final steps of setting up the Outlook account, her body remained completely motionless. She wondered if he could hear the pounding of her heartbeat.

"Check your email," he stated brusquely. "See if you got the one I just sent you."

"Yes, it's here," she replied.

They spent the next hour going over a handful of files together, and Ryan was pleased to find that she was indeed organized and thorough. At 9:30, he logged off his computer and glanced in her direction. She was bending over a stack of files he'd placed on an empty chair; it took effort to pry his eyes away. He cleared his throat and said, "I'm going to head over to my meeting. Are you good here?"

She looked up. "Yes. This will keep me busy."

"Alright," he smiled. "When I get back, we'll have lunch."

32

The mid-afternoon sun was shining brightly, high in the sky, when Ryan walked Tara over to the park bench where he usually started and ended his runs.

"Do you want to lead?" he asked. "I'll let you set the pace."

"Sure," she smiled.

"Okay, I'll tell you which way to go. How far do you want to run?"

"Maybe four miles or so? Forty-five minutes?"

"Sounds good to me." He turned and pointed her in the direction they'd be going. "Ready?"

She threw him a quick glance then set off at a fast clip, coyly looking over her shoulder to make sure he was following.

He grinned and easily caught up to her, settling into her pace. As they jogged, he mused over the day and considered his next steps. He'd already planned to set aside some time to show her the basics of self-defense, which largely involved learning how to inflict the most damage with the least amount of effort. He felt confident that he could teach her these elements by the end of the week, depending on how hard she was willing to work at it. The next thing was getting her comfortable with a gun, and he'd already broached the topic with her. He knew he could call Brett anytime and get an invite out to his ranch; taking her to a shooting range wasn't an option as he was afraid that doing so would get the attention of anyone keeping an eye on her movements. Going to Brett's, however, offered an easy solution without raising suspicion, and he was happy that she was amenable to the idea. His overall goal was to give her as many tools as possible so she could defend herself should the need arise.

In terms of earning her trust, he felt like he was making some progress in getting to know her, but he sensed that her guard was still up; he could feel a wall between them, and there wasn't much time for finesse in getting it to come down. The one thing in his favor was having her near him for the remainder of the week, giving him plenty of time to solidify a friendship.

He continued his musings as they ran, and the forty-five minutes passing quickly. When they neared the park bench from which they'd started, they each slowed their pace, eventually coming to a stop in front of it.

After a few minutes of stretching, Ryan turned to her and asked, "What would you like to do for dinner? We can go out somewhere if you'd like." He bent down to tighten his shoelace.

"Do you cook?" she asked, arching an eyebrow.

He gave her a sideways glance. "Not really. But I'm pretty good with a jar of Prego sauce and a package of spaghetti."

"Oh," she laughed, subtly.

"What?" he grinned. "You don't like spaghetti?"

"No, I would love spaghetti actually. I just didn't imagine you eating something so...ordinary."

He laughed and responded, "I enjoy simplicity every now and then."

They continued to converse as they walked back to Eastcott Place and entered the lobby. As they stepped into the elevator, Ryan heard her take a deep breath in. He glanced at her and saw that her facial expression was drawn taught, every feature filled with tension. She moved rigidly into the corner and placed a hand on the wall for support.

"Are you alright?" he asked, pushing the button for the 62nd floor.

"Yes. It's just the heights thing. I'm okay with elevators, for the most part, if they're enclosed and not made of glass or something."

"Well," he smiled. "I'm here if you need an arm to hold onto." He wanted to hold all of her, but he quickly cut off that train of thought. *Friends*, he reminded himself. Just friends. That was all he could be to her. Needing a distraction, he said, "Do you really want spaghetti? Because I was joking, you know. Karen always has meals prepped and saved for the days she's not here."

"Oh, I definitely want to try your version of spaghetti," she laughed.

"Alright," he grinned. "It'll be great. You'll see."

A moment later, the elevator doors opened, and he gestured for her to exit first. As soon as they entered the unit, he removed his shoes and said, "I'm going to take a quick shower."

"Me too," she nodded.

He headed towards his room, leisurely whistling a tune. After closing the door behind him, he scanned through his contacts list on his phone then tapped on one of the names.

A few rings later, Brett picked up.

"Hey, Ryan. How've you been?"

"I'm good," he said. "Yourself?"

"Not too bad. I've been breaking in a new horse, but other than that, nothing much going on."

"Are you up for a visit? I bought a new handgun since I last saw you. And I got the latest Colt rifle – the CBX, .308. Thought you might like to try it out."

"Sure," he answered. "When're you thinking?"

"How does this Wednesday sound?"

"Yeah, that should work. You want me to call up Adam and see if he's free?"

Ryan had forgotten that Brett's best friend lived right down the road from the ranch; but more importantly, Adam's sister lived nearby as well, and Ryan was sure she'd be included in the invitation. Brett had been trying for years to set him up with Amy.

"Sure. What time?"

"Let's do five," Brett responded. "We can have dinner after."

"Okay," he replied. "I'll bring some beer." He paused then slowly added, "And I'll be bringing someone with me, if that's okay. She's the niece of one of my business partners – she's staying with me for a few weeks while she's apartment hunting."

"Oh?" Brett responded, sounding more than a little curious.

"Purely as a guest," he clarified. Then he quickly added, "And she's taken."

"Right," Brett laughed, his tone implying that her relationship status was of no consequence. "Is she cute?"

"Don't make it awkward," he responded, grinning.

Brett laughed again. "Okay, so she's cute. I'll see you Wednesday."

Ryan hung up then threw off his sweaty T-shirt and headed for the bathroom.

Well, Tara thought to herself, stepping out of the shower, *things are going okay so far.* The sudden change in her circumstances hadn't affected her mood – beyond the typical fluctuations that anyone would be feeling in her situation. The medication helped with that. However, she knew at some point, it would all catch up to her, especially as Friday got closer. She would need to find time to process her situation and decide whether she was going to return to Jai or attempt an escape – except it wouldn't be an attempt. She would either have to succeed or die trying. The thought suddenly overwhelmed her, setting off a wave of panic that hit her like a flash flood. She took a few deep breaths to steady herself then diverted her focus to toweling off and getting dressed.

Approximately ten minutes later, she emerged from her room and headed for the kitchen. Ryan was already there, dressed in jeans and a T-shirt. Against her will, her heart gave a little flutter. He was leaning casually against the counter, his hair damp and slightly tousled. He'd fully shaved, which didn't subtract from his appeal as it did with some men. He flicked his gaze to her, straightening his lean muscular frame, and threw her a carefree smile. Her hands were shaking. *This is ridiculous,* she thought. How was it possible that he could have this kind of effect on her?

"Alright," he said, opening one of the utensil drawers. "Let's do this."

"Oh, you want me to get involved?" she laughed, ignoring her nervousness. "I was under the impression that I'd be merely a spectator."

"True, but it'll take longer if I end up burning something."

"I'm not sure if it's possible to 'burn' spaghetti." She leaned away from the counter. "But I'll handle the sauce." Laughing as she passed him on her way to the pantry, she added, "I hope you like your pasta al dente. I can't stand soggy noodles, so if you don't, we'll have to make two separate pots."

"Al dente is fine," he called after her.

She stepped into the pantry and scanned the fully stocked shelves. "Do you actually have any Prego sauce in here?" she called out from the recessed space upon not seeing any.

A moment later, he came in behind her and perused the shelves. "So I may have been making a generalized statement about the spaghetti sauce. It's what my mom always used growing up, but I have a feeling that Karen probably has her own special recipe or something." After performing a more thorough scan, he spotted some mason jars on one of the upper shelves. Reaching above her, he grabbed a jar of sauce and handed it to her.

It wasn't long before she had the fragrant sauce simmering on a backburner.

He drained the noodles at the sink then looked over his shoulder at her. "How's it going?"

"Just about done," she smiled.

Roughly ten minutes later, they made their way to the formal dining room, each carrying something; one more trip to the kitchen was sufficient to bring everything else, including a salad that Karen had put together. As Tara arranged the plates and silverware, Ryan grabbed a set of candles from the buffet.

"Here we go," he smiled, removing a lighter from one of the table's drawers. He placed the candles and lighter on the table then pulled her chair out for her. "I'll pour us some wine if you want to light these."

She reached for the lighter and watched as he removed the cork from a 1996 bottle of Charmes-Chambertin Grand Cru; she didn't have to be a connoisseur to know it was expensive. Turning her attention to the candles, she quickly lit them then set the lighter off to the side and watched as he filled their glasses, the wine making a soft gurgling sound as he poured it. With their glasses full, he set the bottle down, returned the lighter to the drawer, and proceeded to take his seat at the head of the table, as he'd done the night before.

She glanced at him playfully then said, "You don't want to go all-out formal?" She swept her hand toward the head chair at the other end. "It would make passing the salt a lot more interesting. Or I guess in our case, the Parmesan cheese."

He grinned, "I weighed the pros and cons, then decided I'd much rather be able to see your face up close."

She blushed and there was a moment of awkward silence before she realized that he was waiting for her to take the first bite. She quickly picked up her fork and started twirling some pasta around it, using her spoon to assist.

"You know," he said, "I never asked if you like to cook."

"I do, for the most part," she replied, smiling.

"Alright." He took a quick bite, followed by a sip of wine. "What's your favorite food?"

She didn't hesitate. "Pizza. I could eat it forever and never stop liking it."

"I know a great pizza place nearby. I'll take you over there sometime." He took another bite then continued, "You like to run, dance, read, and pizza's your favorite food. You like cooking, for the most part. You went to Berkeley on a dance scholarship. Minored in psychology. Organization is one of your strengths. And you have a fear of heights. Your favorite color is blue. What else should I know about you?"

Surprised that he remembered her favorite color, she said, "I think you know more about me than I do about you." She nodded at the Notre Dame logo on his T-shirt and asked, "Is that where you went to college?"

He quickly looked down at his shirt, obviously forgetting which one he was wearing, and pulled the front of it away from his chest so he could see it.

"Yes. I got my master's there." He studied her for a moment. "Do you mind if I ask why you took a break from Berkeley?"

"Well, I..." She stared at her bowl of spaghetti as she searched for a vague response. Oddly, she didn't remember mentioning that she'd taken a break, but she must have at some point. "I went through a difficult breakup." Difficult was the biggest understatement ever, and the breakup hadn't even been the worst of it. She pushed away the memory of her mom finding her locked in the bathroom, crying, with a vial of Vicodin in one hand and a half-empty bottle of vodka in the other.

"It was a little overwhelming at the time." She idly twirled some pasta around her fork and added, "I had some other things I was dealing with too."

306

"Hmm," he replied understandingly. "Do you think you'll go back to finish?"

She nodded, appreciating that he didn't probe into her divulgence. "I plan to. I've had a two-year hiatus, but I'm not really worried about it." She took another bite, contemplating the question she'd been wanting to ask him – she just wasn't sure how to go about it, as there really was no other way than to ask it forthrightly.

They each took a bite then she raised her wine glass, lofting it casually in the air before taking a sip. "So," she began, with feigned nonchalance, "I'm just curious – and it's none of my business, and you don't have to answer...." She trailed off, swallowed, then asked blankly, "Are you married?"

He raised his eyebrows, leaving his fork in mid-air. "No," he laughed quickly. "I am most assuredly not married."

"I mean, it doesn't matter if you are," she rushed. "I just didn't want you to feel that you have to hide anything from me." She could feel her cheeks growing flush. "I'm very good at keeping confidences."

"Well, I appreciate that. I don't think I have any secrets worth keeping though." He took a slow, deliberate bite then asked, "What about you?"

"Hmm?" She flicked her eyes in his direction then quickly replied, "Um, no, nothing that I can think of. I'm an open book." Which was generally true of her, the current context being the exception.

"Me too," he replied, taking a sip of wine. He set his glass down and slowly added, "If there's ever anything you needed to talk about, you can trust me."

She glanced suspiciously at him.

307

"What?" he responded, smiling. "You don't think you can trust me?"

"I don't know," she replied honestly. "I mean, please don't take offense, but your type doesn't exactly inspire trust."

"And what type is that?" he asked playfully, cocking his head to the side.

"The type that knows how to say all the right things." She gave him a faint smile, tucking a loose strand of hair behind her ear, then after reflecting, added, "I think you're the leaving type. I'm guessing once the initial excitement fizzles out, you move on to the next."

"Well," he leaned back in his chair. "That's..." he laughed and finished, "insightful." Pondering for a moment, he added, "I suppose this is the part where I attempt to refute your opinion of me?"

"Yes, please," she quipped, casting him a beguiling smile. He didn't seem to be upset with her for the semi-accusation regarding his character, and her hand stopped shaking under the table as she gave a little laugh.

He leaned forward, and she glimpsed what might have a been calculating look in his eye; however, with the exception of a somewhat anxious crease in his forehead, his facial expression was genuine enough. He rested his elbows on the table, placing his hands under his chin in a thoughtful manner. "I guess it's hard to refute something that's common knowledge. But I will have you remember that I did say I was turning over a new leaf the other day. And, as a slight defense, I will add that when I'm in a serious relationship I fully invest myself to sustaining it." He fixed his eyes on her. "And I don't look at anyone else."

An electric current ran down her spine, her heart fluttered violently, and she lost the ability to breath for a moment. She proceeded to give the utmost attention to her half-empty plate, ignoring the feeling that he was observing her.

There was a moment's silence then in a low voice that had a slightly seductive edge to it, he softly asked, "What would it take to gain your trust?"

The question caught her off guard, and she took a moment to reflect. And to steady her heart rate.

"Time," she replied simply. "And that's not something we have." She took a quick bite then reached for her glass of wine. Before taking a sip, she asked, "Does it really matter that I trust you?"

"Yes. I want to know what you're thinking. You're hard to read." He grinned and with an air of gravity added, "It's frustrating."

"You're generally good at reading people?" She looked at her plate and gently speared a leaf of lettuce with her fork.

"Usually," he nodded, giving her a narrow look.

His unwavering gaze sent her thoughts scattering. "Well," she replied, taking a quick breath, "I plan to remain an enigma."

He cocked his head to the side and raised an eyebrow. "Then I accept the challenge."

"You know," she responded with a half-laugh, "I should really be wondering why on earth you trust me, a total stranger, to live in your home and work for you."

He thought for a moment then shrugged his shoulders and replied playfully, "I guess I just trust you." He smiled and added, "That's the definition, isn't it?"

"Yes, but it's nice to have a little information, along with some evidence, ahead of time before submitting to blind trust."

"True," he nodded. "But intuition is equally important. After all, some people are very good at lying." He glanced at her. "And hiding things."

Tara's gaze flicked to his then she stated, "I believe it's a universally accepted truth that time is the best judge of character."

He gave her an arched smile. "And how long do you think it would take for you to trust me?" It was more a statement of fact than a question. He leaned back in his chair and set his napkin on the table. "I'm a patient man."

With an equally arched smiled, she replied, "A long time. And, like I said earlier, we don't have enough of that."

"We might," he said, "Depending on whether you want to see me again after this." His eyes flicked to hers, and he managed to hold her gaze for more than a second. "So how long is a long time?" he repeated.

She took a sip of wine, then delicately placed one elbow on the table, peering at him over the rim of her glass. Ignoring the question, she asked, "Would you tell me the truth, no matter what I asked?"

"Yes," he replied promptly. "Unless…" the hint of a frown played at the corner of his mouth, "Unless the truth wasn't in your best interest."

"That sounds vague," she responded, her forehead wrinkling, "and very inconducive to the trust gaining process."

There was a drawn-out silence then he slowly said, "Could you trust that I would never withhold the truth unless absolutely necessary? And in that event, I would tell you in due time?"

She smiled and tilted her head to the side, searching for a good response.

Their eyes met, and he gave her the most imploring look. He almost seemed pained, which surprised her. This mattered to him, on a deeper level, and something in his eyes indicated that her trust would not be misplaced.

She broke away from his gaze, and said simply, "I suppose I could accept that." The air of solemnity that had fallen over them suddenly had her searching for a shift in topic. "So," she started, idly reaching for her wine glass, "can we talk about what we'll be doing for the rest of the week?"

"On Wednesday," he replied, "we'll go out to my friend's ranch. We can do some target practice."

Her eyes instantly widened, and she asked warily, "What do you mean by 'target practice'?"

"Don't worry," he laughed gently. "I'll show you exactly what to do. You'll be fine."

She sighed, resigned. "You seem very adamant about this. I thought we had settled on you giving me a self-defense lesson."

"Oh, you're getting that too," he laughed. In a more serious tone, he added, "I feel strongly about a woman being able to handle a dangerous situation." He reached for the wine bottle, concentrating as he refilled his glass, then continued, "My dad signed my sister up for karate when she was five. She didn't exactly enjoy it, but it made him feel better." He set the bottle off to the side then stared at his glass, brooding. After a moment, he cleared his throat and said, "My mom was sexually assaulted in college." His eyes darted to Tara's then to the table. "My parents wanted my sister – along with me and Andrew –

to have agency if we ever found ourselves in a vulnerable situation like that. For me and Andrew, it was more about being able to come to someone's aid."

Tara was momentarily stunned, but she recovered from her surprise and quietly responded, "I'm sorry."

His carefree air had disappeared, and there was an edge to his voice when he said, "I want you to feel that you have some power over a situation if you end up in that kind of circumstance, and that you'll be prepared to take action." He flicked his gaze to her.

"Alright," she smiled faintly, silently agreeing with him and suddenly feeling grateful that he wanted to teach her something she could use.

33

At 6:00am the following morning, Ryan walked down the hall and past Tara's bedroom, slightly relieved that she didn't appear to be up yet as he was needing a little time to himself. After toasting a bagel and brewing some coffee, he walked over to the nook with his plate and mug. He spent twenty minutes scrolling through the headlines on his phone as he ate then started his morning read: *Zen Mind, Beginner's Mind* by Shunryu Suzuki. Eventually, he drained his cup of coffee and strode back into the kitchen with his empty plate and mug.

By the time he sat down at his desk, it was just after seven. He opened his planner and wrote down the quote he most liked from the chapter he'd read:

"The best way is to understand yourself, and then you will understand everything. So, when you try hard to make your own way, you will help others, and you will be helped by others. Before you make your own way, you cannot help anyone, and no one can help you."

The other quote from the book humored him so he wrote that one down as well:

"Life is like stepping onto a boat which is about to sail out to sea and sink."

Closing the planner, he turned his attention to the handful of emails that needed a response; upon completion of the task, he decided to give Anna a call to go over the week's agenda.

"Will you be in for your 10:00am on Wednesday?" she asked, after a brief greeting.

"No," he replied. "See if you can move it to next week sometime."

"Will do." She moved on to the next bullet point. "I've selected three candidates for your temporary assistant position. Shall I schedule interviews for next week?"

"That won't be necessary." Smiling to himself, he added, "I happen to have found someone I like."

"Oh, good," she responded. "I'm happy you found someone. I'll let the temp agency know that the position has been filled." There was a brief pause as she made a note then she continued, "Moving on to the next item: the gala."

"Gala?" His mind was drawing a blank.

"Yes, the fundraiser for Action Against Hunger? It's at seven this Thursday, at the Finchers' residence."

"Oh, right." He'd forgotten all about the fundraiser that his family attended every year. And if he was remembering correctly, he was supposed to give some sort of speech.

"Do you still plan on going?" she asked, her tone sounding slightly perplexed.

He thought for a moment then replied, "Yes, I'll be there." He didn't think Tara would mind accompanying him to the event. "Is there anything else you needed to go over?"

"No, I believe that's all."

"Okay, I'll be working from home for the rest of the week, so call me if you need anything. I'll check in again on Friday."

After hanging up, he ruminated for a moment then decided to call Karen, who answered promptly.

"Hello, Ryan."

"Can you do me a favor?" he asked, getting straight to the point. "I'm taking Tara to the gala with me Thursday night, and she doesn't have anything formal to wear. Would you be able to pick up a dress for her?" He cleared his throat and added, "I think I'd like to surprise her with it."

There was the briefest of pauses then she replied, "I should be able to find something. Do you know her size?"

He thought back to their shopping trip then said, "I believe a size four."

"That seems about right. She's a tiny thing. Skin and bones, really."

Ryan agreed with her, but he knew it was the result of the strict diet that Tara had been forced to follow; he'd been happy to see her display a hearty appetite over the last few days whenever they'd eaten together. And she didn't seem self-conscious about it either, which he liked.

"Does she need anything else to go with the dress?" Karen continued.

He thought for a moment then said, "Yes, she'll need a complete ensemble."

"Alright, I'll ensure she has everything she needs."

A thought suddenly occurred to him, and he added slowly, "See if you can find something blue."

"I'll do my best," Karen nodded. There was a moment's weighted silence then she carefully added, "I don't want to pry, but has something developed between the two of you?"

Feeling a small degree of frustration that he hadn't ended the call by taking advantage of the silence right before she asked that question, he simply replied, "No."

"She's very attractive," Karen continued, "and she seems like a nice young woman."

"Yes, she's both of those things...." He sighed, raking his hand through his hair. "I'm too busy right now to pursue anything."

"I see."

He pictured Karen with her hands on her hips, lips pursed. He wondered exactly what it was that she "saw."

"Well," she said, with a little harrumph, "don't go leading her on if you don't intend to follow through."

He knew she was right. "Noted," he replied brusquely, ending the call.

As he reached for the binder he'd created for the rainwater project, a light rap on the office door interrupted him. He glanced up and smiled as Tara walked forward, holding a mug of coffee. She was wearing a white blouse tucked into a pair of slim navy slacks. A belt with a wide buckle circled her waist, and her hair was pulled back into a tight ponytail, high on her head. To top off the look, she was wearing a pair of glossy, navy heels.

He managed a quick "good morning" as he gathered his thoughts then said, "You look ready for work. Did you sleep well?"

She nodded. "I wasn't sure how dressed up I should be. Is it okay if I bring my coffee in here?"

"Of course," Ryan replied. "And please feel free to dress casually if you want to."

She walked toward her desk, which had been delivered and set up the night before, following their dinner. "I see you're wearing a dress shirt," she commented, eyeing him quickly as she set her mug down. "I want to be professional too." She was grateful that their desks were far enough apart to not be distracting – for the most part.

Ryan swiveled his chair in her direction then folded his arms across his chest and slowly rocked back, planting his feet a little wider. "I'm going to have you start with scanning that stack of reports over there." He nodded towards a large pile of papers sitting on a chair. "After that, I'll show you how I like my files organized." He gestured towards a metal filing cabinet to his right. "I have a filing system for all the different LLCs and entities I'm involved in."

"Alright," she responded, settling into her chair as she opened her laptop. She was suddenly feeling quite aroused, her body's direct response to the way he'd instructed her. He was authoritative and – she exhaled slowly – commanding. She kept her eyes on the computer screen as visions of him bending her over his desk suddenly flooded her mental space. She imagined him behind her, slowly unbuckling his belt....

She almost spilled her coffee, setting it down more forcefully than she'd intended.

"Everything alright?" Ryan asked, quirking an eyebrow as he glanced her way.

"Hmm?" she responded, hoping he would think that he had imagined something. She cleared her throat and asked, "Where's the scanner?"

"Next to you." He smiled and raised his eyebrow again. "It should be plugged in."

Tara glanced to her left and saw the scanner perched on a bookshelf a few feet away. She traced the cord with her eye and replied, "Yes, it's connected to the computer." With that, she brusquely rose from her chair and retrieved the stack of papers he'd directed her to scan. She felt his eyes resting on her but paid him no heed – at least not externally.

They worked quietly together for the rest of the morning, with occasional conversation. Around noon, they were both interrupted by the sound of Ryan's phone vibrating, buzzing loudly against the hardwood surface of his desk.

He reached for it and saw that it was his mother. Again. She'd called twice yesterday, and both times he'd let it go to voicemail. The message she'd left after her second call was short and vague, but he was fairly certain about her reason for wishing to speak with him.

"Hey," he said, answering the call as he rose from his chair. He walked quickly around the corner of his desk then strode toward the door and out into the hall. He didn't exactly want Tara overhearing his mother lecturing him. Or scolding him. Or both. He took a breath, preparing himself for the worst.

"I just thought I'd check in," his mother began, her tone airy. "Am I interrupting anything?"

"No, I'm free at the moment," he replied carefully. "Sorry I couldn't answer the other day. Things have been busy lately."

There was a moment of awkward silence then she simply stated, "Rachel said you had a guest staying with you. A young woman?"

He was surprised that his mother went straight to her agenda, not wasting time with small talk.

"Yes, I do," he replied quickly. "As a favor to her uncle. It's just for a few weeks while she's apartment hunting."

"Oh." She paused then said, "Well, she'll need a lot longer than that, with the way housing is up here."

He held in a sigh. "I wouldn't worry about it, Mom. Like I said, I'm only assisting temporarily." He thought quickly and added, "She doesn't have any family close by, and her uncle wanted her to stay with someone he trusts." There, he thought, that should settle it.

"Well, I'm sure he'd be happy for her to stay with us, or Rachel."

A heavy silence ensued, and he knew where this was going.

"Ryan," she continued, "I just don't think it's appropriate for you to have a young, single woman staying with you. She doesn't have anyone else?"

Doing his best to keep his mounting frustration at bay, he answered calmly, "No, she doesn't. And she's fine where she is." Clearly, his emotions were getting the better of him and he thought it best to wrap up the conversation. "There's no reason for concern, as I have the best of intentions in her regard, if that's what you're worried about. Nothing is going on and it will remain that way." He riffled his hand through his hair and exhaled. "Look, I have to run. Sorry to cut this short."

"Alright," she responded in a clipped tone. "I'll talk to you later."

Ryan hung up and took a moment to process his frustration. Why did his parents have to be so old-fashioned? He didn't like that he was doing something they disapproved of, but on the other hand, he was a fucking adult.

He strode back into his office and stopped next to Tara's desk.

"Ready for lunch?" he asked, putting the phone call behind him.

She nodded, giving him a smile that made all his frustrations melt away.

Ryan followed her into the kitchen where they proceeded to make sandwiches.

Their conversation was minimal as they ate, and it was obvious to Tara that Ryan was anxious to return to his work, so once they'd finished eating, she offered to clean the dishes; he nodded his gratitude and rose from the table. Out of the corner of her eye, she watched as he strode down the hallway and disappeared into his office.

It only took her a few minutes to load the dishwasher and clean the counter. As she wasn't quite sure what to do with the rag she'd used, she simply wrung it out and draped it over the front-facing edge of the sink. She then made her way back to the office and seated herself once more at her desk; Ryan acknowledged her return with a brief look then went back to the report he'd been reading.

Eventually, he glanced at his watch and shifted his gaze in her direction. "I don't think I have much else for you to do," he stated, "once you're done with that spreadsheet. How's it coming?"

"I'm almost done with it," Tara replied.

"Okay, I'll take a look when you have it ready.

She nodded and continued typing.

Ryan went back to his own project, raising the height of his desk so he could stretch his legs and stand for a bit. After another ten minutes, Tara announced that she'd finished the spreadsheet.

"Perfect," Ryan responded. "Would you mind bringing me two files from that filing cabinet before you go?" He pointed toward a large, metal cabinet a few feet from her desk. "I believe they're the only two files under the 'J' tab."

She walked around her desk, opened the draw, and easily located the files.

As Ryan took them from her, he tried not to notice the slight opening of her blouse, and instead shifted his eyes to her face.

Tara looked quickly down at her hands then vaguely glanced around the room. "Is there anything else you need?"

"No, not at the moment. Thanks for this."

He placed the files on his desk then allowed his eyes to linger on her retreating figure. If he had to describe the way she moved in musical terms, it would be "vivace:" graceful and unhurried. He'd noted the slight unsteadiness of her hands when she'd handed him the files, and it gave him an inner satisfaction knowing that his presence had an effect on her. But perhaps her reactions were merely surface level? If she truly believed her assumptions about his character, then surely she wasn't seeing him in any sort of romantic light. First impressions were hard to overcome, and right now she thought he was a player who wasn't worthy of her trust. He didn't know how long it would take to undo that, and time was eating away. He gritted his teeth and opened one of the files. After a quick glance, he slammed the folder shut and flopped it back on the desk. He needed a good, long run. Alone.

Returning to her room, Tara slipped off her heels and lounged across her bed, reluctant to change out of her work clothes. She reflected on her time with Ryan that morning, glowing inwardly as she thought about the admiring look he'd given her when she'd walked into his office earlier that morning. She closed her eyes and took a deep breath in, basking in the euphoric feeling of contentment that filled her. She loved being a part of his work, even if her duties weren't terribly important, and it had somehow felt strangely natural to be at his side. Her mind began to drift to the authoritative bearing he'd displayed, and the sensation it had stirred within her. She quickly willed her mind to think of something else. Anything else. But as that proved to be impossible, she rolled over and reached for her book on the bedside table. It was one she'd selected from the library right before going to bed the previous night, happening to be the only Jane Austen novel she hadn't read: *Mansfield Park*. Grasping it firmly, she rose from the bed and quietly slipped into the hallway, heading for the pass-through lounge area behind the breakfast nook. When she reached it, she cozied up into the corner of the sectional and picked up where she'd left off.

An hour later, the pinging sound of rain on the window uprooted her from Austen's picturesque world of early 19th century English gentry. As she watched the gloomy raindrops dribble down the windowpane, her thoughts returned to the present. Maybe this was a good time to start thinking about an escape plan. Somehow, she would need to warn her family before Jai found out she was gone – that had to be the very first step before doing anything else. Next, she would need to find somewhere to go where Jai, or any of his associates, would never find her. Since she had no driver's license or passport, she would need to have a very solid plan in place before making any moves. And planning meant that she needed a computer. Perhaps Ryan wouldn't mind letting her use the work laptop for her personal use? With an inward sigh, she closed her book and twisted her body around to glance at the collection lining the shelves above her. Stretching, she pulled down a rather heavy volume titled *Impressionism: Art, Leisure and Parisian Society*. She slowly flipped through the pages, stopping when she landed on Renoir's familiar painting of a merry group of individuals clustered around a dining table, enjoying the outdoors on a summery day. "The Luncheon of the Boating Party" was printed underneath the image. She continued to flip aimlessly through the book then eventually returned it to the shelf.

Her thoughts turned once more to escaping. During their previous day's run, she'd noticed a sign for an Amtrak station not far from Eastcott Place. Perhaps that could be her means of transportation, and she liked the idea of taking a train over a bus. She'd need to alter her appearance to avoid recognition....maybe a drastic haircut and some dye?

Idly, she looked once more at the rain streaking down the windowpane and briefly considered telling Ryan what was really going on, but she knew she couldn't bring herself to do it; besides, she didn't need his help. His *"I don't intend to pursue anything with you"* statement still invaded her thoughts.

Tossing her head, she rose from the sectional and wandered back to her room where she proceeded to change out of her work clothes and into a pair of black leggings and a tank top. A few minutes later, she heard footsteps in the hall; she caught a brief glimpse of Ryan as he passed by her room on his way to his. She guessed he would take a shower before dinner, which should be soon. It was close to 5:30, and she was getting hungry.

A half hour later, he knocked on her door and they proceeded together to the dining room where they partook of one of Karen's prepared meals: a quinoa, kale, and couscous dish, topped with two chicken breasts that had been marinated in a lemon vinaigrette. Afterward, Ryan did the dishes while she put away the leftovers.

As she was sealing the lid on the last of the containers, he glanced her way and stated, "I think now's a good time for a self-defense lesson."

"Oh?" she replied, arching an eyebrow. She suddenly felt very nervous.

"We can use the empty room I showed you the other night."

A moment later, she followed him down the hallway. As he ushered her inside, she saw that it was far from empty. Mirrors had been installed on the long wall across from the windows, and at one end of the room, a punching bag dangled from the ceiling; on the wall behind it, a set of large, black fitness mats were folded in half and stacked against each other; next to the mats, two rows of free weights had been neatly arranged in a holding stand; a long, vinyl-padded workout bench had been pushed against the wall next to the weights so that it was out of the way.

"Exactly when did you find time to do all this?" she queried, watching as he walked over to a closet and began to remove interlocking grappling mats.

He looked over his shoulder and smiled roguishly. "Late last night. I had everything delivered yesterday afternoon while we were out running."

"Really?"

"Yeah." He glanced at her again. "Thought I'd surprise you."

She smiled, blushing, as her eyes fell on the mirrored wall where a ballet bar had been installed. "Mission accomplished," she murmured before turning to look at the punching bag. "Do you box?" she asked.

"Sometimes." He set the last flooring square in place then said, "Alright, let's get started." He motioned her over then positioned her so that they faced one another, with a few feet between them. "I'm going to show you some simple blocks and strikes."

"Okay," she laughed nervously. "I don't know that I'm ready for this."

"You'll be fine," he grinned. He shifted his stance and stated, "First thing: always keep your hands so they're in front of your face, at eye level. Don't let them drop below your chin."

She lifted her hands and balled them into fists.

"Good," he laughed. "But open your hands. You don't want them fisted, since you'll be striking with the heel of your palm. Next is your stance. We'll work with the right side of your body first, so take a step forward with that leg."

She did as he instructed. "Like this?"

He nodded. "Just like that. Keep your feet shoulder width apart, with your weight on the balls of your feet. Lean your body forward a little...yes, like that. You don't want to get thrown off balance." He took a step back, his stance wide. "Let's start with a basic scenario. I'm the attacker. You want to be able to block the hand that's coming at you. I could be reaching to grab your shoulder or your neck, or I might have my hand in a fist with the intention of punching you. Either way, my hand's entering your personal space and you need to block it. What you're going to do is meet the outside of my forearm with the outside of yours, just above your wrist. Like this." He did a slow-motion demonstration to show her exactly where her hand should be connecting with his arm to achieve an effective outside block. "Then you're going to use that connection to push my arm away from you while stepping around me. You have the advantage now since you're behind me."

She tried it a few times then he said, "I want you to really throw some strength behind it. Don't hold back." He grinned and added, "And remember to keep your hands up."

After multiple repetitions, he moved on to show her an inside block with a strike.

"This should be one fluid motion," he said. "You're going to block the inside of my arm with the outside of your left forearm, just above the wrist, like you did before. Now, with your right hand, you're going to strike against the front of my shoulder using the heel of your palm. Like this." He simulated the motion for her.

"Okay." She gave it a try.

"Good. Now do it a few a more times, then we'll switch to the left side of your body and practice the same maneuver."

An hour and a half later, he decided to call it a night. He'd shown her a few more fundamental moves, and after multiple repetitions of each, her eyes had started to glaze over.

"How do you feel?" he asked as they made their way towards the door.

"Good," she smiled, glancing up at him. "That was fun."

"You're a quick learner. It just takes time before it becomes muscle memory. Your reflexes will get faster with practice." He grinned. "And repetition. We're going to be doing this every day while you're here."

34

Nothing out of the ordinary happened the following morning. It was a typical Wednesday – minus the overall unconventionality of the situation in which Tara now found herself. Despite that fact, she was beginning to settle into a routine. She'd risen at 7:00am sharp, ready to start the day, and had selected a patterned blouse and a high-waisted, black pencil skirt to wear "to work." She'd paired the ensemble with a set of skin-toned heels to make her legs look even longer. After a quick breakfast by herself, she'd promptly joined Ryan in his office where they worked diligently for several hours, only stopping to take a break for lunch.

She was now nearing the completion of the project he'd given her and was feeling quite proud of her ability to stay focused despite his being only four feet away; it was difficult, however, to ignore the tingling feeling he gave her whenever he spoke to her or glanced her way.

Eventually, he looked up from his computer. "I'm almost done here," he stated. "Are you ready to wrap up?"

"I just need to finish proofreading my summary of the reports," she replied, "then I'll email it to you."

"Thanks." He gave her a quick nod then turned back to his computer to finish typing an email. A moment later, he stopped and said, "I think we should plan on leaving here at 4:30 for Brett's."

She glanced up from her summary. "Your friend with the ranch?"

"Yes," he nodded.

"I'll make sure I'm ready by then." She turned her attention back to the document.

Stretching his arms, Ryan lounged back in his seat and added, "We'll have time for another self-defense lesson before we go." He quirked an eyebrow at her.

"If you insist," she said, throwing him a withering glare, although secretly she was looking forward to it. Without further comment, she quickly finished the summary and emailed it to him.

"Thanks," he said, seeing it in his inbox. "I have a few more things I need to finish up here. Meet me in the studio at 3:00?"

"So that's what we're calling it?"

"It sounds better than 'the room'," he stated, grinning.

She laughed at his ominous tone then said, "I think I'll head down to the gym for a workout before then, if that's alright."

"Of course." He subtly watched as she closed her laptop and walked briskly toward the door.

Approximately ten minutes later, and carrying her swimsuit with her, Tara took the elevator down to the fitness club. Upon exiting, she made her way toward the attendant's counter and stopped to see if there might be a pair of goggles she could borrow. There wasn't, so she skipped the lap swim part of her agenda and headed to the gym. Her plan was to do a quick circuit workout, followed by a short dance and stretch session, then she'd have a nice, long soak in the hot tub.

A half hour later, she pulled her hair up in a messy bun and rinsed off under one of the showers, taking care to keep her hair dry. She changed into her bathing suit, grabbed a towel, folded it neatly under her arm, and left the locker room. A few heads turned as she walked down the corridor towards the pool, but she ignored the attention. A moment later, the unmistakable smell of chlorine hit her full on as she rounded a corner and entered the pool area. She spied the hot tub in the back corner and immediately headed for it, taking care to watch her step due to the wet floor tiles. Two of the lanes in the pool were occupied and, out of curiosity, she slowed her gait as she approached then halted altogether when she recognized the figure swimming down the first lane, heading directly toward her, only seconds away. She knew she should move on before Ryan noticed her, but her legs seemed to have forgotten how to walk. He surfaced a moment later, and she watched in fascination as he rose from the water, sweeping his hand through his hair, disheveling it. He tossed his goggles onto the pool's edge, a few feet from where she was standing, and ran a hand over his face, brushing off the water and clearing his vision. He slowly broke into a tilted grin as he registered her presence, his gaze leisurely working its way up her body, to her face.

"Hello," she said simply, trying to calm her heart rate while wondering if his decision to swim had been purely coincidental.

She gave him a small smile, her mouth seeming to be the only part of her that wasn't completely frozen. She took a step back, watching as he lifted his body from the pool, the muscles of his forearms hardening and flexing. He put one foot on the silver grate just below the tiled edge and rose to a standing position. Water dripped to the floor, trickling down his skin, and she couldn't look away even if she wanted to; the defined muscles of his upper body had her riveted. Her eyes trailed to his abs, which were hard and toned, then continued downward to the top of his waistband. She quickly swept her gaze upward and over to the hot tub behind him.

"Did you just finish working out?" he asked, taking a step toward her. His stride brought him just short of the generally acknowledged zone of personal space, and the air between them began to pulse with sexual tension.

"Yes," she answered breathlessly. Her thinking skills had completely abandoned her. "I was just heading for the hot tub," she stammered.

"Right," he nodded, looking over his shoulder in that direction.

She stole a quick glance at his lower abs and the beginnings of groin muscles then distracted herself by unfolding her towel and throwing it around her shoulders. As his eyes returned to her, she saw his jaw clench; a muscle just below his cheekbone ticked, and he appeared to be fighting some inner struggle.

Finally, he just said, "I'm going to head back up. See you in a bit." He gave her a parting glance, then turned and walked briskly towards the men's locker room.

Her knees were wobbling as she glanced over her shoulder, watching him disappear around the corner. After collecting her scattered thoughts, she stepped towards the hot tub, grateful that it was unoccupied.

Twenty minutes later, she headed for the locker room where she proceeded to take a quick shower, rinsing her body of the chlorine. After throwing on a fresh change of clothes, she gathered her things and tossed them into the gym bag she'd brought with her then headed back to Ryan's unit.

Arriving in her room, she transferred her dirty clothing from the bag to the laundry basket in the bathroom. A few minutes later, she exited her room and headed down the hall to meet Ryan in the studio for her "lesson." With each step, she had to fight the butterflies fluttering in the pit of her stomach as memories of their last session began to surface; she particularly found herself thinking about the way his hand had felt on her hip each time he'd adjusted her stance.

Upon entering the room, she saw that he had beat her to it and was now in the process of retrieving the interlocking mats from the closet. She walked towards the stack he'd piled and began to lay them out on the floor, subtly watching him as he lifted another mat from one of the shelves. His hair was wet and tousled from what she assumed had been a shower; the dampness made his hair color appear darker, almost the same shade of black as the T-shirt he was wearing. She tried to unsee the image of him standing in front of her, water dripping from his muscled arms and chest, but it was no use. With a sharp inhale, she reached for another mat. A moment later, he knelt beside her and together they started to interlock them.

Their lesson lasted longer than either of them realized and she only had time to change out of her sweaty clothing, take a quick shower, and don a pair of denim shorts and a grey tank top before switching off the light and leaving her bedroom.

Ryan, who'd been waiting in the kitchen, glanced up from his phone when Tara entered, and as always, he had to force his eyes not to linger on her figure. He reached for his keys and said, "Ready for a bit of a drive?"

She nodded, following behind him into the foyer and out the door. As they rode the elevator down, he did his best to ignore the sexual tension that had ignited between them as soon as the doors had closed. He gave her a quick glance, wondering if she could feel it too, and caught her staring at him; she immediately looked away, blushing, and he couldn't help smiling to himself.

Once the doors opened to the parking garage lobby, Tara followed him to his Audi and waited as he opened her door for her. He then moved around to the driver's side and slid behind the wheel.

"So," she asked, once they were on the road, "exactly where are we going?"

"Brett's ranch is near Lake Cavanaugh," Ryan replied. "About an hour north of here." He checked his blind spot then smoothly shifted lanes.

"It's out in the country then?"

"Pretty much," he replied. "The closest grocery store is a twenty-minute drive, and it's really more of a convenience store than anything else."

He smiled as childhood memories of Illinois began to surface. Tall stalks of corn swaying in a late summer breeze; vivid sunsets against a sky that never ended; big red barns; tractors plowing fields in the early morning light. A place where everybody knew everybody. Sometimes he missed it.

As he continued making his way through downtown, he occasionally flicked his gaze to Tara who was staring at the passing skyscrapers and crowded sidewalks. Eventually, he merged onto the highway.

After a few minutes, he glanced in her direction again and asked, "Do you want to listen to some music?"

"Sure," she nodded.

Keeping his eyes on the road, he tapped through the colorful icons on the Audi's media screen then said, "Can you scroll through my playlists? Pick whichever one you want."

"Okay," she smiled, glancing at the titles as she started to scroll down the list. "What are these summer ones?" she asked a moment later. "'Summer 28'....'Summer 29'..."

He glanced at the screen then replied, "I create a playlist each summer and title it with my age for that year." He shrugged his shoulders and added, "I like to look back and see what kind of music I was listening to."

"I see," she smiled, scrolling for a few more seconds. With a half-laugh, she announced, "I think I want to see what you were listening to when you were twenty-six." She gave him a quick glance. "How old are you now?"

"I just turned thirty last month. I haven't started this summer's playlist yet." He gave her a sideways glance and added, "Maybe you can help me with that."

She nodded vaguely then hit the play button. As the opening chord of Weezer's "Buddy Holly" sounded from the speaker, she decided not to comment on his suggestion of helping him compile a new playlist. Unless he knew something she didn't, their current arrangement was set to expire on Friday, and she would most likely return to Jai unless she could muster the courage to run away. The thought sparked an immediate feeling of anxiety. She turned her attention to the window, digging her fingertips into the side of her thigh until the feeling eased. Her breathing still felt shallow, so she continued to take slow, even breaths as she watched the scenery go by. As the city gradually gave way to suburbs, the traffic became less dense. Tall spruce trees, some steeple-like, others wider, started to become a consistent feature throughout the passing scenery.

As he continued to drive, Ryan's thoughts were on the investigation. He hadn't heard anything from Agent Mitchell since their last conversation on Sunday morning. He'd wanted to call for an update but hadn't when he realized that he himself had nothing new to report. On the other hand, he was anxious to know what would happen on Friday. No matter what Tara's reaction might be when he told her the truth, he had no intention of returning her to Jai, unless, of course, she wanted to go back. He clenched the steering wheel tighter and his jaw hardened. He gave Tara a sideways glance. There had to be a way he could convince her to stay if that were the case. But perhaps more importantly, how would he get her away from Jai if she didn't want to go back? Thoughts of simply running off with her to someplace they'd never be found quickly dissipated. He couldn't just think about her, as much as he wanted to. What about all the other women under Jai's control? With an inward sigh, he turned down the volume of the music and fixed his attention on Tara.

"I think we should get the shooting lesson out of the way first," he said, "before it gets too dark outside. Is that alright with you?"

She hesitated then replied, "I guess so. Might as well get it over with."

Inclining his head, he gently asked, "What exactly is it that scares you about guns?"

After thinking for a moment, she replied, "The noise, I suppose. The sound it makes when the trigger's pulled. I guess maybe the unexpectedness of it too? Like when I'm opening a can of biscuits – I know it's going to make that popping noise, but it makes me jump every time."

"That makes sense." He smiled at her reassuringly. "We'll just stick to handguns, okay?" He turned the volume up slightly but kept it at a level that was conducive to conversation.

Eventually, he exited the highway then drove for another twenty minutes down a narrow, two-lane road that turned off onto an even narrower stretch of road.

"Are we getting close?" she asked, giving him a quick glance.

He nodded. "Almost there. Just a few more turns."

A few minutes later, he turned left and drove down a long dirt driveway with a farmhouse at the end of it. He pulled up to a shed that was adjacent to the house and parked next to a rusted-out, blue and white striped Chevy truck.

Tara unbuckled her seat belt and turned to open her door but stopped when she felt him tap her on the shoulder. She gave him a quizzical look.

Grinning, he stated, "I thought you knew by now that when you're with me, I will always insist on opening doors for you."

"Oh," she responded, a faint blush rising to her cheekbones. So far, they'd mostly walked to places, and on the occasions that he'd opened doors for her, she hadn't given it much thought. However, now that she did, she realized what he said was true. And he always pulled out her chair for her.

Tara watched as he walked lithely around the front of the Audi and over to her door; when he opened it and extended his hand to her, she gladly took it. For one fleeting moment, there was only a sliver of air between their bodies as she stepped out, facing him. Slowly, he released her hand then turned toward the back of the car.

Slightly breathless, she followed him around to the trunk then stepped to the side as he popped it open. He handed her a black plastic case, light enough for her to carry, then reached for his rifle bag. Looping his arm through the strap, he slung it over his shoulder and shut the trunk.

The bang of a metal screen door caught Tara's ear, and she glanced at the farmhouse where a tall, lanky figure had appeared on the porch. Hands in his pockets, he descended the steps and sauntered in their direction, a wide grin on his face.

"Hey, Brett. Good to see you, man." Ryan gave him a brief hug, accompanied by a thump on the back.

"It's good to see you too," Brett responded.

Ryan turned and introduced Tara, refraining to mention the nature of their relationship and leaving it to Brett to remember that he'd said she was taken. The last thing he wanted was for Brett to think she was single and unattached...although technically this was true. He brushed the thought aside.

"Nice to meet you." Brett stepped forward and gave Tara a firm handshake.

Before Tara could respond in kind, another figure waltzed down the porch steps and sidled up to Brett.

"Hi," she said, glancing at Tara, "I'm Amy." She abruptly turned her attention to Ryan and imparted a winning smile.

Tara gave her a quick once over and admitted to herself that Amy could easily be Ryan's type. She had a perfect tan, with straight blonde hair that was tied back in a sporty ponytail. Her well-fitting Mariner's T-shirt was accompanied by a pair of denim shorts that barely covered her upper thighs. Out of the corner of her eye, she saw Amy give her a sideways glance – a glance which was both assessing and calculating.

"Adam couldn't make it?" Ryan asked, turning to Brett. He thought it strange that Amy would have shown up if her brother hadn't been able to come, but then again, it fit with his theory that Adam and Brett were trying to set the two of them up.

"No," Amy interjected with a smile. "He flew out of town this morning for a high school reunion. But he told me I should go ahead and come anyway."

With that, they all followed Brett inside the house and over to his gun rack, which was positioned just inside the living room. Tara's eye roamed over the outdated space, which reminded her of her deceased grandmother's house in Illinois. A brown shag carpet covered the floor, and the wood paneling and faded floral sofa both looked like they were from the seventies. The tan recliner adjacent to the sofa seemed to have arrived a decade later; it was positioned next to a red brick fireplace which was marred with stains from smoke and soot.

Tara shifted her gaze back to Ryan, watching the way his shoulder blades moved under his T-shirt as he reached for a rifle and lowered it from the rack. She took a step back as he handed it to her.

"Hold onto this one for me."

"Okay," she responded, not sure exactly how she was supposed to hold it. Out of the corner of her eye, she saw Amy give her a quick smirk.

"Here," Ryan grinned, "put your hand around the barrel, like this and hold it upright. Don't put your fingers near the trigger when you're carrying it."

"Right," she murmured, feeling embarrassed.

Brett removed two handguns and handed one to Amy before closing the case. Turning to Ryan, he said, "All set?"

"I think so," he replied. "You want to go over by the corral?"

Brett nodded. "I already got a table set up with some ammunition."

Tara and Amy followed the two men outside to the fold-out table, which was positioned next to a tall cottonwood tree. After carefully setting the gun down, Tara stared at the empty field in front of them, watching as a gentle breeze rifled through the tall blades of grass. Her gaze shifted to the large, rectangular board nailed to a distant tree near the back of the field. She eyed it nervously.

A moment later, Ryan came alongside her with a .22mm pistol in his hand. "We'll start with this," he said. "There's virtually no recoil."

She felt a quick flutter of nerves in her stomach, and her heart started to beat faster. She wasn't sure if it was due to her fear of guns or if it was because he was now standing close enough for her to feel the heat from his body.

He first pointed out the gun's features then showed her how to load it. "Before you pull the trigger," he explained," you have to cock it, like this."

She nodded as he handed it to her.

"Alright," he continued, keeping an eye on the gun as she took it. "Put both hands around the handle."

"Like this?" She had no idea where to place her fingers. She only knew that she preferred not to have any of them near the trigger.

"Not quite," he smiled. "Here, I'll show you." He stepped behind her then wrapped his arms loosely around her body. "You don't mind?"

"No," she said breathlessly, "I don't." She inhaled sharply as his chin gently grazed her check, and her concentration broke completely when she felt his hands close over hers. The light and heady scent of his cologne wafted over her, and she had to remind herself to breathe.

"Alright," he continued smoothly. "Grip it like this." He arranged her fingers, aligning her left index one along the side. "Good, keep it right there. You'll use your right to pull the trigger." He stepped away. "Okay, raise the gun to eye level and keep your arms straight. Don't bend your right elbow." He came alongside her again and adjusted her arms so that her right was completely extended while the left bent slightly at the elbow. "Good. Now, look through the sight and line it up with the target."

She squinted her left eye and saw what he meant. She adjusted her aim so the green dot at the end of the gun aligned with the bull's eye on the target board. She slowly exhaled and pulled the trigger. There was a small snapping sound, like that of a rubber band, then she lowered the gun.

"Sounds like you hit the board," he grinned. "Let's go take a look." After double checking that no one else was getting ready to shoot, he nudged her forward.

Breathless and with a glow of pleasure, she fell into step beside him, following him through the field and over to the tree.

He glanced at the board. "There it is."

She could see a small hole not far from the bull's eye. "Oh," she said surprised. "I didn't think it'd be that close."

He grinned and said, "That wasn't so bad, right?"

"It wasn't as intense as I imagined it would be." Feeling his arms around her was a different story. She followed him back to the corral where he had her fire off the remaining rounds.

For the next hour or so, everyone in the group took turns shooting the variety of guns, and before it was time for dinner, she had tried all the .22mm ones, which included two of the rifles. In the same amount of time, she had also learned three things regarding Ryan: the first being that he was almost a perfect shot, hitting the bull's eye dead center nine times out of ten. And it didn't matter which gun he used.

The second was that he did not seem to have any interest in Amy who, conversely, seemed quite taken with him. Tara had deduced this based partly on Amy's lukewarm attitude towards herself and partly by how often she'd caught her gazing in Ryan's direction. Furthermore, Amy seemed to make a point of excluding her in almost every conversation.

The third thing she learned was that Brett had assumed she was Ryan's girlfriend because Ryan couldn't take his eyes off her (according to Brett). The conversation in which she'd explained to Brett that she wasn't his girlfriend had thankfully taken place out of Ryan's earshot. When she'd asked Brett what had given him that impression to begin with, he'd laughed and made the comment about him not keeping his eyes off her. Then he'd pointed out that Ryan was acting a little possessive. These two pieces of information had caused her to glow inwardly, a state that she was finding difficult to hide.

She turned her attention back to the fold-out table and watched as Ryan and Brett began to put away the ammunition. After a second, she jumped lightly from her perch on the split rail fence where she'd been ruminating and walked the few feet to the table. "Anything I can help with?"

Ryan handed her three boxes of ammunition then she followed behind him as he headed for the farmhouse, two of the rifle bags slung casually over his shoulder and a cardboard box full of empty casings in his hand. She watched the way his body moved as he walked in front of her, his gait smooth and even. It was hard to look away, but she eventually shifted her eyes to the farmhouse.

A second later, Amy came alongside her. "So," she asked casually, "how long have you known Ryan?"

"Not that long," she responded vaguely. "We're just friends." She hoped that Ryan had overhead her. If she could make him believe that she wasn't attracted to him, perhaps she wouldn't be at risk for any future incidents of rejection. Additionally, she had vowed not to fall for him, which meant she needed to make it clear to him that she too "had no interest in pursuing anything."

It was nearing 8:30 by the time they stepped off Brett's front porch and walked over to the Audi. Ryan opened the passenger door for her then turned around to say a final goodbye to their host. Tara watched as Amy took a step towards Ryan and proceeded to give him a hug. The exchange was brief, and Tara thought she saw his back stiffen, an observation which caused her to smile satisfactorily. As he walked around the car, she fixed her attention on the tall oak in the middle of the yard where a half-dozen fireflies were flitting underneath it's leaves, twinkling on and off in the gathering darkness.

Ryan opened his door and eased himself into the driver's seat. After starting the engine, he extended his arm along the edge of her headrest and turned to look over his shoulder out the rear window. Tara's breath caught for a moment at the raw masculinity in the way he kept one hand on the wheel while twisting his body to look over his arm. He smoothly veered the car into an empty space behind them, then whipped the wheel back around and proceeded to drive forward down the long driveway. She leaned contentedly back in her seat, smiling to herself as she recalled the way his arms had felt around her when he'd shown her how to hold the gun. The memory caused her face to flush, and she was thankful for the darkness.

After a second, she turned her head slightly in his direction and said, "Thank you."

"Yeah?" he responded.

"Yes," she smiled, "I had a great time tonight. It was fun."

She blushed again, thinking about how many times she'd caught him staring at her. Brett had been right. And there'd been a brooding intensity to his gaze throughout the evening. A deliberateness. But then again, maybe she was reading into everything too much. After all, she'd been wrong before. And she'd learned the hard way that having a man attracted to her didn't mean a thing. For all she knew, he looked at her like a new toy to be played with and enjoyed, then quickly tossed aside when someone more interesting came along. Thus far, that pattern had defined every relationship she'd been in. She found it hard to imagine that it would be any different with Ryan.

35

When they arrived back at Eastcott, Ryan gave her a brief good night and headed to his room. Tara, on the other hand, wasn't tired yet so she decided to curl up on the living room couch with the work laptop that he'd assured her she could use whenever she wanted. After spending some time catching up on a few week's worth of news, she determined that she hadn't missed very much. Next, she looked up the cost of Amtrak tickets then researched a variety of different destinations. After a few minutes, she let out a sigh, unsure if she could really follow through with a plan. The last few days had afforded her with enough distractions to keep her mind occupied, but now that she was actually giving it some thought, she began to feel conflicted. Could she really run away and not feel guilty about deserting the other women at the complex? Because that's what she'd be doing. Deserting them. Especially the younger ones, the ones still in high school. Angry tears pricked her eyes, and she rubbed at the corners before they had a chance to spill over. Maybe leaving was the best way she could help, if she went to law enforcement with her story. But perhaps she needed more evidence? Her thoughts started to run together as she felt the claws of anxiety begin to clutch at her chest, squeezing tighter.

Her breaths were getting faster now, uneven and shallow. She gripped the arm of the sofa, digging her fingernails into the fabric. The memory of Ryan standing behind her, his hand covering hers as she held the gun, suddenly pierced through the wall of anxiety. She grounded herself in the memory, focusing on the scent of his cologne, forcing herself to remember the smell of it, clean and crisp, like fresh laundry mixed with a hint of pine. Slowly, she took another deep breath. Then another. And another. Everything would be alright, and she would figure something out. And if worse came to worst, she would simply tell him everything. She felt like she knew enough about him now to know, that at the very least, he would do what he could to help.

Feeling much calmer, she set the laptop aside and gazed through the wide windows at the twinkling city lights. The only noise amidst her solitude was what she could hear of the nightscape outside. She gazed at the looming skyscrapers for a few minutes then shifted her attention to the piano. She'd been longing to feel the polished keys beneath her fingertips, but the instrument was positioned too close to the windows for her comfort. The piano bench was only three or four feet away from the glass, and additionally, she didn't like that the window would be to her back if she took a seat.

She pushed herself off the sofa, her legs stiff from sitting. She eyed the piano again. Perhaps she could just stand near it. Feel the grain of the wood, look at the rows of taught strings lying beneath the raised lid. She took slow, measured steps in its direction. A moment later, she leaned her body against the solid instrument, feeling only partially satisfied at having reached her goal. Perhaps if she kept her hand on the curved wood of the rim, she might be able to slowly make her way to the front of it. She stood rooted in place for several minutes, struggling with herself as she gazed out the window, just a few feet from where she was standing. How was she supposed to be brave enough to attempt an escape when she couldn't even manage her fear of heights? Determined now, she made her decision. She would get close enough to the window to see down into the street below. After a quick look around to confirm that she was alone, she let go of the piano's edge and carefully sank to her knees. Slowly, she began to inch her way forward to the wide wall of glass. Her breathing became more rapid as she drew haltingly closer, and her heart, which was already pounding in her chest, felt like it might stop altogether. She paused and reached her hand out. The glass was about two feet away. She crawled forward another six inches then very slowly lifted her eyes from the floor. It wasn't as bad as she thought, and she had a partial view of the Space Needle. She stayed still for a few minutes, taking in the view. If she could get close enough to touch the glass, she'd count it as a win. She scooted forward another six inches, laughing to herself at how ridiculous she must look. She stopped again and reached her hand out, this time feeling the glass pane, solid against her fingertips. She closed her eyes and steadied her nerves, waiting until she felt ready before gradually inching forward another six inches. With her eyes still closed, she attempted to bring her heartbeat back to a normal rhythm by inhaling and exhaling slowly, a handful of times. Once her heart rate had calmed down, she slowly opened her eyes.

Her head began to spin as she cautiously peered out the window, feeling as if she were looking over the edge of a cliff.

Thousands of feet stretched between her body and the bustling street below her. It was terrifying. She kept her body completely motionless, barely breathing; only her eyes moved as they roamed over the panoramic scene. After watching the microscopic people and traffic for a few minutes, she shifted her gaze back to the Space Needle. A full moon hovered above it. She looked beyond the city, past the wharf and out over the sound where the light from the moon shimmered on the water. She imagined herself riding on one of the ferries, bound for the nearest island.

After what seemed like an age, she scooted her body backward until she felt a leg of the piano bench. Slowly, she began to inch her way up, keeping one hand on the bench for support. Once she was standing again, she kept her eyes on the piano keys. If she could focus all her attention on what was in front of her, perhaps she could forget about the towering skyscrapers behind her. She lowered herself on to the bench then cautiously scooted it toward the piano a few inches. There was a book of classical pieces resting on the music stand; it was dog-eared in a few places, and she peeked inside to find that it was enormously beyond her skill level. She could read a little music, but she mostly played by ear. After pondering for a moment, she decided to fall back on the song she knew best: "Gravity" by Sara Bareilles. She lifted her hands to the keys, and with a light touch, quietly awakened the beautiful instrument. She remembered the first few chords then had to resort to trial and error to jog her memory. Eventually, she began to hum the melody as her fingers continued to glide over the keys. She'd forgotten how good it felt to play. As she began the bridge, she looked up and suddenly realized she wasn't alone; Ryan was leaning against the end of the kitchen counter, watching her in the dim light. With a sharp inhale, she immediately lifted her hands off the keys.

"I'm sorry," she apologized quickly. She started to stand, pushing the bench out from under her as she did so, but she lost her balance and fell back onto the cushioned seat causing it to tilt precariously toward the window. She reached for the edge of the piano with one arm and desperately tried to steady the bench with the other. Just when she was on the verge of tipping over, she felt a strong hand on her back, pushing her forward. Her left elbow crashed on top of the piano keys as the bench lurched back into place with a loud screech.

"Are you alright?" Ryan asked, concerned.

The clashing tones of the piano reverberated throughout the room, shattering the monastic silence that had enveloped her.

"I'm fine," she replied. "Just a little startled." She could feel her face turning bright red as he took a seat next to her on the bench, which was just the right length to accommodate both of them.

"Let me see your arm," he said gently. "Sounds like you hit it pretty hard."

She extended the limb for his inspection. The side of his body was touching hers, and she could smell the freshly laundered scent of the shirt he'd changed into. A tingling sensation ran down her spine.

"It looks like you'll definitely have a bruise," he commented. "I feel bad. I think I overcompensated when I pushed you upright."

"It's okay," she responded quickly, withdrawing her arm. "How long were you standing there?" She could still feel herself blushing.

"Not long," he replied. "I didn't know you could play. You never said anything."

"I only play a little," she said, glancing at the keys.

"Did you teach yourself?"

"No, not exactly." Her memory flashed back to the first time Justin had sat next to her at the piano, patiently showing her how to play a short chord progression. "A previous boyfriend got me started. And then I began to pick it up a little here and there on my own. I can only play by ear though." Leaning slightly away from him, she inclined her head and said, "Karen told me that you play."

"I do," he responded. "My mom taught the three of us for a while, then I went on to take lessons with a more advanced instructor for several years."

There was another pause, a gentle lull between them. Out of the corner of her eye, she saw him hunch forward, resting his elbows on his knees, his feet planted wide. She could feel his gaze resting on her, and she suddenly felt self-conscious.

"I'm curious," he said, letting the words linger in the air for a moment. "Would you want to stay here longer with me? Not go back to Vancouver at the end of the week?"

She gave him a furtive glance, usure how to respond. "I wouldn't mind it, but I know Jai is expecting me back." Nervous energy coursed through her body as she felt his leg brush hers.

"Hmm." He rubbed his jawline idly. "Do you want to go back?"

After swimming in the deep end for a good response, she finally replied, "I'm kind of tied to the contract right now. I don't have much of a choice."

"I see," he responded grimly. He hesitated for a moment then continued, "Can I ask what made you want to work for Jai? Is it the appeal of the yacht?"

"I suppose, for the most part," she lied. Thinking quickly, she added, "And I was given the opportunity to dance." She needed to change the subject. Fast. She shifted her body slightly, turning so she had a better view of his face. "Speaking of dancing, you seemed curious earlier about why I left Berkley."

Ryan nodded slowly. "You don't have to go into it if you don't want to."

"It's alright," she replied, faking a smile. She really didn't want to, but she'd rather talk about that than anything having to do with Jai Kumar. "I think I told you earlier that it was mostly due to a bad breakup."

He nodded and she continued, "I met him in my freshman year. We had a music class together." She momentarily lifted her gaze to Ryan's jawline, which had a fresh five o'clock shadow, then resorted to staring idly at the piano keys as she continued, "He was the lead guitarist in a band and I was drawn to him, in a way I hadn't been to anyone else. I guess he kind of mesmerized me." She reached her arms behind her to the back of the bench, propping herself up.

"This is the same guy who taught you piano?"

She nodded. "We had an on-again, off-again relationship. He was gone a lot, touring. He dropped out of Berkley in the middle of my sophomore year to pursue a record deal." She rubbed her elbow, which was starting to hurt a little. "Anyway," she continued, "we officially ended things in the spring semester of my junior year, right before mid-terms." Her jaw hardened, and she did her best to keep the acidity out of her voice as she stated, "I caught him cheating." She followed this disclosure with a long exhale. "One of my friends showed me a sex video that he'd made with some woman, and I didn't handle it very well. He tried lying about it, but it's kind of hard to lie when you're caught on film." She laughed abruptly. "But that's the kind of person he was. He thought he could talk his way out of anything." Her throat suddenly felt dry. "You would think I would have been the one to call things off at that point, but I didn't. I wanted to forgive him, to work it out….to take him back like all the other times." Feeling the need to justify herself somewhat, she added, "I think I'd become very emotionally dependent on him. And he knew that about me; he knew he could manipulate me." She paused, trying to decide how much of the story she wanted to reveal. "The night we broke up wasn't pretty." She glanced vacantly at the page of music on the piano stand and took a shallow breath. "It ended up turning into a domestic dispute and the police were called." Wryly, she added, "Apparently, that's what it took for me to officially end the relationship."

"Did he hurt you?" Ryan asked, his voice deathly calm.

"Well, no….not really." She looked down at her hands. "I mean…" She gave Ryan a quick glance. His expression had considerably darkened, every facial muscle drawn taught. The anger that burned in his eyes caused her to quickly add, "I was fine, really. It wasn't that bad, and besides, it was my fault. I shouldn't have started an argument with him."

"That's not the point," he said through gritted teeth. "Was he arrested?"

"He was charged with a misdemeanor assault. 'Fear of harm' or something like that." She gave him another glance to see if his anger had dissipated. It had not. Moving on, she said, "I was stuck paying the rent and the bills. We'd moved in together a few months prior, against my parent's wishes." As an aside, she added, "My dad really didn't like him, but I didn't much care what he thought at the time – we had a strained relationship, to say the least." She took a breath then rushed on, "But anyway, after Justin was out of my life, I had a hard time adjusting. I just got overwhelmed by the void he'd left, and I...." she paused, searching for the right wording then concluded, "Both my parents thought it best that I take a break from school for a little while." She tilted her head to the side and shrugged her shoulders. "So that's pretty much the story there."

"I can relate," Ryan said, "to the needing-to-take-a-break part, anyway." He leaned forward and placed his elbow on the ledge above the piano keys so that his head was level with hers. "I decided to take some time off in my sophomore year."

"Really?" He didn't seem to be the type of person that took breaks.

"Yeah." He glanced at the floor then tilted his head toward her. "I was starting to get depressed. And what made it worse was that I couldn't figure out why." He paused, musing, then said, "Looking back, I suppose it makes sense. I was pursuing a law degree, which hadn't been my first choice." His shoulders slumped a little. "I only chose that track because I thought it would earn my dad's approval." As an aside, he added, "He was always comparing me to my best friend, who was also pursuing a law degree, and nothing I did seemed to be good enough. Except for maybe football."

"You played in college?" she asked, not surprised.

His face was shrouded in shadow and for the first time, Tara felt like she could look at him, without giving anything away.

With the faintest hint of a smirk, he replied. "Quarterback."

"Of course you were." She rolled her eyes. "I told you that you were good at everything."

He quickly laughed then added, "Well, not to my dad. I was constantly trying to live up to his expectations, and it was a lot of pressure." He paused, then said heavily, "I'd originally wanted to do something involving criminal justice."

"Really?" Her eyes widened in fascination; she most certainly hadn't expected him to say that.

"Yes," he nodded, giving her a quick glance. "You seem surprised."

"A little," she responded. "It's just seems so far from what you do now. What exactly did you want to do in that field?"

"There's a lot of options I could have pursued," he mused. "Crime scene investigation....detective work....forensics. Or criminal intelligence."

"You mean like the CIA?" Her jaw dropped a little.

He nodded, cocking his head to the side. "I could have chosen to be a special agent for any number of federal agencies, like the DEA or the FBI. I also considered local law enforcement." He ran his knuckles along his jawline, momentarily lost in thought, then said, "Anyway, to make my dad happy, I chose to pursue an English degree, with the intent to go on to law school after I graduated, but I couldn't handle both football and the academic rigor. I ended up failing two mid-terms. And then I sprained my ankle right around the same time, so I couldn't play." He hesitated then finished, "Things sort of spiraled."

Her eyes fluttered to his for a millisecond then she reverted to speaking to his chest. "How bad was the spiral?" she asked softly.

A moment of tense silence ensued then he cleared his throat and answered, "I'd have to say pretty bad. The depression made me lose my appetite, and I felt tired all the time. I remember basic things like walking felt hard. It was as if there was this weight constantly holding me down – I couldn't find joy in anything anymore." He ran his hand through his hair, disheveling it, then with a subtle laugh, said, "It's coming back to me. I remember that making simple decisions was almost impossible. Even taking a shower was hard. There was just no motivation behind anything. It was kind of like, what's the point?" He reinforced his rhetorical question with a shrug of his shoulders. "And not being able to be decisive about anything just put more pressure on me and made me feel guilty for doing nothing." He straightened his back for a second, stretching, then leaned forward. "I'm the type of person that always has to be doing something productive, so I wasn't okay with just sitting around watching TV or staying in bed all day. It was honestly the worst kind of feeling." He stared vacantly at his hands for a moment then said, "It felt like I had an endless black hole inside my chest, consuming me." He flicked his gaze to her and added, "Sometimes, I wake up with that feeling, and I have to remind myself that it's only a dream. That the feeling has no association with the present."

Instinctively, she leaned a little closer. "I don't have dreams about it, but I know exactly what feeling you're describing. I've felt that hole too when I've gone through depressive episodes."

"Yeah?" It was his turn to be surprised.

"Yes," she replied quietly. "I've had my own struggles with depression."

He glanced at her, idly stroking his jawline, then continued, "I started questioning the point of it all. My purpose in life. Everyone else around me seemed to have it all figured out."

She nodded, shifting her focus to his shoulder. "Did taking a break help?"

"Sort of," he answered. "Things got worse though before I got to the point of recognizing I needed some time to work it all out. The depression caused my girlfriend to break up with me. I had really pushed her away. Then the sprained ankle further exacerbated the situation since exercise was the one thing that had been helping me cope with the depression. Having to watch my teammates play from the sidelines didn't help." He kept his head down, staring vacantly at the floor.

"Did you try to... to...?" She didn't want to ask him outright, but there really wasn't a delicate way to ask someone if they tried to kill themselves.

"Commit suicide?" He laughed quietly. "No, but I thought about it. That's when I knew I needed help. I ended up seeing a therapist, and I took an anti-depressant for a while. Things gradually started to get better." He tilted his head toward her and continued, "It was a painful process. And of course, my dad didn't provide any support." In a brittle tone, he added, "I think he thought I was weak for not being able to handle everything on my own. He's never really wrapped his mind around the fact that not everything can be solved by sheer willpower. Or by praying harder.

She nodded, shifting her gaze back to the piano keys. "So the anti-depressant helped....and you've been alright since then?"

"Yeah, I'm good now, for the most part." He nudged her knee with his. "Your turn. How did you deal with your situation? Did the break from college help?"

"Sort of," she replied, trying to cover her unease with a laugh. A little shiver went through her at the touch of his knee. She really didn't want to disclose further details about what happened – it was too embarrassing. But now that there was this shared experience between them, maybe she could tell him just a little more. She felt like he would at least be understanding and non-judgmental; as to whether he would look at her the same was a different story. She couldn't be sure if it was his disarming smile or the genuinely attentive concern in his voice that compelled her to keep going. "I...I came close to a suicide attempt." She took a deep breath. "But I didn't do it. I got help at that point." That wasn't the embarrassing part of the story.

He nodded. "That must have been hard. Were you diagnosed with anything?"

This was the embarrassing part, the part she'd been trying to avoid telling. It took her a moment, but she quietly answered, "Yes."

After a long silence, she finally asked, "How much do you know about bipolar disorder?"

"Not much," he replied, giving her a sideways glance, "other than that it involves mood swings?"

"It's a little more dramatic than mood swings." She took a shallow breath then continued, "There's a pendulum ranging from depression, on the low end, to manic on the high end."

She hated that word. Manic. It was right up there with "insane" in her opinion.

"Finding the right combination of meds can be a long process," she continued. "If a normal anti-depressant is used to help with the depression, it can boost the mood too much, tipping the brain toward the more" – she hesitated – "energetic end. A mood stabilizer helps even things out, but it's still hard to treat the depression. Right now, there are only one or two anti-depressants on the market that are okay for people with bipolar. In my case, I was fortunate enough to find a good combination of meds without having to go through a lot of trial and error." She glanced at her hands. "I've been stable for a while now, and I feel pretty normal on most days."

There was a moment of silence, then he cautiously asked, "So when you say manic, what does that mean exactly?"

Dread pulled in the pit of her stomach as she tried to determine how best to describe it without having to reveal anything too personal. Or making it sound like she was crazy. "Well, first you feel really great, and you have all this energy. You don't need as much sleep and you're just busy doing all these things, multi-tasking. I could dance for six hours straight, without needing much of a break. I would forget to eat because I wasn't hungry. And then I could stay up until two in the morning studying. Do my laundry. Clean. Go for a run. And then do it all again the next day. It's the exact opposite of depression. You feel great about yourself, on top of the world. But clearly, that's not sustainable, and for people with severe bipolar, it can be dangerous. A prolonged period of not sleeping and eating properly can cause..." She really didn't want to say the word, but there was no way around it. "...psychosis." She nervously twirled a strand of hair around her finger and hurried on. "Hallucinations, etc. Anyway, you can have grandiose thinking, like you're the queen of England, or a movie star, or something like that." She laughed, trying to shrug off her inner embarrassment. "Clinicians also love using the term 'racing thoughts.'" She rolled her eyes. "I wish they would come up with better descriptions of the symptoms, so you don't sound like a crazy person when you try to explain it to someone. But anyway, that's about it in a nutshell."

"Well, it doesn't sound that crazy to me." He hesitated then asked, "Did you ever have a severe episode?"

Her body tensed, and for a second she was tempted to simply lie. It would be so much easier. She struggled with herself for another moment then slowly nodded and said, "It happened a week or so after Justin and I broke up. I suffered some memory loss after the episode, from the psychosis part of it, so my memories are very jumbled, but I know it happened after the break-up." She took a deep breath. "I was basically alone in my apartment for three or four days, without sleeping much or eating. I just remember having all this energy and feeling really good about life in general. Everything seemed perfect, even though it was far from it." There was no way she was going to tell him about all the online shopping she did for new clothes and other items she didn't need. Like a plane ticket to Paris that she had charged to a newly opened credit card. Or the fact that she'd decided to write a memoir and had spent hours on end just writing incoherent gibberish. Typical manic behavior. "I sort of experienced a small degree of psychosis." She bit her lower lip and rushed on, "I was posting a lot of random, weird stuff on social media. I basically had no filter." Swallowing, she continued, "It was really, really embarrassing later when I realized what had happened. And then of course I had to wade through all my posts, and actually read some of what I'd written so I could figure out what to delete. It was so humiliating." After a long exhale, she added, "But it was honestly the thing that also got me help. A friend saw what I was posting and came to check on me." She swallowed the lump in her throat, then with her eyes cast down, said, "She took me to the hospital."

She focused her attention on the piano pedals next to her feet, feeling long buried emotions stirring in her chest. He would never look at her the same after this, and the ensuing silence seemed to confirm it. She stole a quick glance in his direction, but his expression was blank. Maybe he just didn't know what to say? Wishing to break the silence, she continued, "I was hospitalized for a week, and that's when they told me I had bipolar. Type two. Apparently," she added dryly, "it's the more severe of the bipolars." It was getting harder now to force her emotions to stay put so she kept her eyes on the floor. "It took me a while to process what had happened." Tears began to form. *No,* she told herself. *You will not cry.* She breathed in and steadied her voice. "I've been on medication for a while now, and I'm fine. Everything's fine now."

She glanced at his chest, focusing on how white his T-shirt was. "I just learned that I ..." She hesitated briefly. "That I can't do relationships very well. Romantic relationships. I think my relationship with Justin was the catalyst that caused the

episode, and I'm afraid of that happening again with someone else. And I'm scared that the rush you get at the beginning of a relationship might boost my mood too high."
The tears were starting to come to the surface again, and
her throat felt tight and dry. "The whole thing with Justin
put me on an emotional roller coaster, and my brain chem-
istry just became imbalanced, I guess." *Yes, everything was
scientific and not her fault.* She shifted her gaze to the hem
of his shirt, and continued, "I don't know if I can handle
an actual relationship. I think I'd have to know it wouldn't
end badly." Ruefully, she added, "They seem to always come
to an end for me. It's just a matter of how bad it will be."
She hated that word - relationship. It represented shame
and humiliation. "And I have major trust issues too, as you
already know." She could feel the corners of her eyes becoming moist again. Clearing her throat, she added wryly,
"I'd be a lot of work. I don't think most men would consider
it to be an enjoyable pursuit."

She forced herself to smile, keeping her eyes on the piano
bench, but a small tear escaped and ran down the side of her
face. Blinking quickly, she swiftly brushed her hand across
her cheek then trailed her fingers through the hair draped
over her shoulder, hoping that the entire movement was
fluid enough to be interpreted as nervous fidgeting. "But I
guess that's just relationships in general. They all seem to
have their ups and downs."

Deciding that she'd talked enough about herself, she gave
him a quick glance and asked, "So, what about you?" She
hoped her tone sounded playful and not genuinely curious.
"You think you'll get married someday? Maybe start a family?"

She blushed, wishing she hadn't asked. "I mean, it's probably none of my business."

"No," he laughed quickly. "I don't have any plans at the moment, but I might want to start something serious with someone at some point in the future." He paused, staring at the music resting on the piano stand, then slowly turned his head towards her and quietly said, "It sounds like you've been through a lot." He leaned down so that his eyes were level with hers. "And Tara," he said, almost whispering, "any man would think you were well worth the pursuit."

Her heart beat faster when she heard him say her name, but she laughed weakly and responded, "Just any man but you." She'd meant it as a quip, but it came out sounding very different than it had in her head. She swiftly veered away from her remark and said, "Anyway, some people just know innately how to do things right the first time, like they were born with some inner compass that always points them in the right direction. And then there's people like me who seem to have to figure it all out as things happen to them."

He nodded. "It seems that way sometimes, from the outside. But I don't think any of us can say that we have everything perfectly figured out or that we have all the answers."

He paused for a few seconds, and this time, the silence didn't feel uncomfortable. Eventually, he added quietly, "I think the process of overcoming pain and loss is what helps to grow us into better human beings. It gives true depth to things like joy and love because we've known true suffering. It makes you appreciate the good times more than you would have otherwise." His body tensed, then he muttered, "Trust me, I know. I've had my share of heartache too when it comes to relationships."

"Forgive me, but it's hard for me to imagine you having relationship problems." She lifted her eyes to his face, preparing to give him a wry look, and found that his usual easy-going expression had vanished, replaced by a vacant shadow; the hollowness she saw behind his eyes drew her in.

He quickly looked away, glancing at the floor then turned back a split second later with a youthful grin on his face and no trace of the emptiness she could have sworn she'd just sensed. "I thought I was ready to settle down once," he said. "I really believed she was the one."

Great, she thought. Now he's going to talk about some amazing woman that she would never be able to compete with, even as a memory. "What happened?" she asked reluctantly, not sure if she really wanted to hear the story. It seemed unreasonable that she should suddenly be feeling jealous....and yet she was.

"It was a difficult relationship from the beginning," he responded. "We dated all through high school, but she broke it off in my senior year." He paused for a minute then added, "I don't think that relationship went as deep as I thought it had, even though it was painful." He inclined his head and lifted his eyes to meet hers. "I'm beginning to realize that my past relationships may have left me hurt, but I don't know if I can honestly say that my heart's ever been truly broken."

Tara ignored his gaze and glanced down at her hands. "Do you think she'll ever come back into your life?"

"No," he responded firmly. "She's happily married now, with a family." His voice trailed off and there was a long pause before he took a deep breath and stated flatly, "I got her pregnant."

"Oh," Tara responded, taken aback.

His shoulders slumped, and with his head lowered, he continued, "The conversation with my parents did not go well. They were very disappointed with me, to say the least. And I already felt enough shame over it." He glanced at her and added stiffly, "I think I mentioned that I grew up in a very religious family."

Tara nodded and said, "I'm sure that made it worse."

"It took a while to work through all the guilt later, as an adult."

"I'm guessing they expected you to 'do the right thing'?"

He nodded then said tonelessly, "I wanted to, and I would have, but she didn't want the relationship anymore." He shifted his weight slightly and added, "I don't know exactly what happened with the baby. She told me she had a miscarriage, but I don't really believe that." He brushed the memory away, ready to move on, and with a light laugh nudged her knee again. "What about you? Do you want a family someday?"

"Yes, I think so," she replied. "Someday. But I'll probably need to work through my fear of relationships first if I want to achieve that." She gave a little half-laugh. "It's not my main focus at the moment."

"You said you wanted to go back to Berkley the other day. To finish?"

"Yes," she nodded. "But I'm not sure I'll go back for dance. I might minor in it."

Tilting his head to the side, he asked, "What do you want to do instead?"

With some hesitation, she replied, "Lately I've been thinking I might want to be a counselor."

"Oh?" He raised an eyebrow, encouraging her to continue.

"Yes," she nodded. "I feel so much appreciation for the mental health profession in general, and then on a personal level for the help I've received. The therapists that I've met along my journey have impacted my life in so many ways, and I'm incredibly grateful. It makes me want to help others in the same way, I guess."

"I think you'd be a great therapist."

"You do?"

"Yes," he smiled, watching as her cheeks turned a delicate pink color. "You're a great listener. And you have this..." He paused, trying to put into words what he was feeling. "You have a way of drawing people in. I think there's something about you that makes people feel safe."

"Really?"

"Yes." He nodded, then with a quick laugh, added, "I've shared things with you that I've only talked about in therapy."

"Oh," she replied. "I wasn't prying too much, was I?"

"No, that's what I'm saying. There's just something about you that encourages people to share themselves with you. You don't have to pry." He smiled and added, "I think that's a rare gift."

"I guess so," she responded, her cheeks still flushed.

He watched as she gently bit her lower lip; his breath hitched, her mouth instantly becoming the subject of his deepest fascination.

"Well," she said, giving him a quick glance, "I should probably get ready for bed." She eased herself to a standing position, holding onto the piano for support.

He reluctantly slid off the piano bench so she could exit after him. As she stepped around him, her body briefly brushed against his, causing what little coherence he had left to vanish. A wave of desire hit him full on, heating him to his core.

He was certain she was oblivious as to her effect on him as she glanced over her shoulder, giving him a parting smile before heading down the hallway. He lingered on her retreating figure, mesmerized, then with a shake of his head, decided he needed a glass of water before going to bed. An ice-cold glass of water.

Once in her room, Tara picked up her phone and called Jai; since it went straight to voicemail, she left a brief message then set the phone on her nightstand. So far, she'd been religious about checking in with him nightly; sometimes he answered and sometimes he didn't, which she'd taken to mean he wasn't that concerned about her.

She headed for the bathroom where she went through the routine motions of brushing her teeth and washing her face. A few minutes later, she crawled under the covers, and after checking her phone one last time, flicked off the lamp. As she lay awake, waiting for her medication to make her drowsy, she thought through her conversation with Ryan, analyzing it from every angle. But the words that rose from her subconscious as she drifted off to sleep were from a different conversation.

"I have no intention of pursuing anything with you."

The phrase was starting to become her own twisted mantra, repeated internally when she needed to remind herself that this would never go anywhere. Tonight, he seemed to have let her see a side of him that he didn't share with many, but it didn't mean anything. It was a conversation and that was it, and she had shared way more than she had intended to.

36

While Tara fell into a fitful sleep, Ryan remained restless. He rolled over and adjusted his pillow for the hundredth time then closed his eyes again; however, after several minutes, he determined it was useless. He sat up and turned on his bedside lamp with the intention of jotting down his thoughts. He reached for a notepad on his nightstand then settled back under the covers. He'd only written a few sentences when a piercing scream emanated from down the hall. He dropped the pad, threw the covers aside, and quickly opened the drawer of the nightstand to retrieve the handgun he kept there. As he sprinted to the door, his immediate thought was that Jai had sent one of his men to fetch Tara. He proceeded down the hall with caution toward her room, but when she screamed again, he set aside his wariness. Thrusting her door open, he quickly scanned the room then lowered his gun when he saw that she was the only occupant. She was still asleep, but there was a pained expression on her face and her hands were fisted around the covers. She cried out again, and he quickly strode toward her, setting the gun on the dresser. When he attempted to wake her, she sat up and hit him hard in the chest with her fist.

"Reuben," she cried, continuing to jab at his chest. "Please. You...you have to...."

Her body shuddered then relaxed as he pulled her close and wrapped his arms around her. He waited a moment to see if she would continue talking, hoping that she might reveal something, but then realized she was crying.

He gently rubbed her back. "It's alright," he whispered. "It was just a dream."

She buried her face in his shoulder and continued to cry quietly. After a few minutes, he felt a tug on the sleeve of his T-shirt, and he glanced down; she was using it to dab at her eyes, which he didn't mind in the least. Once she'd finished, she slowly lifted her eyes to his.

"I...was I dreaming?" she asked, still clinging to his arm.

"Yes," he reassured her. "Are you alright?"

She began to shake uncontrollably, as if she were cold, and he started to rub her back again.

"Take some deep breaths," he said. He could feel the pulse of her heartbeat against his chest as he continued to hold her. Eventually, her heart rate returned to a normal rhythm, her breathing smooth and even once more. He glanced down and saw that her eyes were closed. Since she appeared to have fallen asleep, he began to carefully extricate his body from hers; however, she strengthened her grip on his forearm.

"Please," she said. There was a slight pause, then in a barely audible voice, she whispered, "Stay."

"Alright," he whispered back. "I'll stay."

Without letting go, he lowered her back to the mattress, then with one hand, pulled the blanket up, adjusting it so she was mostly covered. As he settled in next to her, he spotted her phone on the nightstand; he waited a moment then gingerly reached over her body, checking to make sure her eyes were shut before picking it up. It was a simple flip phone, and when he opened it, the screen provided only a handful of options. He checked her texts and found nothing. Next, he checked the call log which revealed that she had dialed one phone number in the evenings, every night that she'd been with him. There was no history before that. He was almost certain this was the object in the box that Jai had handed her just before they'd left the yacht. He placed the phone back on the nightstand then carefully eased his body next to hers. With one arm pinned beneath her, he wasn't quite sure where to place his free arm, other than around her waist, which was what he wanted to do; the other option was to simply roll over to the other side of the bed...which was what he should do. Momentarily putting off a decision, he closed his eyes and slowly breathed in the scent of her hair. It consisted of floral notes with hints of citrus, and it wafted over him like a breeze from a tropical garden. After two years of being single, it was excruciatingly satisfying to have a woman in his arms again. And not just any woman – her. He didn't want anyone else.

It was that realization that finally tipped the balance in favor of his doing the right thing. With one long exhale, he prepared to extricate himself and roll to the other side of the bed; however, she chose that exact moment to arch her back into him, pressing against his groin. His cock instantly hardened, and a quiet groan escaped him. He hesitated for a moment more then gave in to his longing, draping his free arm gently around her waist, pulling her close. As long as he stayed on top of the covers, all would be fine. And he would remain above the covers. Of that much he was sure.

37

She felt Ryan's body pressed against her back as he lay beside her, his hand running along the side of her thigh then over her hip, pulling up her T-shirt. He stopped when he reached her waistline, and she arched into him, communicating her need for him to continue. He pulled her closer, holding her for a moment before shifting his body so that she was on her back. He hovered above her, and of their own accord, her hips began to writhe beneath him, begging him. "Not yet," he said, his voice low and commanding. He held her in place with one hand then leaned down and kissed her, hard. As his lips moved against hers, he nudged her leg to the side. She moved her other leg, giving him free access. A moment later, she felt his erection against her inner thigh, then at her entrance, slowly rubbing against her underwear. She kissed him back, deepening the connection, and placed one hand on his chest, which was bare to her touch, as he continued to move against her, grinding. Finally, he yanked her underwear out of the way and entered her with one slow thrust. He pulled out again, waited a second, then thrust once more, deeper this time. She pressed her hand against his chest, feeling the strength of his body as he began to move –

Tara awoke suddenly, disoriented and with her heart pounding in her chest. It took her a moment to realize she'd been dreaming. However, the fact that she was wet was thoroughly grounded in reality, as was the excruciating urge to touch herself. Somehow, she sensed that she wasn't alone, and turning ever so slightly, she peered over her shoulder to see Ryan lying beside her, atop the covers and shirtless – a sight that only intensified her arousal. With a deep inhale, she forced herself to divert her thoughts in a different direction. Something had happened that had caused him to end up in her bed. She closed her eyes and pushed all thoughts of Ryan out of the way. Gradually, scattered fragments of her nightmare began to fill the void, but before she could fully recall the dream in its entirety, she remembered that Ryan had awakened her from it. She looked over her shoulder again, giving him another glance, and realized that she must have asked him to stay, as she was almost certain he wouldn't have otherwise; she might not know everything about him, but he had proven himself a gentleman in every interaction they'd had.

Not wishing to wake him, and not that desirous of leaving the comfort of his presence either, she decided to remain beneath the blanket, enjoying the warmth of his body and the feeling of his arm around her waist. She thought about their conversation the night before and went through it again in her mind, picking it apart. He'd been as equally vulnerable as she had, sharing parts of himself with her that she sensed most people didn't know about. And the fact that he'd been interested in criminal justice got her to thinking that it might not be such a bad idea to tell him the truth. She continued her musings for another few minutes then reluctantly scooted out from under the covers to sit on the edge of the bed. She twisted her body and glanced at Ryan, who had rolled onto his back. His hair was slightly disheveled, and she imagined what it might be like to run her fingers through it. Her eyes roamed over his exposed chest and abdominals, every muscle perfectly sculpted, then trailed downward to the band of his boxers. He began to stir, and with a surprising amount of alacrity, she jumped from the bed, feeling flushed.

Slowly, he sat up, propping up his torso with his elbow, and raked a hand through his hair. His eyes flicked to hers, then with a somewhat sheepish expression on his face, he simply said, "Hey."

She gave him what she hoped was a composed smile and replied, "Good morning."

"How're you feeling?" he asked, his facial expression transitioning to one of concern.

"Good," she responded weakly, averting her eyes from his bare chest. "Did you sleep alright?"

"Yeah, I did."

They were both silent for a moment, and she was certain they were thinking the same thought. "We didn't..." she slowly hedged in a questioning tone. She let her words linger, waiting for him to respond.

"No," he replied emphatically. "We didn't." He flashed her a quick smile then sat up straighter and asked, "What time is it?"

She reached for her phone on the bedside table and responded, "Almost 7:30."

With a groan, he fell back onto the pillow, lifting his forearm to his eyes to block out the soft sunlight.

Glancing at him, she half-laughed then said quietly, "Thanks for staying with me. You didn't have to."

He peeked at her from underneath his forearm. "You were pretty shaken up."

"I guess I must have been," she slowly acknowledged. "I honestly don't remember that much from last night." Suddenly curious, she asked, "How did you know I was having a dream?"

"I heard you scream."

"Oh." Her pulse quickened. "Did I say anything? Out loud?"

"No, not really," he responded, glancing at her. "Except for something about 'Reuben.'" He quirked an eyebrow.

She remained silent for half of a second, then simply said, "That's strange." Assuming a nonchalant air, she asked, "That was all?"

He nodded, sitting up again. "Can I ask who he is?"

"Reuben?" She gave him a puzzled look, stalling as she thought through a response.

"Yeah," he said, inclining his head. "I think you thought I was him."

"Oh?" She now wondered what exactly she had said.

"Yes," he repeated, glancing at her. In a tone that was more curious than probing, he asked, "Do you remember the dream?"

"Not, not really," she replied vaguely, pretending to muse. "And oddly, I don't believe I know anyone named Reuben." She swept her hair over her shoulder then flicked her eyes to his, daring him to challenge her.

Since it appeared that he just might, she quickly said, "I think I'll take a shower."

He studied her for the briefest of moments, then slowly nodded and rose from the bed.

She walked toward the bathroom then stopped when she saw the gun on the dresser. She glanced at him. "Why is this here?"

"It was instinct," he replied, throwing on his T-shirt, "when I heard you scream." He casually retrieved it from the dresser then said, "See you for breakfast?"

She nodded, feeling suddenly turned on by the site of him standing in her doorway with a gun in his hand.

"I shouldn't be too long," she added quickly, turning towards the bathroom.

As she lathered shampoo through her hair, she tried not to dwell on the nightmare, which she did in fact remember in detail. She shuddered and tried to push away the all-to-real memories that the dream had invoked. *Don't think about it, don't think about it, don't think about it.*

When she was finished with her shower, she joined Ryan in the kitchen, giving him a brief hello as she headed toward the refrigerator for a carton of eggs.

"You want some coffee?" he asked, reaching for a mug. She was wearing a patterned blouse with a slim, navy skirt; he could still feel the shape of her body against his.

"Yes, thanks." She placed the eggs on the counter. "Do you mind handing me a bowl?"

He opened the cabinet again and handed one to her. "Want a bagel?"

"Sure," she smiled.

Roughly ten minutes later, they both made their way to the breakfast nook and set their plates down.

"I have a conference call in about twenty minutes," he said, taking a sip of his coffee. He wasn't sure how long his call with Agent Mitchell would take, so he added, "I can come find you when I'm finished. I was also thinking we might mix things up a bit today. Do a self-defense session first, then work."

"Alright," she nodded. She took a bite of her bagel, chewing it slowly, then asked, "Is Karen here today?"

"Yes," he replied, taking a quick sip of coffee. "I told her we'd make our own breakfast, and she decided to go grocery shopping. That's usually what she does on Thursdays, after breakfast." He took another sip of coffee, knowing exactly where Karen was, and it was not grocery shopping; she'd texted him earlier to let him know that she was picking up Tara's dress and was just waiting for it to be boxed up before heading back. He figured he could keep Tara occupied with the self-defense lesson to give Karen a chance to slip the box inside his office, unseen. As to how he would present the gift to her, he wasn't quite sure yet.

Finishing his bagel, he glanced at his phone and said, "I should probably head to my office for the call."

"Okay," she replied. "I'll change into some workout clothes and meet you in the studio."

He nodded, taking his plate to the sink, then headed for his office, coffee in hand.

A moment later, he took a seat at his desk, set his mug down, and picked up his cellphone. He didn't actually have a scheduled call with Mitchell, but he felt he should provide him with an update; more importantly, he wanted to know what the plan was for the following morning.

His call was answered quickly, and after a brief greeting, Ryan said, "I'm planning to talk with Tara tonight. How much should I reveal regarding the investigation?"

"You can tell her about your role, and how you're assisting," Mitchell responded. "But don't share any details until I've had a chance to interview her."

"Right," he replied. "And what do we do about tomorrow? I haven't heard anything yet from Kumar's people about logistical details. I'm guessing I'll be getting a call sometime today."

"Good," Mitchel responded vaguely. "Let me know when you get the call."

There was a long pause then Ryan said, "Please tell me that giving her back to Jai is out of the question."

The agent's silence continued for a moment longer than Ryan would have liked.

Finally, Mitchell replied, "The task force has been discussing several options. One of them involves both you and Tara going aboard the yacht in Vancouver, as Jai is expecting, to gather more intel. Of course, that plan depends on what Tara can tell us beforehand about Kumar and his operation. And obviously, we would never force her to return, but the more information we have, the stronger a case we'll be able to build for prosecution."

"I don't like the idea of her going back," he responded heatedly, "even if I'm there with her. The situation's too volatile."

"You might not like it, but it's not your choice to make. It will be up to her. Besides, have you thought about how Kumar will react if she doesn't show up with you?"

"I'll just tell him that she left, of her own accord and that I wasn't aware." He'd thought through the scenario ahead of the call, and he hoped he could make it sound convincing. "I can tell him that she told me her intention was to return to the yacht. He can hold me liable, and I'll pay him whatever – "

"This isn't about money to him," Mitchell cut in. "He wants to exert power and control over these women, and he's not going to part with any of them without a struggle, I can guarantee it. And I doubt he'll entrust you with Tara, or any of the other women in the future, if you show up without her. I'd be willing to bet your membership would end abruptly."

Ryan had no immediate response to that. He sighed then said, "You're probably right."

"This is a tough situation to navigate, and I appreciate what you've been able to do so far. With that said, you need to keep in mind that you're a non-agent helping us with an investigation, and I need you to follow whatever plan is decided upon by the task force. Do I have your word on that?"

He ran a hand through his hair. "Fine. Yes."

"Good." There was a moment of silence then Mitchell asked, "Does Tara have a phone? A way for Jai to keep tabs on her?"

"Yes. I actually had a chance to look at it last night. She's been dialing the same number every night since she's been with me. There aren't any other numbers saved in the phone. And I remember that Jai handed her a small box just before we left the yacht – I'm guessing it was the phone."

"Perfect. Do you have the number?"

"Yeah, I memorized it." He waited while Mitchell found something to write with, then dictated it.

"No texts?" the agent asked a moment later.

"No, just the calls," he replied. "No voicemails either."

"Okay, I'll get a trap and trace on it. How long were the calls?"

"Very brief. The first one was only a minute or so, and that was the longest duration. It looks like some of them might have gone unanswered."

"And she's just called once a day?"

"Yeah, at night. Looks like she's been checking in with him, or whoever the number belongs to, before she goes to bed."

"Okay. Going back to last night, you mentioned Tara had a dream involving someone named Reuben?"

"Yeah, she denied knowing him, but I think there's something there – she was a little too worried about what she'd said while she was dreaming, but then she shrugged the whole thing off as if it had no significance." He paused then added, "As to whether the dream has anything to do with what she's experienced in recent months, I have no idea."

A moment of silence ensued then Ryan asked, "How's the investigation going? Anything new?"

"Yes," Mitchell replied. "We were able to track the yacht to both complexes."

"Both?" His pulse quickened with a surge of elation.

"Yes, the yacht went to Complex One Sunday night, after the clients disembarked, and stayed there for a few days. We got satellite images of the area, and the location matches what Kristen described – wooded, with an estate and expansive grounds. From the outside, it looks to be a private residence. We set up surveillance on Tuesday." He paused then continued, "The yacht left yesterday morning and headed north towards Vancouver. It stopped just short of the Canadian border and docked at what we think is Complex Two. That's the yacht's current location, and the locale is similar to that of the other complex – remote, with a lot of acreage. Nothing around for miles." He paused again, then added, "This place seems more like a small resort though than a private residence, from the satellite images. There's a three-story building that looks like a hotel of some sort. And they have a helicopter pad."

"Interesting," Ryan replied slowly, dragging out the word. "You have surveillance there too?"

"We're setting it up later tonight."

With a long exhale of relief, Ryan sat down in his chair and asked, "So what comes next? I get on the yacht tomorrow with Tara and then what happens?"

"We first need whatever information Tara can provide," Mitchell replied, "before we can decide on the best plan."

"Right." He would simply have to convince Tara not to go back on the yacht before she talked with any of the agents, providing that she was willing to talk at all. Frowning, he reached for a scrap piece of paper on his desk, crumpled it in his fist, and aggressively tossed it into the small trashcan by his desk. "Anything else?"

"Call me with details when you hear from Jai. And call me after you've talked with Tara tonight."

"Got it."

He ended the call then placed the burner phone back in its hiding place. Feeling the full weight of his mission, he strode towards the studio where he found Tara ready and waiting, the mats already interlocked together.

"Looks like you're eager to get started," he said, grinning.

"Well I just thought I would save us some time," she replied coyly, giving her head a little toss.

Finding himself just as eager to teach as she was to learn, he commenced the lesson and for the next hour demonstrated a handful of new maneuvers until he was satisfied she had them down; he then led her through various combinations that mixed the new moves with the ones she'd already learned over the course of the week. They practiced for another half hour before he decided she'd had enough.

Stepping off the mat, he threw her a quick glance and remarked, "You've come a long way in one week."

"Thanks." She brushed away some wisps of hair from her face then used the sleeve of her T-shirt to wipe the sweat from her forehead.

Ryan caught a glimpse of skin as her shirt rose above her midriff.

"I'm going to take a shower," he said. "Meet me in the office when you're ready?"

She nodded, giving him a smile.

38

As she didn't realize she'd be so sweaty from their session, Tara was forced to take her second shower of the day. She twisted her hair into a bun, ensuring it would stay dry, then quickly rinsed off. When she stepped out of the bathroom a few minutes later, she ignored the navy skirt and blouse that she'd left lying on the bed. Wishing to wear an outfit that Ryan hadn't seen her in yet, she chose a simple, forest green dress that fell just below her knees. It was sleeveless, but the straps were wide, giving it more of a professional look, and it reminded her of one that Audrey Hepburn had worn. After selecting a pair of nude heels, she left her room and headed down the hallway. A few minutes later, she rapped a knuckle on Ryan's open office door, announcing her entrance.

He glanced up, his gaze lingering on her for a moment before he motioned her inside.

She took her seat at her desk, and asked, "What do you need me to do today?"

"Can you read through some reports for me?"

"Of course," she replied, opening her laptop.

"You don't have to read them in detail," he explained. "I just need you to glean enough information to know which file they pertain to."

Tara took the stack of reports he handed her and began the task.

After an hour or so, and needing a break from his own project, Ryan slouched back in his seat, folding his hands behind his neck. He slowly rocked his chair with one foot, studying her for a moment, then said, "I have a meeting at 3:30 at my office. The building's not far from here, and I should be done by 4:30 or so." He glanced at her. "Any thoughts on what we should do when I return?"

She quirked an eyebrow. "Do you have something in mind?"

"Perhaps," he grinned. "That is, if you want to go to a boring fundraising gala tonight."

"A gala?" she responded, inclining her head. "That could be fun." She glanced at her computer screen for a moment, then arching her eyebrows, gave him a coy smile and added, "Unfortunately, I don't have a date."

His brows furrowed in mock perplexment. "That is a problem." The corner of his mouth twitched as he flicked his eyes in her direction.

"And," she continued, assuming a prim air, "I don't believe I have a suitable dress."

"That part is easily solved," he replied, doing his best to keep his expression neutral.

"Oh?" Her eyes widened with curiosity.

He broke into a boyish grin, then swiveled in his chair to reach around his desk. A moment later, he handed her a large rectangular box wrapped in pure white. A cream-colored ribbon encircled the box, with the ends meeting on top to form a giant, intricate bow.

She took it, her eyes flitting to his, and warily asked, "What's this?"

"Open it," he said, hunching forward and giving her an encouraging smile.

She fingered the ends of the ribbon. "This is from you?"

"Partly," he replied. "Karen did most of the work."

She slowly unwrapped the bow and opened the lid. Midnight-blue chiffon fabric tumbled over the edges of the box, unfurling and falling in wispy billows all the way to the floor. Tiny sequins embedded in the skirt's folds glittered as they caught the light, and an intricate belt, studded with two sapphire gems in the front, circled the waistline. The velvet bodice parted in two as it neared the chest area, forming a V-shaped split designed to expose skin while still covering each breast, like two molded petals.

"Do you like it?" he asked anxiously.

She met his gaze, her eyes glassy. "I think this is the most beautiful thing anyone's ever given me."

"It suits you," was all he could manage as she held it up to her. Clearing his throat, he added. "Now we just need a solution as to your date." He casually rocked back and forth in his chair then, with a straight face, said, "I'm sure Brett is free."

She stared at him, blank-faced, trying to determine if he was joking. Slowly, she said, "Is Amy coming?"

"Amy?" He stopped his chair mid-rock, his expression puzzled. "I hope not. You know I was joking right?"

"Well..." she trailed off with a little laugh. "I thought so, but you looked so serious."

"To be quite honest, I'm not sure if I could let anyone else take you." He glanced at her, straightening in his chair. "You do want to go, though? You don't have to if you don't want to." The deep blue of the dress looked stunning against her flawless skin as she continued to hold it in her arms, and he very much hoped she would say yes.

"I would love to go," she replied, smiling. With a little hesitation, she added, "As long as I'm going with you."

"Of course," he replied, giving her a reassuring nod. He rose from his chair and walked toward her. "I would consider myself to be quite fortunate if you accompany me." He stooped to pick up the large empty box, which had fallen to the floor near her feet, then set it on top of her desk. He took a step back, letting his hand fall to his side. "I'll have to keep my eye on you tonight...make sure no one steals you away." He watched as her cheeks flushed pink then stated, "I'll pick you up at five, Miss Hayes."

39

Tara stood in the middle of her enormous walk-in closet and glanced in the mirror, once more checking her hairstyle for the evening. She had decided to straighten it, then curl it loosely so it fell in soft waves; she'd then taken a side section and pulled it to the top of her head, in line with her ear, holding it in place with a jeweled clip. The style had a touch of 1940's glamour, reminiscent of Veronica Lake's signature look, with a part on the side instead of the middle so that the hair fell across one eye as it trailed downward. For make-up, she'd gone heavy on the mascara but had otherwise kept it minimal, with a neutral eye shadow and some light blush.

Stepping into her gown, she pulled it up to her chest, holding it in place while she reached around for the zipper, which didn't require assistance as it only went halfway up her back. She then turned to gaze at her reflection once more in the full-length mirror, running her hand over the chiffon folds of her dress. This must be what prom is like, she thought, as she quickly twirled around. She'd been sick with the flu for her junior one, and then the following year the only guy she was attracted to had asked her best friend to go with him. She'd made up an excuse not to attend.

Satisfied with her appearance, she turned away from the mirror and walked over to the vanity. A square velvet box, along with an unopened note, had been placed on top of it; next to the box, were a pair of heels that she guessed had been purchased to go with the dress. Her eye had been drawn immediately to the items when she'd first stepped into the closet, but she'd decided to wait until now to open the envelope. She broke the seal and pulled out a simple, ivory-colored card with black handwriting on the front of it.

I know you don't mind walking around barefoot in evening wear, but I figured you'd at least like to start the night with shoes on. I'll gladly carry these for you if they start to hurt your feet.

She stared at the note and tears welled in her eyes as she thought back to the night she'd met Ryan on the yacht. It had only been a week ago, but it felt like months had passed since then. And in that time, he'd been nothing but thoughtful, considerate, and kind. He was also intelligent, with a sense of humor. And of course, he was physically attractive. Why did he have to be all those things? She didn't want to like him. And why was he doing all this for her? None of the men she'd met up to this point had ever been this kind to her without expecting something in return. She quickly brushed away angry tears with the back of her hand.

"Tara?"

Karen's voice, followed by a light rap on the open door, interrupted her thoughts. She hastily wiped away her tears before turning around with a bright smile on her face. Avoiding direct eye contact, she nodded for Karen to enter.

"I put some fresh towels in your bathroom." Karen paused to give Tara a quick look-over then, satisfied, said, "It looks perfect on you."

"Thanks," she replied, making sure to keep her voice steady.

Karen tilted her head. "Your mascara's a little smudged."

Darting to the mirror, she saw with dismay that it was obvious she'd been crying.

"I'll get you a wet washcloth," Karen responded, stepping out of the closet.

Tara rubbed at the skin under her eyes, trying to wipe away the smudges with her fingertip.

A few minutes later, Karen reappeared with the wash-cloth. As she handed it to Tara, she said, "I don't want to pry, but is everything alright?"

Fresh tears pooled in the corners of her eyes at the motherly concern in Karen's tone. It reminded her of her own mother, and her eyes began to sting as she struggled to keep the tears from spilling over.

"Yes," she answered, her voice quivering despite her best efforts. One tear escaped and slid down her cheek. "Yes... and no." She brushed away more tears. "It's just that..." she trailed off, unable to put her thoughts into words. How could she even begin to explain the situation she was dealing with?

Karen's eyes narrowed suspiciously, and she asked, "Did he do something?"

Despite her tears, Tara couldn't help but laugh at the bristle in Karen's tone. "You mean Ryan? No, he hasn't done anything, at least not intentionally." A fresh wave of emotion rolled over her. "I don't know." She suddenly felt drained. "I need to sit down." She gathered up the folds of her dress and lowered herself to the carpeted floor.

Karen closed the closet door behind her then slowly eased herself downward, her knees creaking as she stooped.

"Oh," Tara exclaimed, "you really don't have to..."

"Nonsense." Karen cut her off with a wave of her hand, then using the door for support, continued to lower herself toward the floor. Once she was comfortably situated, she leaned her back against the door and said, "So, what has he done?"

Tara dabbed at her eyes with the washcloth. "He hasn't done anything, per se, and maybe that's the problem." She'd been hoping he'd do or say something to indicate that he wanted more than just a friendship. "I think I..." she looked down at her hands. "I think I like him." She wiped away another tear with her fingertip. "And I don't want to."

Karen merely nodded, waiting for her to continue.

Tara didn't want to admit her feelings out loud, but her need to talk outweighed her desire to suppress so she reluctantly asked, "Is it obvious?" Her forehead creased as she raised her eyebrows in concern.

"I can't really say," Karen responded, "but I don't think you have anything to worry about. He's clearly attracted to you."

Tara dabbed at her eyes again. "But do you think he's more than just attracted to me?" She swallowed, and added, "I'm so tired of guys simply liking me for my looks. That's not what I want." She cleared her throat, fighting to keep the tears at bay, and continued, "The initial attraction is the easy part, but somehow it always seems to fade – like they could take me or leave me." She continued to stare at her hands. "Whatever spark was there, it's like I did something to put it out." A shudder swept over her body, and she folded her arms across her stomach.

Karen scooted towards her. "Whatever's happened in your past, Tara, it is *not* because you did something wrong." She gave her arm a quick pat.

Tara glanced at her. "I don't know about that. I trust too easily. And I allow myself to be taken advantage of."

"Most women do," Karen said, her voice reassuring. "It's sad that there's men out there who are not deserving of our trust – along with our time and attention – but that's how it is, unfortunately. It just takes experience to see through the bad ones."

She nodded, fingering the chiffon fabric of her dress. "I think I've had so many negative experiences that I've come to believe they're all bad."

"Well," Karen replied, giving her a smile, "I can assure you that's not the case – Ryan's a good man. And," she added wryly, leaning towards her, "he's available."

Despite her mixed feelings, Tara couldn't help but laugh. She tucked a strand of hair behind her ear then asked, "Have you known him long?"

"Yes," Karen smiled. "His family moved into our neighborhood years ago, and my husband and I have been close with them ever since." As an aside, she added, "Bob and I never had any children of our own, and over time, we developed good relationships with all three of the kids as they grew up. They've all turned out quite well, if you ask me."

Tara continued to stare down at her lap for a moment, still holding the washcloth in her hand, then she gave Karen a sideways glance. "You really think he might be interested in me?"

"I can't say for sure, but I think he's just being cautious and taking his time. He's always been intentional about relationships, and I know he wouldn't start something unless he was ready to completely devote himself. He's not the type to date someone just for the sake of dating."

"Really?" Tara tried to assimilate this new information with what she knew about him so far. It seemed incongruous, especially given where she'd met him. She began to wonder just how much Karen really knew about the man she worked for.

They lapsed into silence for a moment then Karen said, "I want to tell you something my mother told me. She repeated it often to me and my sisters growing up." She shifted her weight, stretching her legs out in front of her and flexing her feet. "Ah, that's better." She settled her shoulders against the door, folding her thin, bony hands in her lap. "When I was a teenager," she began, "we lived way out in the country, about a half hour from the nearest town. All the boys were crazy about us." She sighed happily, eliciting a quick laugh from Tara, before she continued, "But then there was my father. He was the size of a bear and just as intimidating. He had that John Wayne type of personality. Quiet, but strong. Didn't waste words." She crossed her ankles. "Mind you, it was a small town. The pickings were slim, and we were always afraid my father would scare them off before they even had a chance. So when we did get a 'suitor' courageous enough to ask one of us out on a date, we didn't want to be an inconvenience by asking to be picked up at our house, especially since they'd already overcome one obstacle."

Tara laughed again, pressing the damp washcloth against her cheek.

Karen continued, "The temptation for any one of us girls would be to jump in my father's pickup and drive the twenty miles into town to meet the young man." She shook her head, laughing, then cleared her throat and continued, "But here's what my mother would say, and she always said it very slow, so that each word had weight to it. She'd say, 'Girls, you are worth the drive; if they aren't willing to make the drive out here, then they're not worthy of you'." Karen patted her on the hand and said, "Tara, you are worth the drive. Don't ever forget that."

Fresh tears gathered at the corners of her eyes, and she couldn't prevent a few from spilling over. She glanced up at Karen, no longer embarrassed by her display of emotion. "Thank you," she whispered. "I'll remember that."

"And you know," Karen added dryly, "I'm pretty sure that man out there," she rapped her knuckle against the back of the closet door, "would drive any distance to pick you up for a date."

"Maybe," Tara replied quietly. "But tonight isn't a date. I'm just his plus-one."

"Well," Karen smiled, "give it time." She slowly pushed herself up off the floor, muttering something under her breath that sounded something like "don't know what's taking him so long."

Tara felt a gentle warmth settle over her, feeling hopeful for the first time in a while that something good might lie in the path ahead of her. Slowly, she began to lift herself up off the floor, allowing Karen to assist by holding the wispy, chiffon billows of her dress so she didn't step on them as she rose.

"Alright, Cinderella," Karen said, releasing the folds of fabric. "I don't want to make you late for the ball."

Tara laughed weakly as she followed her out of the closet.

Before leaving, Karen turned and said, "I don't think you have my number." She removed a sticky note from her apron pocket and handed it to her. "I keep forgetting to give this to you. Feel free to call anytime, alright?"

Tara placed the note on top of her dresser. "Thank you."

With a brief nod, Karen walked to the door.

"Wait a minute," Tara softly called after her.

She paused, one hand on the doorknob, and looked over her shoulder.

"I just wanted to say thanks for everything you've done to make me feel at home here....and for understanding. And," she added, "especially for this." She lifted one of the chiffon edges of her dress, holding it out in front of her. "It's beautiful."

Karen merely smiled. "Have fun tonight."

"I will." She thought quickly then added, "I probably won't be here for too much longer." *How was she supposed to say goodbye?* She swallowed then slowly said, "In case I don't see you before I leave..."

Karen nodded and replied, "You have my number."

40

Leaving Tara to herself so she could get ready for the gala, Ryan departed for his 3:30 meeting. As he exited the lobby, his phone rang, and he glanced at the number. The caller ID was blocked. He was doubtful it was Mitchell, since all of their conversations had been facilitated through the burner phone.

He picked up the call with a good idea of who it might be, and a moment later his hunch was confirmed. Kumar's voice was hard to mistake: deep and resonant, with a seductive, unassuming lilt that belied a restrained sense of stealth.

"Good afternoon, Ryan. I trust all is well?"

"Yes," he responded, continuing down the sidewalk. "Tara and I have had an enjoyable week together."

"I'm delighted to hear that," Jai replied. "We look forward to having you back on the yacht tomorrow."

"I was planning on calling you tonight to get details," Ryan responded. "We're to meet you in Vancouver, correct?'

"Yes. I'll send a chauffeur to your residence to pick you both up at noon tomorrow."

"Perfect," he stated, making a mental note of the time.

"It's settled then. Enjoy the rest of your day, Mr. Harker."

The call ended, and he glanced at the time. If he hurried, he could give Mitchell a quick update before his meeting. He strode back through the lobby, entered the elevator, and returned to his unit so he could call Mitchell on the burner phone. Neither Karen nor Tara were in sight, and he walked uninterrupted to his office to provide the update. After reassuring Mitchell once more that he would call immediately after his talk with Tara later that night, Ryan hung up and headed back down to the lobby, anxious to get to his meeting.

When he reached his office building fifteen minutes later, he hurried past the reception desk, only slowing his gait to glance at the clock on the wall as he approached the elevators. He was right on time. With a satisfactory smile, he hit the up button.

Before heading into the meeting, he stopped by Anna's office.

"Is everyone here?" he asked, poking his head through the doorway.

She glanced up from her computer screen. "Not yet. We're still waiting on Mr. Romero."

"Alright," he nodded. "Just send him in when he arrives."

Although he was keen to get back to Tara, he managed to keep his thoughts on the meeting and not elsewhere as he gave the board members the latest update regarding the rainwater project. When he was finished, he listened as each one provided input, causing the meeting to drag out a little longer than he wished; however, since everyone was pleased with the progress being made, he really couldn't complain, and upon the meeting's conclusion, he breathed a sigh of relief. Before leaving, he stopped in with Anna for a brief rundown of the week then headed back to Eastcott.

When he arrived, he went straight to his room where he found Karen laying out his tuxedo for him. She waited outside his closet while he donned it then helped him with the cufflinks and bowtie.

"There," she said, giving the black bowtie one final adjustment. She took a step back and nodded approvingly.

"Thanks." He glanced at his watch and saw that it was almost five. "Feel free to go home once we've left," he said with a smile.

Karen nodded, walking toward the door. "I hope you both have a good time." She gave him a pointed look before exiting his room.

Not bothering to reflect on whatever Karen had just meant to impress upon him, he grabbed his phone and stepped into the hall. Everything will be fine, he thought. Tara can handle the truth. However, he still had no idea what he would say. How was he supposed to explain to her that his purposefully established playboy reputation was only a front? That pretending to be something he wasn't had been the only means for him to get to her. With a sigh and a shake of his head, he closed the bedroom door behind him, hoping that the words would come to him at some point during the evening.

When he reached Tara's door, he paused, then gave it a light rap.

She opened it a moment later, smiling breathlessly. "I'm almost ready. I just need to grab my purse."

He lounged in the doorway, spanning his arms across the opening and leaning his body slightly forward through the frame. As she turned back around, purse in hand, he admired her openly for several seconds, speechless.

"Thank you," she responded playfully. "You look nice too." She flashed him a head-turning smile as she ducked under his arm and stepped into the hallway.

Grinning, he spun around and followed her, lengthening his stride to catch up to her. "I hope you're not planning on being this elusive when we arrive."

"I am allowed to leave your side, aren't I?" she quipped lightly, glancing over her shoulder at him.

"I'll let you go where you like as long as you don't leave my line of sight."

The edge in Ryan's voice caused Tara to wonder if he was half-serious. "That seems like something a parent would tell their child at an amusement park."

"Or a zoo. Which is what this will be like."

They stepped into the elevator, and he hit the button for the lobby. Once they were moving, he gave her a sideways glance. "You really do look beautiful, you know."

The huskiness in his voice, and the hooded look he gave her, caused her mind to go momentarily blank.

"Thank you," she managed, giving him a glance. "You look quite sharp yourself." And he very much did, in his sleek black tuxedo, with a pair of silver, initialed cufflinks peeking out from the edges of his jacket sleeves. His five o'clock shadow was meticulously trimmed, and it looked like he'd had a fresh haircut. Her eyes were drawn to his hands, which were smooth and masculine, with large knuckles and long fingers. She quickly shifted her gaze to the passing floor numbers illuminated above the elevator doors before her thoughts wandered to what he could do with them.

A few minutes later, they emerged and entered the parking garage where Ryan retrieved his Bugatti. He lent Tara his arm as she folded herself into her seat, ensuring her dress was completely inside before he closed her door.

The street was quiet as he exited the garage and pulled out onto the road; traffic became heavier, however, when he turned down Union Street a few minutes later, and he took his time merging into the flow of traffic.

Eventually, he leaned towards the dash and tapped a few times on the touchscreen. "Music?" he asked, giving her a quick glance.

"Sure," she replied absently, absorbed with watching the downtown scenery as it flew by.

Keeping one eye on the road, he quickly scrolled through the playlists until he reached the one he wanted.

She was still captivated by the scenery when Norah Jones's "Come Away With Me" began to play. Her eyes darted to his. It was the song she'd chosen when they had waltzed together.

"I thought that might get your attention," he smirked, glancing at her before returning his focus to the road.

Midway through the third song, Tara turned her head ever so slightly in Ryan's direction, peering at him from the corner of her eye. He seemed to be lost in thought, one hand mindlessly on the steering wheel, and she would have given almost anything to know what was running through his head.

Suddenly, his eyes shifted from the road to her, as if a sixth sense had informed him that she was watching him. He started to grin, and she quickly looked down at her hands then out the window, feeling herself blush. What was happening between them?

For one moment, she imagined what it would be like to be in a legitimate relationship with him – to have a commitment that went beyond mere words. He'd told her that he didn't look at anyone else when he was in a relationship, and Karen had essentially confirmed that to be true. What did that kind of devotion look like? She began to sift through her memories of their time together, reimagining the scenes as if she'd been his all along.

Eventually, she brought her thoughts back to reality, sighing inwardly. Even under normal circumstances, it would never work. His life was here, and hers should be back in California. However, now that her circumstances had completely changed, it seemed even more unlikely that they would ever end up together. If she chose to run away – something she would have to do within the next twelve hours, if she were to do it at all – she'd be leaving Seattle for good. And if she stayed, she'd be getting back on the yacht, most likely never seeing him again after the weekend voyage.

She was still feeling conflicted over whether to tell him the truth. If she did, she'd be pulling him into a situation where he would most likely endanger himself to help her, as he didn't seem to be the type of man who would simply go to the police and be done with it. Therefore, she should not tell him. However, on the other hand, she longed to divulge everything just for the mere sake of having someone to confide in. She glanced out her window again, suddenly feeling utterly helpless, weighed down with what felt like a backpack full of rocks. She had a strong desire to scream into a pillow.

The drive remained quiet, except for the music which became white noise whenever they engaged in occasional, brief conversation. Eventually, the scenery changed from boisterous city nightlife to quiet residential suburbs. Tara gazed in awe as they drove past several large homes, only partially visible beyond their gated entrances.

As Ryan rounded a corner, he remarked, "A lot of these houses were built for Boeing executives."

"They must be worth a fortune," she murmured. She hadn't exactly grown-up poor, but she'd certainly never lived anywhere this lavish.

"The one we're going to was once owned by Bob Hope," he continued.

"The comedian?" she asked, surprised.

He nodded. "I don't know much of the home's history beyond that, but I'm sure our hosts could tell us more." He glanced at her, smiling. "You'll like them. They're good friends of mine."

The road twisted sharply in front of them, and Tara waited until he'd rounded the turn before asking, "What will the funds from the gala go toward?"

"The proceeds will be split between Action Against Hunger and the Water Center at Columbia University."

"A water center?" she responded quizzically, curious as to what exactly that meant.

Keeping his eyes on the road, he explained, "It's a program in their Earth Institute. Students research ways to help solve the water crisis, at a local level, in a handful of third world countries."

"Interesting." She was silent for a moment, searching for a follow-up question, but as she couldn't think of one, she nonchalantly asked, "Will any of your family be coming?"

"No, I don't believe so. My parents are out of town, and Rachel's busy with an art class. There's a slight possibility that Andrew might come, but he tends to shy away from these types of things, especially if his presence isn't required." He shrugged and added, "Since my dad's not coming, he won't be obligated."

She glanced at him. "But you are?"

"Yes," he replied. "At least for this event." Not wishing to dwell on the subject of his father, he added, "I'll be giving an update on the rainwater project I've been working on." He gave her a quick glance and added, "Some students from the university have been heavily involved as well, and they'll be speaking in more detail about it once I'm done."

Tara raised an eyebrow. "This is the project you were telling me about the other day, how you've just finished phase three?"

"Yes," he nodded, rounding another corner. He slowed to a stop in front of a wrought iron gate, rolled down his window, and showed his invitation to the gate attendant who waved him through. He then proceeded down the winding drive, slowing as he neared the residence. After parking next to a large circular fountain in front of the house, he handed his keys to the valet then walked around to Tara's side, assisting her as she emerged from the car. Offering his arm, they began their ascent up the winding walkway, which was lit by delicate paper lanterns hanging from nearby trees. As they climbed the steps, he kept one eye on Tara, enjoying the way the light illuminated her high cheekbones, heart-shaped chin, and slender nose. Her make-up looked natural in the light, and he hadn't noticed how long her eyelashes were until that moment. For fear of missing a step, he pried his eyes away and concentrated on his feet.

When they reached the portico, they were greeted by one of the staff and ushered through the doorway. Ryan instantly spotted the hosts, the recently retired Ed Fincher and his red-headed wife, Marcia. They were engaged in conversation with another older couple, but they quickly caught Marcia's attention; she broke away from the others and began walking towards them in a glittering gold dress. As she was somewhat stout, and was wearing heels, it took her a minute.

"Ryan," she said with a wide smile. "It's good to see you again." She gave him a quick hug then pleasantly asked, "And who is this young lady?"

Ryan lowered his gaze to Tara and introduced her.

Marcia eagerly leaned forward, clasping Tara's hand in both of hers. "I'm Marcia Fincher, Ed's wife." Her gold earrings swung back and forth like see-saws as she gestured behind her to the group from which she'd departed.

"It's nice to meet you," Tara responded, smiling politely.

"Have you met the Bishops, Ryan?" Marcia asked, tilting her head in the direction of a well-dressed, middle-aged couple standing in front of a floor-to-ceiling mural.

"No, I don't believe so," he responded.

Her hazel eyes sparkled. "I'll introduce you. They're wonderful, both professors at Seattle Pacific." She motioned for them to follow, her heels clicking loudly on the marble tiles as she walked.

Ryan glanced at Tara and gave her a reassuring smile before taking her hand and pulling her gently alongside him. Her heart fluttered wildly as her hand slipped into his, and she had to take several calming breaths as they followed behind Marcia.

Several minutes later, she found herself engaged in a side conversation with Laura Biship; however, she only half-listened as she was more interested in hearing the others discuss a recently added program at the university. Eventually, a server approached holding a tray of hors d'oeuvres, and their respective conversations dwindled as they each turned to take something. Tara glanced idly around the expansive reception hall and noted with a sense of pride that Ryan was the most attractive man in the room, devastatingly charming in his crisp, black tux. She caught several women giving him furtive glances, and she had to stifle a frown. With the intent to discourage them, and feeling slightly possessive, she leaned into him, just a little.

A half hour later, Ryan turned to ask Tara a question but was interrupted when he felt someone step on his toe. He moved his foot to the side then threw a quick glance over his shoulder. A tall, rather skinny man in his mid-sixties or so, was staring at him. Ryan had never seen him before.

"Oh, I'm sorry," the man apologized quickly. "Very clumsy of me."

"Don't worry about it," Ryan murmured, ready to return his attention to Tara.

"You're Ryan Harker, aren't you?" the man asked quickly. "One of my friends pointed you out as you came in, and I thought the name sounded familiar."

With the suspicion that the man's "clumsiness" was not accidental, Ryan reluctantly turned and faced him. "I don't believe we've met before."

"No, I don't think we have," he replied uncomfortably, wearing the expression of someone who knew they were imposing. "I don't go to these things very often." Extending his hand, he introduced himself then continued, "My friend was telling me that you own the Platt building downtown?"

"Yes, that's right," Ryan slowly replied, watching as a small bead of sweat rolled down the man's neck, disappearing into the collar of his shirt.

A passing server with a tray of macaroons caught the man's attention, and he motioned for the server to stop. After lifting one from the tray, he took a nibble then turned his attention back to Ryan. "My friend mentioned something about a recent acquisition of yours. Some sort of manufacturing plant that you're converting over for biotech purposes, or some such thing?" The corners of his mouth pulled upward into a half smile, and he added, "I'm only asking since I'm in the health industry. Pharmaceuticals. We're almost ready to take a new drug to market." He popped the rest of the macaroon into his mouth then said, "I'd like to have a means of distribution in place before then. Perhaps you could spare a few minutes to talk?"

Ryan turned and glanced at Tara, who was still holding onto his arm. All the color had drained from her face, and her eyes were wide with fear.

Alarmed, he quickly stooped and whispered, "Is everything alright?"

Her eyes darted to his. "I think I just need some fresh air. Can you...." She glanced nervously over her shoulder then back at him. "Would you come with me?"

"Of course," he replied, relieved to have an excuse to walk away from the conversation, which had been off-putting from the beginning. He vaguely instructed the man to call his secretary then turned and maneuvered his way around a group of women, with Tara still clinging to his arm. He led her out to the terrace, and as soon as he'd found a secluded spot along the balustrade, turned to examine her.

Finding that her face was still a concerning shade of white, he asked, "Are you alright? We can leave if you need to."

She took a deep breath and replied, "That man you were talking to..." she trailed off, lowering her eyes to the stone balustrade. "I thought he was someone else, someone on the yacht with us." She glanced out over the balustrade at the sprawling grounds, which were lit by the same paper lanterns as those hanging from the trees along the front walkway.

Slowly, it dawned on him. "You mean he looked like that old guy who was trying to outbid me at the auction, right? Raymond Colt?"

She nodded, keeping her eyes down.

Stooping so that his head was level with hers, Ryan searched her face then quietly stated, "You're afraid of him, aren't you?"

She bit her lower lip, hesitating, then softly whispered, "Yes."

He stepped closer, wanting to pull her into his arms, but managed to keep himself from doing so. Instead, he fisted his hands at his side, trying to keep his rising anger in check at what he feared the man might have done to her. Through clenched teeth, he asked, "Did he hurt you?"

"No," she hastily reassured him. "I've never had any interactions with him, but I've heard stories from the other women."

She crossed her arms over her stomach and leaned against the balcony. "I'd rather not talk about it right now, if that's alright." She took a shallow breath and added, "I think I could use a glass of water. Would you mind getting me one?"

"Not at all," he replied, still concerned.

"Thank you," she smiled. "I'll just wait here."

"Are you sure you don't want to come with me?" He gave her a skeptical look, his eyebrows drawing closer together as his forehead creased.

"Yes, I'm fine now." She touched his arm and playfully added, "I'll stay within your line of vision."

He leaned his head toward hers, and hoping to lighten her spirits, responded roguishly, "I suggest that you do."

She flashed him a smile then tossed her head in a coy manner, sweeping her hair over her shoulder so the soft waves trailed down the front of her arm.

As he walked away, Ryan could feel her eyes on him and, eager to return to her, he stopped at the first refreshment table he came to. He hoped that she didn't mind flavored water because the pitcher he found there was filled with cucumber slices, and as he didn't wish to prolong his time away from her by searching for one that was vegetable-free, he simply poured her a glass.

As he turned to leave, Ed stepped beside him, smiling. "Are you having a good time?" he asked.

Doing his best to hide his reluctance to converse, Ryan nodded and replied, "You and Marcia always throw a good party."

"We try," Ed chuckled. "Marcia's the one that does all the work. I'm just the opinion giver."

Ryan gave him a half-laugh then glanced in Tara's direction. He did a quick double-take when he saw that she was engaged in a conversation with a young man who, in his opinion, appeared much too attentive. The observation caused his jaw to clench.

Ed followed his gaze and asked, "Who's the young lady you brought with you tonight?" He took a sip from his wine glass and added, "She seems quite lovely. Marcia's still raving about her dress."

"She's a friend," Ryan responded distractedly. "I was just fetching her a glass of water."

Ed chuckled, glancing towards the terrace, then with a twinkle in his eye, said, "I advise that you return with haste."

Ryan mouthed a quick "thank you" then turned on his heel and headed straight for Tara. However, he'd only covered a short distance when a tall brunette angled herself into his path, stopping him with a light touch on his forearm.

"Hello," she said, her face stoic. "Remember me?" Her hair was piled high on her head, and her black velvet dress draped elegantly to the floor.

His memory failed him momentarily then he recognized her as one of the escorts he'd hired while he was looking for Darin Robson, as a means of finding Tara. He hadn't the faintest clue as to her name, although he vaguely remembered their interaction at Darin's club. He'd been half-drunk that night and kissing her had been a huge mistake, a moment of weakness.

Before he could put together a response, she touched him playfully on the arm and said, "I'll forgive you for not texting me back if you dance with me tonight."

408

His eyes swept back to Tara who was now standing across from another enraptured male. He glanced back at the woman in front of him and gave her a fake smile. "Of course. I'm sure we'll run into each other again before the night's over."

He didn't wait for a reply as he turned and walked briskly in Tara's direction; she seemed to have attracted the attention of a third male, and he cursed lightly under his breath.

41

Despite his determination to keep her close, Ryan couldn't prevent Tara from mingling with the other guests, and they were separated several times. His simultaneous efforts to keep her within view and participate intelligently in conversations began to give him a headache, and he was relieved when, an hour later, dinner was announced.

Walking side by side, they joined the other guests who were leisurely making their way to the banquet tables set up outside on the wide veranda. As they approached their table, Ryan was dismayed to see that the tall brunette was occupying one of the chairs directly across from their assigned seats. He was still drawing a complete blank as to her name.

Once seated, Tara leaned towards him and whispered, "I've been warned that you're a world-class player, and that I would be smart to stay away from you."

Ryan didn't have to ponder who had given Tara that advice; his eyes swept briefly to the brunette.

Tipping her head in the woman's direction, Tara whispered, "Former girlfriend or just a hookup?" With a tight laugh, she added, "She's been glaring at me with daggers for eyes since we sat down."

"She's neither," Ryan muttered, "unless you want to count one drunken kiss as a hookup." He exhaled then mischievously added, "Nevertheless, you should watch your step. I can't guarantee that she didn't hire an assassin."

Tara quirked an eyebrow at him. "I'm not sure if I should tell you to stay away from me, or if I should keep you close for protection."

"Well," he replied, "I'd hate to deprive you of an opportunity to practice your self-defense skills. However," he added, leaning closer and lowering his voice, "I have no intention of staying away."

Breathe, she told herself, as her heart skipped several beats. The scent of his cologne, subtle and masculine, threatened her ability to think clearly. With a quick inhale, she stated, "Maybe you should go on offense and ask her to dance or something." Her thoughts went to the terrace below where she'd spotted a band setting up their equipment. A brief vision of Ryan with his arms around the woman across from her caused her spine to stiffen.

"That might be a problem," he replied with a sheepish grin on his face. He flicked his eyes to the brunette then back to Tara. "I honestly don't remember her name."

"Well," she responded primly, "from what she told me about you, that doesn't surprise me." She smiled sweetly before turning her head the other way, feigning interest in the topic under discussion to her left. A moment later, she felt him nudge her elbow. Ignoring the spark of exhilaration from his touch, she turned back around. "Yes?"

Extending his arm along the back of her chair, he leaned towards her and whispered, "I think if I'm to go on offense, you're going to have to play defense and get her name for me."

Tara's eyes narrowed. "Did I fail to mention that sports aren't really my thing?"

He shrugged his shoulders.

She rolled her eyes.

A moment of silence ensued, then Tara hissed, "Oh, alright. Fine. I'll see what I can do." She turned away and focused her attention on the server heading their way with a tray of elegantly plated food.

Throughout the course of their dinner, several keynote speakers took to the small stage that had been set up at the back of the tent. Using a large screen, they each provided a power point presentation to show what their respective organizations had achieved that year to support Action Against Hunger. When these had concluded, the attention shifted to the Water Center and Ryan was called up. He gave Tara a quick smile then rose from his chair and made his way to the podium where he made a few general remarks about the Rainwater Project before introducing the group of college students who had contributed their efforts. After handing off the mic to one of the students, he walked back to their table and took his seat next to Tara.

Upon the conclusion of the students' presentation, dessert was served, and an hour or so later, the chairs at each table gradually began to empty. Tara kept one eye on the servers clearing away their dinnerware and the other on the brunette who had just risen from her seat. Subtly, Tara watched as she leisurely walked towards a set of stone steps at the other end of the veranda. Once she'd disappeared from view, Tara shifted her gaze to Ryan who was conversing with an elderly woman seated in the chair next to him. From what she could hear, it sounded like they were wrapping up the conversation, and a few minutes later, the woman rose, giving Ryan a pat on the shoulder before departing with a farewell to them both.

Grinning, Ryan turned to her and said, "Alright, Miss Hayes." He cleared his throat in a dramatic manner. "Do you still think you can manage to get that name for me?" With feigned concern, he added, "Frankly, I'm a little afraid to leave the table until I have it."

"I think I would be too, if I were you," she quipped, trying not to smile. She began to scoot her chair out.

Ryan rose quickly from his to assist her. "Did she go downstairs?" he asked.

"Yes," she nodded.

"Alright, I'll wait up here."

She swept her hair over her shoulder and smiled archly. "You're not planning on hovering?"

"Oh I will be," he grinned, nodding towards the balcony. "I've got a good vantage point."

"Well, don't worry if I disappear for a few minutes. I plan to use the ladies room on my way down." She threw a quick smile over her shoulder as she glided away.

Her retreating figure captivated his attention for several moments, as always, then he rose and walked toward the end of the veranda. The sound of a saxophone drifted from the lawn below, and he peered over the balustrade at the couples dancing on the makeshift dance floor, which had poles at each corner and a latticed grid for a roof. String lights with large bulbs dangled from above, along with strands of ivy leaves and white roses that had been woven through the lattice. His eyes shifted to the expansive grounds then upwards to the full moon then back to the dance floor and the glowing paper lanterns hanging from the limbs of the trees that bordered it. He continued to watch the couples, shifting his gaze every now and then to the wide portico below and the terrace that led from the house to the dance floor. Finally, Tara emerged from under the eaves of the portico, and his heart skipped a beat; however, his elation was short-lived when he saw that she was accompanied by the gentleman who had unintentionally frightened her. Frowning, he pushed away from the balcony only to find that the brunette was standing between him and the stairs. When she locked eyes with him, he realized there was no getting around her. As she made her approach, he slowed his gait to a leisurely stroll and met her halfway.

"Are you on your way down?" he asked, giving the stone steps a brief glance. "I'm headed in that direction." He smiled and added, "Care to join me for a dance?"

She nodded, her eyes brightening, and replied, "I'd love to."

When they reached the bottom of the stairs, Ryan's eyes went straight to Tara, and he sighed with relief. She must have managed to break away from the gentleman, since she was now dancing with someone else. As the band began to play "Fly Me to the Moon," Ryan pulled the brunette in close then began to slowly maneuver in Tara's direction, moving in time with the music. A moment later, he came alongside her and grazed her shoulder with his arm.

She glanced up and her expression changed from boredom to relief when she saw it was him.

Raising his eyebrows and, taking care to enunciate, Ryan subtly whispered, "Name?"

With a mischievous gleam in her eye, Tara quickly whispered back, "Starts with an 'A.'" Her partner drifted to the left, spinning her away.

Eventually, they were brought within close proximity of each other once more.

"Next letter," Ryan mouthed.

"Really?" she hissed, arching an eyebrow, "You need another one?" Clearly enjoying herself, she smiled beguilingly back at him just before her partner swept her away again.

When the last notes of the song faded, Ryan released his dance partner who by this time had imprinted herself in his mind simply as "The Brunette." He thanked her quickly then turned toward Tara who had ended up a few feet away from him and was, surprisingly, alone.

"Hey," he said lightly, stepping to her side. The next song began, and he pulled her into his arms.

"Hi," she whispered back, her voice soft and her lashes lowered.

Ryan pulled her closer as the band began to play "Unforgettable," and a moment later, he felt her head against his chest. His breath hitched.

She glanced up at him and asked, "Does it look like she still wants to murder me?"

He grinned and whispered, "I wouldn't know. I haven't given her a second thought." He moved his hand to her lower back.

"Do you still want to know her name?" she asked, her forehead wrinkling slightly.

"No," Ryan replied, breathing softly into her hair. "Game over."

She looked up at him, smiling. "Who won?"

Ryan paused, stopping mid-step, then said blankly, "I think I did."

"Oh?" she responded with a quirk of her eyebrow.

"Yes," he stated, lowering his gaze to hers, "because I got what I wanted."

For the first time, it felt like her heart was truly beating as they began to sway to the music again. She leaned into him, resting her head against his chest. Despite her best efforts, her body would not stop trembling.

"Are you cold?" he whispered.

"No," she replied softly, not caring if he knew that he was the reason for her body's response. As long as he was holding her, nothing else mattered.

Minutes later, the song ended but he didn't release her. Instead, he dropped his other arm so that both his hands encircled her waist. He inclined his head toward hers, his chin grazing her ear, and said, "Is it alright if I don't allow anyone else to dance with you tonight?"

She laughed quietly, unable to meet his gaze, then slowly nodded yes. She tightened her fingers around the lapel of his dinner jacket, hoping she could keep her tears at bay by focusing on the feel of the fabric in her hand. In this one moment, he wanted her. And that would have to be enough. Whatever was happening between them right now was the most she would ever have with him.

As the band began to play John Legend's "All of Me," she felt his hold tighten, and once more, her body was pressed against his, the world around her fading away.

42

It was shortly after eleven o'clock when they left the gala. The drive back was quiet, and Tara found it difficult not to succumb to the lull of the engine. It wasn't long, however, before they pulled into The Eastcott's parking garage. Ryan cut the engine and stepped out. She watched quietly as he came around to her side of the car and opened her door. He offered his hand, and a tingling sensation swept through her when their fingertips touched, and again when his hand closed over hers.

As soon as she was standing, she let go and stepped away. The night was coming to an end and so was this. Her feet throbbed with pain from wearing the heels all night, and her legs were stiff after the drive. Despite her best effort to walk evenly, she stumbled into him. "Sorry," she murmured.

Ryan slipped his arm around her. "I see you decided to keep your shoes on tonight." Without warning, he scooped her up into his arms and carried her into the foyer. She protested, but only because it seemed that she ought to. A moment later, they reached the elevator. Grinning, he slowly lowered her back to a standing position. Her heart raced wildly as he leaned forward and reached around her for the elevator button. She pressed her back into the wall as he pushed it. There was less than six inches between them now, and she waited for him to step away, but he didn't. Instead, he raised his arm and firmly placed his hand on the wall, just above her shoulder. If she looked up at him now, she wasn't sure what would happen next. Suddenly, the elevator doors opened. She glided quickly out from under his arm and stepped inside. She heard him push the button for their floor then his arm brushed against hers as he took a step back. She kept her eyes on the floor, knowing her cheeks were flushed.

Watching her from the corner of his eye, Ryan wondered if she had any idea how difficult it was for him to think straight when she was this close. His heart was pounding in his chest, and he hoped the hum of the elevator was loud enough to drown it out. Suddenly, her eyes lifted to meet his, and for the first time she held his gaze, drawing him in. A fraction of a moment passed and that was all it took to undo his resolve. The next instant, his arms were around her, and she offered no resistance as he gently pushed her against the elevator wall. He kissed her roughly, overcome by raw need and want. Her body arched against his, welcoming his touch, and he pressed her closer. He knew he should pull away, but when she kissed him back, equally desperate, his mind went numb. He wanted more of her, all of her. He suddenly realized how easy it would be for him to simply take what he wanted, and the thought helped to summon what little strength he had left.

Breathless, he pulled away and took a step back, placing a hand on the wall for support. "Tara," he whispered finally, his eyes lowered. "I can't." He exhaled, his breath ragged. "I shouldn't."

Tara was stunned, his words breaking into a thousand slivers around her, each one piercing to her core. With her heart still pounding relentlessly, she finally managed to say, "Oh."

A tidal wave of emotions filled her chest, just as the elevator doors glided apart. She lunged threw the opening and walked quickly down the hallway.

"Tara," he said, following behind her. "Wait. I..."

He caught up to her at the door.

Even though it felt like the wind had been knocked out of her, she managed to give him a quick smile. "It's fine," she breathed. "It was nothing. Don't worry about it." Somehow, she was able to laugh. "Please, just open the door."

He attempted to respond, but she held her hand up and shook her head. "Really, it's fine. There's no need to say anything." As soon as the door was open, she pushed past him. "I had a great time tonight. I'll see you in the morning." She turned on her heel and headed for the hallway.

"Tara," he called after her. "I – we need to talk."

The desperation in his tone wasn't lost on her, but in that moment, she didn't care if she never saw him again. She closed her door behind her and locked it. Leaning against it, she listened for his footsteps to come after her down the hallway. Hoping she would hear them, she strained her ear and tried to quiet her breathing, but there was only silence. Eventually, she heard the clatter of his keys on the kitchen counter and her emotions turned to ice, numbing her. Turning away from the door, she angrily kicked her heels off then walked to her closet where she proceeded to methodically unzip her dress and step out of it, leaving it in a pile on the floor. After changing into a T-shirt and leggings, she sat down on the edge of the bed, waiting for the tears to come, but nothing happened. She felt nothing at all. There was no urge to analyze or process. Her mind was surprisingly clear and focused, and in a matter of minutes, she had made her decision. She rose and went to the closet again for her duffle bag. After retrieving it, she glanced at her phone. 11:46. The last train for the night was gone. Her only choice now was to wait until the earliest morning departure, which was at 5:00am. She didn't foresee any trouble making it, since the Amtrack station was only a fifteen-minute walk away.

She filled her bag with the bare essentials: two T-shirts and some shorts, followed by a pair of pants, toiletries, and her medications. Lastly, she slipped her purse inside the bag and was just about to zip it closed when she remembered the pair of scissors that she'd hidden. Taking the bag with her, she glided toward the nightstand and retrieved them from the back of the drawer, placing them on top of her clothes inside the bag, just in case she encountered Jai, or anyone else who might be nearby, keeping tabs on her. Turning around, her eyes fell to her book, which she'd been keeping on the nightstand. Grabbing it, she held it in her hand for a moment then fluttered through the pages and watched as the notes Ryan had written her floated to the floor. Without giving it further thought, she crumpled them up into a tight wad and walked into the bathroom where she had a strong desire to flush them down the toilet but decided against it in favor of making as least noise as possible. She tossed the wad into the wastebasket, still surprised at how levelheaded she was feeling. She knew the emotions would catch up to her later, but for now she was focused entirely on one thing: getting out of Seattle. As soon as she was on the train, she'd find a way to call her parents and tell them everything. She'd convince them it wasn't safe to stay where they were. She'd meet them somewhere and everything would work itself out. She flicked the bathroom light off then stood in the doorway, perusing the bedroom once more. This time, her eyes landed on the laptop. She would leave it, making sure to clear her browsing history. Next, she glanced at the phone resting on top of the dresser. That too would be left behind. Satisfied that she was ready, she crawled into bed and set the alarm on her phone for 4:30am.

She slept fitfully through the remaining hours and awoke twenty minutes before the alarm went off. Her heart began to race as she remembered the task before her, but she ignored the palpitations and set her feet firmly on the floor. Everything was packed, and there was no need to change out of her leggings and T-shirt. Reaching for the duffle bag, she slung it over her shoulder then cautiously stepped to the door. She put her ear against it, listening. All was eerily quiet, with no sound of movement. Slowly turning the doorknob, she opened the door one inch at a time, expecting to hear the hinges creak at any moment. Finally, she peered out into the hallway and glanced down to the end of it to find that the master bedroom door was open. She stood at the threshold, quickly considering the odds of Ryan being awake. After a moment, she stepped forward. Silence enveloped her as she made her way stealthily down the hallway. Upon entering the kitchen, she saw with dismay that the light above the breakfast nook was on. She stopped, frozen, but it was too late to turn around. He'd already seen her.

She watched as he rose stiffly from the table.

"We need to talk," he stated quietly, walking toward her. "There's something I have to tell you."

"We can talk when I get back," she responded evenly. "I'm going down for a workout."

He took another step toward her, narrowing the gap between them. "I haven't slept at all," he said, imploringly. "Could we please talk now?"

For the first time, she saw how drained he looked. He was still wearing his tux, minus the dinner jacket; his collar was loose, a few of the buttons undone; the cuffs of his sleeves were rolled up, and she noticed his silver cufflinks lying on the counter beside her. The stubble along his jawline looked rough, like sandpaper, and his eyes were tired, the skin underneath puffy.

"Alright," she replied, her tone clipped.

"Thank you," he sighed, relieved. "I think we should sit down."

She nodded, following him back to the breakfast table where they sat on opposite sides, both remaining silent.

"Your hands are shaking," he said softly.

She looked him straight in the eye, holding his gaze. "I think you should just say what's on your mind."

"Yes." He cleared his throat and took a deep breath. "First, I'm sorry for pushing you away in the elevator."

The air around them suddenly felt denser as she waited for him to continue. She felt there ought to be more for him to apologize about, but she couldn't think of what else it should be.

He cleared his throat again. "I just want to..." He paused then started over, his voice deeper this time. "It was never my intention to hurt you."

A sick feeling suddenly swept over her. Nothing good had ever come after the line, "it was never my intention to hurt you." This was starting to feel all too familiar. *Deja vu* of every horrible conversation that had left her feeling embarrassed and humiliated.

Deciding that she didn't need to hear anything further, she drew a hollow breath and rose from her seat. She swallowed hard, then in a cold, calm voice that she didn't recognize as her own, quietly stated, "I'm leaving."

The heavy silence between them grew thicker, and she felt a stinging sensation in the corners of her eyes. With her throat feeling dry and constricted, she continued, "This has simply been a business transaction. There's nothing to apologize for." She grabbed her bag and left the table, walking quickly toward the door.

He caught up to her in the foyer and reached for her arm.

"Don't touch me," she snapped. She lunged for the doorknob, but he moved in front of her.

"Please, just hear me out," he stated hoarsely, his eyes darting to hers, begging her.

"There's nothing more to say." She glared at him and gritted her teeth. "Please. Move."

"I'm not who you think I am, Tara." His voice was calm and controlled, which somehow aggravated her more.

"I don't care. You can be whoever you want to be." She was almost yelling now in her desperation to simply leave. "If you don't move, I'll..." She wasn't sure what she would do. "I'll scream for help."

"Alright," he replied, his voice ragged. Reluctantly, he stepped out of her way.

Without looking back, she opened the door and headed straight for the stairs. She had no desire to stand awkwardly in front of the elevator doors, waiting for them to open, not when she knew he was still standing in the doorway watching her leave. She took the stairs down to the floor below then got on the elevator and pushed the button for the parking garage. In roughly five minutes, she'd be in the garage headed for the narrow set of side stairs that she knew led to the back alley. She could feel her emotions starting to catch up to her. Not now, she told herself. You can cry about this later. Suddenly, she felt as if she were being torn in two. Everything within her longed to go back and hear him out, but it was too late for that. If she wanted to move forward with her life, she couldn't look back. She had to stay levelheaded and force all thoughts of Ryan Harker out of her mind entirely. Brushing away angry tears, she told herself that leaving was the right thing. The best thing. She needed to put the events of the last week far behind her and never look back. And yet there was something within her, some inner voice deep inside, that was trying to tell her something; what it was, she couldn't even begin to guess, but she had a sudden premonition that whatever force of nature had caused her orbit to collide with his wasn't about to let her go.

Book 2 of the Ryan Harker set will be releasing in 2026! Visit my website and subscribe to my newsletter for the official cover reveal, updates, and giveaways! If you loved *The Medallion Client*, consider leaving a thirty second review on Amazon, Goodreads, or BookBub. Reviews go a long way toward an author's success, and I thank you in advance for leaving one!

amazon

BookBub

goodreads

Acknowledgements

There are several people I would like to thank, the first being my Aunt Anita. She has been on board from the early drafts to the final stages, and without her encouragement, editorial support, and overall availableness, this book would not be what it is. She always confirmed that I was a writer, especially on the hard days when it felt like I was just pretending to be one. I would also like to thank my adopted Uncle Faron who provided the verbiage and insider knowledge for the poker scene. Additionally, I owe a thank you to my dad for never failing to ask me on a monthly basis – over an eight-year period – when I was going to publish. And lastly, I would like to say a special thank you to my boyfriend, Ian:

You helped me see this book across the finish line, and I feel like I won a trophy in more ways than one. Thank you for all the support you've given me, and for the time you've invested in helping me be successful. You fostered and facilitated connections with key individuals, and you saw the bigger picture. You also went into the weeds with me, standing over my shoulder while I asked if I should use a comma or a semicolon in a particular sentence (and then I changed my mind later). You patiently let me be my most perfectionistic self, and you were always available to simply listen. Thank you, my love, for being the man you are. I'm looking forward to doing this all over again with book two.

I've always been drawn to books and films that feature iconic espionage characters, government operatives, and heroes with alter identities – but add in some spicy romance, and I'll be completely engrossed. Given my prior experience as a criminal paralegal for both the D.A.'s Office and the U.S. Attorney's Office, it was only a matter of time before I felt inspired to write some stories of my own. Formerly a resident of Alaska, I now reside with my two children in Rochester, New York, where we enjoy spending time at the lake, hiking adventurous trails, and roller skating at the neighborhood tennis court.

www.ingramcontent.com/pod-product-compliance
Lightning Source LLC
Chambersburg PA
CBHW010512100726
47903CB00009B/2716